What Readers are Saying About Mark Shaff's
Redemption Road

"This fast-moving thriller proves that revenge is a dish best served red hot! "—*Lewis Perdue, New York Times Bestselling Author of more than 4 million copies sold.*

"From the very first scene, Mark Shaff propels the reader into what must be every husband and father's nightmare, never letting us forget that the effects of world-wide terrorism can easily hit closer to home than we think. The action never lets up in this absorbing thriller that makes us wonder what we would be capable of under similar circumstances. "—*Charles Salzberg, Shamus award nominee, author of Swann's Last Song, Swann Dives In,* and *Devil in the Hole.*

"So many twists—most unexpected, a novel that gets your pulse racing. Shaff delivers a high-speed thriller that was nearly impossible for me to put down."— *Todd A. Zalkins, author of, Dying for Triplicate and The Most Selfless Love*

"Redemption Road is a riveting page turner chock full of thrilling twists and colorful detail. A wonderful accomplishment for a debut novelist, looking forward to more."—*Diane Dennis, Inspired Media Communications*

REDEMPTION ROAD

MARK SHAFF

Moonshine Cove Publishing, LLC

Abbeville, South Carolina U.S.A.
FIRST MOONSHINE COVE EDITION APRIL 2013

This book is a work of fiction. Names, characters, places and incidents are products of the author's imagination or are used fictitiously. Any resemblance to actual events, locals or persons, living or dead, is entirely coincidental.

ISBN: 978-1-937327-21-7
Library of Congress Control Number: 2012935462
Copyright © 2013 by Mark Shaff

Book design by Moonshine Cove; cover photograph by Jeremie Schatz, used with permission.

Forthcoming Works

Saint or Sinner, the second Marcus Diablo book, Winter 2014 release.

Life in a Box
South Southerland

Dedication

To Carol Ann who has stood by me, with me, and on top of me when required; this book could never have happened without you. In one way or another you are part of every word I write. Your love and friendship are as essential to me as the air I breathe.

With our words we paint tales short and epic, of love and heartbreak, of happiness and despair, of triumph and tragedy. Stories of this world, and beyond, pictures of the past, the present and the future. If we practice our craft well, we can, for a time, hold the reader's heart in our hand, feel its beat and let our heart pulse in rhythm with theirs, and for those brief moments, we are one—
Definition of a writer, Anonymous

Author's Note

In reference to distance, I have used both miles and kilometers. This is, in part, a distinction between civilian and military terminology, but also a distinction between the U.S. standard of measurement and the metric standard, which is used around the rest of world.

Acknowledgements

The process of writing a first novel is, I suppose by definition, a solitary endeavor. And for me the writing was, but the time to write, that was a privilege given by others. There are many people to thank, first and foremost my wife and sons. This book would not have happened without their understanding and encouragement as I sat for hours on end, sprawled across the dinning room table, iPod connected, and oblivious to the life going on around me. To all those who read the many drafts and offered advice, and free editing, you know who you are, and also know you have my heartfelt thanks for your love and friendship. To my editor, Michael Carr, not only did you make my manuscript better, by leaps and bounds, you took the time and interest, to make me a better writer. I will be forever in your debt. Lastly, to my publisher, Gene D. Robinson and Moonshine Cove Publishing LLC, not only did you give my work generous consideration, you put up with my overbearing personality, and provided steady, patient and experienced direction. That my novel is going to see the light of day, and in such a first class, professional manner, is all due to you.

CHAPTER ONE
August 4
Diablo Family Cabin, Eastern Sierra Mountains

The steam rose in lazy wisps from the mug cupped between Annie Diablo's hands as she gazed out the cabin windows, at the morning light awakening the grey granite peaks of the Sierra Nevada Mountains. Turning away from the view, she looked at her husband Marcus, who was kneeling on the stone floor, methodically placing gear, arranged in ordered piles, by the four backpacks lying in front of him. This morning, they and their sons, twelve-year-old Bodie and eight-year-old Garrett, would be heading out for six nights in the Hoover Wilderness.

Annie walked toward Marcus, reached down and as she mussed his long, curly brown hair said with a smile, "Why don't you wake the boys and I'll go get breakfast started."

Marcus looked up, returned her smile and replied in a kidding tone, "Oh yeah, give me the hard job."

As Annie pulled eggs and milk from the fridge, she heard Marcus call up to their sons asleep in the loft, "Hey, sleepy heads, time to get up!" Annie counted the seconds off in her head, one hippopotamus, two hippopotamus . . . before she got to ten, after not hearing any sound of movement from the boys, Marcus switched to what Bodie and Garrett referred to as his *Drill Sergeant's* voice. "All right, men, if you aren't both down here pronto, I'm gonna make you double-time it for the first half of the trip—which, as you know, is all up hill."

As Annie cracked eggs into a stainless steel bowl, Marcus came up behind her and wrapped his arms around her waist. Squeezing, he whispered jokingly into her ear, "Maybe we should have started having kids a bit sooner?"

Annie turned away from the counter to face him. Staring deep, into Marcus's blue eyes, Annie thought, even though she was forty-three, and Marcus forty-five, their children had come into their lives at just the right time. As Marcus hugged her, Annie nestled her face into his chest and murmured, "Everything in our lives has always happened when it was supposed to."

Annie felt Marcus's fingers glide through her straw blond hair, heard him inhale deeply, and let out a contented sigh. Annie knew that she and Marcus were on the same page. For the first ten years of their marriage, they had pursued careers with a vengeance, had a hyper-obsessive commitment to physical fitness, and worked twelve hours a day, often six days a week. When they weren't working they had an almost reckless sense of adventure. They dove with sharks off the Great Barrier Reef, trekked to 19,000 feet in the Himalayas, explored the Pyramids, and the Jungles of the Amazon, mountain biked across New Zealand,

and did most of it while managing to run fifty miles a week, all things that, would have been difficult with young children.

Annie had built a medical management-consulting firm that she had sold earlier in the year for a handsome profit, plus a lucrative two-year consulting agreement. Marcus imported centuries old timber, limestone slabs, and hand-made terra cotta floor and roof tiles, primarily from Western Europe, for resale to the high-end U.S. housing market. Their successes had made their dream cabin in the mountains, and an adventurous lifestyle with their sons, a reality. And though they were keeping the adventures closer to home, Annie was sure that in a few years, when the boys were bit older, globetrotting would be back on the menu.

Annie drew back from Marcus as she heard the sound of feet shuffling across the wood floor of the loft. Then one by one, with hands and feet sliding down the rails of the ships ladder, the boys landed like pouncing cats on the native flagstone floor. Brushing past their father, the boys hugged Annie good morning

"Go on you two, get your packs loaded then we'll have breakfast," Annie said, giving them each a playful push toward their dad.

Bodie and Garrett, their sandy blond hair sticking up and out every which way, gave their dad a quick hug, and then set to their task. Annie stood there a moment longer, leaning against the counter, and watched the three most important men in her life. It was curious she thought, how her husband, who in so many ways was *non-conventional*, was *so-conventional* when it came to any type of adventure trip. He insisted on routine and repetition—doing things the same way every time—like loading a backpack.

When he had first introduced her to his brand of adventure, and then when the boys came along, Marcus, though he had no military background, had a habit of equating being in the mountains to being a soldier. He had said the words so many times she could recite them verbatim. "To be a good soldier, you must follow orders, adhere to a chain of command, have an established routine, plan and train, know your strengths and limitations, and those of your fellow soldiers, and so it is when you are in the mountains. The goal is to live to fight, or in our case, adventure another day."

At first, especially with the boys, Annie was worried Marcus was going to scare them to the point that they wouldn't want to go. But during the summers when they hiked and backpacked exploring the mountains, seeking out remote lakes and streams to fly fish, and looked for routes they could access and ski in the winter and early spring, Marcus played the *what if game* with them. He would explain the topography, pointing out features that indicated slopes that frequently avalanched, or where a particular fall line terminated in a drainage that would be very difficult to get out of, and then he would pose a *what if* scenario to the boys.

And Annie had to admit, the boys were eager to prove to their father that they understood and were excited about the challenge, and more often than not, their answers seemed to be out of context with their age and so in line with Marcus's golden rule: *When you have only seconds to react, when you only get to make one decision, follow your instincts. React, don't hesitate, if it turns out you made the wrong choice, deal with it then.*

Marcus thrived on taking calculated risks, and had a knack for selling those risks to others, including her and the boys. It was one of his talents, Annie mused, getting people to buy into his vision. He liked to say, "We never dwell on, or contemplate failure. That's why we have a game plan, because your survival and the survival of others may depend on your ability to make hard decisions and follow orders."

Annie's reminiscing was broken when Marcus walked in, grabbed plates and silverware and began setting the table. Glancing from the stove to the living room, Annie saw her youngest son Garrett sitting on the floor, staring at his pack. Marcus saw it too. He returned to their son and in one smooth motion sat down on the stone floor next to him. "What's up bud?" he asked as he reached over and put his arm around Garrett's shoulders.

Annie heard Garrett ask with a hint of trepidation in his voice, "Are you sure Mom's up for almost a whole week in the mountains?"

Annie smiled at her son's question. Garrett could always sense her nervousness, especially at the start of one of their family adventures. For whatever reason Garrett was attuned and connected to her, in a way no one else was, not even Marcus.

Marcus tousled Garrett's shaggy hair. "Mom's fine. You know she's tougher than the three of us combined," Marcus said with a quick wink at Annie. "What's really bothering you?"

Sheepishly Garrett looked up at this father, then quickly over at his mom, "Oh nothing, really. Just a feeling I have."

Turning back to the cooking eggs, Annie heard Bodie say to his younger brother, "Hey, we've been backpacking lots of times. So quit worrying and get your pack loaded."

Then Marcus, his voice encouraging, "Yeah buddy, let's get done. I wanna to be outta here within the hour."

Garrett got back to his packing as Marcus went to help Annie get breakfast on the table. Forty-five minutes later, with packs on their backs they set out from the cabin toward the trailhead that would lead them into the wilderness.

CHAPTER TWO
August 6
Eastern Sierra Mountains

Around noon, Marcus and the boys had caught some nice golden trout. It was time to head back to base camp. Bodie and Garrett, their sun-bleached mops bouncing in the light breeze, led the way, a good twenty yards ahead of their father, eager to give their mother a blow-by-blow account of their morning.

Their brotherly banter was as constant as the babbling stream beside them as the boys approached a spot where the trail narrowed to wind through a dozen car-size boulders. At the end of this rock-walled section, the trail took a hard right, and their campsite would come into full view some fifty yards ahead. The boys reached the end of the boulders and stopped abruptly. Marcus was expecting them to scamper ahead, yelling over each other to their sunbathing mother all about what splendid fly fishermen they were. Instead, they turned back and looked at him, worry and concern on their faces.

They expected to find Annie after her trail run, spread out on her favorite rock on the bluff overlooking Hardin Lake, catching some sun and reading. What they found instead were two young men, tearing their campsite apart.

To Marcus they looked Latino, perhaps, or eastern Mediterranean. There were always a lot of young backpackers in U.S. wilderness areas and national parks during the summer, but they didn't usually behave this way, he worriedly thought to himself.

Something was very wrong, and the boys knew it instantly. There was no sign of their mother. She should be right there, lounging on her favorite rock overlooking the lake, waiting for her three mighty anglers to return.

The boys were scared. "What's going on, Dad? Where's Mom?" Bodie whispered.

"Look, Dad!" Garrett murmured. "Those guys are tearing our stuff apart. Look what they did to the tent and the sleeping bags—the stuffing is all over the place! What are they looking for?" He paused. "They have guns, Dad! Look!" Garrett said as he pointed to the holsters at their waists.

Marcus's mind was running at hyper speed. None of this made sense. These guys weren't just a couple of young vandals tearing stuff up for the hell of it. They were looking for something, and with every passing second, it became apparent to him that the something just might be them. But *why*? And why the guns?

"What's that language they're speaking?" Bodie asked. Until he said it, Marcus really hadn't paid attention to what they were saying—he had been too focused on what they were *doing*.

It wasn't English, not Spanish or French or any of the other western European tongues he was accustom to hearing. It sounded Middle Eastern, and that in itself seemed odd—not something one expected to hear in the high Sierra.

"What are they saying? What are they *doing*?" The boys whispered. Marcus had no idea what was going on, but whatever it was had something to do with Annie. They were almost fourteen miles from the nearest real outpost of civilization. Whatever was going on, wherever Annie was, the answers were here, and he needed those answers now!

Marcus motioned for the boys to follow him back the way they had come. He wanted to put a little more distance between them and the two young men at their camp.

They stopped near the far end of the boulder-enclosed trail. "All right, guys, listen up," Marcus said, as the three of them hunched down in the shadow of a gigantic granite rock. "I know you're worried about Mom—so am I! I don't have a clue what's going on. But count on this. I'm going to find out. So here's what I need. I want you both to go back down the trail to where we saw that little game path this morning, the one that cuts back above us on this side of the mountain." He pointed that way. "Remember yesterday when we went up above camp to get snow?" They both nodded. "Remember that big rock we looked at, the one that's just hanging there ready to go?" They nodded again. "Okay, I want you guys to make your way up the game trail and come in around and above that rock. Stay low, and don't talk—your voices 'll carry, and I don't want these guys to have any idea where you are."

The fear on their faces was enough to break his heart.

"What are you gonna do, Dad?" Garrett said.

"I don't know, buddy, but I have a bad feeling about this, and right now I need to get you guys outta here."

"What do you mean 'get us outta here' "? Bodie said.

"Listen, I don't know where your mom is. All I know is, she's not here. These guys, they're looking for something or someone. Since we don't have anything of value, just our personal gear, I have to assume they're looking for *us*. What that means, I don't know, but I sure as hell plan to find out."

Marcus took off his daypack and dumped the contents on the ground. He grabbed the first aid kit, a flashlight, binoculars, a couple of two-way radios that they used to get National Weather Service reports and to communicate with each other, some trail mix, a half-dozen granola snack bars, and his pistol.

He motioned for the boys to shuck off their small hydration packs. Each had a compartment that would hold a small amount of gear. Opening the first aid kit, he stuffed some Band-Aids and an elastic bandage in one pack with some of the food, and put the flashlight and one of the radios in the other. Then he crammed all the remaining gear and food, as well as their fishing gear, back into his daypack and stashed it just off the trail in a rock crevice.

11

He glanced at his watch as he reached for the nine-millimeter Smith and Wesson semiautomatic—almost two in the afternoon. He set the pistol along with an extra nine-round clip on the rock beside him. The pistol was standard gear anytime the family was backpacking in the mountains—not so much as protection against bears or mountain lions—but rather, as protection against the two-legged predators that seem to favor remote wilderness areas for whatever sick, freaky thing might float their boat. Until today, Marcus had never been in a situation that even remotely made him consider taking the pistol out of his pack.

Now the boys were freaking. The guys at their camp had guns, and now their dad had a gun—what was going on? They had to think that the situation was deteriorating with every passing minute, which it was.

"How long do you think it will take you to get up behind that rock?" Marcus asked.

Bodie thought for a second. "Well, we oughta be able to get up around and come in behind it in about fifteen minutes."

"Okay, this is what's going to happen. You guys are going to head back down and turn up the game trail, like we said. You're going to get yourselves behind that rock. Twenty minutes from the time you leave, you're going to push the rock down the mountain. Then you're going to turn tail and head out of here. If you cut up and across to the right, you'll hit the trail that brought us in—you guys have been on that trail lots of times. I want you to stop at the creek, fill your water bladders, and then you haul ass out of here. Let's say it's about two thirty when you push the rock. You should be able to get back to the High Sierra Lodge by no later than seven thirty or eight, before it gets dark."

Bodie looked at him. "But, Dad, what about—"

"You don't stop and chat with anybody. Now, people are going to think it's strange for an eight and twelve-year-old boy to be this far in the backcountry by themselves. If anyone says you have to stay with them or go with them, you run. You know as well as I do, there isn't a person in these mountains who can keep up with you, let alone catch you. Once you hit the summit, you go nonstop all the way down the other side to the Lodge, then find Jake and Bonnie. Explain to them everything you know. Tell them something bad has happened to your mom and they need to get a hold of the police and the park rangers right away." Jake and Bonnie had spent most of their lives in these mountains and operated the High Sierra Lodge. They had known the boys since they were born, and were close family friends. Marcus knew the boys would be safe with them and that Jake and Bonnie would know whom to contact.

"All right, take a breath," Marcus said. "We're going to figure this out. No matter what, your mom and I are coming out of here tonight. You stay with Jake and Bonnie till we get back. Bonnie will know exactly where we camped, so she can tell the police and the rangers where we are. I'll be fine."

To say that his sons were scared and badly shaken would be a gross understatement. Marcus knew to give them too much time to think about something, like how steep the chute they were going to ski was, or how steep and difficult a climbing route was, would only make it tougher to convince them they were ready and could handle it. Better just to make a plan and then quickly execute it. The problem was, Marcus didn't have a plan—but he couldn't let them know that.

His sons stared at him with a deer-in-the-headlights look as their father continued. "In a few minutes, I'm going to cut down off the trail and make my way along the bushes by the lake and come in under our campsite. You two are going to head for the rock and do just as we planned. No matter what you hear, gunshots, whatever, don't you dare turn around. You get your butts out of here, and I'll see you sometime tonight. Got it?"

"But, Dad, what if it takes us longer than twenty minutes to get to the rock?" Bodie asked, his lip quivering.

"No worries, I'll wait until I see the rocks coming down the mountain. I need the distraction if I'm going to get close enough to these guys to get the information I want."

"But, Dad, they have guns!" Garrett said, choking back his tears.

Marcus could see he was losing them. If this was going to happen, it had to happen now! He was also concerned that the two visitors back at their camp would decide they had stayed long enough. It was time to send the boys on their way.

"Okay, okay, calm down. I need both of you to buck up! You know me. I'm not going to let anyone hurt me—or you, or your mom. So let's do this! You guys are the key to making this happen. I need you, and so does your mom. Now, come over here."

As they fell into his open arms, tears welled up in Marcus's eyes. He held them, their heads tucked into his chest, and he was overwhelmed with a sense that they may never see Annie again.

"I love you guys! Now, it's time to roll." Marcus looked at his watch, 2:10. "Okay, two thirty should be just about right, but don't rush. If you need a little more time, don't worry—I'd rather you were safe and quiet than on time. I'll be in position in fifteen minutes, and I'll wait for the rock to start moving."

"We love you, Dad," they both croaked. Then twelve-year-old Bodie looked his dad in the eye and said in the clearest, most confident voice he could muster, "Dad, we got it. We won't let you down—you can count on that. We'll take care of each other, and as soon as we take off, we won't stop for anything. You go take care of this and find Mom. Let's move, Garrett." He put his arm on his brother's shoulder. They turned toward their father and, in unison, each touched their right palm to their chest, tapped twice over their heart, and then pointed their finger at him.

This was their little thing. It signified *from my heart to yours—I am always with you, always!* Marcus returned the gesture. No more words were spoken as the boys turned and headed down the trail.

13

As he stood there staring at his young sons walking away, they never once looked back. He was so proud of them. In less than a minute, they were around the bend and gone from sight.

CHAPTER THREE

From his position below the bluff, Marcus had a clear view of the two men, who appeared to be in their early to mid-twenties, average height, lean, definitely not Hispanic, maybe of Middle Eastern or central Asian descent. He could hear them talking animatedly in what he assumed was some Middle Eastern dialect. They wore khaki hiking pants and loose-fitting long-sleeved shirts. The taller one, the older looking of the two, wore a red ball cap with YOSEMITE on the front. The other guy wore the same cap in blue.

Their daypacks lay on the ground. Like his, they were big enough for a day excursion but not an overnighter. This told him they had probably come from a base camp within a few hours hike, and he had to assume they were not by themselves. The whole thing seemed unreal. One minute, he's in the back country with his wife and sons, and the next, hiding in the bushes with a gun, staring at two guys who look like poster children for Islamic Jihad.

He pulled the pistol from the back of his shorts, thumbed the safety off, and waited for the rock to move. The two men were too busy speaking with each other to pay any attention to the mountain right in front of them.

As he watched, the rock started leaning outward, as if in slow motion. He wasn't sure, maybe his mind was playing tricks on him, but he thought he glimpsed two small figures scrambling away.

In just seconds, the two camp visitors were staring up the mountain in front of them, at a huge boulder, and other rocks it had knocked free, bounding down the mountainside. They were in no danger from the slide, but the noise and feel of the raw force was so compelling, they never noticed Marcus slipping up behind them.

It took about fifteen seconds to cover the distance, with the rock slide muffling any noise of approach. By the time they heard him, he was standing five feet behind them. They looked surprised, which was good because his heart was racing and he was struggling to keep his composure. This was the first time that he had ever pointed a firearm at another human being.

"All right," Marcus said, "slowly take your weapons out one at a time, and toss them down there." He tilted his head at the lakeshore, a stone throw away.

For a moment, they just stood there looking at him as if they didn't understand English. He fired a round past the older guy's ear, its report reverberating off the granite peeks.

"Now, boys, I'm not fucking around. If those guns are not out of those holsters and in the lake in five seconds, the next shot is going to blow off a knee. First you...." Marcus motioned to the one in the red hat, who eased the pistol out of its holster and pitched it into the water. "And now you," He said to the one in the blue hat. "The knife, too."

Having disarmed them of all the weapons he could see, he wasn't quite sure what to do next. "Where's Annie?" He said, his voice desperate. "My wife—where is she?"

As he held the gun on them, the younger guy, in the blue hat, turned to his partner and started jabbering in an unintelligible language. His partner yelled back, "English, speak English."

"What do we do now? You said this would be simple," said the guy in the blue hat.

"Shut up. He's not going to shoot us," the older guy said. "Good Christians like him don't do that kind of thing."

Marcus stepped around a little farther to his left and trained the pistol on Red Hat. "Now, I am going to ask you only once, and if you don't answer, then I *will* shoot you. Where is my wife?"

"You mean that infidel whore? She is about to find out how women are supposed to behave in the presence of men of Allah. Women in this country are so full of themselves that they believe—" That's as far as Red Hat got before the back of his head exploded, spraying blood, bone, and brain matter across the face and torso of his partner. By the time his body hit the pine needle–covered ground, Marcus closed the distance to the younger man and slammed the side of the pistol into his face. He felt the crunch of bone and cartilage, as the young man dropped like a poleaxed steer.

Heart racing, and hyperventilating he willed himself to stay under control. The boys had to have heard the pistol shots. What were they thinking?

One man was dead, the other out cold. If he was to find out where Annie was, he needed him awake, but restrained when he came to. There had been some rope in the pack inside the tent, but all their stuff was strewn about like a yard sale. Marcus looked about at what else he had—lots of exfoliated slabs of flat, weathered granite, weighing anywhere from twenty to seventy pounds. He dragged Blue Hat by his feet over near the torn-down tent. He then took the rocks they had stacked as a windbreak around the tent and placed one under each ankle and another under each wrist, so that his feet and hands were suspended off the ground. Next he laid rocks over his ankles and shins, his knees and thighs, and gathered more rock and did the same with his arms. It took about fifteen minutes, and Blue Hat had been out cold the whole time. Worried, Marcus checked his pulse—he wasn't dead.

With his legs and arms pinned beneath several hundred pounds of rock, he wasn't going anywhere once he came to. Grabbing two water bottles that had been tossed from the ransacked tent, he filled them with icy lake water and poured them over the young man's bloody face.

After the second bottle, Blue Hat began to stir. His eyes blinked, and he grimaced in pain from his destroyed nose. The dark-brown eyes looking back didn't look like the eyes of someone ready to be a martyr just yet. It was more like looking into the eyes of a very scared young man who, only a few years ago, was just a boy.

"Let me explain how this is gonna go," Marcus said. "I'm going to ask you a question, and every time you give me some *jihadist* bullshit or you start spouting off or getting all full of yourself, I'm going to break one ankle, then the other, then your wrists. Then I'm going lay rocks on your chest, and I will continue piling rocks until I crush the life right out of you. If you think I give a shit what you think or believe, that would be a painful and fatal mistake. Do you understand me? Nod your head, God damn it!"

He nodded.

"Good! I hope we understand each other, because if you fuck with me, when I am done, you will wish you were the one who got shot. Okay, I'm going to clean your face up a little bit. And if you think it's hard to breathe with your nose smashed all over your face, imagine how hard it'll be with a few hundred pounds of rock on your chest."

Marcus picked up a T-shirt that had been thrown from the tent, wet it and wiped the blood and gore off his pinned captive's face. Blue Hat winced and whined, trying to move his head side to side, but Marcus had it wedged between two watermelon-size rocks.

There was still about four and a half hours of full daylight left, and if he was going to find Annie it had to be while it was still light out. He wasn't worried about trekking out of the mountains in the dark—the trail was clear, he knew it well, and he had a good headlamp. He just needed to find her.

Marcus knelt down close to Blue Hat's face. "Where is my wife? What have you done with her?"

The look in his eyes was not so much wild as crazed. He couldn't breathe through his nose, and his gasps sounded ragged and strained.

"I don't know," he rasped. His voice was distorted with pain, but there was not even a hint of an accent. This guy sounded American.

"Wrong answer," Marcus said through gritted teeth. Getting up, he picked up a fifty-pound rock, lifted it to head level, and brought it down onto Blue Hat's left foot. The snap of his ankle seemed to echo off the mountains. He screamed as best he could. His foot was turned inward at an angle that was just not right. *Go on,* Marcus thought, *scream all you want. It's just us.*

His mind was whirling, thoughts tumbling over each other. Had he chosen wrong? Had he shot the wrong guy? He had assumed that Red Hat was the alpha, but had he reacted too quickly after letting his anger at Red Hat's remarks about Annie cloud his judgment?

Walking back to his prisoner, he poured a bottle of cold water on his face. The eyes that looked up now were unfocused and bloodshot. There was no resistance in them, only agony and undiluted fear.

"One more time. Where is my wife?"

"They . . . took her," he grunted.

17

" *Who* took her?"

"My…team."

"What team? How many? Where did they take her?"

Marcus was getting rattled, asking too many questions at once. His captive was in excruciating pain. He had to slow down, keep him focused on one question at a time.

"What team?"

"She ran up on us as we were setting our...."

"Our *what*?"

"Our...firestorm."

"What the fuck are you talking about? What firestorm? If you don't start making sense in a hurry, I'm going to break you into little pieces and leave you for the crows.

"Okay, we're going to take a different approach. You're going to tell me everything from the time you saw my wife, and I'm going to listen. If you haven't figured it out yet, I'm not a patient man, and I won't hesitate to start breaking every bone in your body."

From his raspy breathing, Marcus sensed Blue Hat was at the point of passing out. "Talk!" He yelled into his face.

His voice was low, his tone halting, "She was running...off trail...through the big timber down along Buck Creek. We were...setting our incendiary devises. They are set to...ignite at a specified time and start a fire." He sucked in a couple of strained breaths, and Marcus poured a sip from the water bottle into his mouth.

Swallowing, he continued. "Ricky, our team leader, talked to her. They just… chatted about the mountains and...what a nice day it was...and how beautiful the whole area is. She told Ricky about you and your boys, and how you guys had gone fishing. She told him...the area where you had your camp. It wasn't hard to find it on a topo map. I thought everything would be okay. Then your wife asked Ricky about what we were doing. She must have seen us...burying the devices to start the fires. That's when Ricky hit her. She was pissed. We restrained her… and tied her to the back of one of the mules."

Marcus wasn't sure he if was ready to hear more. *Stay calm,* he reminded himself. "Go on," he said.

"We came in on horseback a week ago… with a team of mules. There are five on my team. We entered at the base of Buck Creek… just off the highway. This was our last plant...and we were out of here." He didn't need to say the next words. "Just a few more hours, and none of this would have happened!"

To Marcus the kid sounded totally American, maybe not born here, but he had certainly lived most of his life in the States.

He went on. "Ricky sent me and Alex to find you...and your kids. We were supposed to...." He paused for a few moments and then croaked, ". . . kill you."

"What's your name?" Marcus asked.

"Kevin. Kevin Alahda."

"Where are you from, Kevin?"

"Colorado Springs."

"Where are they taking my wife?"

Tears welled up in Kevin's eyes, and he began to sob. "I don't know. Please don't hurt me anymore—I really don't know. Once we got to the highway, we were all supposed to split up...and never see each other again...ever. You have to believe me."

He did. "How long ago did you last see your team?"

"What time is it now?" he asked his teeth chattering as if he was cold.

"Almost three o'clock."

"We left them around twelve thirty...got to your camp just before two."

Marcus reckoned, since Annie ran into them, it had to be at least an hour to the trailhead at the Buck Creek parking lot. Shit! If they headed out when Kevin and his partner set out for their camp, they could already be out of here.

"What was the plan for you and Alex? Were they going to wait for you?"

"Yeah. Ricky said they'd wait till two...and then head out. We all had our own individual arrangements once we got to the highway. So even if we missed them...we were supposed to follow our plan and scatter."

Marcus stood, grabbed the two men's packs, and dumped them out on the tarp that they had spread under the tent. He didn't know what he was looking for. There was only the usual stuff: snack food, first-aid kit, flashlights, rain jackets. There was one thing that was a little unusual: five cell phones in a heavy-duty Ziploc bag. Why would two guys need five phones? Not to mention that almost nowhere in these mountains could you get a signal.

He walked back to Kevin. He was in bad shape, and his eyes were rolling up into his head. Bending down, Marcus slapped his face a couple of times. "Kevin. Kevin! Look at me. What's with all the cell phones?"

Kevin was having difficulty focusing, and it looked as if he was going to lose consciousness any minute. "Cell phones?" It sounded like a question.

"Yeah, cell phones. You guys have five of them. Why?"

As he faded from consciousness, he was trying to say something. In a voice that was barely more than a whisper, Kevin said, "Not...cell...phones. They're...." And he was out.

CHAPTER FOUR

Marcus had no more time to waste with Kevin. He would have to come back this way on his way out. Right now he needed to get to the ridge that would give him a view down into the valley of Buck Creek Canyon. If Kevin's team were headed out, there was no way he'd catch them. But he had to see if they had Annie. He felt in his gut that she was alive, but he needed to be certain.

Grabbing one of the packs that belonged to Kevin or his dead partner, he gathered up a few supplies. The last thing he tossed into the pack was the bag with the five cell phones—or whatever they were. He wasn't sure why he took them— he just didn't want someone stumbling into camp and taking them. For some reason, nothing else seemed as important as those phones—except for Annie and the boys.

He took off his boots and changed into a pair of shorts and trail shoes, all the while thinking, *this can't really be happening.*

Kevin was out cold. His breathing seemed shallow, as Marcus took off at a steady trot down the trail toward Buck Creek Canyon.

He made good time and reached the ridge in thirty-five minutes, shucked off the pack, pulled out the binoculars, and began scanning. He could see the trail as it wound down out of the mountains, into the foothills and then the valley.

Near the bottom of the trail, where it dropped steeply off, out of view, into the parking lot, he spotted five horses and three heavily laden pack mules. He could make out three people with dark hair. This had to be the rest of Kevin's team, but where was his straw-haired Annie? He could feel the panic rising in him. Had they left her behind? Alive? Injured? Dead?

Staring through the binoculars he wondered how had he gotten here? In the space of just a few hours, he had sent his sons on a fourteen-mile trek out of the mountains alone, killed a man dead, and tortured another. Strangely, he didn't feel bad about anything he had done. He was worried about the boys and Annie, but mostly he was anxious. It felt somehow wrong that he had so little emotion about killing a man and, quite possibly, sentencing another to death.

From the ridge, he couldn't see the parking lot where the trail ended. But he knew that they were less than half a mile from it. The parking lot was an area where people could leave their trucks and horse trailers. It was specifically for those wishing to enter the wilderness on horseback.

Backcountry outfitters ran pack stations in this part of the eastern Sierra. They provided guides, horses, mules, and gear and took groups into well-established backcountry camps, where they could enjoy the splendor of the wilderness from the comfort of a well set-up base camp, complete with big wall tents, cots, and home-cooked meals.

Marcus knew that there were outfitters who rented livestock and gear and provided permits to people wishing to have an unguided wilderness experience. It had to be what this group had done.

Concentrating so hard his eyes hurt, he could see they were stopped. The three men were walking around at the back of the mule train. Still no Annie! Where the hell was she! She had to be there! Then he saw it: movement on the back of the last mule. It looked as though the three men were trying to offload something. Then he saw the blond hair; they must have had her covered. Then they had her on her feet. He couldn't quite make it out from that distance, but it appeared that her hands and feet were bound. If they hadn't been tied, she would be raising holy hell—and for sure wouldn't be standing in one place.

She was alive! All he could figure was they were going to hold her up on the trail until they could get the horses, mules, and gear returned. He assumed that the outfitter was waiting with a stock trailer in the parking lot. And there was a good chance that other people would be there. Maybe she could get away, run, and yell for help. God, he hoped so! *Please, get away, Annie! Run!*

There was no way he could get to her before they were gone. From where he was on the ridge, it would have taken him two hours, maybe more, to cover the distance.

He watched as one of the men moved Annie off the trail and into the timber. Then the other two men gathered the horses and mules, mounted up, and made their way down the trail, around the bend, and out of sight.

He waited, alert for any movement. Nothing! He sat on that ridge for another thirty minutes all the time thinking, *what the hell have you guys stumbled into Marcus?* No one ever came back out onto the trail.

He felt so helpless! Had they left her in the woods? Killed her? Were they doing unspeakable things to her? But Kevin had said they were all going their separate ways, never to see each other again. So maybe the one named Ricky had taken her with him.

"What should I do?" He asked himself out loud. Should he head down and see if they left her in the forest? For some reason—again one he couldn't explain—he was almost sure she wouldn't be there. But what if he was wrong and she was there, hurt? What if she had been left for dead?

Experience had taught him never to second-guess himself. Make a decision and go. If you spent time on every little thing, mulling over every contingency, you only ended up wasting time. As Annie would say, "The rest is just dirt."

He had already wasted more time than he could afford. Hefting his pack onto his shoulders, feeling more inadequate than he ever had before, Marcus stood on the ridge, and yelled as loud as he could, "I'm coming, Annie! Hold on, baby, I'm coming!" As the words echoed down the canyon, he turned around and headed back to camp and to Kevin.

CHAPTER FIVE

Marcus looked at his unconscious captive. Kevin's breathing was coming in shallow gasps, and Marcus was a bit startled by just how barbaric the whole scene appeared. Crazily, he thought, *good thing no one had come upon him while he was gone.* Marcus removed all the rocks he had piled on him, removing the ones from his broken left ankle last. Kevin let out a low animal moan. Marcus needed to wake him up.

Pouring water on a T-shirt he squeezed drops onto Kevin's parched lips and into his mouth, trying to rehydrate him a little. He started to stir, groaning and mumbling.

While he was coming around, Marcus gathered his gear. He pulled on his lightweight pants over his shorts and put his hiking boots back on. He was going out with a daypack only. Everything else, he gathered up and stuffed under a tree, covering it with the tarp, making a halfhearted attempt to hide it with some branches and loose pine needles.

As he was walking back to Kevin, he remembered the two shots he had fired. Looking around in the fading light, he spotted the brass casings, picked them up, and put them in the front pocket of his pants.

He returned to Kevin. Just looking at him, it was obvious to Marcus, that his fear and adrenalin fueled smash to Kevin's face had done a lot more damage than a mere broken nose. It was clear to him, this boy was not leaving these mountains alive. But before he died, Marcus intended to find out all he could. He rifled the pockets of the dead guy, Alex, not looking at his exploded head. Then went through Kevin's pockets. There wasn't much: a pocketknife, a lighter, a few coins, and a matchbook. Neither was carrying a wallet or identification of any kind. He stuffed it all into the small front pouch of the pack and forgot about it.

He knelt down next to Kevin and dripped a little water into his mouth. Most of it ran down his chin. Putting his left hand behind Kevin's head, he lifted gently, pouring a little more.

"Kevin! Kevin, I need you to stay with me. Come on, man, look at me. Focus on my face." Kevin's eyes were red, pupils dilated. After a few seconds, their eyes met. This was as awake as he was going to get. "Tell me everything you can about Ricky," Marcus demanded. "Where is he from?"

"No...I—I don't know...where he is...from."

Kevin's slurred speech made him sound drunk, and it was hard to make sense of what he was saying.

"How old is he?" He asked. "Older than you?"

"Yeah...older...I think twenty-five, twenty-six."

"Okay, this is important. Did he ever say anything that would indicate where he was from?"

Kevin's eyes were starting to roll back up into his head. Marcus tilted his head up and gave him some more water. Kevin was in shock—hell, he had been since he'd been hit with the gun.

Kevin's voice was weak, the words broken, barely audible. "One night we were talking about rivers. I'm from Colorado… we have some big rivers. He said something about the Columbia...and, I think, a river called the Willamette...something like that. That's all I know. We never talked about...our homes or our families—it was strictly forbidden."

Marcus knew these rivers, the Columbia and the Willamette. They were both in Oregon. "Kevin, is there anything else you remember about Ricky? Anything at all?"

"Rivers were important—besides the fire, there was something...about the water...I don't know what. We only knew about the fire, but there was something else. I think...only Ricky knew."

He was fading fast. "Anything else?" Marcus asked.

Kevin's voice was now a faint whisper, and he had to lean close to hear. "Ricky...he's a true believer. . . an important person...important to the cause."

"What cause? What are you talking about?"

"The fires—fires everywhere, I think. And something more, something big, but I don't know what. None of us knew…except maybe Ricky. All I know...the fire is just a part of it." He hissed this last bit of information out, and in the fading light, with the sun sinking behind the mountain, he asked Marcus with maybe the most pleading look he had ever seen, "Am I going to die?"

Marcus, look at the young man. This guy was no Al Qaeda trained terrorist. No, he was just a college kid who'd been sold some load of fanatical crap, Marcus thought. Then in a voice devoid of emotion he said, "Yes."

Kevin struggled to move his hand and touched Marcus's arm. His fingers were cold. With his last breathe, he said, "I am going to Paradise...to be with Allah."

Marcus felt for a pulse but couldn't find one. He left the two bodies where they lay. He considered trying to hide them, but what was the point? These guys were on a mission to kill the boys and him. Why should he care if the rodents and the crows ate them? And at the end of the day, did it really matter? He had nothing to hide. He had done what he had to do. He would have to tell the police and whoever else got involved what had happened here, and this was not the time to try to cover something up. No matter, you couldn't lie yourself out of this kind of shit anyway.

***

Marcus reached the ridge above Upper Trout Lake just before midnight and keyed the talk button on the radio, hoping the boys had remembered to turn theirs on. "Bodie, do you copy?" He waited. "Bodie, it's Dad. Do you copy?" He tried to keep the desperation out of his voice.

"I copy. This is Bodie. Dad, where are you? Do you have Mom?"

Marcus let out a huge sigh of relief. They had made it out, and they were safe. "I'm just above Upper Trout Lake. I should be to you in about another hour or so. Is Jake there? Over." He had intentionally ignored the question about Annie knowing full well that in a moment Bodie and anybody else with him would hear what he had to say.

"Yeah, he's right here."

"Marcus, this is Jake. What the hell is going on? These boys are scared to death!"

"Jake, are the police there?"

"Yeah. Sheriff Watkins, out of Bridgeport—I'll put him on."

"This is Sheriff Watkins, over."

"Sheriff, this is Marcus Diablo. My wife, Annie, has been kidnapped. Over."

"Okay, settle down, Marcus. I need you to take a minute and collect yourself—you've been pushing pretty hard. Just sit down for a minute, compose yourself, and tell me what happened, over."

Taking Sheriff Watkins's advice he sat down on a rock and gathered his thoughts. The sheriff needed enough information so that he could get his people and whoever else he might need to the Buck Creek Canyon trailhead right away.

Knowing that his sons were listening, and that he would have to give the sheriff all the details when he got down, Marcus told a condensed version of what had happened. After a pause in his transmission, the sheriff broke in, "All right, Marcus, you get down here safe. I'm going to head on down to the parking lot at Buck Creek Canyon. I need to get a hold of the search-and-rescue team and my deputies and arrange for some lights."

After a brief pause, the sheriff said, "When you get here, Jake will bring you and your boys down. Now, you listen to me. We're going to do everything possible to find your wife. I really need to go, but you hold it together, you hear me? Are you okay, Marcus? Do you need any assistance?"

"Thanks, Sheriff, I'm okay. Go find Annie! And I think you might want to call in the FBI. I'll be at the parking lot in less than two hours. Please find my wife, Sheriff. Find her."

"I hear that, Marcus, and I'm on it. See you soon. Here's your son."

Bodie's voice trembled, "Dad, what about Mom?"

"I saw her buddy. We'll talk when I get there. Take care of your brother. Dad out."

He changed headlamps and set out at a steady jog down the trail, his mind was reeling, trying to sort out what all this was about. Annie was the toughest woman he'd ever known, and she could outwork, outrun, outhaul anyone he knew—including him, most of the time. She came from tough stock. Marcus thought his family ancestral history was amazing, but compared to Annie's, his forbears had come to America on the good ship *Lollipop*.

When he thought of the struggles and risks that her people took to come to America, from a little town in the Ukraine, across Siberia and the Bering Sea, it explained much about her: how she looked at the world, her love of the wilderness. Annie thrived on hard work and challenge. Physical exertion, to her, was like a drug. If anyone could survive this, it was her.

CHAPTER SIX

Annie lay on her side, facing the back of the rear seat of the car, her legs tied together at the ankles, her arms bound behind her back, and a cloth gag in her mouth. She squirmed around to clear a space so she could get more air. She could hear and see little else. She knew if she let it, fear would soon consume her and that if an opportunity did come for her to try and make an escape, she would be unable to. Marcus was always so good at this, the staying calm in the face of danger and adversity thing, at being level headed when they were out in the backcountry, skiing or climbing. Because of the boys, she too had come to see the value in it. Marcus always said "Find strength in the struggle, or you lose the battle before the fight even begins." So his words, that had so often infuriated her, now echoed in her mind, giving her a calming, steely resolve.

The driver's door opened, slammed shut, the car started, and began moving. She assumed the driver was the only one of the men she had talked to—the one who introduced himself as Ricky. Whoever it was, he didn't say a word. Annie forced herself to concentrate. She could tell they were on the gravel road that would lead to the highway. She felt the vehicle slow and turn right. South she thought, toward LA. She felt the steep downgrade as she fought to keep her face from being slammed into the rear seat. Minutes later the car slowed again and turned left. Left she thought, what the hell? If she was correct they were now headed almost due east. Shit, all there was in that direction was desert. So that was it. Instead of killing her up on the mountain, in an area where her body might be discovered rather quickly, he was going to take her into the middle of the Nevada desert and dump her in an area where her rotting corpse might go weeks and even months before someone stumbled upon it.

Find strength in the struggle, she said to herself over and over, until somehow, she drifted off into a restless sleep. When she awoke it was dark and the car was moving at what seemed like a fast clip.

A few hours later she began to notice the sounds of traffic and light shining through the dark tinted windows as if maybe they were driving through a town or a city. Then she heard the driver speak. "Hey this is Ricky. I have a package for you. I think you are expecting me." A pause. He must be on the phone she thought, "Yeah I have it plugged into my navigation system. I should be there in about thirty minutes." Then the conversation ended.

A short time later the car came to a stop. The back was opened and a man Annie had never seen before yanked her from the car. She looked around. They were in some kind of industrial park, the kind with lots of warehouses. She also noticed how hot it was outside. Even though it was the middle of the night or very early morning it had to be at least a hundred. Without a word, she was hopped to a door and led into one of the buildings.

Once inside the bonds on her ankles were removed. She was led to another door. Before she entered, her wrist bonds were cut, the gag removed, and she was pushed through, the door slammed shut and locked behind her.

It was pitch black inside. Standing there she attempted to adjust her eyes but it was no use. She moved awkwardly forward, stooped over, feet taking small shuffling, probing steps, her arms sweeping the air in front of her. Her foot bumped into something on the ground. On her knees she searched with her hands, it felt like a mattress. It was then that she realized the stifling, still heat. It was like a sauna. Crawling onto the mattress she felt the ground around the perimeter. At one end and side a wall, so the space was small, then off to the right side some kind of carton covered with plastic. With more careful inspection it felt like a case of water bottles. Annie was beyond worrying that these men, whoever the hell they were, might try and poison or drug her. She tore through the plastic and pulled out one of the warm bottles. Her first sip was tentative, but then satisfied she finished off the bottle and opened another.

For a long time she sat in the center of the mattress, trying to make sense of what had happened. She took off her shirt, poured water over it, and carefully probed her swollen eye and split lip. She replayed the scene in her head. Everything seemed okay when, while running, she had come upon the five men with mules and horses. They often encountered groups exploring the wilderness this way and she didn't think twice about stopping and saying hello. That is until she had asked what it was they were doing, digging around at the base of the big trees. Then out of nowhere Ricky had struck her with his fist in the side of the head while ranting about the faults of American women. Then she was bound and tied, laying on her stomach, across the back of one the mules.

Pouring more water onto her shirt she washed some of the sweat and grime from her body as a sense of panic swept through her. She was certain she had seen five men, but when a few hours later, she had been taken off the mule, she only saw three. It was possible that the other two had already moved out of her sight. So why didn't she think so? Another thought popped into her mind, and it surprised her that it had such a calming effect. For all the things she loved about Marcus, there was one aspect of his personality that drove her crazy most of the time, and on a few occasions scared the shit out of her.

The single-minded focus that he preached to her and the boys when they were on an adventure, especially in the mountains, was for Marcus more about a state of mind than an actual physical location. Throughout their twenty years together, she had seen Marcus, on many occasions, whether business or recreation, focus on a task or a goal so completely that he could tune out almost everything around him. And Annie knew that what Marcus might consider as a viable option, most people couldn't remotely envision. So if those two men had been sent to their campsite to find him and the boys, they were up against an adversary whose wrath could be fueled by an imagination without boundaries.

Using the damp shirt to cool her skin, she laid back exhausted on the mattress. As she closed her eyes and tried to picture a happy ending to her nightmare, she knew Marcus was out there, and that he would never stop looking for her.

CHAPTER SEVEN
August 7

It was almost one a.m. when Marcus arrived at the front door of the High Sierra Lodge and found Jake and the boys sitting on the front porch. After a brief, tearful reunion they loaded into Jake's truck and headed down the mountain to meet Sherriff Watkins at Buck Creek trailhead parking lot.

Driving down the dark mountain road, Marcus's adrenaline buzz began to fade. The boys' worried voices echoed from the backseat, "What's going on? Why would they take Mom? Where are they taking her? Is she going to be okay?"

The fatigue of the last eighteen hours was crashing down on him like a wave on a beach. Two men were dead, he had covered close to twenty-five miles, and he had no answers.

The boys were fighting off sleep in the backseat, as the truck rumbled up the gravel road into the trailhead parking lot. The dashboard clock read just before two a.m. The sheriff's department had set up a command post, and the high-powered road construction lights had the parking lot lit up like a small-town football field on Friday night. Jake pulled up, and Marcus jumped out of the truck to find a big man in a kelly green jacket walking toward him.

"Marcus?" A big hand reached out. "Sheriff Bill Watkins."

The boys piled out of the back, saying in unison, "Have you found our mom?"

The Sheriff took a step forward and rested a big hand on each boy's head, tousling their hair. "No, but we aim to. Now, we're doing everything we can. And right now I need to talk to your dad. Why don't you go over there?" he said, pointing to a table set up under one of the floodlights, with coffee urns and a few large pastry boxes. "Get yourselves some hot chocolate and a cookie. You both look like you could use it. We'll be right over."

Marcus nodded at them, and reluctantly they headed for the table.

Sheriff Watkins was a big man, six four and maybe two fifty. He looked to be somewhere in his late-fifties. He had salt and pepper, military cut hair and a thick, well-groomed gray mustache. His dark, intense eyes and beginnings of a paunch suggested a good'ol boy manner that Marcus instantly took a liking too.

They walked over to a well-lit table covered with a large topographical map.

The area where he had last seen Annie was circled in red. Marcus was anxious and impatient. He wanted to go tearing off up the trail to look for Annie himself. But he forced himself to stay calm. Starting at the beginning he replayed what had happened. The sheriff listened without interrupting.

"Well, son, sounds like you had a full day," he said when Marcus finished. "Any idea why they would want to take your wife?"

"No. I just think she was in the wrong place at the wrong time. Why they decided to take her, I don't know! I think maybe she saw something she wasn't supposed to." Saying it to himself didn't seem so bad, but now, saying it to someone else, it sounded lame.

Just then Sheriff Watkins's radio squawked. "Sheriff, we have something here. Roscoe found it."

"I read you, Willy. Is it the woman? Have you found her?"

"No sir, but we found some rope with what looks like blood on it."

"All right, sit tight. No one touches anything. I'm on my way up—be there in about fifteen."

Sheriff Watkins turned to Jake and Marcus. "Let's go and see what we have. Marcus, I think it would be best if your sons stayed here." It wasn't a suggestion.

Marcus looked to the boys standing with cups in their hands talking to a grandmotherly woman with short, wavy gray hair, dressed in jeans and brown boots and a lightweight navy blue ski jacket. Jake noticed Marcus's gaze, "That's Maggie, Bill's wife. They're good people. Let the boys be for a minute—they're in good hands."

Marcus turned toward the boys, their pleading eyes drilling holes through him. Too loudly, he said, "I am going up the hill with the sheriff and Jake. You guys stay here with Maggie."

Before they could protest, he turned away and headed up the trail, right behind Sheriff Watkins. His big frame moved in long, easy strides up the trail. He pulled a high-intensity LED flashlight from his Sam Browne belt. Marcus was feeling dead on his feet and struggled to keep up.

They arrived at the location where Marcus had seen Annie taken into the woods. The man they now met was a tall, rangy, thirty-something with a wiry build and long, straight hair pulled back in a ponytail wearing a head lamp similar to the one Marcus had worn just hours earlier. He had a solid-black German shepherd on a leash beside him.

"Sheriff...Jake," Willy acknowledged with a slight nod.

Willy extended his hand, "Willy Wardlow. This here mutt is Roscoe."

"Good to meet you," Marcus said shaking his hand.

"What have we got?" the sheriff asked.

"Just in off the trail, no more'n thirty feet, next to that big fir." He pointed with his flashlight. "We found some rope...looks like there's some blood on it. Also, just over there"—again he pointed with his flashlight—"there's a silver necklace with a small medallion on it."

Marcus felt the knot in his gut harden. "Annie's St. Christopher," he said. He reached up to his neck and pulled out his medallion, the flashlight now shining on him. "We all wear one, me, the boys, and Annie. This is the original. I had one made for each of them."

"Are you a religious man, Marcus?" Sheriff Watkins asked.

"Not really. My great-grandmother gave it to me. I've worn it for as long as I can remember. We wear them to protect us in our travels. I know it sounds kind of weird, but it's like our good-luck charm. We never take them off—never."

This was bad. A sense of doom settled over Marcus like a thick, dark cloud. He couldn't get the thought out of his head. Annie's St. Christopher, her personal guardian angel, was here, not with her.

"All right, Willy, good work," said Sheriff Watkins. He reached into his jacket and pulled out a pair of latex gloves and a couple of large plastic evidence bags. He asked Jake and Marcus to wait, and while they watched, he and Willy walked into the woods by the beam of his flashlight.

They returned a few minutes later with the rope in one bag and the St. Christopher in another. Sherriff Watkins handed the bag with the necklace to Marcus. "Do you recognize this? It's an unusual shape. Most of the St. Christophers I've seen are round."

Marcus took the bag, his hands trembling from fatigue and now dread. He forced himself to look at the contents. It was Annie's. He had never seen another St. Christopher medal of the same rectangular shape. Handing the bag back to the sheriff, he reached up and took his necklace off, slipping the whole chain over his head, and handed it to him. "Just compare the two—one's an exact copy of the other."

The sheriff examined them both. "Yup, look identical to me." He continued addressing Willy. "Are you sure the woman isn't here?"

"No way, Sheriff, if she was, Roscoe would have found her. You know that dog can sniff out someone under eight feet of snow."

"Okay, at first light I want Search and Rescue to do a grid search. I want you to go over every square inch from here to the back of the parking lot. Let's see what else we can find. Anything you find, tag and leave it—nobody touches a thing except the CSI guys. I called the FBI and they'll have a team here in about four hours. I'm going to leave a deputy here, and until further notice, this parking lot is shut down. We'll have to reroute everybody south to the pack station at Tioga Pass, or north to the one at Sonora. Don't overlook anything, and I want you to keep your eyes out for any of these." He took out an evidence bag holding the four cell phone–looking devices Marcus had given him.

"I don't know what they are, but from what Marcus here has told me, I want you to treat them as dangerous, possibly *very* dangerous. Whatever you do, I don't want you or any of your people fucking around with them."

Marcus had given Sheriff Watkins four of the five "cell phones" that he had taken from the two dead men's backpacks. But before he arrived at the lodge, he stopped at the old pump shed a hundred yards above the lodge, got one of the phones from the plastic bag, took out its battery, wrapped it all in his rain jacket, and stashed it under a pile of rocks, making sure it was completely hidden from sight. Marcus's constant companion, the nagging voice in his mind, kept telling him that as soon as he turned those devices over to the sheriff, he might never see them again or learn what they were, and that the time might come, at some point in this ordeal, when he needed to know. Perhaps he watched too many movies.

On their way back to the parking lot the sheriff said, "Jake, I need to speak to Marcus and his boys back at the office in town. Think you could bring them in and wait till we're done?" He stroked the iron-gray mustache thoughtfully. "It could take an hour or so. If you can't wait, I'll get one of the deputies to bring them on back up to their cabin."

"No problem, Bill," Jake replied. "I'll hang out as long as needed. If something's going on up in the mountains, the sooner Bonnie and I know, the sooner we can figure out what to do."

As they came into view, the boys ran toward their dad.

"Did you find Mom?" Bodie said, the hope and need undeniable in his voice.

Kneeling down on the gravel, Marcus spoke to his sons, "No but she was there."

The look in their faces asked the question, *how do you know?*

All his harping to them about being honest, about facing the reality of a situation, he just couldn't lie to them. And even though he knew the effect his words would have, he said them anyway. "They found your mom's Saint Christopher." And as if someone had opened an air valve, their small tired bodies sank to the gravel and they sobbed. Marcus took them in his arms and cried with them, and for the first time since becoming a father he felt like he had failed them.

Marcus knew though, that as surely as he couldn't lie to his sons, also he couldn't let them fall into the pit of despair. Annie was alive and was out there alone, so he slowly pulled back from the boys getting them to focus on him. Keeping his voice calm and controlled he said, "We need to go back to town and talk with the sheriff. It shouldn't take too long. Then we need to get back to the cabin and try to get a little rest."

As they all stood, brushing gravel off their pants Marcus saw Jake and the sheriff standing a short distance away. Before the boys could launch into a *Q&A* session, Marcus asked Jake to take the boys so he could ride alone with the sheriff. "Go on with Jake, guys," he said. "I need to speak with the sheriff. It's only a fifteen-minute drive into town."

The boys with their heads hung down, looking small, fragile, and worn out, shuffled off and followed Jake to his truck. Marcus got into Sheriff Watkins's SUV.

"What now?" Marcus asked in a monotone.

"I need you and the boys to get the facts down, in writing, while everything is fresh in your minds. I know you're tired, but we need all the information we can gather now. The FBI forensic team is in route and they're dispatching a team of agents that should be here around noon. I hate to bring in the feds, but if you're right—and to be honest, I can't take the chance of assuming you're not—this is bigger than my small department can handle. We don't have the resources, especially the forensics. These phone things you gave me need to be analyzed right away."

He went on. "Now, Marcus, I want to warn you, when the FBI get here, the suits, shit's going to change. They're going to take over, and they're going to take a long, hard look at you, so if there's *anything* about this whole situation that isn't right, now's the time to tell me." Before Marcus could reply he went on. "Don't get me wrong. I'm damn good at evaluating people, especially the ones trying to feed me a line of bullshit, and I don't think you had anything to do with this. But these FBI guys, by and large, are a bunch of by-the-book pricks, and they'll be crawling up your ass with a microscope."

Marcus shook his head wondering just how much worse things could get.

"You have the gun?" The sheriff asked.

Marcus reached into the backseat and grabbed his pack. He took out the pistol and the spare clip, and set them on top of the large console between the front seats. Then he reached in his front pant pocket and pulled out the spent cartridge casings and dropped them into the cup holder.

Marcus remained silent for a moment, staring ahead at the dotted centerline rolling hypnotically past. "I couldn't care less how far up my ass they wanna crawl. All I want is to find Annie. I'll give 'em any information they want—take a lie detector, give them DNA, whatever." Marcus knew he was rambling, but the sheriff seemed content to let him get it off his chest.

"I'm glad you mentioned DNA," he said. "We're going to need oral swabs from the boys and from you for comparison to the blood on the rope. So, Marcus, I'm interested in what *you* think is going on. What you think the guy, what was his name? Kevin?"

Marcus nodded.

"What he meant by 'firestorm' and the other, big thing."

Marcus desperately needed caffeine. He was having a hard time focusing, keeping his thoughts straight. "I don't really know, Sheriff. All I can figure is that whatever these cell phone things are, somehow they can start a fire. It sounded like these guys had been in the backcountry for a week or so. I'm assuming they've planted these things in other places. I know the route Annie was running, and on the topo map I should be able to figure out the general vicinity where she went off trail. You know as well as I do that this whole area is not a big timber zone—any significant stands are below eight thousand feet. So using a topo, you should be able to identify potential danger zones."

"Do you think this is the only area they were targeting?" Watkins asked.

Massaging his temples and fighting to stay in the moment Marcus answered. "That I don't know. On my way out, I realized there were quite a few other questions I should have asked Kevin, but I needed to find Annie before it got dark. And when I got back to him, he was in a bad way. I smacked him in the face with my pistol really hard—I think I did a lot more damage than just break his nose."

The sheriff gave him that "Ya think?" look. Marcus had told him everything. Well almost everything. The one thing he withheld—at least the one thing he could remember at the time—was that he had found five cell phones, not four.

Just then, they pulled up to the sheriff's office in the small Sierra foothill town of Bridgeport, California. It was one of those purely utilitarian buildings in a county with a low tax base: Slumpstone block, painted light gray, with a flat roof and a single glass door that read, MONO COUNTY SHERIFF'S OFFICE, in black block letters. Jake and the boys pulled in right behind them. The boys were quickly out of his truck and by their father's side.

Annie and Marcus had tried to cultivate a strong sense of independence in their sons. The boys were accustomed to spending time away from them, and now, in the space of twenty-four hours, they were scared to let Marcus out of their sight.

They entered through the glass door and followed the sheriff through another door the dispatcher had to buzz before it would open. The sheriff led them through a large open office area with unoccupied desks. Marcus glanced at his watch. It was almost four in the morning.

He took the boys and Marcus into a small conference room with a big rectangular folding table surrounded by folding chairs. "I'm going to get you each a pad of paper and a pencil," he said. "I want you each to write down everything you can remember, starting when you left on your fishing trip. Try to be as detailed as possible, take your time, and write neatly. Don't worry about the order. If you forget something, just add it when you remember." Recognizing that the task might be a bit difficult for an eight year old, the sheriff, with his hand on Garrett's shoulder said, "You just help your brother remember, and let him write it down, okay? "

Garrett looked back over his shoulder and nodded wearily.

Marcus looked at Bodie and Garrett; he knew that if they even shut their eyes, they would be out like a light. The sheriff must have also noticed that they were all fading fast, because he returned with the pads and pencils, a cup of coffee for Marcus, and two Mountain Dews for the boys. There was also a woman with him who took oral swaps from them.

For the next half hour they sat in silence, with the only interruption the questions the boys asked each other about their trip out of the mountains. At four thirty they finished, handed their pads to the sheriff, and left with Jake to head back to their cabin.

No sooner had they loaded back in Jake's truck than the boys were asleep. "You know, Marcus," Jake said, nodding at the backseat, "if you need to leave them after they get some sleep, they can stay at the lodge with Bonnie and me. I'll put them to work to keep their minds off what's going on. You're going to need to spend some time with the sheriff, and if the FBI or anyone else wants to talk to the kids, they can sure as hell come up here to do it."

As the first hint of dawn stole into a cloudless eastern sky, Jake dropped them off at their cabin. Marcus sleepwalked the boys inside, and put them to bed in his room. There was no way he could sleep, so he put on a pot of coffee, got out his laptop, and sat down to outline the events of the past day. He figured that the more he went over the events, the easier it would be for him and others to make some sense out of all that had happened.

CHAPTER EIGHT

At noon, Marcus dropped the boys off at the lodge and talked for a minute to Bonnie and Jake. Under normal circumstances, leaving the boys with them at the resort would have been a special treat and no problem at all. Today however, things were far from special or normal. Driving away, in route to Bridgeport, he couldn't recall a time he had felt more reluctant to leave them.

Marcus was buzzed into the sheriff's office, where he found him, looking as though he hadn't been to bed either, speaking with three suits.

"Afternoon, Marcus," he said, extending his large hand.

"Afternoon," he replied. "Any news about Annie?"

"Nope, Marcus sorry, but you have good timing, the FBI just arrived. I'd like you to meet Special Agent in Charge Nathan Reynolds, Special Agent Mike Gibson, and Special Agent Sherri Wu. I was just explaining to them that the bodies have been recovered along with all your gear as well as the weapons from the lake. It's all being flown to their facilities in San Francisco as we speak."

As Marcus shook hands all around, he had the feeling of being profiled, quantified, assessed. He also realized that he was doing the same thing to them.

Agent Reynolds and Agent Gibson could have been clones. Both wore dark blue suits, starched white shirts, different versions of the same blue-and-cream-striped club tie, and highly polished wingtip shoes. They were big men, six three or so, somewhere in their early thirties, with expensive haircuts. Both looked to be a very fit couple of hundred pounds: not a wrinkle in their suits and not a hair out of place—all in all, a little too clean-cut–white-bread to suit Marcus' taste.

Agent Wu was striking, and tall for an Asian woman, maybe five eight, with shoulder-length jet-black hair and exotic dark-brown eyes. She wore a tailored dark-blue pantsuit with low-heeled black shoes. They must have all shopped at FBIattire.com.

The Sherriff moved toward the conference room, where just hours earlier, Marcus and the boys had written out their statements. "You guys can set up in here. We have coffee, water, and sodas. Just let me know what you need. But first . . ," he gave the evidence bag he was holding, containing two of the four cell phones Marcus had given him earlier that morning, to Agent Reynolds, "I want you to get a good look at these things. We suspect they may be some kind of incendiary device, and if the forests around here are going to erupt into flames, the sooner I know, the better. As you can see, we're a small department, and we rely on a substantial amount of support from a largely volunteer force, not only for search and rescue but for firefighting as well. Any heads-up we can get will be greatly appreciated. Also, as you may know, I sent a courier to San Francisco with two of these devises as well as the evidence recovered last night, DNA samples from Mr. Diablo and his sons, and the gun."

Agent in Charge Reynolds, responding in a clipped, *you can relax now; the professionals are here* tone, said, "Seems you've been very thorough, Sheriff. As soon as we have talked with Mr. Diablo and evaluated the information, we'll decide just how important these phone things are. Until then, thank you for your cooperation, if we need anything else, we'll ask. It might be best if you just went back to business as usual."

Marcus could see Sheriff Watkins stiffen ever so slightly at Reynolds's supercilious attitude, but he just gave a nod of the head.

Business as usual? What the hell was that? Did this young hotshot think people got abducted every day from the backcountry? Did he think the sheriff and basically everybody else who lived and worked in these mountains were a bunch of ignorant hayseeds? Marcus didn't like Agent Nathan Reynolds, and was pretty sure that in the next minute or so, the feeling would be mutual. They all took a seat at the table: Agents Gibson and Wu on one side, he on the other, and Agent Reynolds at the head of the table with his back to the far wall. Marcus pulled the UBS drive from his shirt pocket and slid it across the table to Agent Reynolds.

"What's this?" he asked.

"It's a detailed outline of everything that has taken place since my wife and I left with our sons for our backpacking trip on Monday morning. Everything in italics is supposition based on my observations; everything else is exactly what happened. I've tried to be as accurate as possible in reference to the timelines."

"Seems that you are also a very thorough man," Agent Reynolds said in a tone that implied he was perhaps a bit *too* thorough. From TV and crime novels Marcus knew there were three credos that all law enforcement believe in and live by. One: the first forty-eight hours of any investigation are the crucial time for gathering evidence, obtaining forensics, interviewing witnesses, and following leads. Two: anytime a spouse or child goes missing, the most likely suspect is the other spouse or the parents. And three: everybody lies—everybody.

"I'm tired, Agent Reynolds," Marcus said, not even trying to hide his frustration. "My sons and I are worried to death about Annie. I needed to make sure I got everything down, every detail I could remember."

"Okay, settle down!" Reynolds said in the same tone Marcus used with his sons when they got themselves all sideways about one thing or another. "All right, we're going to go through everything, from the time you and your family left your cabin on your backpacking trip." He reached down and took a small digital recorder out of his briefcase and set it on the table. "We're going to be recording this." It was not a question.

For the next couple of hours, Marcus went through the events of the past two days. Occasionally, Agent Reynolds, Gibson, or Wu would interrupt him for clarification. The only matter that he left out was that he had found five of the cell phones but had turned over only four to Sheriff Watkins. They listened impassively, giving no indication of whether they believed him. Marcus got the impression they didn't.

"Okay, Mr. Diablo—do you mind if I call you Marcus? Now, let's leave this for the time being. We'll come back to it. There are a few other items we'd like to touch on." He didn't wait for a response. "Marcus, have you and your wife, Annie, been having any problems? You been gettin along?"

So here it was, just as Sheriff Watkins had said.

He looked right at Agent Reynolds. "No, Annie and I are fine. And just what the fuck has that got to do with her being taken?"

Reynolds looked right back at him, not the least bit intimidated by his rising temper and less than civil language. "Well, Marcus...." His first name again. "That is the question, now, isn't it? What *does* your relationship with your wife have to do with her going missing?"

Marcus took a deep breath—a huge sigh, really, of weariness over what he could see coming. And even this small act of self-control seemed to be interpreted as an act of deception.

"Listen, Agent Reynolds"—he hadn't been told to call him Nathan—"I didn't have anything to do with this mess. My only concern is finding Annie. Now, in my view, you are wasting valuable time. If you think that you and these other agents were pulled away from your office, and sent out to Bum Fuck Egypt only to accuse me of staging some elaborate scheme to get rid of my wife, then you're barking up the wrong tree."

Without missing a beat, Reynolds moved to another topic. "Let's talk about the gun. Do you always go everywhere with a loaded pistol?"

"No. Call it paranoia, whatever, it just seems like a good idea to have a pistol when I am in the middle of nowhere, with two young sons and a beautiful wife." He answered, but got the impression they weren't buying it either.

And just like that, Agent Reynolds rose from his chair and said, "Let's take a quick break." With a slight twitch of his head, he indicated that he wanted Agents Gibson and Wu to follow him from the room. They all went out into the main office, shutting the door behind them.

As Marcus sat there in the sterile, plain conference room, and finished off what must have been his fifteenth cup of coffee, he felt tired and weighed down by an all-encompassing feeling of doom. If he thought his life sucked yesterday, this was a whole new level of suck. The caffeine-induced buzz of his body seemed to be in sync with the sound coming from the overhead fluorescent tubes, that high-pitched, almost subliminal reverberation just one notch more bearable than fingernails run across a chalkboard. He laid his head atop folded arms on the table and closed his eyes.

Grandpa Charlie, his dad's father, had this saying: "Keep a string tied on it, boy!" When he was young, he really had no idea what he meant, it just sounded cool. But as he got older, he took Grandpa Charlie's words to mean, "Keep your head, boy, and don't let your mind and your mouth outrun your common sense."

He was certain that the saying applied to his current situation, but it looked as though it was going to require a very long string.

***

It was five o'clock when Marcus got back into his truck to head back to the cabin. Checking his phone he saw a message from his brother-in-law, Mario, he had driven through Bridgeport a few hours ago. Marcus had talked to him that morning, explained what had happened and that he was on his way to meet the sheriff and the FBI. Mario said he would come down to the cabin and that if Marcus wasn't there he would pick the boys up at the resort. He had also informed Jake and Bonnie and that Mario might be up to get them. This was a good thing. His boys loved their uncle Mario, and it would be good for them to have more family close at hand.

Driving up the grade Marcus replayed the scene with the FBI. After Agent Reynolds had called their little break, Agent Wu returned, by herself, to have a run at him. When Marcus lost his cool and began to shout, Agent Reynolds entered the conference room and threatened to charge Marcus as an "Enemy Combatant," under a provision of the Patriot Act. It seemed that the suspension of civil rights and due process, habeas corpus and other little constitutional inconveniences, were of no concern to the FBI. And in truth, Marcus had no problem with the detention of suspected terrorists. He didn't even give a great, steaming heap of horseshit if their rights were ignored and violated, but when it came to his rights, the rights of a regular, hardworking American—that was a different story altogether.

Over the course of the remainder of the afternoon Marcus was accused of being a wife-hating husband, and Agent Reynolds even alluded to the idea that Marcus might be some cunningly disguised closet Wahhabi terrorist. The whole thing to Marcus was beyond reason. When he finally had enough, there was a moment when Marcus was certain that Agent Reynolds was not going to let him leave. Now, driving back to his boys he couldn't help but wonder, again, how much worse the situation would get?

CHAPTER NINE
Canby, Oregon

Ricky arrived back at his home in Canby, a little over twenty-four hours after he had taken off from the parking lot at Buck Creek. He should have been exhausted especially after the four hundred mile detour. Instead, after dropping off the American women he felt quite proud and content with himself during the long drive back to Oregon. Everything had gone according to plan, well, almost everything.

While he was retuning the horses and mules to the outfitter, he had called his father, Dr. Abdurrahim Faradi, and explained the situation, and by the time he had the woman loaded in his vehicle he received a text with instructions. It seemed, if played right, they might be able to use this woman not only to further their cause but, perhaps, also deliver another blow into the hearts and minds of their enemy. And what better place in all of America to make a definitive statement than the glaring, neon lit, mecca of depravity and avarice?

Ricky drove around behind the house to the barn, parked, and went directly to the special room, a self-contained shelter located twenty feet beneath the barn's dirt floor. His father, dressed in his customary grey wool slacks, starched white shirt and black sweater vest, was standing, facing him, when the electronically activated door swished open. Dr. Faradi appraised his son. With beard stubble and clothing that hadn't been attended to in over a week, along with a smell to match, Ricky had a rugged, hardened appearance. "Jihad suits you my son," his father said, while clasping a firm hand on each side of Ricky's shoulders. "In a small way you now know firsthand the struggles our brothers must endure." Ricky knew his father was referring to life as a *jihadist* in the mountains and rugged plains of Afghanistan and Pakistan. As a child and teenager he had always held a romanticized vision of these men. He learned, in this very room, the tenets of Islam and of the commitment and struggles of those who sacrificed all, who lived and trained in a harsh land in hopes of being chosen to fight and die for Allah.

"After you called I made contact with our friend. It seems he has many allies. Now come, take a few moments to compose yourself while I finish my report and then you and I must speak and pray," Dr. Faradi said, as they both sat, in matching rolling office chairs.

Ricky leaned back into the leather of the ergonomic chair, and ran his hands over his unshaven face. The adrenaline rush of the last forty hours was fading as he reflected on the man he knew his father was speaking of, Adad al-Mohmoud, the wealthy young Syrian who controlled one of the largest financial empires in the world. The previous February, his father had received an invitation to attend an Ethics of Bioengineering in Genetic Manipulation conference in New York

City. Inside the gold embossed invitation there was a cryptic message, hand written in Persian, requesting that Dr. Faradi bring his son, Abbas Majid, with him. This was a name that had never been uttered, or for that matter was even known, to Ricky's knowledge, by anyone other than himself and his parents. During their stay in New York, while Dr. Faradi was attending the conference, Ricky had received a visit while in their hotel suite. With his hands still covering his face, he recalled that day.

***

The second day of the conference, a knock on the door of their hotel room roused Ricky from an unplanned afternoon nap. Upon opening the door, he was greeted by a tall, strikingly handsome, well-dressed Middle Eastern man. In his tailored suit, his jet-black hair cut very *GQ*, he was the definitive picture, at least in Ricky's mind, of success and power. "Abbas Majid, Lion of the Glorious Sword," the man said, evoking the English translation of Ricky's Persian name. "It is my great pleasure to meet you. *Assalamu alaikum,*" the man said, extending his hand. "May I come in? We have much to discuss, and time is short."

Ricky stared in recognition. Although he had never met this man, his face was well known in the Arab world, Adad al-Mohmoud. The man before him spoke impeccable English with an accent suggesting many years of education in the UK. Attempting to compose himself and shake off the effects of his sleep, Ricky made a lame effort to straighten up the room.

"Leave that, my young friend and come sit. The warriors of Allah must sleep when they can," Adad said, as he motioned for Abbas to take a seat at the small table.

Feeling awed and suddenly not very confident, Ricky took a seat across from Adad. With legs crossed and hands clapped in his lap, Adad spoke. "You see Abbas, I am a student and great admirer of the late Shah of Iran. If I had not become obsessed with finding his private papers and been willing to pay a small fortune for the privilege," a wicked smile creased the chiseled features of his face, "I would never have come upon this brilliant plan—this *Petit Amérique*—that led me to your father… and you."

Startled by the mention of *Petit Amérique,* that like his Persian name was something, he believed, was a special secret shared by only a very select few, Ricky started at Adad, his mouth agape.

Seeing the surprise on Ricky's face Adad said, his tone casual, "What Abbas, do you not believe there were others who supported this plan to not simply prepare educated Iranians ready to emigrate to the United States, but to prepare educated Iranians *dedicated to the establishment of a worldwide Muslim caliphate* ready to emigrate to the United States."

"No…no…," Ricky stammered, "I did not mean…."

Adad smiled at Ricky and gestured with both hands, palms up, "It is all right my young friend. It is one thing to plan for a holy jihad, and another entirely to

41

see that plan on the very edge of fruition, is it not? So tell me Abbas, are there others who share you and your father's commitment?"

Unsure how he should address this man, this icon, before him, Ricky began, his tone halting. "Yes your—"

"Please Abbas, you and I are brothers, call me Adad."

"Yes Adad, we have kept our faith strong, but hidden. We have put on all appearances of joining the multitude of foreigners who have embraced America's corrupt and immoral ways."

Gently shaking his head, and with a smug smile, Adad indicated for Abbas to continue.

For the next few hours, Abbas explained, in detail, everything to Adad. His father had located every member of Little America who still lived in the United States. Out of the group, he found forty-eight couples who shared the commitment. The sons and, in some cases, daughters of these members were eager to be part of a holy crusade.

Rubbing his hands together, Adad appraised Abbas. "You have done very well my brother. How glorious is the will and foresight of Allah? One man's grand scheme to avenge the dishonor of being played the puppet of America is now, thirty years later, thanks to true believers like you and your father, and now *me*," Adad paused a moment and rested his hand over his heart before continuing, "going to deliver the blow that will bring the mighty Satan to its knees. And how ingenious to use you and your father's fields of expertise in the formulation of an attack, that will strike fear and distrust into the hearts of *all* Americans. Imagine their surprise when they realize it was their own blind arrogance that prevented them from comprehending the simplicity and scope of this…wonderful plan. While the authorities are making watch lists and monitoring airports we will attack from within. We shall strike in locations that are…how do they say…American as apple pie." Adad chuckled at his own joke and his zealous, infectious excitement made Abbas smile.

Uncrossing his legs and leaning forward in his chair Adad continued. "Please, pass my praise on to your father. Now it is time to put this plan into effect. As we speak a system is being put in place by where we can communicate, and funds will be put at your disposal. Sadly to say, you and I shall not meet again unless you survive the aftermath. I fully expect you to lead one of the teams and to ensure that the other leaders are your equal. And should it be Allah's will and you come through unscathed, you shall become a member of my personal staff by the year's end. Your commitment and effort shall be rewarded, and your keen intellect put to work, furthering the proliferation of Islam."

The two men stood and Adad embraced Abbas. "My brother, words cannot express my gratitude. May the light and blessing of Allah go with you."

As Adad took his leave, the wheels had been put in motion.

***

Opening his eyes, Ricky saw that his father was just finishing up. Sitting up in his chair he asked, "What has Adad planned for the woman?"

Swiveling away from the computer monitor to face his son, Dr. Faradi said, "That I do not know. All he said is that it would be the grand finale in our fight and that in a few days the whole world would know about the *New Islamic Dawn.*"

Adad himself had come up with the name, and Dr. Faradi rather liked it.

"Now we must resume our daily routines and wait. It is very important that you return to your normal life. Even after the destruction begins we must appear as shocked and angry as any American."

Ricky thought about his father's comment. He found it ironic that terrorism, at its base, was so much like a theatrical production. Everything staged, controlled, and planned to elicit a specific emotional response.

Standing Ricky's father grabbed two prayer rugs that were folded on one of the shelves, and father and son knelt to perform the Salaat.

CHAPTER TEN
Damascus, Syria

Seated side by side on a leather covered bench, inside the centuries old al-Srouji bathhouse, Sheik Nazir al Mohmoud said to his son, Adad, "Your visits, are to infrequent these days. Your son and your wife miss your presence."

Adad knew from his father's tone that he too missed him. For Adad, this bathhouse within the walls of the "Old City", always reminded him of how little some aspects of life had changed in the last fourteen hundred years. Here in the world's oldest inhabited city, the divisions between Arab and non-Arab were as pronounced as ever. And the fact that in this neighborhood of Al-Shaghour lived Syria's largest Jewish population, that too seemed to typify the root of the struggles and conflicts in *his* world. And now with Syria in the midst of a civil war his people were fighting amongst themselves and it was by the grace of Allah, and some very wealthy and powerful Syrians like his father, that his simple place of refuge was still accessible.

"I know father," Adad began, his tone clam and yet commanding. "But our business demands much of my time. Have we not doubled and redoubled our holding since I took control?" The rhetorical question was stated without a hint of boast.

"Yes my son, the requirements of wealth are a great burden, but you have borne them well. So tell me, what is so important that I had to return to Damascus from Palmyra?"

The yearly trip to the oasis at Palmyra was an act that symbolized the Mohmoud family's willingness to endure the hardships of their faith. It severed as reminder of the sacrifices required, for centuries, of their Bedouin ancestors crossing the inhospitable Syrian desert, on their way to the lush Euphrates valley. And was all the more important now, given the current state of affairs in Syria. Shifting the shawl of his horizontally striped, cotton robe, Adad turned toward his father. They had already sat in the hammam, the traditional steam bath, and were now cooling down in the sitting area. Adad fixed his gaze upon the patriarch of the Mohmoud clan. "I am sorry father, I know how you value the yearly sojourn to the oasis, but there are events which are about to unfold that will not only affect us, but all Muslims."

Nazir questioningly raised his eyebrows, "There are things in motion that demand my personal attention. In fact, I may need to stay away for an extended period of time. My son, Jabril and wife, Mishael must be understanding," Adad said to his father in a tone of voice that made it clear he was asking his father to make sure his wife and son were looked after.

"What else might I do to assist you?" Nazir asked, with his hands clasped in his lap.

Standing, Adad walked to the window that looked into the interior courtyard. With his back to his father, Adad stared at the shimmering waves of heat rising from the limestone paving stones, and thought how the spewing fountain provided a false sense of coolness to the harsh reality of a Syrian summer. In that instant it struck Adad that America, just like the fountain, provided a false sense of comfort and security to her people. Still looking out the window, Adad spoke. "We must trust in Allah, father. We are embarking upon the path of righteous glory. In a matter of days the world will view all of Islam in a new light." Turning to face Nazir, he continued. "For too long have the nations of Islam been looked down upon by the West. Our resources are the only things of interest to them. Our peoples, our beliefs are of no concern. But thanks to your good friend, the Shah of Iran, that is about to change." Approaching his seated father, Adad knelt before him, his knees cushioned by the thick carpet. Taking his father's hands in his, "You must be patient, I will get word to you. But do not worry if our communications are few. I do not mean to be cryptic, but for your safety and the safety of my son, the less you know, for now, the better."

Nazir looked intently into his handsome son's, deep brown eyes, "You have done well my son, your sense of faith, family and business is a source of great pride to me. I will continue to look out after our interests here in Syria," the implied reference to Adad's family clear, "and will leave the rest to you."

Standing and urging Adad to his feet, Nazir embraced his son. "Go with God, and be well in the knowledge that it was by the hand of Allah that you were chosen to lead."

CHAPTER ELEVEN

Marcus stepped onto the native flagstone floor of the cabin to find his brother-in-law Mario and the boys preparing dinner. So typically Italian Marcus thought, the one sure fire remedy for any ill, food.

Their chore immediately abandoned, the boys turned to their dad. "Did they find Mom?" "Where is she, Dad?" both of them saying the words in unison, as if rehearsed. He could see and hear their need for an answer that would make the events of the past few days seem like just a bad dream. *Just tell us Mom is okay and everything can go back to the way it was before—please, Dad!*

Marcus sat tiredly on the bench at the dining table, indicating with a pat for the boys to sit on either side. Trying to sound confident, he said, "The FBI is here, and they're going to find your mom. Now we need to hold ourselves together and be ready to help in any way we can. Can you guys do that for me?"

They both nodded hesitantly. Their expressions indicated the doubt they heard in their father's voice.

Mario came to his rescue. "Hey guys, I'll finish up here you go out back and start the coals for the steaks while I talk to your dad." Reluctantly the boys did as they were asked. Marcus grabbed a beer from the refrigerator and took a long pull as he sat back down. He stared at Mario without speaking. Mario Mattucci was the quintessential Italian. He was built like a fireplug, five feet eight and 220, head sitting on his shoulders and never mind a neck, short, powerful arms and legs. But his most imposing feature was his dark brown eyes, which bulged as if they might pop right out of his head at any moment. Along with his brother Glen, Mario was one of the smartest men Marcus knew, and he was glad to see him.

Breaking the silence Mario said, "I have a basic idea of what's going on. I talked to Jake. He told me what happened, and the boys filled me in on what they know. Are you holding up okay?"

Marcus took another long pull from the bottle of pale ale. "I don't know what's going on. Yesterday the boys and I went fishing. We were all supposed to go, but in the morning Annie decided she wanted to go running instead. If only she had just come fishing with us...." His voice trailed off.

"Well, Marcus, that didn't happen," he said. "So there's no sense in beating yourself up about it. It won't help, and now we have to focus on what we know and what we can do." Mario responded, stepping seamlessly from concerned brother-in-law to lawyer.

"Okay, walk me through everything," Mario said. "I'm particularly interested in how everything went with the FBI."

By the time he finished, Marcus was well into his second beer and the alcohol was creeping up on his exhausted, underfed body. This time he left nothing out—nothing. Now only he and Mario knew about the fifth cell phone.

***

As the four of them were eating Mario said, "Marie and the girls will be here first thing in the morning. Your brother Harold is coming with them. Also, Glen called Marie, apparently he couldn't reach you, and he's coming in on Qantas from Sydney with Ellie and the kids as we speak. Looks like we're circling the wagons." Between bites he continued. "As for Annie's family, Marie called them and said she would keep them in the loop." Annie's was the youngest in her family, her next sibling, almost ten years older. Consequently, her family was not nearly as close as Marcus's. Hell, Marcus thought with a sad smile, his family's closeness was a big part of the reason Annie fell in love with him in the first place.

For a moment, Marcus thought about protesting, but Mario put his hand up to stifle any reply. "Right now you and the boys need your family." It wasn't what he said, but what his words implied that bothered Marcus the most. *What if this ends badly? What if Annie doesn't come back alive? How would he and boys handle that?*

Just as they were finishing their meal, they heard a vehicle pull into the gravel driveway. Marcus got up from the table walked to the windows at the front of the cabin, and noticed not one but two cars: the sheriff's SUV and a nondescript dark-gray Crown Victoria—that had to the FBI. He grinned. The sheriff would have had no trouble navigating the road with his high center and four-wheel drive, but the Crown Vic must have taken quite a thumping coming up the steep, rocky incline.

He walked back to the table and sat down. "We've got visitors," he said. "Looks like the sheriff and the FBI." The boys looked up, as if for a cue that they should stop chewing.

"Go on, finish up," Marcus said gently. "Whatever they want can wait till we're done."

***

Sheriff Watkins and the FBI agents looked around at the old wood covering the walls and ceiling, the huge exposed timbers, and the antique knickknacks and furniture. After a moment of wondering silence the sheriff stepped forward.

"Marcus...boys," he said, smiling. He turned to Mario and extended his hand. "Sheriff Watkins."

Mario stood up from the table and shook his hand. "Mario Mattucci. Good to meet you."

"Agents Reynolds, Gibson, and Wu from the FBI," the sheriff said to Mario. Mario nodded but made no move to shake their hands. "They have some questions for you, Marcus, and for the boys. Is it all right?"

"Sure, Sheriff. Let us just finish up." Marcus said. "Make yourselves at home, cold drinks and beer in the fridge."

"You know what, Marcus?" the Sheriff said, heading for the fridge. "Officially, I'm off duty, and after the day I've had, I'd love a beer."

"Agent Reynolds, can I get you guys anything?" Marcus asked, certain he would decline, which he did. As the three agents made their way out to the front deck Marcus thought that he was perhaps not the only person in the world who considered the FBI's attitude predictable.

The boys got to cleaning up, washing the dishes, putting away the leftover food, and doing anything else they could to hide their renewed and rising anxiety.

***

On the sofa, Mario sat next to the boys so that they were between him and their father. Sheriff Watkins sat in Annie's rocker, leaving the agents to grab patio chairs from the deck. After some brief sparing between Agent Reynolds and Mario as to what and what would not be allowed in terms of the boys, the interview began. Reynolds picked up right where had left off in regard to Marcus and Annie's relationship. Staying true to form he bounced from one topic to another hardly taking a breath. One minute Marcus was a man responsible of getting rid of his wife, the next an Islamic sympathizer, and the next a left wing environmental wacko.

When their attention turned to the boys it was agent Wu who took the lead. Yeah, Marcus thought, let the women talk to the boys. Their mom's gone missing, and their dad is the chief suspect—let's go for the motherly connection. There must be some handbook these guys were all required to read and memorize—something like *A hundred and One Truisms of Crooks, Criminals, and Wife-Hating Husbands.*

All in all the boys did fine, considering their ages and the circumstances, but when Agent Wu made Garrett cry, Marcus was done. "Okay, Agent Reynolds," Marcus said standing, "let's get to the heart of this dog-and-pony show. You think I hired a team of guys, with horses and pack mules to be in the backcountry to coincide with our backpacking trip. Then somehow, maybe using my well-honed psychic powers, I subliminally convinced my wife to go running and not come fishing with us. Then these guys, these *Arab* guys, come to our campsite and ransack it. Then I kill them both, send my sons out of the mountains by themselves, and hang out for the next seven or eight hours just to make the whole ruse complete. Hike out of the backcountry in the dark, get hold of the police, *and* suggest that they call the FBI—all to put the finishing touches on the perfect crime. I think maybe, you spend too much time watching TV."

Agent Reynolds replied, "I'll admit that it would have required a lot of planning and coordination. It seems like a lot of coincidences, and we haven't connected all the dots yet." He said this "yet" part intimating that in time they would. Hell, in time they could probably link him or anyone else, to the assassination of JFK, the disappearance of Jimmy Hoffa, and conspiracy to commit global warming.

Marcus was ready to leap across the Red Rider sled that served as a coffee table, at agent Reynolds, when Mario stood and placed a restraining arm out and across Marcus's chest. Looking at Reynolds, Mario said, "If you don't have anything useful to ask us, or evidence that can support your far-fetched theories, I think it's time for you all to leave."

With that, the three agents got up, gathering their notes and briefcases. Agent Reynolds said, "Okay, Mr. Diablo, we're going to go, but this isn't over. I need you to be available. I'm sure we're going to be seeing a lot of each other over the coming days, so just stay close by."

"Listen to me. I'm not going anywhere until we find Annie. And if anything happens to her because of your pigheadedness, you're going to see a lot more of me than you want to." For emphasis, he tapped Agent Reynolds in the chest with his finger.

CHAPTER TWELVE
August 8

In the dark of the early morning, Marcus was awakened, by the sound of "Dad, Dad," coming from the loft. He found his sons both on the bottom bunk in animated, excited conversation, while below, undisturbed by the commotion, Mario snored on the sofa bed.

"He keeps saying he saw, Mom!" Bodie said.

Marcus sat down on the edge of the bed and took his youngest son in his arms, "Hey buddy, everything okay? What's goin on?"

"Dad, I talked to Mom!" Garrett said, looking up into his father's eyes. "It wasn't a bad dream Dad. I talked to her. I *saw* her," he continued, more excitement than fear in his voice. "She was in a room with no windows, and it was dark. But there was this light, kind of like a glow around her. She told me she was okay. But, Dad, she said...." Here, he began to quietly sob.

"It's okay I'm here. Take a breath and tell me what she said." Marcus said, as he hugged Garrett to him.

Garrett looked up at his father, the tone of hopeful excitement, of just moments before, gone. "She said she was okay. She told me not to worry about her, and told me to tell you to keep looking for her, that she was close, and was waiting for you. That's all I can remember. What are we going to do, Dad? We have to do something! We have to help her! We have to find her!" Garrett finished, his small voice filled with frantic anxiety, as Marcus held him, wondering to himself, *where the hell are you Annie?*

***

Annie bounced in and out of her nightmare-filled sleep. The darkness of her prison was absolute, and combined with the suffocating stillness of the hot air, it required all her concentration to suppress the panic. Drenched in perspiration, she wet her sweat-stained tee shirt with tepid water and lay back on the mattress. As she swam through a fog of exhaustion and fear, she first heard then saw her youngest son sitting on the bed next to her.

"Hey Momma," Garrett said.

"Garrett, is that you baby? Where are you?" Annie had a sense that she was speaking aloud but somehow knew she wasn't.

"I'm right here Momma." Garrett said as Annie's eyes found his. "I'm with Daddy and Bodie at the cabin. Are you okay?"

"Yes, baby, I'm all right. I'm glad you're okay." Annie replied, with an intense sense of relief that Garrett, Bodie and Marcus had made it out of the mountains.

"Don't worry Momma, Daddy says we're going to find you."

50

"Garrett," Annie said, as her dream-hand touched his, "tell your dad, I think I'm pretty close, and that I'll be waiting for him. Now I want you to go back to sleep. I need to get some rest too, but we can talk whenever you want."

Annie smiled at her young son, as he sat next to her, bathed in a gentle light. They reached out, as if to embrace each other, and as Garrett's angelic face faded, Annie slipped off into a more peaceful and relieved sleep.

CHAPTER THIRTEEN
August 10

Over the next few days, the thousand square foot cabin filled beyond capacity. But Marcus didn't mind and with the boys' cousins there it helped keep their minds, a least somewhat, off their mom.

Marcus was the oldest, and was close to all of his siblings. But of all his brothers and sisters the one Marcus needed the most was his brother Glen. They were just fifteen months apart in age. They grew up together, went to high school and college together, had many of the same friends, lived and adventured together. And even though Glen lived on the other side of the world, they spoke by phone every couple days and managed to fit in a couple "guys" adventures every year.

Glen was the managing director of one of the worlds' largest manufacturers of slot machines, South Pacific operations, headquartered in Sydney. He and his family had lived in Australia for the past eleven years, although his income allowed them to keep their house in Reno.

Annie and Marcus had visited Glen and Ellie their children, Renée and Charlie several times before the boys were born, and all four of them had spent last Christmas together Down Under.

Glen and his family had been here for a couple of days now. As Mario had said, they were circling the wagons. His middle sister Marie, Mario's wife, and their daughters, Kelly and Karen as well as Marcus's youngest brother Harold were also there. His oldest sister Ruth and youngest Lynn who lived in Seattle were planning to arrive in a few days, as was his mother who lived at Lake Tahoe.

***

The FBI did come back but not so much to talk or put forth some off the wall supposition as to Marcus' culpability in the disappearance of Annie. Agents would search the cabin and the property. Thankfully, at Mario's suggestion, they took the phone, and hid it well above the cabin amongst boulders and jumbled granite talus, where it would stay hidden no matter how big a search the FBI mounted.

They served Marcus warrants to search their home in Reno and both Annie's and Marcus's offices. From their respective managers Marcus knew the FBI had seized all of their personal and business records, including financial statements and tax returns. They froze their bank accounts, which Mario was sure was illegal, and made life more of a living hell than it already was.

***

On that Sunday morning, the entire family went up to the resort to see Jake and Bonnie and have breakfast. They had all been spending too much time in the confined space of the cabin, obsessing about Annie, worrying about who had her, where and why they were holding her, all things they had no answers for. At 9:37 a.m. PDT, while eating pancakes and omelets, the first backcountry fire was reported over Jake and Bonnie's radio that monitored park and forest ranger activity.

The location was Mariposa Grove, a stand of ancient giant sequoias near the south entrance to Yosemite National Park, the entrance used most heavily by summer visitors coming from the Sacramento Valley and the Bay Area. The fire spread quickly and was soon threatening El Portal, California, a small community of mostly national park employees and their families. The Forest Service was mobilizing its firefighting crews, air support was en route, and all volunteer firefighting personnel were on standby to defend the houses in greatest danger.

The fire's origin was undetermined. Since there had been no lightning storms, it was assumed that the cause was human.

Marcus listened, from his stool at the counter while he pushed his food around the plate. He couldn't escape the feeling that this was just the beginning. Over the next two hours he and the rest of his family remained frozen to their seats as fires were reported in a half-dozen areas in and around the Hoover Wilderness and Yosemite. There were fires in the Stanislaus, Toiyabe, Sierra, and Inyo National Forests, which surround Yosemite. And unlike national parks, national forests had thousands of year-round residents living within their boundaries. The fires were miles apart, all in areas of heavy timber, and in close proximity to access points for the park and the wilderness area.

As they were getting ready to leave the café the radio squawked, reporting that Interstate 395, five miles east of the cabin, was closed both north and south. They were trapped. On the way out the door, Marcus shared a look with Jake and Bonnie—a look that said, *oh my God.*

***

In a mood of collective disbelief, the family returned to the cabin. One of the few creature comforts Marcus had in their off grid cabin was satellite TV. He had rationalized the need because the boys required satellite Internet service to keep up on their schoolwork when a big dump of snow meant fresh powder, and those opportunities did not always coincide with the weekend. Ellie had turned on the TV to see what was being reported on the national news.

By noon, the CNN header in the upper right corner of the TV screen read, FIREWATCH. There were no commercial breaks, no Wall Street updates, and no gossip on the latest scandal involving some film star, singer, or pro athlete. All attention was on the fires.

For decades, fire in the Lake Tahoe Basin had been a topic of serious speculation. The likely impact of a major blaze in this densely wooded and populated area was frequently debated, though all agreed on the potential for devastation on an unprecedented scale.

The area was dense with timber and billions of dollars worth of homes. It was a place where fire, *big fire*, could do enormous monetary and environmental damage, and more than ten fires were being reported there, rimming the whole two hundred square miles of lake.

Marcus had been so focused on Annie that that he had almost forgotten about his mother. The matriarch of the Diablo clan lived on the North Shore of Lake Tahoe, at the family motel her parents had built. She was planning on coming to the cabin the next day, but now…

Glen called her and learned that they had started to evacuate all their guests, but just as in Yosemite, all roads in and out of the Tahoe Basin were cut off. The situation was grim. Entire subdivisions of homes built in the woods surrounding the lake were burning to the ground. Firefighting crews had been mobilized, but were hopelessly outmatched by the size and number of fires. The situation was not a matter of containment but of survival. People were gathering by the thousands along the lakeshore. Visibility was down to mere feet, and the smoke made breathing difficult. In the end, the smoke and ash that filled the air would be responsible for far more deaths than the scorching heat.

But even in the face of imminent disaster, their mother remained her practical, motherly self. She told Glen that they were not to worry about her. They were to keep safe and find Annie. She said she would be okay and that their aunts and uncles would all stay safe, that they were to take care of themselves and her grandchildren. She didn't act panicked or afraid—in Diablo fashion the females stood strong in the face of danger.

Fires were raging throughout California: in Sequoia, the second oldest national park in the United States, and Kings Canyon, its sister park. Both parks were not so far from the Los Angeles Basin and were part of the massive watershed that supplied the sprawling metropolis.

In Northern California, fires were burning in Lassen National Park and the wilderness areas surrounding Mt. Shasta. The small towns of McCloud and Mount Shasta were being ravaged, while other fires blazed in the Siskiyou and Trinity Alps Wilderness areas, and in western Oregon from Bend to Portland.

From Washington to West Virginia, New Mexico to New Hampshire if there was a national park or forest with large stands of timber it was on fire. Major interstates from coast to coast were impassable. Helicopter footage showed images of roadways choked with panicked families trying to escape but now trapped, unable to move forward or backward on the gridlocked asphalt. The estimates of the fires' size were doubling and doubling again as fires that started in national parks or forests spread miles beyond their points of origin.

The news bounced from one commentator to another with pictures of towering flames, burning homes, buildings, and in some cases entire towns. It felt as if they were watching an end-of-the-world science fiction movie—not the real thing.

Evacuations in most areas were restricted to gathering citizens in schools or other large, defensible public buildings. Local municipalities outside the fire zones were weighing their options and debating shutting off access into their counties for those seeking refuge. The arguments were starkly simple: it was not a humanitarian issue but an issue of survival for their own citizens. Numerous Governors were declaring huge portions of their state disaster areas and requesting federal assistance. Meanwhile, the sheer volume of smoke and airborne ash were choking aircraft engines and seriously hampering the aerial firefighting operations. Local resources were being pulled out of the backcountry to defend the larger towns and cities.

Marcus couldn't help but think that for at least a decade, much of the western half of the United States had suffered from an extended drought combined with record growth. Add to this that August was historically the hottest, driest month of the year, and the busiest month of summer vacation, a perfect setting for destructive, deadly fire on an unimaginable scale. It was clear to him, that whoever these people were, they too had thought the same thing.

At the time, no one gave any thought to the fact that many of the fires were in forests that contained the nation's largest and most important water shed systems. Rivers like the Columbia, Snake, Salmon, and Colorado were all in fire zones. From a strictly firefighting analysis, the proximity to large, accessible bodies of water in the form of lakes, reservoirs, and rivers was a huge advantage when mounting an attack on a forest fire. Ignored was what a massive delivery system these waterways would turn out to be.

News reports were interspersed with weather forecasts for the affected areas. Except for the Pacific Northwest, which if the forecasters were right, would get a heaven-sent reprieve in the form of a wet cold front, the rest of the West was slated to be hot and dry. Alternately, the newscast switched from fire coverage to go to Capitol Hill, where Congress was in joint session and the President was scheduled to address the nation at any moment.

In over an hour, no one in the family had moved or spoken. All eyes were glued to the screen, as the news anchors reported that federal resources were being mobilized to provide assistance. Congressmen and Senators spoke on camera, and then the President came on assuring viewers that help was on its way and that the most useful thing anyone could do was to remain calm, stay tuned, and obey local authorities. At this comment, Marcus couldn't help thinking that the government's track record at managing major disasters was less than stellar.

Marcus stood, no longer able to contain his rising anxiety and agitation. All faces were on him waiting for him to say something, anything. Walking behind the couch he leaned over his hands resting on the shoulders of his sons and continued to watch the nightmare play out. A detailed map of the United States was now the backdrop for the CNN newscast, with little glowing licks of flame representing locations where fires had been confirmed. In some areas, the little flame symbols were too thick to count, and the little flame indicators were popping up like spam notices on a computer screen.

By now, many of the reported fires had been burning for four or five hours and, driven by strong westerly winds, had spread many miles from their points of origin. With so many fires in so many places, traditional firefighting techniques, such as the clearing of firebreaks were useless and as a result, fires from one area were meeting others to form huge conflagrations. It was like a video game where the monster consumes everything in its path, increasing in size with each bite until it eventually becomes an unstoppable force.

And the reports of new fires continued. The largest boreal forest in the continental United States, Minnesota's Superior National Forest, was in flames. This massive area, encompassing the pristine Boundary Waters wilderness, was a key watershed system and vitally important to the industrial Northeast.

As they watched it became easier to count the states not affected. Then the news information began to report the first deaths and speculate on the potential for many more.

The female anchor was describing the scene in the Great Smoky Mountains National Park that sat in both Tennessee and North Carolina. This park, within a day's drive of a third of the U.S. population, was the most visited in the country, with over nine million visitors a year. The perky blonde newscaster reported that an estimated twenty to thirty thousand people were now stranded in the park and that many deaths were expected. And this would turn out to be just one of dozens of locations where people were trapped, and where many would die. Leaning on the back of his couch, Marcus's breath caught in this throat as the reality and despair of the situation hit him head on—whatever attention had been focused on finding Annie would now, surely be directed elsewhere.

CHAPTER FOURTEEN
August 18

Late in the morning on the eighth day of the fires, the Highway Patrol reopened Interstate 395 to Reno. At last Marcus and his family could pack up and head home. They had done all they could to protect the cabin, and if it was going to burn, there was little more they could do about it.

The boys headed home with Glen and Ellie and their kids. Marcus needed to stop in Bridgeport to say good-bye to the sheriff. From Jake and Bonnie, he knew that the sheriff and Maggie had lost their home, located in a heavily timbered canyon west of town. They had just made it out with only a few boxes, mostly pictures and keepsakes, before fire closed the road.

The sheriff had no news about Annie—indeed, he apologized for that. It was clear from his pained and tired expression that the FBI was sharing no more with him than they were with Marcus.

They talked for a few more minutes. Marcus told him that he and his family were heading back to Reno and would stay in touch. Leaving the sheriff's office, he found Agents Reynolds and Wu set up in the conference room. "Hey," he said to Reynolds, "my boys and I are going home," not asking permission.

"Well, Mr. Diablo," Agent Wu said, "it seems you were right about the fires." Just the way she said it implied that she thought Marcus knew a lot more about the fires than he had shared.

Looking up from the large folding table that served as his desk, Reynolds said, "Marcus, we are going to be a fixture in the lives of you and your sons—and, I guess, your whole family—for a while. Agent Gibson is already in Reno. We need to set up a phone tap, just on the off chance that someone calls with information or a ransom demand for your wife. I'll be along in another day or so. We're getting teams in place throughout the area as we speak, and will be coordinating for the time being out of a temporary field office in Reno."

Marcus bit back the urge to make a sarcastic retort, instead he replied, "By the way, you do remember what I said about the fire being just one part of this thing, right? If I were you, I'd spend a little time pondering that, and maybe while you are at it you could put some energy into finding my wife." Feeling lost and ineffectual, and not wanting to be drawn into a lengthy debate, Marcus turned and walked out.

***

The drive home should have been a glorious summer palette of mountain woods and meadowlands but instead the landscape lay muted under a ghostly pall of acrid gray smoke and white ash. The road was choked with traffic, people who had been trapped were doing as Marcus was: going home.

Driving through the small towns that dotted the eastern slope of the Sierras, he could see how many roadside businesses were shut down. The closer he got to home, the more he wondered whether they all should have stayed in the mountains.

When he hit Reno at five-thirty the temperature was in the high nineties, and the air was so thick with smoke he could almost chew it. The two dark blue Crown Vics at the curb may as well have had neon signs flashing, THE FEDS ARE HERE.

Dragging himself out of the truck, Marcus felt empty inside. If the cabin exuded Annie's presence the house that she designed, where her children were conceived and raised was going to scream it. How would he and the boys be able to carry on when everything they saw or touched had Annie's indelible imprint?

He hadn't gone three steps toward the house before the boys were on him. Did the sheriff have any news? Had they found Mom? When was she coming home? It was his job to have answers, and he hated that he didn't.

Inside he found Agent Gibson and two other men turning the dining room table into a kind of high-tech work station: computers with high-definition monitors, and a contraption that all their phone lines were rerouted through. All incoming and outgoing calls would be recorded, and they could trace any call within about thirty seconds. Gibson laid down the spiel on what to do if a call came in that had to do with Annie, how Marcus needed to stay calm and keep the caller on the line long enough for Gibson's people to trace the call.

After Gibson's tutorial, Glen grabbed Marcus by the arm and led him to the master bedroom. Closing the door behind them, he walked into the bathroom and returned seconds later. "Here, take this," he said, handing Marcus a small white pill and a glass of water. "It's from your first aid, kit, the one we take when were out in the mountains. Now take it. If you don't get some sleep you won't be worth a shit to yourself, your boys, or anybody else."

Too tired and depressed to argue, Marcus took the pain pill that was guaranteed to put him out for eight hours, jumped into the shower, and then crawled between the sheets.

CHAPTER FIFTEEN
September 21

With FBI teams working three eight hour shifts, the house felt to Marcus like a dark version of a three-ring circus: the big cats snarling in one ring, frown-faced clowns in another, and, in the center ring, the boys and him on the flying trapeze, working without a net. High-definition monitors, carrying the major news networks as well as two "FBI only" feeds, showed graphically the spread of mutual distrust and sense of protectionism that even pitted neighbor against neighbor. And all the while, the fires were raging, growing, gobbling up forests and croplands, towns, homes and businesses at an alarming rate.

The images of rioting, looting, and citizens killing citizens turned the country into a frenzied, lawless frontier. Bodie and Garrett did their best to try and comprehend what was going on, but their personal fears made the world's problems seem a little unreal. The schools were still closed and Glen and his family couldn't go back to Australia, because only "essential" flights were being allowed in and out of the States. So Marie and Ellie, wanting to establish some semblance of normality for the kids, worked out a way for them to get their schoolwork online. The surrogate schoolmarms gave assignments, checked work, and prodded any slacking in their makeshift study hall in the den.

On the morning of September 10, while the kids were diligently studying, the first reports of widespread sickness came in from Los Angles. Marcus was on the sofa, reading the script at the bottom of the screen, because he couldn't stand another second of the news anchor's earnest voice. A hundred people had shown up at L.A. area hospitals complaining of severe stomach cramps, nausea, diarrhea and dehydration.

Marcus switched off the mute button. The initial reports were presented matter-of-factly, as though this were nothing to be alarmed about. But Marcus couldn't get it out of his head that this just might be the other "something big" that Kevin had mentioned during his interrogation that fateful day in the mountains.

The suspected cause was giardia. The female reporter explained that giardia was very hardy parasite, protected by an outer shell allowing it to survive outside the body and in harsh environments for a long time. It was a common waterborne disease that could be passed in the feces of animals and humans, and even though symptoms took a couple of weeks to appear, it could pass from one person to another by mere hand contact.

Officials were speculating that one of the municipal reservoirs was contaminated. But the reporter, who seemed a bit cavalier to Marcus, did not connect the outbreak and the fires in the Sierra Nevada watershed.

Marcus remuted the TV and went to the dining room where he found Reynolds and the other two agents glued to the monitors. Reynolds was on the phone, doing more listening than talking, as if maybe he was getting his ass chewed. Hanging up the phone, Reynolds stared up at Marcus.

"It would appear Marcus, that this just might be the other 'something big' you mentioned. Although it hasn't hit the air yet, we're getting reports of the same sickness across virtually every fire zone that was in a major watershed."

Surprisingly Reynolds didn't look nearly as alarmed or tired as Marcus thought he should, but the look in his eyes was the first real chink he had seen in that polished exterior. Without a word, he went back to the sofa thinking this was one more thing that would take priority over finding Annie.

***

Today, September 21st was Marcus's forty-sixth birthday. Normally, this would have been a day of celebration in the Diablo household. Annie and the boys would have shopped for some great new gift, any of the thousand things that he would love to have but wouldn't dream of buying for himself. But there was no joy today, no jubilantly shouting boys bringing him an odd-shaped package sloppily gift-wrapped with the Sunday funnies. This birthday, the boys gave their dad a handmade card, and the gift they promised him was the safe return of their mother. What should have been a special day only ignited their sense of loss and desperation.

At one-fifteen in the afternoon, while Marcus and the boys were watching a DVD, the computer monitors flashed with an incoming Internet feed, putting Agent Reynolds and the computer technician instantly on high alert.

Bounding off the sofa, Marcus and the boys swooped down in front of the table to stare at the monitors. At first, the picture was all shadows, and it was hard to make out what they were looking at. Then the light rose slowly, and the picture came into focus. Someone with a black hood covering their head and face was seated in a wooden chair in front of a banner with three broad stripes: one red, one white, one black. In the banner's center were a red star and crescent.

Marcus could feel the boys' tension, as they stood transfixed in front of the screen. They were both digging their hands into him as they stood at his sides. "Is that Mom?" Bodie asked in a voice that sounded meek and unsure and, at the same time, hopeful.

Before Marcus could tell him he didn't know, someone walked into view and stood behind the person in the chair. This person was dressed in a black djellaba, a full-length garment that hid a body's physical contours. A black kaffiyeh was wrapped around the face, leaving only the eyes exposed.

"Are you tracking this?" Agent Reynolds yelled.

"Trying, sir," the techie replied. "But it's being bounced off routers all over the world so fast we can't pinpoint the signal. Whoever's sending this knows what they're doing."

In the next moment, the audio came on. "We are the New Islamic Dawn," the standing figure said in an unaccented male voice. "By now you have felt our fire and tasted the bitter ashes of defeat. Soon you will know the length of our reach and the power of the one true faith. The might of Allah will be known throughout America. Your imperialistic, arrogant hold on the Muslim peoples of the world will no longer be tolerated. We are among you. We are in every corner of your racist country, and we cannot be stopped. Your support of the Zionists is evidence of your blasphemous, misguided policies. Not only are you feeling the wrath of Allah, but as you can see, your leaders cannot protect you. We are holding one of your godless citizens."

With the last word of his rant, he reached down and, in one swift motion, whisked off the hood from the seated figure. The camera zoomed in, and there, in the flesh, was Annie. Bound around her waist to the chair, she was shaking her head from side to side. Her mouth was covered with what looked like a piece of duct tape, and her eyes were blinking, trying to adjust to the sudden brightness.

"Hold it up," the black-clad man ordered.

Annie lifted a copy of the *Wall Street Journal*. The camera zoomed in on the date: September 21. Then the feed cut abruptly to black.

"Dad, that was Mom!" Bodie shouted.

"Where is she? Are they going to let her go?" Garrett asked, beginning to cry.

"I don't know, buddy," was Marcus's lame response.

Agent Reynolds yelled again, "Did we get it?"

"No sir. We have it narrowed down to maybe a couple of dozen possibilities from Chechnya to Istanbul. Sorry!"

"So now what, Reynolds?" Marcus asked, his tone low and hard. "Still think this is all part of my big plan? You got any more brilliant theories that'll explain *this*? Come on, let's hear it! Where did all that confidence and swagger go, Mr. Cocksure Terrorism Expert? You've spent the past five weeks with your head up your ass and you have absolutely no idea where my wife is! You know, you really suck at this whole investigating thing."

Not in any mood to hear Reynolds's response, Marcus led the boys back into the living room. He could see the renewed sense of hope in their faces. Annie was alive. Last week he and the boys had *the* talk, the one about the possibility that their mother might be dead. It wasn't easy, but it was a conversation they had to have, and to his surprise, the boys took it better than he had expected. But now they had seen her with their very own eyes, that had to be a good thing, right? So why didn't *he* think so? Hope could be such a powerful force for someone seeking a ray of light in a desperate situation. But if that hope should be crushed, the effects could be all the more devastating. For Bodie and Garrett, it was as if they had just been granted their dearest wish. They were going to be able to deliver on their birthday promise to their dad. Their mom was alive, and surely now the FBI would find her and she would be restored to them soon.

CHAPTER SIXTEEN
October 28

Annie had been counting the days of her captivity by the switching on and off of the lights. She had been in her prison cage forty-four days, give or take, and in that entire time she had not exchanged a single word with anyone. Not that she hadn't tried. Several times a day she cycled through her rage phases, beating on the door, kicking the walls and screaming increasingly vile streams of words at anyone who might be in earshot.

And someone *was* in earshot because food was delivered every day, and after complaining about the need for a more varied diet, she sometimes found chicken or lamb added to her rice and sometimes yogurt or fruit. She got fresh water, and she had toothbrush, toothpaste, tampons and nondescript clean T-shirts and gray gym shorts, all pushed through a little door at the bottom of the wall. Also in one corner of the small room were a toilet, a sink, and an oscillating fan that gave some small relief from the stifling heat of her windowless prison.

During the first days, she kept herself awake and waited until the supply door was opened, hoping for a glimpse of a face. But every time she did, the door never opened, and she got no food or water that day. It didn't take long to figure out that she must be under surveillance by some cleverly hidden camera in the ceiling, which she couldn't reach, even if she knew where it was. She was handling the intensity of being alone as best she could and probably better than most. As the youngest of five, with her next closest sibling, a sister, almost ten years older than her, Annie had been raised like an only child. Her parents had divorced when she was seven, the same year her sister left for college. It was just Annie and her mom, who had to work two jobs to make ends meet. So Annie learned to be alone, to fend for herself.

It wasn't that she was antisocial or introverted. She just liked her time by herself. In high school she was introduced to trail running, and from that time on she found solace in running for hours alone, over desert and mountain trails. She learned to let her mind exist independent of the discomfort and exertion she was putting on her body. Right after she graduated university she had meet Marcus. He too was an avid, addicted trail runner. And as they grew closer and made a life together they pursued their careers with the same commitment and intensity.

It seemed they spent all of their time together. They shared adjoining office space, ran together each day, and returned home together almost every evening. And it was that time, the end of the day time, when they would eat dinner and maybe watch a little TV, without ever saying more than just a few words to each other, that she looked forward to the most. They communicated simply by being near each other. As Marcus was so fond of saying, "conversation is over rated."

Both Marcus and Annie believed that being alone was a learned skill. It was one of the things they discussed with the boys in regard to their time adventuring in rugged, remote areas. There was always a risk that you might get trapped, due to injury or weather, and have to survive for days, weeks, possibly even months completely alone. Food and shelter were tangible requirements; sanity on the other hand was a product of a person's mental conditioning and toughness. But unlike your body, where the results of physical training were evident, with your mind, you only really knew if you were up to the challenge when you were knee deep in the shit.

Now, over six weeks into her captivity, it was requiring every ounce of will she had left to not crack. She forced herself to stay as occupied as was humanly possible in a twelve by twelve box. She was given a steady supply of reading material, dog-eared novels, and outdated news and fashion magazines. Ironically, she even found solace in the Koran, a copy of which she had found beside the mattress on her first day.

But the only thing that was really keeping her from losing her mind was her nightly dream visits with Garrett. They were never quite the same. Sometimes he would come to her, other times she went to him, and sometimes it was just their voices. She never could connect with Marcus or Bodie, but Garrett, her little angel, always kept her informed. As weird as it seemed, Annie was convinced that she and her son were communicating in real time. She had no doubt that he, his brother and Marcus, were safe. Also she knew, or rather she felt, that Marcus was doing everything he could to find her. So she would spend her days reading and doing yoga and anxiously waiting for the lights to go out, and her son to visit.

If her day count was even close to accurate, it was mid September. She was about to do a long yoga session when suddenly the lights went out. The next instant the door opened and she heard the sound of rushing feet; then hands grabbed her and pinned her to the floor. Before she could yell, the hands duct-taped her mouth and pulled a cloth bag over her head, hauled her to her feet, and led her out of the room.

During this time no one spoke a word. She hadn't walked far before she was forced to sit on a hard chair. She was lashed to the chair back, arms tight to her sides, hands in her lap. Then the first words she had heard in six weeks: "Hold this." Something was thrust into her hands. It felt like paper, a newspaper perhaps. Then the voice began to speak, and with each passing word the reality of her situation became shockingly clear. Someone yanked the bag from her head.

"Hold it up," the same man's voice commanded.

It was the *Wall Street Journal.* September 21, Marcus's birthday. Then, just like that, the bag was back over her head.

***

After her one and only experience with her captors, Annie settled into a resigned, almost melancholy mood. The days passed, each one the same as the next. She now found herself bouncing in and out of the despondency and depression phase of her extended captivity.

Her connection with Garrett was as powerful as ever. It was the only thing that kept her going. Her abductors were terrorists, and from the rhetoric she concluded that something terrible had happened. But what?

By her lights-on-lights-off calendar, it was approaching the end of October. Her birthday was today or tomorrow. They had waited until Marcus's birthday for the proof-of-life contact, but why? Had Marcus done something and these assholes were sending him a message. She hoped so. Marcus was a formidable opponent. Not because he was big and strong, although he kept himself very fit, but it was his mind. He had the uncanny ability to assess situations, and make decisions without the slightest hesitancy. Even when he was wrong, he just owned it and, without another thought, moved to plan B. He had an unshakable self-confidence. It was the thing she found the most attractive about him.

Sitting on the floor in a yoga pose, letting focused body and relaxed mind take her away, she hardly noticed the door open. Two men walked in. This was the first time she had seen them without their faces covered. Jumping to her feet, she faced them. "Come," one of them said.

They took her to a larger room where there were cots and a makeshift kitchen, but it was the banner on the wall, the chair in front of it, and the video camera on a tripod another ten feet from the chair, that consumed her attention. The taller and older of the two tossed her a black robe and ordered her to put it on. Then the other man bound her hands behind her back.

The man, who had spoken at her proof-of-life appearance said, "You will be allowed to speak for two minutes. Make that time count. Do not speak until you are told to do so. Do you understand?"

Still standing, Annie nodded.

For the next several minutes the men made preparations, checking the camera, changing into robes that concealed them from head to toe. These men seemed to be of the same ethnicity as those who abducted her in the mountains. And as before, the man who spoke sounded as American as she.

Her two tormentors wrapped scarves around their heads so that nothing but their eyes showed. So this is it, the end had finally come. She thought it strange that she could be so calm. Shouldn't she be on the verge of hysteria? Be struggling or show some sign of distress? *No way. Not now.* She would never give them the satisfaction of seeing her afraid or weak.

The men approached her. That's when she noticed the sword that one carried. Her gorge rose involuntarily in her throat at the realization of *how* it would happen. *No you don't Annie,* she chided herself. *You've come too far. Your boys and Marcus are safe. Hold it together.*

The man, without the sword, led her to where the chair once sat, and made her kneel on the concrete floor. Then, standing behind her, he began to speak. Annie used every fiber of will that she could summon to keep herself composed. Her focus grew so single pointed that the words of the man speaking into the camera became mere white noise.

As if on cue, she heard, "She will be allotted two minutes to speak, to say whatever she wishes."

Looking up at the camera, Annie spoke to Marcus and her sons. At the end, she felt a tremendous sense of strength and calm settle over her. In that instant before everything dissolved into a brilliant white light, she smiled and thought, *You bastards have no idea what Marcus will do when he finds you.*

CHAPTER SEVENTEEN

Marcus knew from his daily talks with the boys that, since the night in the cabin almost ten weeks ago, his youngest son, Garrett, had been dreaming about his mother almost nightly. Usually he only remembered little bits, but the night after Annie's Internet appearance, she came to him and told him how glad she was that he had got to see her. She told him she was okay but that it was important for him and his older brother, Bodie, to be strong and brave. She wanted them to take care of each other and watch over their dad. They mustn't stop looking for her, but if they didn't find her, they were all to "do as I know you will." Garrett gave the instruction to his father very deliberately, as if repeating it word for word as directed.

To do as I know you will—what the hell was that? Marcus wondered. Whatever it was, Garrett assumed it meant that they would find her as long as they didn't lose hope.

Since the proof-of-life Internet feed, Marcus and the boys lived as if they were strapped into an endless roller coaster ride, long, slow, rattling rises of anticipation followed by crashing, stomach-in-your-throat plunges. There had been no further contact, and the FBI had made no headway in locating where Annie might be.

With Glen's Reno house only two doors away, Marcus's home had become a base camp of sorts during the day for most of them. They were all beneficiaries of the round-the-clock FBI presence. That meant access to food, uncontaminated water, and medicine. What they learned of the outside world, they gleaned from television news. And it seemed that every minute of broadcast time was dedicated to updates on the rising death toll, and ever-increasing estimates of the billions in losses.

Marcus couldn't seem to pull himself away from the broadcasts and the constant stream of news. The short-term prognosis was encouraging. With autumn in full swing, Mother Nature would contain most of the fires that man could not. But it was the longer-term situation that was more troubling.

Expert after expert was trotted out in front of the cameras to theorize on the months-long inferno that had left almost no state untouched. The consensus, however, was unanimous: the devastation of vast ecosystems would be felt for centuries to come.

The wide-open nature of Marcus's household meant that everything the FBI said and did was in plain view. The current topic among the agents and the computer techs was the giardia parasite. Even though the fires would soon be under control the microorganism that had been planted in the nation's water systems to coincide with the fires was proving stubborn. According to Agent

Reynolds, the biggest problem was a woefully inadequate supply of antibiotics for the thirty-day regime required to kill the bug, much longer than the seven-to-ten-day regime usually required.

Today was Annie's birthday, and Marcus felt an ominous sense of dread that this was the day that would finally, once and for all, change his and the boys' lives completely and irrevocably. The terrorists had chosen to broadcast her proof-of-life on his birthday. "It was a message," Agent Reynolds said. "A message to you for the killing of their two comrades."

And despite what Marcus thought of Agent Reynolds's powers of deduction, he had to admit, it had a ring of logic, and for over a month he had been dreading this day.

Late that morning, when Agent Reynolds arrived, to spell Agent Gibson, Marcus needed to vent. Dread and anxiety weighed on him like cold, wet earth over a coffin. As Reynolds removed his jacket and took a seat at the dining table, Marcus sat down across the table from him.

"Something on your mind, Marcus?" He asked in a tone that ratcheted up Marcus's level of agitation.

"Well, let me see," Marcus said. "How about almost eighty thousand dead and the number still climbing? How about mass chaos, riots, neighbors killing neighbors over clean water, medicine, and food?" No longer able to sit still, Marcus stood and leaned his palms heavily on the table. "How about cities that look like war zones, people living under martial law, curfews, food and fuel rationing? This attack makes Nine- eleven look like a skinned knee. How about the fact that people can't travel, can't work, can't go to school? And how about the fact that you have no fucking idea where Annie is, let alone who has her?"

Just as Marcus was about to launch into round two, Glen, his wife Ellie, Harold, Marie and her husband, Mario, and their children showed up with lunch. They laid out the food and paper plates, and everyone sat down to eat when they heard the agent charged with monitoring all the hardware on the dining room table say, "Hey, Agent Reynolds, we have some magic happening,"

"Okay, let's make sure we get the son of bitch this time around." Reynolds ordered as, lunch abandoned, everyone gathered before the monitor.

The monitor came to life, and the same banner that had been the backdrop for Annie's proof-of-life appearance filled the screen. A man—Marcus assumed it was the same man from over a month ago—walked in front of the banner, dressed, as before, in a black djellaba and black kaffiyeh, that veiled his face. He began to speak. "You have felt the fire of Allah and tasted the bitter air of defeat. Now, his wrath lives in your bowels as well."

The man stood still, arms folded across his chest. "Now you see just how weak you truly are. Our power is unstoppable, for we are the chosen of Allah, and you are merely arrogant nonbelievers. You will hear no more from us, but watch as fear and distrust take hold. The Great Satan has been brought to its knees. How does it feel? Is your government able to protect you? Our commitment is beyond your narrow ability to comprehend. Our ranks are strong; when one true follower falls, there are ten to take his place. Nothing you can do will change our resolve. But lest you take us for an uncompassionate people, we have granted our captive one last wish. She will be allotted two minutes to speak, to say whatever she wishes. We know the value you place on women, and will, this time, defer to your misguided ideals so that you can see we are not without feeling for our enemies."

Agent Reynolds turned to Marcus. "The kids…the boys." He said with a nod, "Maybe they shouldn't be watching this."

Marcus thought for a second, and even though he had a terrible feeling about what was going to happen, and knew it wasn't a good idea, he said, "No, my boys will stay."

The camera panned out and focused on Annie, dressed in a back robe, this time with her head uncovered, kneeling on the floor her back to the banner. Her hands were bound behind her back. The face that stared at them was not what Marcus had expected. It was certainly Annie, but there was no fear in her gaze. She looked exhausted, and yet there was steely determination in her eyes, in the way she held herself. She knelt straight and strong, no sitting back on her heels, and began to speak.

"Marcus, Bodie, Garrett, I have missed you all and I love you, but now is the time for us all to be strong. I will not beg these pigs for my life. I wouldn't give them the satisfaction of seeing me weaken. Boys, now is the time for you to stand together. Take care of your dad, you hear me?"

"What does she mean, Dad?" Bodie whimpered. "What's going to happen?"

Marcus held up his hand to indicate that he would speak to him in a moment.

Annie went on. "Marcus, pay attention. The best I can figure, I'm within eight hours of the Buck Creek parking lot. But now that doesn't matter. What matters is...." Her eyes narrowed as if she were looking right through him, into him and only him. "You take care of this. It's time for that old Marcus, the unreasonable, terrible, at-all-costs Marcus. Listen, baby, you bring it—no regrets, no looking back. It's your job now to protect our boys. Make sure they stay safe; make sure they have a good life and grow into fine, strong young men. Don't you dare waste time grieving for me. You deal with these bastards. Whatever it takes, I know you will find a way. You always do. So you dig deep, put your mind and body to work, find out who is responsible, and you make them pay!"

Taking a deep breath, she continued. "Marcus, I love you. You make sure. You promise me! Say it! Say, I promise!"

Tears leaking down his cheeks, his stomach in a knot, Marcus whispered, "I promise."

"You tell my precious boys every day how much their mother loves them. I will always be near them." She paused a second and hurried on, a smile gracing her face, "This is much bigger than just me Marcus. You keep that in mind." Her tone was hard, as if she was trying to make a point. "Whatever these people have done it threatens not just us but everyone. You were right, baby, I did find strength in the struggle. It's time for you to do the same, Marcus. Don't be afraid—I'm not. I love you!"

Just as Annie uttered these final words, out of the corner of his eye, Marcus saw Glen and Ellie each grab one of the boys. They spun them away from the monitors and hugged them in a tight embrace. At the same time Marcus stared at Annie, her head held straight and tall, a blur appeared on the left side of the screen, and her head tilted forward, as if she were praying...and then dropped to the floor. Twin geysers of blood spurted once, twice, as her body slumped sideways to the floor.

In his mind, the whole scene played out in ultraslow motion. Although his eyes could not see the sword, his mind saw every fraction of every second of its movement. As he screamed, "No-o-o-o-o-o-o-o-o!" in a ragged howl, like the baying of a sick hound, the image of Annie's face etched itself on his memory: smiling, unafraid, proud and strong even as her body fell in two parts onto the floor.

Marcus was dimly aware of the mass chaos going on around him, but he heard none of it. All he heard was the exhalation of Annie's last breath.

Just as the final guttural moan left Marcus's throat, in a motion that seemed to take place outside him, he reached up with his left hand and grabbed the Windsor knot of Agent Reynolds's tie, and with a windmill motion as if pitching a softball, he slammed his right hand into the agents groin, grabbing his crotch. And before Reynolds could even make a sound, Marcus lifted him up as if he weighed no more than a backpack, and slammed him down on the dining room table, scattering keyboards and monitors. He brought the full weight of his body to rest on top of him. Marcus had his face so close to Agent Reynolds, he could feel his breath spilling rough and ragged onto his cheeks.

"Now you lame little excuse for an FBI agent," he snarled, "you are going to take these other two Cub Scouts and leave my house. This whole thing—you did nothing to prevent it. The whole crock about the life of one person sometimes being the cost to protect the greater good is bullshit. I told you weeks ago that if you couldn't take care of this, I would. Now it's my turn."

Strong arms pulled Marcus off Agent Reynolds. The sounds of screaming and crying assaulted his senses. It was as if he had been somewhere else and, in the blink of an eye, had been jerked back into the present. Breathing in panting gasps he stood there looking like a rabid animal, teeth bared, and a thread of spittle dripping from his tense and quivering jaws.

Glen hugged Marcus to his chest, biting back his tears. "Marcus the boys...the boys!"

The words were like a hard slap to the face. Marcus looked around, searching the tormented faces of his family, eyes settling on his sons. If horror had a face, this was it. They were on their knees, holding each other. Vomit was spewed all over the floor and on their clothing. They were sobbing, retching, their little bodies convulsing.

Marcus dropped to his knees on the wood floor and scooped them into his strong arms. He had no words, and for the first time in his life, he could not find the resolve to face the situation.

"Oh, Dad, what just happened?" Bodie's voice shrieked. "Did those people kill Mom? *Did they?* Although they hadn't actually seen the beheading, no thanks to him, his anguished cries and angry words, had left no doubt that something very bad had happened.

Garrett couldn't speak. His face was buried against his father's chest, dry heaves jerking his little body rigid, then letting it collapse.

The only thing Marcus could say was, "We need to get out of here now." He pulled himself up off the floor, reached down, and lifted first Garrett, then Bodie up onto their feet. Ellie came over, her mascara streaking black down her tearstained face. "Come on, guys," she said in a broken voice, "let's get you washed up and into some clean clothes."

Agent Reynolds was rearranging his tie and trying to shake off the effects of being slammed in the balls. Marcus walked over to him. "Out. Now!" He pointed to the electronic equipment on the table. "You can gather your toys later. I want her body, so I'd suggest you do everything you can to find it—now! You owe me, Reynolds! You remember that!"

Agent Reynolds nodded to the other two agents to follow him, and they left.

When they were gone, Marcus turned to his brother. "Glen, I need you to take the boys to your house, I have to go for a while...I have to be alone. I've got to try and figure out what I'm supposed to do next."

As Marcus paced, trying to wrap his mind around the meaning of Annie's final plea, Ellie brought the boys out. Their hair was still wet and they wore clean clothes.

He knelt before them. "Listen guys, he said. "You're going with Uncle Glen and Aunt Ellie over to their house. We're all going to be staying there for at least the next few days. I need to take off for a little while. I need some time alone. I know my timing sucks, but if…" He didn't finish as his anguished sons clung to him.

Disengaging himself, he let Ellie take the boys by the hands. Too traumatized to argue, they followed her and their aunts and uncles and cousins out of the house. Marcus stood there alone in the home where he and Annie had planned their future, dreamed together, made love, where they had laughed and cried, and now, he felt nothing. It was as if some huge part of him had died with Annie. It was that part of him that made him a father, that enabled him to be the man his sons knew and needed. His life, Bodie's and Garrett's lives, depended on his finding and resurrecting that part. But how was he going to that? Was it even possible? He quickly changed clothes, grabbed his coat and truck keys, stuffed a couple hundred dollars into his pocket, and left.

CHAPTER EIGHTEEN

Ricky sat with his father, in the confines of the underground shelter watching the large HD monitor, with rapt fascination as the woman's head separated from her body. Unlike the majority of Americans watching the live Internet feed, they felt neither horror nor revulsion, but excitement and the thrill of victory. They had not known Adad's plan for the woman but this…this was spectacular.

All during the time the fires were raging, the Faradis had feigned disbelief and shock that such an attack could happen in *their* country. Ricky had gone out of his way to stay connected with his friends and colleagues. Without exception, all conversation, centered on the devastation being wreaked on the United States.

To Ricky and his father, it was the will of Allah that had spared their region from the worst of the fires. Yes, there were burns in the western forests of Oregon and Washington but the fires raged for days, not months. As for the parasite that was a different story. The region's vast watershed system, among the largest in the nation, supplied water to millions, and as many fell sick here as anywhere in the country. But at least *they* had an adequate supply of antibiotics.

"All we must do now is wait, my son." Ricky's father said, flicking the television off. "Soon the call will come and your destiny will be fulfilled."

Ricky could see the pride in his father's face. Everything had happened even better than planned. The beheading of the women was the climactic act that would usher in a new era of fear and distrust, which would fester and grow for years to come. No longer were the effects of such an attack limited to a major city, removed by distance from much of the population's psyche. Now every American had felt the sting.

"It will be only days until you are contacted." Ali Faradi said to his son. "You must be prepared to leave."

"My things are in order." Ricky replied. Then he said, "Do you think the infidels will ever figure out that the battle for our faith is waged by men, not nations?"

"Inshallah. Abbas no."

CHAPTER NINETEEN
Aboard the Takbir, somewhere in the Mediterranean Sea

Adad sat in the plush club chair, in his private salon, aboard his six hundred foot mega yacht, that served as his mobile base of operation, and watched the big HD monitor with more than a little sadistic satisfaction, as the infidel's head rolled from her shoulders. Turning to his second in command, Fazil Rafanjani, Adad said, "Did I not tell you that we could use this women to our advantage? This final act, on top of the fires and the infection that has sickened hundreds of thousands, imagine the outrage the citizens of America must be feeling." An evil smile crossed Adad's face, "Today's outrage will turn into tomorrow's paralyzing fear and paranoia."

"Yes," Fazil said, with just a hint of shame in his voice, "Adad, as always you were right."

"Do not patronize me Fazil. Have you such little faith, that it is beyond comprehension that American born Muslims can carry the same fire of Allah within them that we do? Do you not see that a small group of true and faithful believers has created an America where neighbors mistrust neighbors?"

Fazil cast his gaze at the floor. "Yes, I see that they are a powerful force, but are you sure it is wise that we welcome one of them into our inner circle? It is one thing to use them to further the cause, and another all together to make them a part of the cause."

Adad looked at his friend, the man who had been by his side since he took control of the family financial empire, more than a decade ago. His face softened, "Fazil, you are my man on the shoulder, that voice in my ear," Adad taped his right ear with his finger, "and for that I am grateful. I know you have only our best interests at heart, but in this you must trust me. American citizens as our allies, is in itself the blow that will strike the most fear into the hearts and minds of our enemies. We have succeeded where our predecessors have failed, not just one city has been affected, but an entire country, and not just any country, but the United States of America, a nation filled, for the most part, with unbelievers."

Fazil hesitated, choosing his words carefully. "I would only ask that you leave the details of determining the loyalty of this individual to me, should he survive, and actually make it to Istanbul. And that you trust *my* judgment in the matter."

"Oh course, I will leave those details to you. As to my trust, you have always had that. And how goes our arrangement with the Saudis?"

"Your substantial investment has made it possible for the satellite to be completed ahead of schedule, the launch date is set for spring of this coming year. All is on track, the very best engineers in the world are working around the clock to ensure an April launch."

Sitting back in the leather chair, Adad took a drink of water from the crystal glass resting on the end table. Fazil continued to talk. "Once we have the link established here on the Takbir, you will have real-time information and surveillance capabilities at your finger tips that will surpass that of any government or intelligence-gathering agency in the world. Planning the future of an Islamic world will become a reality."

Adad relaxed and closed his eyes. "When we can unite the planets one and half billion Muslims, what a different world it will be." Adad's voice had a dreamy, distant quality, "And with me as the leader, all the world will know that there is but one God, and that God, is Allah."

CHAPTER TWENTY
October 29

Marcus went back to Glen and Ellie's house the following morning. He had thought he could somehow drink the past three months out of his head, but it felt more like drowning, the more he drank, the more his life flashed before his eyes, with Annie in every scene. As always the boys were on him before he made it into the house.

He was so preoccupied with this sons, he missed the dark blue Crown Vic parked across the street. Inside, he found Glen and Agent Reynolds at the kitchen table. He sent the boys upstairs to find their cousin Charlie, as the two men gave him the once-over. Clearly, they could smell last night's whiskey coming through his pores.

Not caring how he looked or smelled Marcus said, "What a singularly unpleasant surprise! I thought I made it clear that you were to say the hell out of my family's life."

"Marcus, sit down." Glen said, his face grey. "You need to hear this."

Marcus pulled out a chair and sat.

"They found Annie—her body," Glen explained.

Marcus looked at Agent Reynolds. "Okay, Reynolds, let's hear it. Let me guess—you didn't find her in Yemen or Mogadishu or some other Middle Eastern shit-hole, did you?"

Agent Reynolds spoke in a low, almost contrite tone. "No, Marcus, we didn't. We found her body in North Las Vegas, dumped in an alley in a warehouse district."

Marcus came out of his chair, equal parts grief and rage. "I kept telling you she was close, but you had it all figured out. The whole time, she was less than five hundred miles from where she was taken. The whole time you were flailing around with your head in your ass, my wife was in *Las Vegas.*"

His yelling brought the boys down from their air hockey game upstairs. "What's going on, Dad?" Bodie asked.

Marcus just didn't have it in him to gloss it over, knowing that it wouldn't shelter them from all the pain and horror of what was going on. "Guys, they found your mom's body."

There, he'd done it. Whatever faint hope they may have held that what had happened over live Internet feed was just someone's sick idea of a joke, was now quashed.

Ellie stomped in from the kitchen, grabbed the boys and, shooting Marcus a backward look that said, *How could you!,* ushered them upstairs and out of earshot.

"That's great, Reynolds. You must be so proud."

Agent Reynolds didn't responded.

"I want to see the pictures—the crime scene photos," Marcus demanded.

Reynolds opened his briefcase on the table, took out a manila envelope, and handed Marcus a dozen eight-by-ten color photos.

No one spoke as he looked at the headless body, and the bodiless head, of Annie. When he came back to the present his face held no emotion. The photos, gruesome as they were, were all the motivation he needed to stop wallowing in self-pity.

"Marcus, there's something else," Glen said.

"We found this note taped to her body." Agent Reynolds said as he handed him a copy.

He read, "Mr. Diablo, be warned to leave this be. Your wife was but a woman and, therefore, insignificant. But your sons would be another matter entirely. We know where you live, and we will be watching."

After giving him a moment to digest the message, Agent Reynolds said, "We'll be keeping an eye on you and your family around the clock, just in case these people try to make a move."

"Thank you, that's so reassuring, Agent Reynolds." He couldn't help the sarcasm coursing through his veins. "You've done nothing but screw this whole thing up since day one, so why should I have the barest scintilla of confidence that you can protect us?"

"Be that as it may, Marcus, we will be shadowing you, your boys, and your family for some time to come. I know I haven't done my best work up until now, but this is coming from the very highest level of the FBI."

"And that should instill me with confidence? Look, do whatever you have to, but you stay out of my way. I will expect my wife's body."

"Her body has already been shipped to San Francisco for a complete autopsy and forensic examination. As soon as that's done I will make sure we get her to you. I'm sorry it has to be that way." And at long last, he looked as though he meant it. He got up. "I'll keep you informed," he said, and left.

Marcus walked to the front door and saw Reynolds talking to two other agents in an identical Crown Vic, parked across the street. The watchers, it seemed, were watching.

***

Marcus's mind was running a mile a minute. He needed to clear his head and since drinking hadn't done it, he thought he would try a more proven method, running. Putting on sweats and running shoes, he headed out into the bleak, gray October morning.

After chuffing along for a quarter mile, he realized how neglectful he had been of something that had been almost like a religion to him. For the first time in months, he felt alive. Now if he could only find purpose. He let his mind wander, knowing he would pay the price for trying to get back in running shape in one day.

Back at his brother's house, he showered and suddenly realized that he and the boys had no clothes. "Okay, Marcus, you have to start somewhere." He said aloud to the haggard, unshaven face staring back at him in the mirror.

Glen insisted on accompanying them to their house. While he helped the boys gather their things, Marcus went into the bedroom. It felt odd, the house, like Annie's body, was now no more than a shell that had once held her.

On a mission, he grabbed the suitcases from the closet and started stuffing them with clothing. Rummaging through the folded laundry piled on the little sofa in the sitting area, he uncovered his pack—not *his* pack really, but the one he had come out of the mountains with.

He hadn't touched it since he got back to Reno, just threw it on the sofa and forgot about it. Taking it over to the bed, he dumped the contents. Inside the main compartment were a first aid kit, flashlight, two headlamps, his rain jacket, and a fleece pullover. He dropped the pack and turned back to the closet, but something caught his eye. The small pouch on the front of the pack was zipped shut.

He remembered hastily stuffing the contents of both dead men's pockets into it. Unzipping the pouch, he pulled the contents out, and for a few seconds he just stared at the miscellaneous stuff: a lighter, a scrap of paper, a Swiss Army knife, forty cents in change, and a matchbook.

One by one, he picked each item up and looked at it from all sides. He even opened every blade on the Swiss Army knife. The last item was the matchbook. Crumpled and worn, and with only three matches left. It was fire engine red with white capital letters reading ALES FOR AILS. He lifted the flap, and on the inside upper cover was printed "Canby, Ore." He pulled the flap back so that the matches stood out, and midway down the flap, behind the matches, someone had written in blue ink "*R. Faradi.*"

Holy shit. "R" as in "Ricky"? The Ricky, Kevin had told him about? It all started to make sense. Kevin had mentioned the Columbia and the Willamette rivers. Canby, Oregon, was in the Willamette Valley, right on the river.

***

Returning to Glen's house, Marcus went to the guest room, booted up his laptop and did a search for "Faradi." There were only a few hundred hits. One was some Arabian historian, dead a thousand years. He scrolled down a few pages to "Abdurrahim Faradi, Ph.D.," who taught bioengineering at Portland State University. His bio ran for four paragraphs. He and his wife, Rahlia, had emigrated, from Iran, to the States in 1980. Rahlia was a professor of Middle Eastern literature, also at Portland State. They had a son, Richard Faradi, born in 1982, which would make him twenty-five. They made their home in Canby, a suburb south of Portland. *Canby, Oregon*—it had to be! He had found Ricky—and maybe a whole lot more.

Marcus spent the rest of the day making a list of what he would need and figuring out how to slip his FBI babysitters.

***

That evening Marcus gathered his brothers Glen and Harold and the boys at the kitchen table and laid out his plan. He didn't mention the matchbook to anyone, but he had to redirect the boys' grief and get them started on the process of healing. Marcus knew they were still in shock, the reality hadn't hit home yet. But it would, and he could only hope he had the fortitude to deal with it.

"I'm going away for a few days, maybe a week," he said. "I just remembered something one of the guys at our camp told me. Now, I can't tell you where I'm going or what I'm going to do. The FBI is watching us, and I can't risk them finding out. But if I'm right, this is the first step to doing what your mom asked me to do."

"Do you think you can find out who did this to Mom?" Bodie said.

"Yeah, I do!" and this time real confidence was in his voice.

Garrett said, "When are you going?"

"Soon, in the next day or two. I have some things to work out and a few things to get. So this is how it's going to work: When I do leave, you guys are to go about your daily routine, do your schoolwork, hang out, act as normal as you can."

"What if the FBI guys want to know where you are?" Bodie said.

"If you have to talk to the FBI, tell 'em I'm just a wreck about your mother and haven't left my bedroom for days. I'll talk to everybody else, they'll know what to say, too."

"Okay, so that's it. We have a plan. Now, you better get to it, Dad, the sooner this is over, the better."

And that was it. Bodie and Garrett left to find their cousins.

Seeing Glen's and Harold's stunned expressions and not wanting to get sucked into a debate about just how stupid it would be to go anywhere, Marcus barreled forward. "Just hear me out. I'll explain what I can and the rest…well, you'll just have to trust me."

CHAPTER TWENTY-ONE
October 30

The next afternoon Harold returned with his truck, along with some other things Marcus wanted. Last night Marcus had given him a list and an envelope full of cash that he had recovered from the safe he and Annie kept under the house—a safe the FBI knew nothing about. Of all the Diablo siblings, Harold was by far and away the oddest. And his eccentricities had gotten him a distinct set of friends and acquaintances. Given the time and the money, there was nothing Harold couldn't lay his hands on.

In the garage, Harold, Marcus, and Glen went through an inventory of what he needed for cold-weather camping. Harold laid out the items he had procured: a Taser with ten extra cartridges and two sets of replacement pins, a brand-new Sig Sauer P250 .45-caliber pistol, along with three fifty-round boxes of what he called "knock 'em down, they stay down" ammo, and a pre-paid cell phone.

"Now," Harold said, "are you gonna tell us what's really goin' on? And maybe you'd like to explain how you're gonna get outta here with the man parked outside, not to mention the travel restrictions?"

"Hey, little brother," Marcus said, resting a hand on his shoulder, "I've told you all I can. As to the travel restrictions, I'm working on it. And I'll finally get to see if all that bragging about your truck is true."

Outside of his restaurant supply business, Harold spent time riding his mountain bike, whitewater kayaking, and fly-fishing in the most remote places he could find. To this end, he had invested a small fortune on a Toyota Tundra, specially equipped for his particular brand of adventure. It had a beefed-up frame with a big winch on the front, and dual tanks that gave it a capacity of over sixty gallons of gas. As if this weren't enough, he had an additional sixty-gallon tank fabricated to fit in the bed, against the backside of the cab. Harold had always boasted that he could travel from coast to coast without ever needing to fuel up. Since this truck was used only for his "excursions," as he called them, he kept it full of gas so that it was ready to roll when the spirit moved him.

"Okay Marcus, anything else?"

"Now that you mention it, when I leave I need you to stay here with Glen and the family. Pretended you're me, completely distraught about Annie and unable to get out of bed."

Glen said nothing, just shook his head.

***

At seven that evening the doorbell rang. Marcus opened the door to find Agent Reynolds, whom he had called, and asked over.

"What's up Marcus? Why all the urgency?"

Without answering, Marcus led him to the table, where Glen and Harold were seated. "Harold needs to see my sisters and their families, up in Seattle—make sure they're all right and explain to them in person what's happened to Annie. He needs to reassure them that the boys and I are coping and that, hopefully, all the turmoil will be behind us soon and we can get together and mourn Annie's death."

"Well, you guys know that there are still travel restrictions, especially crossing state lines." Reynolds replied. "Besides, even if Harold could travel, getting fuel would be next to impossible."

Before Marcus could respond Harold broke in and gave Agent Reynolds a brief rundown on what his truck could do, and assured him that he could easily make it there and back without gassing up.

"You know, Marcus," Reynolds said, in his *I'm the boss here* voice, "much as I'd like to help you out, I don't think there's anything I can do."—exactly the response Marcus was expecting.

"You *can't* make it happen, or you *won't?* First of all, Agent Reynolds, understand me—he's going, with or without your permission. And it would ease my mind if I knew that my brother had, at the very least, some sort of official sanction to travel. Considering that I haven't once asked you or your organization for one blessed thing and, moreover, that due to your utter lack of competence my wife is dead—I would think it's the very least you could do!"

For a few moments, Agent Reynolds just sat there staring through the dining room window into the darkness of the backyard. Then he pulled his cell phone from his inside jacket pocket and punched in some numbers. A half hour later, someone showed up at the front door with a permit for ten days travel.

CHAPTER TWENTY-TWO
October 31

In the predawn, Harold pulled up to Glen's house, backed his truck into the garage, and came into the house to find everyone very much awake.

About five a.m., Harold walked out the front door and brought the two agents on duty coffee in Styrofoam cups. He went back inside, and immediately changed clothes with Marcus, who put on the baggy pair of sweats and the Points North hat that Harold had been wearing.

Marcus said his goodbyes, and promised to check in as often as he could. He thought it a bit strange that the boys should be so on board, but then, that was how they had been raised. Whatever they decided as a family, everybody got behind it all the way.

Marcus quickly checked the gear in the back of the truck and added a small chainsaw and a five-gallon can of fuel. Then after tossing in some climbing gear and his daypack with the cell phone device, he got in the truck, pulled out, and, from behind the tinted windows, waved good-bye to the two FBI agents. Next stop: Canby, Oregon.

***

It was almost three in the afternoon when Marcus arrived in Canby. He drove around and located the brewpub Ales for Ails, then went to find the residence of one Dr. Abdurrahim Faradi, provided by the same search engine that had given him directions to the pub.

On the way, he passed a county park less than a mile from the Faradi residence. Satisfied that he had the right house he returned to the park and changed into his running clothes. Having no clue what he was looking for, or what he would do if and when he found it, didn't bother him in the least. This willingness to fly by the seat of his pants was one of his many personality traits that had driven Annie crazy. Even more infuriating, he usually pulled it off.

While pretending to stretch his leg on the three-rail fence, Marcus took in the colonial two-story with its big covered front porch, sitting maybe a hundred yards back from the road. In back was a big gambrel-roofed barn, painted white with green trim to match the house. There were a few cows, a horse, and some sheep in the pasture. The broad lawn in front of the house was set about with lofty pines and spreading maples and several fruit trees. There were flowerbeds, too, now colorless in the autumn gloom. It looked like an all-American homestead, Marcus thought.

No one appeared to be home yet, so Marcus continued running up the road a couple of miles before turning around. Coming back he found lights on, a Mercedes SUV, and a Lexus sedan parked in the paved circular driveway. The drapes were pulled on the windows facing the street, so that all he could make out were indistinct shadows moving about inside.

He found a spot in the drainage ditch, about fifty feet past the driveway entrance, that allowed a clear view of the front door. From this vantage point, he could see while staying out of sight. The dirt was wet and smelled of rich loam and leaf mold. Pulling a pair of lightweight knit gloves and a fleece cap out of his jacket, Marcus settled in. He needed to get a look at the people who lived in that house. He was convinced that if he could just see their faces, he would know whether they were Middle Eastern. Racial profiling, pure and simple, he thought, feeling a small twinge of conscience.

From his jacket pocket, he pulled a night-vision monocular—last year's Father's Day gift from the boys, which, until now he had never quite found a use for—and scanned the house. After a half hour he was getting a cramp in his calf, his eyes hurt from gazing into the eerie green light of the night-vision scope, and the damp of his hiding place was beginning to seep into his bones. But as he considered bagging his vigil for the evening, the front door opened and a man walked out onto the porch with a basket under one arm, turned and waved back to someone inside, and went down the steps.

Marcus strained to get a good view of him. He appeared to be somewhere between five-ten and six feet tall, slender, with dark hair and a close-cropped beard. Wearing jeans and a heavy, dark sweater, he had the build and carriage of a young man. By Marcus's reckoning, Dr. Faradi had to be in his late sixties. Was this Ricky? Was this the animal who had killed Annie?

He watched as the young man put the basket on the backseat of the Lexus, then drove around the house and parked in front of the barn, got out, and entered though a side door. Moments later, a light came on in the area that would be considered the loft. An apartment? *What kind of terrorist is this? Your mom still does your laundry and you live at home.*

Marcus now knew where Ricky lived and what kind of car he drove, so he jogged back to the truck and waited. He called his brother's house to talk to the boys on the pre-paid cell. He didn't use his regular phone, from which he had removed the battery, on the off chance that the FBI had discovered he was missing and tried to track him via the cell's GPS.

***

He started the truck and ran the heater to warm up. Tuning the radio to a news station he sat and listened. The reporter launched into a story about the giardia epidemic. According to him, experts were predicting that within another few weeks the infection would level off and that by early December the contagion should be under control.

For a few hours Marcus just sat in the truck, gazing into the darkness though the windshield. The local news reporter signed off, and a syndicated national news show talked about the ongoing fight against various extremist groups. It seemed that the recent attacks on the United States had given a shot in the arm to the Taliban, al-Qaeda, Hezbollah, al-Shabab and every other radical fundamentalist Islamic group. U.S. troops still stationed in Iraq and Afghanistan were facing a revitalized enemy. According to the commentator, attacks against American aid workers and civilians working in the numerous Islamic countries and regions throughout the world were at a level never seen before. And in Israel the conflict with the Palestinians was to use his words, "at a fever pitch."

Just as a senator from some state, Marcus didn't catch which one, started talking about the public outcry over the necessity of the war, and the greater need to protect the homeland, the Lexus that Marcus had seen parked in the Faradi's driveway, went by heading toward downtown Canby.

Marcus pulled out to follow. When the Lexus pulled over in a residential neighborhood a few miles away, and the young man he had seen earlier got out, it occurred to Marcus that maybe Ales for Ails wasn't Ricky Faradi's hangout after all. But less than ten minutes later, the guy was back on the road. Marcus followed him straight to the alley entrance to the parking lot behind the brewpub. Staying a safe distance behind the Lexus, he watched as it entered the alley and parked in the lot behind the pub; the young man got out and entered the bar through the back entrance. It seemed Marcus's stars were aligned.

When he first hit Canby, Marcus had spent some time reconnoitering the area around the pub and peered though the street-side windows on the pretense of reviewing the posted menu. It was a comfy old-style pub in a brick building, built in 1929, according to the cornerstone. Stylish without being pretentious, it had a long hardwood bar with a clear glass back, and behind this, six shiny copper brewing vats.

Another parking lot, directly across the alley, serviced some type of accounting business. Marcus parked there and changed from his running gear into a pair of dark jeans, dark blue fleece top, lightweight navy blue ski jacket, and leather hiking boots. He looked Oregon born and bred.

He poked around downtown, grabbing a gyro at a Greek takeout and just sort of blended into the background. Around eleven, he was back in the truck. The Lexus still in the parking lot. Patrons began leaving the bar in twos and threes, some dressed in costumes. It was, after all, Halloween. In normal times, the place was no doubt hopping, but in this post apocalyptic time, things were pretty slow, which suited him.

Marcus pulled the pistol and the Taser from his pack and laid them on the seat next to him, still with no clear idea what he intended to do.

Just before midnight, his guy came out the back of the pub, walked into the parking lot and got into his car. Marcus started the truck, turned the lights on bright, and pulled forward, across the alley stopping five feet behind the Lexus.

He grabbed the Taser off the seat, got out of the truck, opened the rear driver's door on the crew cab, and acted as if he were rearranging something, which in a way he was. He pulled off the knit cap he was wearing and slipped on a pair of leather gloves, keeping his head down inside the cab. He heard the honk once, twice, three times. A pause for a moment, then the engine shutting off, a car door slamming with a little more force than necessary, and approaching footsteps, and jangling keys.

"Hey man, what are you doing? You're blocking me in!" A male voice said, in a tone more agitated than angry.

Marcus ignored the question—he wanted the guy right up at the truck.

"Hey buddy, did you hear me?" The voice was right behind him.

Turning, Marcus looked Ricky Faradi square in the face, "Hello, Ricky."

The recognition was instantaneous. Marcus's face had been on the news, especially during the early part of the investigation, and his and the boys' pictures were frequently on screen during the days after Annie's beheading. Marcus raised the Taser and fired the pins, point-black into Ricky's chest. Fifty thousand volts of electricity arced through him, and the keys flew from his hand. As he slumped forward, Marcus grabbed him and forced him into the back seat.

Before Ricky came around, Marcus scooped up the fallen car keys, jumped in the truck, and backed up into the spot he had occupied earlier. He put a new cartridge in the Taser and, climbing over the seat, zapped Ricky again, then quickly duct-taped his legs, arms, and mouth.

Sliding back over to the front seat, he sat shaking. The whole thing had taken less than a minute and a half. He had been so focused he never considered that someone else might walk into the parking lot. Well, sometimes fate was with you, Marcus thought—or not, if you were Ricky—as he pulled out of the parking lot.

Driving down the alley, he stopped and lowering his window. "Hey, Ernie," he called out to the pile of cardboard leaning against the back of a brick building. "Yo, Ernie, you in there?"

The sheets of cardboard moved, and in a moment a middle-aged man came crawling out of the pile, wearing several layers of clothes. Marcus had run into him earlier, while casing the pub. He had hit Marcus up for spare change, all the while lamenting the cold damp, of Oregon Fall.

"Hey man." Ernie said, trying to focus his alcoholic gaze.

"You know how you were talking about a warmer place? Well, these keys are to the Lexus in the parking lot behind the pub, and here's a little money to help you out."

Marcus didn't think that Ernie would require a detailed explanation or be overly concerned about any legal fine print. He was not disappointed. Without so much as a thank you, Ernie took the keys and money, grabbed a battered old suitcase, and shuffled down the alley while Marcus drove away.

CHAPTER TWENTY-THREE
November 1

Marcus drove north out of Canby on Interstate 5, past Portland, and caught I-84 heading east. This would be the quickest way across Oregon to his next destination. As a light drizzle shrouded the oncoming lights with misty halos, Marcus felt for the first time in months that he was in control.

Pulling into the first rest stop, he parked in a secluded area away from the big rigs. Ricky had recovered some from the double Tasing, but Marcus had him well taped. Pulling him out of the back seat by the tape around his feet, he let him thump hard onto the asphalt and dragged him around to the back of the truck.

He rummaged though his pack and pulled out a Nalgene bottle of water. Prepared before he left home, it contained water and a good dose of ipecac, Ex-lax and four 500 mg Valium that he had crushed into powder. Ricky stared up at him with hate more than fear. *Well, we'll soon change that,* Marcus thought. Reaching into his jacket pocket, he pulled out a small stainless steel vial. One of the things that he, Mario and Glen had discovered about the phones was the compartment under the antenna held a small metal vial. But it wasn't until a news station reported that the vial contained the parasite infesting the nation's water system that they knew what it was.

Holding the vial between thumb and forefinger, he wagged it in front of Ricky's face. Then he unsealed it and poured its contents into the bottle. Although, he was fairly certain the parasite would take more than a day to make its presence known, he wanted it for its psychological impact—a sort of placebo effect in reverse. Then, reaching down, he tore the tape, with quite a bit of beard attached, from Ricky's mouth.

"You have no idea who you're fucking with...you ...." Ricky yelled, as Marcus hit him in the mouth with the hard plastic bottle, opening up Ricky's lower lip.

"Here's what's going to happen," Marcus said matter-of-factly. "You're gonna drink this down, and then you and I are going on a little road trip. Then we're going to get to know each other better."

Marcus put the bottle to Ricky's lips, but he refused to drink. "Be that way." Marcus said, and grabbing a fistful of hair, he forced Ricky's head back. Then with his left hand shoving down on Ricky's forehead while pinching his nose shut, he let go of the hair, grabbed the water bottle, and poured the concoction down his throat. Then, while Ricky coughed and gagged, Marcus rolled him onto his stomach and hog-tied him so that his ankles almost touched his wrists, then rolled him back over and re-taped his mouth.

Manhandling him into the back of the bed of the truck, into a spot he had prepared up against the fuel tank, Marcus covered him with gear bags, closed and locked the canopy cover, and drove.

***

By ten in the morning Marcus had crossed into Nevada. He called his brother's house. Bodie was in good spirits—better, in fact, than he had been in weeks, which struck Marcus as a bit strange. He talked to Garrett next.

"Hey, Dad, you okay?"

"Yeah, I'm good, bud. You sleep well?" He cringed at what a stupid question it was, but he couldn't have been less prepared for the answer.

"I slept good—better than in a long time. Mom visited me last night." Garrett paused as if waiting for his father to say something about it just being a dream. When he didn't, he went on. "She's good. She told me to tell you you're right on track but that you need to be careful—this is only one of many steps you'll need to take. She said you would know what that means. She said the direction would be clear, that you just had to listen. She said, to really listen, Dad." He emphasized this last part as if to imply that his dad didn't always listen intently. Fair enough.

Garrett's voice was clear and confident, with no sorrow or regret.

"Okay pal, I'll listen. Thanks for the heads up."

"No problem, Dad. Here, Uncle Glen wants to talk to you. I love you. Be safe!"

"Hey, Marcus, everything okay?"

"Yeah, all's well. How do the boys seem?"

"It's the damnedest thing. I don't know what happened, but they're good—*great* compared to how they have been. They both look more rested, more alive. Oh, hey, Agent Reynolds stopped by yesterday. I told him he couldn't talk to you. He wasn't very happy, but I think he bought the story."

"Okay, let's just hope we can keep those bozos at bay for a few more days. I have to go. I'll check in later today if I can, tomorrow at the latest."

"All right, brother. Just remember, I'm not there to watch your back, so you mind the rules, plan for the unexpected, and talk to me when you can."

***

In the early afternoon, Marcus arrived at his destination: Dead Man's Hole.

As teenagers growing up in the small ranching and farming community of Eureka, Nevada, he, his brother Glen, and their friends had spent countless hours roaming and hunting in the Diamond Range of the Ruby Mountains. Scattered throughout the hills were hundreds of abandoned mines from the gold rush days. During high school, some of these old tunnels and shafts, up miles of rugged, rutted dirt roads and far from prying eyes, were their favorite places to hang out.

By far their favorite of these derelict haunts was Dead Man's Hole. It was one of those perfect, eerie, scare-the-shit-out-of-you places where the moon cast ominous shadows and the wind blew in moaning voices across rock and sagebrush, and the rickety wooden ladder down into the depths of the shaft awaited anyone foolish enough to test his courage. It was just the setting Marcus needed!

As the sun was dropping to the western horizon, Marcus backed the truck up to a spot where the canyon wall came down steeply to a rock overhang that provided shelter from the wind and cold. Mule deer season had just begun, and on the off chance somebody came upon him, they wouldn't think twice about someone out scouting potential campsites for an upcoming hunting trip.

Opening the back of the truck, Marcus almost gagged at the stench. Ricky was sick all right, though probably not from the parasite.

Marcus pulled out all his gear and set it under the overhanging rock wall.

Hooking his arm around Ricky's folded knees he hauled him out of the truck, dumped him on the stony dirt. Then he cut the duct tape and rope hog-tying his ankles to his wrists. Ricky's pants were shit-soaked, and vomit trickled from a narrow gap in the tape over his mouth. Whatever remained in his alimentary tract was on its way out.

Propping him up against the rear tire, Marcus again ripped the tape off his mouth. The fall air quickly chilled as the last rays of the sun winked out behind the mountain. Marcus suddenly realized how tired he was. He hadn't slept in more than thirty-six hours. He cut the tape from Ricky's wrists, letting him bring his hands around in front of him. His eyes were bloodshot, the agony of the gastric spasms evident in his grimace. Ricky rubbed his hands and wrists.

"What the fuck do you think you're doing?"

"Well, you see, Ricky, that is your name, isn't it? My name is Marcus Diablo. I think you knew my wife?" Again the flash of recognition.

"I'm glad we understand each other. Let me explain what's going to happen. I need some rest, and then you and I are going to have a nice, long chat. You're going to tell me everything you know, starting from the beginning. I want the name of the person who controlled this operation. I want to know everything you know about it. And I want to caution you about lying to me. Every time I think you're being less than honest, I'm going to fuck you up in a nasty way—testing me would be a big mistake. So that you don't think I'm *completely* insensitive to your situation, I'm going to give you some time to think about it."

Marcus detected just the slightest relaxation in Ricky's posture. He was probably thinking, *this crazy bastard is going to leave him alone for a few hours, and by then I can figure out what to tell him, or escape.*

Smiling, Marcus put on a pair of heavy rubber gloves, pulled Ricky to his feet, slamming his back into the side of the truck, and used the knife to cut the tape from his torso, releasing his arms. He stripped off the young man's jacket and shirt and retaped his arms to his body, then repeated the process with his pants. He was a mess—shit everywhere. Then he taped his legs together at the thighs, knees, and ankles.

Hopping him over close to the mine shaft, Marcus made him sit bare-assed on the rough ground, then pulled the front end of the truck up to the shaft's edge, leaving about four feet from the front bumper to the edge of the hole. Ignoring Ricky's protests, he pushed him down onto his back and tied a figure-eight knot around his ankles and feet, then clipped a carabiner to the loop in the knot. He took two water bottles from the case in the back of the truck and forced them down Ricky's throat. Whatever water he didn't drink spilled on his skin. Within minutes he was going to get very cold.

Marcus positioned him with his head leaning just over the edge of the shaft, then clipped the carabiner at his ankles to the lock hook on the winch cable.

"Now, Ricky, you're going to spend the next few hours hanging fifty feet deep over a bottomless pit. Here, listen...." Marcus dropped a fist-size stone and waited quietly. "See what I mean? Never heard it hit. As you hang there, all the shit spraying out of you will drip down to your head, your mouth, your eyes and nose. Don't worry, though, I'll pull you out before you drown in it or die of exposure, or fear. But when I do—and heed these words, boy—you are going to tell me what I want to know, no bullshit, no games. And one more thing: if I don't get what I want from you, your parents will be my next stop."

Marcus pulled an iPod from his pack. Before leaving Reno, he had the boys load a hundred of the most obnoxious, discordant head-banger rock tunes they could find. He knelt down and slipped the buds into Ricky's ears, wrapped duct tape around his head to hold them secure, cranked the iPod up, and then secured it to his chest with more tape. Taking off the rubber gloves, he put on a leather pair and slowly played out the braided steel winch cable, using the remote, and lowered Ricky over the edge of the shaft. Then he got back in the truck and pulled forward until the front tires were inches from the edge. This allowed the winch cable to hang free away from the ragged rock edge of the hole, preventing Ricky from banging against it as he descended fifty feet into hell, screaming in fear the whole way down.

Marcus went back to his campsite and built a small fire, pulled his sleeping bag around his shoulders, and waited. Ricky would survive for a couple of hours at least, and he needed some rest. For the second time in many weeks, he felt in control.

CHAPTER TWENTY-FOUR

When Marcus opened his eyes, it was almost seven thirty. The fire had burned to embers, and he could feel the chill of the late October night. Ricky had been down in the hole for over two hours. Marcus restoked the fire and went to get him.

Engaging the winch, he brought Ricky up. His olive skin was streaked with his own excrement, and he dangled from the winch cable still as a side of beef. Marcus spread an old packing blanket on the ground at the edge of the shaft, backed the truck up, and pulled Ricky's limp body onto the blanket. His skin was cold, his breathing labored. Rolling him in the blanket, Marcus dragged him over near the fire and propped him up against a couple of gear bags.

Ricky looked bad. His face was ashen, his dark hair and scraggly beard matted with his own effluvia, and his lips had a faint bluish tint, but he wasn't going to die—not just yet. Marcus pulled out the camp stove and heated water, added a couple of chicken bouillon cubes, and spooned the warm broth into Ricky's mouth. His tongue licked hungrily out, seeking the salty liquid. It took a half hour, but Marcus finally got him revived and fairly coherent.

Marcus sat back down and pondered what a strong motivator fear could be. The best torture, he thought, was not the actual physical pain so much as the *anticipation* of it, and now, he was capable of imagining the cruelest, most horrible atrocities. Marcus hoped that was equally true for Ricky, because not only could Marcus now imagine them, he was certain he could also commit them.

Marcus had the fire roaring and Ricky was slowly coming around. He had left his legs and feet bound, and his spasms were now continual, gut-wrenching tremors. Marcus sat, waiting for him to speak first.

Ricky raised his bowed head, and looked at him with pleading, pathetic eyes, "Man, I need medicine," he said. "This thing is tearing me apart from the inside. You gave me an entire dose—there was enough in there to contaminate a *lake*!" His voice trailed off as another spasm racked his body.

Marcus removed a prescription bottle labeled, "Cipro" from his pack and tossed it to him, along with a bottle of water. With shaking hands, Ricky removed the top, spilled four or five of the fat white pills into his hand, and swallowed them, draining the bottle of water.

He could take the whole bottle, as far as Marcus was concerned. He had replaced the Cipro tablets with extra-strength Tylenol. The only benefit Ricky was going to get, besides possible liver damage, was some very temporary pain relief.

A few moments passed in silence and then Marcus said, "Okay, Ricky, I guess by now you've put together who I am. What you may not know is that I really don't give a shit what you believe or how noble or sacred you think your motivations are. I want to know who's responsible for my wife's death, and the attack on *my* country. You are going to tell me everything you know about the operation. Got it?"

He didn't wait for a response. "You want to get out of this? It's simple: tell me what I want to know, and I'm outta here. I'm sure a resourceful, intelligent guy like you can figure out how to make his way back to civilization. And anyway you're no real terrorist. You've never been trained. You're just fucked up and misguided."

In the firelight, huddled near the flames, with the blanket wrapped around his naked body, Ricky had a sinister, evil look. "You think if I just tell you what you want, you can do something about it. You have no idea how strong we are, how committed we are to our cause. So if you want to know, I'll tell you. None of it will matter anyway, because you're powerless. The righteous will prevail."

"Oh, Ricky, Ricky," Marcus chided. "Just so we're clear, I don't give a shit about the righteous, the chosen ones, or whatever, but if you keep rambling on about the great cause, instead of telling me what I want to know, I'm going to fuck you up. Look at me, Ricky. Do I look worried or scared? This can go down only one of two ways, and I really don't care which—either I get what I want from you, or I get it out of your parents!"

***

Ricky spoke in a tone more instructional than emotional, sounding like a teacher who had told the same story hundreds of times. "In the late 1960s, the Shah of Iran started a 'Westernizing' program in his country. He gave women the vote and began an education program called Sepah e Danesh, or 'Army of Knowledge.'" Here Ricky had to pause while a tremor went through his insides. "The idea was to bring elementary schools into remote areas of Iran. But what the United States and its allies didn't know was that, included in the Army of Knowledge campaign, which ironically, they financed, was a program known as *Petit Amérique*—French for 'Little America.'

"Two hundred miles southeast of Tehran, in the city of Isfahan, a small community was established, where young professional Iranian couples were placed, among them my parents. Here they ate, spoke, and breathed everything American: books, clothes, music, movies, and television programs. Iran's best and brightest—engineers, doctors, lawyers, scientists, scholars in literature and philosophy, economists, and sociologists—were chosen.

"They lived as Americans, in American-style, stucco homes with lawns and backyards. They even had white picket fences," Ricky said with an air of historical irony.

He moved uncomfortably, the rumblings of his gut audibly evident even over the crackling fire. "Rigorous indoctrination in all things American took place day in and day out, as the couples continued their formal education in English, within their various academic disciplines. Once the indoctrination was complete, the plan was they would emigrate to America, embed themselves in the culture, raise their families, and patiently await the call of Allah."

Marcus could stay silent no longer. "Are you out of your mind? How could something like that remain a secret for thirty years?"

Now Ricky's face took on a look of mild amusement, as if one of his students had just asked a question that indicated he hadn't read the book. "You see by the late 1970s, things weren't going so well for the shah, and he was ultimately deposed in February 1979. But *Petit Amérique* was a highly secret project, known only to the shah and a few of his closest advisors. And thanks to the Iran hostage crisis, which captivated the world's attention for almost a year and half, Little America escaped the notice of the new fundamentalist regime of Ayatollah Ruholla Khomeini—and everyone else for that matter. And by late 1980, all the members of *Petit Amérique* had emigrated legally to the United States."

Ricky squirmed a little closer to the fire. Marcus could see that his discomfort was growing by the minute. Although the parasite couldn't be affecting him yet, he was spewing from both ends, thanks to the ipecac and ex-lax. Ricky leaned over and dry-heaved. Marcus added wood to the fire and as Ricky wiped the bile from his mouth with his hand, he continued in a voice inflected with righteous indignation. "Had it not been for a quirk of fate, that was all that would have happened. My parents and the other couples would have raised their families, and by the time my generation reproduced, we would simply have been absorbed and assimilated into American society and culture. We would all have become grateful immigrants joining the largest Iranian population in the world outside Iran."

Ricky just kept on talking, the words tumbling out of him, as if the two hours he had spent dangling by his ankles had given him an indelible vision of hell itself. "My parents were granted political asylum, and arrived in the States in 1980. They were the first," he said proudly. "They both got associate professorships at Portland State University, completed their doctorates, and became U.S. citizens. I was born in November of 1982. And to anyone watching, I was raised just as American as the next kid.

"My given name is Abbas Majid. It translates as 'Lion of the Glorious Sword,'" he said lifting his head arrogantly. "My parents always remained true and made sure that I would be prepared when the time came. We avoided any public profession of our faith, or any association with an organized Muslim community." Ricky laughed quietly. "As far as anyone knows, we are practicing Lutherans."

"So where did you do this practicing of your faith then?" Marcus asked.

Sneering at Marcus, Ricky explained. "In our barn is an underground shelter. In Oregon, where the citizenry is known for a fierce, freethinking independence, bomb shelters aren't that unusual."

Ricky explained that it wasn't precisely a bomb shelter, however, but more of a classroom hidden away underground. It was in this room that he learned the five pillars of Islam, studied the Koran and, as regularly as possible, practiced the ritual prayers.

Ricky smugly stated that his father, because of his commitment to the proliferation of Islam as the one true faith and because he and Rahlia were the first *petits Américains* to immigrate, was the only one who knew the names and locations of every other couple placed in the United States.

From his story, Ricky seemed to have lived a pretty normal upper middle-class life. But Marcus sat a little straighter when Ricky said he had done his master's thesis, at the University of Oregon in Eugene, on climatic change in the twentieth century and the effects of fire on biodiversity and urban development.

"For three years, my father and I planned and strategized on the faint hope that one day the call of Allah would come. My father located and recruited all of the original members who remained in the U.S., and who still shared our vision of a holy jihad."

So Kevin had been right about Ricky's being important to the cause. The whole fire thing had been his idea—the concept, the method, maybe even the timing! Marcus put another stick on the fire and tried to calm his building rage. And Ricky, sick as he was, kept on talking.

"At the start of this year, my father got invited to attend a bioengineering conference in New York City. A note accompanied the invitation, asking him to bring me.

"For over twenty years my father has been working in biochemical engineering involving 'super bugs'—viruses and invertebrates that mutate so rapidly that, within a year's span, they can become resistant to the antibiotics and chemicals that would have killed them the year before."

Now it all made so much sense. The giardia parasite infesting the nation's water system had been altered—it was stronger, tougher, more resistant to antibiotics. This explained why the normal seven-to-ten-day regime wasn't knocking it out. It was at this point in Ricky's narrative that Marcus realized he would definitely be returning to Canby again before going home.

They had been at it for several hours. Between Ricky's spasms and his own lack of sleep, Marcus was anxious to get to the end of the story. But this was no time to push—the kid was telling him everything he wanted to know and then some, without provocation. Marcus boiled some water and made two hot mugs of strong green tea. Handing one to Ricky, he sat back down by the fire and wrapped his sleeping bag around his shoulders as Ricky kept right on spilling his guts.

"My father and I went to New York. He attended the conference, and I hung around the hotel. One afternoon a man came to visit me." Marcus had to restrain himself from eagerly leaning forward. This was it—the information he'd been waiting for.

Ricky spoke in a hero worshipper's tone about Adad al-Mohmoud. Syrian by birth, he was rumored to be one of the richest men in the world. His family controlled vast resources in oil, mining, timber, shipping, technology, and real estate, scattered throughout every continent on the planet.

"During his university years in the UK, Adad, became a great admirer of the late shah of Iran, who had been a good friend to Adad's father, and studied his regime extensively. And his wealth and connections got him the location and access to the archives that included the shah's most intimate and private papers. While sifting through the mountains of material, he found a couple of references to '*Petit Amérique.*' He became obsessed by the concept of deep-cover sleeper cells as potential weapons to be used against the infidels in America, and the more time he spent gathering information, the more interested he became. He tracked down some of the shah's closest friends in Egypt and, over time, obtained one family name: Faradi." Ricky's face held a look of intense pride. "After a few false starts and cold trails, he tracked my family down in Oregon."

Ricky doubled over in ever-worsening stomach spasms. But he still had more to tell. "Adad promised me that if the attack was successful and I survived the aftermath, I would be joining him as a member of his personal staff by the end of this year." There was a note of disappointment in Ricky's voice, which Marcus took as a grim realization that this wasn't looking like such a sure thing now.

Marcus walked over to Ricky and handed him the cell phone he had taken from the mountains months before. "Tell me about his thing. How does it work?"

With shaking hands Ricky removed the back and saw that the battery had been removed. He looked at Marcus, who held the battery up in his hand.

"That's' the Key, that battery," he said. "We redesigned it. Less than half its volume is the actual power supply. The rest contains equal parts potassium permanganate and car antifreeze, separated by a strong, thin latex membrane. We used the electrical charge from the battery side to break down the latex membrane and bring the permanganate into contact with the antifreeze."

Marcus shook his head. It was chemistry 101: mix potassium permanganate, available at any chemical supply store and used every day in water filtration systems, with antifreeze, and the mixture bursts into flames. The combined ingredients made a gel rather like Sterno, which burned slow and very hot.

"Here, I'll show you how it works."

Marcus gave him the battery and he put it in the phone. "That's the beauty of the whole thing: the advanced lithium-ion technology let us redesign a battery and still have plenty of room for the accelerant. And we chose a cell phone because everybody's got one."

Ricky had all the enthusiasm of a child showing off a cool new toy. Marcus leaned over to watch as Ricky began punching buttons on the phone. "By using the menu we regulated the strength of the charge, so that we could start fires from one end of the country to the other in a fairly narrow time window. All we had to do was bury them in duff—pine needles and leaf litter—in stands of big timber, in remote locations and ..." Ricky held up both hands. "Well, you can see the results."

Marcus took the phone back from Ricky, powered it off and walked over to the truck. He grabbed his laptop from the backseat. There was one more thing he needed Ricky to do, leverage for when he confronted the boy's parents.

CHAPTER TWENTY-FIVE
November 2

It was after midnight when Marcus started loading gear back into the truck. Ricky was spent. He had been a gold mine of information, but the vein was about played out. One of the last things he mentioned about Adad al-Mohmoud was that he spent much of his time on his ship, the *Takbir* which, Ricky explained, was the Arabic name used to refer to the phrase "Allahu akbar"—"God is the greatest." He couldn't say where the ship was, though either the Persian Gulf or the Mediterranean would be a good guess.

As for who had killed Annie, he knew only that he drove to Las Vegas and turned her over to one of Adad's people. Once he delivered her, he returned to Oregon. Having heard everything else, Marcus was sure Ricky spoke the truth about this.

Marcus pulled two cans of Crisco from his supplies and scooped them into an empty five-gallon bucket, poured in some gasoline, put on the heavy rubber gloves, and mixed it up. Ricky paid no attention, as he lay curled up on the ground, wrapped in the blanket, next to the dying fire. Marcus went over to him, and Ricky looked up, his face lit by the orange glow of the coals.

"You're going to help me now?" he moaned. "I've told you everything! You said you'd let me go if I did that!" His voice was desperate.

Marcus had nothing more to say. For the first time in many hours, he thought of his boys. He needed to get out of this place and back to Oregon, get the information on the terrorist cell, and get back home.

He pulled the blanket away from Ricky's body, retaped his mouth and arms, and, in the cold predawn darkness, began rubbing the mixture of lard and fuel over Ricky's entire body. Sitting him up, Marcus made sure Ricky could see his every movement. He held the phone up and, just as Ricky had shown him, set the timer for thirty minutes, which would provide the strongest electrical charge to the latex membrane. Then he taped the device to Ricky's chest.

On the packing blanket, Marcus pulled Ricky back over to the edge of the mine shaft and tied a rope around his ankles, again leaving a loop in which to hook the end of the winch cable. Smearing some of the lard and gas mixture on the length of rope, he played out the winch, and dangled Ricky over the side. Then, pulling the truck forward as before, he lowered him almost to the end of the winch cable. With the cable fully extended and the added ten feet of rope, he had Ricky some ninety feet down in the shaft.

As morbid, and as wrong as he knew it was, Marcus had no problem sitting and waiting. The thirty minutes passed without notice until, he heard the winch cable rattle. Marcus walked over to the edge of the hole, and saw the glow of fire.

From this distance, it didn't seem so ominous—just a flickering light shining up from deep in the earth. Marcus just stood there, numb, watching the light, barely taking note of the faint heat rising up the shaft. In less than a minute, the glowing light fell away, and disappeared into the darkens, and Marcus thought, the cold, bottomless emptiness of the mine shaft, matched the gaping hole that Annie's death had left in his soul.

CHAPTER TWENTY-SIX

Fourteen hours later, Marcus arrived back at the county park, less than a mile from the Faradi residence. Other than a short catnap, he had been up for over forty–eight hours, yet he felt awake and energized. He couldn't escape the feeling that some force, some unseen hand, was directing him.

He parked the truck, put on his rain jacket and knit cap, and stuffed the Sig .45 in the inside pocket, then walked at a brisk pace through the drizzle, back to the Faradi home, breathing in the scents of wet grass and fireplace smoke. The same Mercedes was in the driveway. The front porch light was on, and lights were on throughout the house. This was not to be a clandestine approach, no sneaking or reconnoitering. This was a walk-right-up-and-take-what-you-came-for plan.

He knocked, and a shortish, heavyset, middle-aged man opened the door.

"Professor Faradi?"

"Yes, my I help you?" he said in lightly accented English.

In response, Marcus shoved his way inside, shutting and locking the door behind him.

"What is the meaning of—!" the man sputtered, stopping his demand as Marcus turned from the door, and removed his cap.

Marcus pulled out the pistol. "I see you recognize me. We need to talk. It's about your son. Get your wife—now!"

The elder Faradi called for his wife, and a woman with black hair streaked through with gray came out from what must be the kitchen. At the smell of food, Marcus realized how hungry he was.

"Okay, let's go to the special room in your barn," Marcus said as he herded them toward the back door.

There was an air of resignation in their manner. They just led the way out the door, across the damp yard, and into the barn. At the back right corner, they stopped, and Ali Faradi grabbed a rake from a wall hook and moved some straw aside, bent down, and lifted a small recessed handle. The door opened easily on a hydraulically actuated arm to expose a flight of concrete stairs.

As they headed down the stairs, a motion-controlled light came on. At the bottom of the steps was a steel door with a control panel on the landing wall. Marcus stopped them and returned up the stairs and grabbed the rake. He didn't want to get stuck inside this room, not after coming this far.

Dr. Faradi entered a code, Marcus heard a bolt slide back, and the door opened silently inward. Marcus wedged the rake in the doorway and followed the Faradis in.

The room was about twelve by twelve feet, with a concrete ceiling nine or ten feet high. Marcus knew from what Ricky had told him that it was built like a traditional bomb shelter. The concrete walls, floor, and ceiling were steel reinforced and almost three feet thick. An independent, underground power source not only provided electricity but also ran an air filtration system.

Along one wall were shelves filled with canned and dry food, and cases and cases of bottled water, batteries, flashlights, clothing, and various other items one might need when the end of the world came. But it was all a ruse—they had no intention of using this room as a shelter.

On the opposite wall was a desk area with a computer and two HD monitors. There were shelves holding paper for a printer, packages of disks, and USB drives. There were three rolling desk chairs and, above the desk, a large whiteboard.

Marcus motioned for the two of them to sit in the desk chairs. Then, taking a roll of duct tape from his rain jacket, he bound them securely to the chairs. Marcus had no intention of spending hours and hours with these people. What he needed was simple, and if he approached it correctly, he would be able to get what he wanted and be out of here in under an hour.

He set his backpack on the floor and got out his laptop. The last thing he had done with Ricky before sending him to hell was to have him tape a message to his parents. In simple terms, he had gone over what he wanted him to say, and threatened him with dire consequences if he didn't comply. Marcus had then placed the laptop in front of Ricky and put it in video mode, so that it recorded Ricky's image and voice.

Placing the laptop on the desk, Marcus positioned Ali and Rahlia Faradi in front of it, and hit Play, and their son's face filled the screen.

In a voice that tried to put on a strong front but failed miserably, Ricky said, "Papa, Tata, you must tell this man anything he wants to know. Give him whatever he wants. He is not with the government; it was his wife who was sacrificed. What he wants, what he thinks he can accomplish, he cannot. Do not try and argue with him. He is incapable of understanding our commitment or how strong and many we are. Let him keep his delusions. If you give him what he wants, I will be home soon. This is not the time for me to die for Allah—not yet. I have bigger things to do! You know that! I have been infected with the parasite and will need medical help soon. Please do not waste valuable time."

It wasn't precisely as Marcus had scripted it, but watching it, he had to admit it was much better than what he had come up with. Ricky made him out to be just some crazy grief-stricken infidel who had no clue what he was doing. From Ricky's perspective, anything his parents could give this nut job would be inconsequential

As they watched the video, Ali Faradi's face betrayed no emotion, but the mother broke down at once and would have sobbed into her hands had they not be taped to her sides.

Marcus spun their chairs around to face him. He hadn't considered how he looked—he hadn't slept, shaved, or had so much as a spit bath in days. The picture of a crazed infidel fit.

"What is it that you want?" Ali Faradi said.

"Gee, I don't know, Professor—how about world peace and my wife back?" Marcus's voice took on a hard edge. "But since you can give me neither, I'll settle for the names and addresses of everyone activated from the *Petit Amérique* project, and the names and addresses of everyone they recruited."

At the mention of *Petit Amérique*, Ali Faradi lost his poker face.

"I don't have that information, and even if I did—"

Marcus put his arm around Rahlia Faradi's shoulders. Looking into brown eyes that had become lipid pools of worry and fear, Marcus replied in a calm voice, "That would be too bad, because, you see, I have come a long way and I'm tired and in no mood to play games. So unless you want me to hurt your wife—and please, make no mistake, I will hurt her—then you need to play nice. Give me what I want, or else."

"Oh, yes, I give what you want and then you kill us. You must take me for a fool."

"You are right that I take you for a fool, but not for the reasons you suppose. If I don't make a call in the next ten minutes, your son is going to be dead, and then I will get what I want anyway."

Marcus let that sink in. He really didn't want to hurt Ali's wife, but if that was what it took, he was sure he had it in him.

Marcus started pacing, putting on a show of ever-increasing agitation. He could hear them speaking in what he assumed was their native tongue, his voice strong and arrogant, hers pleading and submissive.

"All right," Ali said, "I will give you what you want, as long as our son is returned safe. You will need to free my hands so I can use my computer. The information is encrypted and I cannot explain to you how to download it, I must do it."

Marcus pulled a fresh thirty-two-gigabyte thumb drive from his front pants pocket, stepped over to Ali Faradi, and cut the tape binding his hands and arms. He leaned over and whispered in his ear while wheeling his chair to the desk, "If you fuck with me, I am going to start inflicting serious injury on your wife, so bring up the information so that I can read it, in English. We will download it. I will check to make sure that I can bring it up on my laptop and, if it works you and I are done. Are we clear?"

Ali Faradi nodded.

Within a few minutes, the file came up on the screen. Ricky had told him that his father was a very analytical and organized man who had embraced information technology "like a teenager." At first glance, the screen was just filled with random numbers and letters. A few keystrokes and entry commands later, the gibberish was intelligible. The information was alphabetical, complete with names and addresses, names of children, educational and professional backgrounds, and even a synopsis—done, he assumed, by Dr. Faradi—of each member's particular talents and suitability for the planned terrorist attack.

Marcus handed Ali the thumb drive, and Ali inserted it into the port and downloaded the information. Marcus took the drive and put it into his laptop, brought up the file, opened it, and was pleased to see that it worked, as it should. Then he put everything back into his pack and prepared to leave the room.

"What about my son?" Mrs. Faradi asked.

Marcus saw no reason to continue the lie. "I'm sorry to inform you that your son will not be returning to you—ever. Consider it the price for the greater cause of jihad. The two of you are going to remain here until the FBI arrives, and then I think you can plan on a little Caribbean vacation in Guantánamo. I hear it's nice this time of year: blue water, white sand beaches, palm trees swaying in the breeze. Hell, if all goes well, within in the next couple of months it'll feel like a class reunion."

He again taped both the Faradis' hands and arms and added more tape to their ankles and around their knees. Marcus went up to the barn and returned with a small sedge hammer he found on a work bench and smashed the computer monitors, keyboards and hard drives. As he walked out the door, Marcus noticed the same type of control pad as on the outside of the door. He smashed them both with the sledge, removed the rake and let the door swing closed. As he had suspected, as soon as it shut, the bolt automatically engaged. With luck, they would not be able to get out until he put the next part of his plan to work.

As Marcus drove south, toward home, the adrenaline that had fueled him for the past two days faded. He pulled into the first rest stop he came to and drifted off into the first nightmare-free sleep in months.

CHAPTER TWENTY-SEVEN
November 3

At seven thirty the next morning, Marcus was ninety miles from Reno. He took out the prepaid cell phone and called Glen.

"Okay, brother, in about an hour all hell is going to break loose around your house. Agent Reynolds is going to show up, and I'm not going to be there. I want you, Ellie and the kids, including Bodie and Garrett, to start packing to head back to Australia."

"Marcus, slow down!" Glen said. "What the hell are you talking about? The airports are still shut down. There's talk about some of the domestic air travel coming back on line, but as for international, it seems like it could still be a while."

"I know, bro, but I'm about to make a deal with the FBI. Based on what I have to bargain with, I think we're going to get out of the United States. I need to get out of here—get the boys as far away from this mess as I possibly can. I'll explain everything when I get there. Just be prepared for a very pissed-off FBI agent."

The next call was to Special Agent in Charge Nathan Reynolds.

"Reynolds...Who is this? How did you get this number?"

"One question at time, Agent Reynolds."

"Marcus, is that you? Where are you calling from?"

"Right now that's not important. You think you can just sit on the line and listen for a minute? I have a gift for you."

"Marcus, don't play games with me!"

Marcus bristled at the remark. All Reynolds had done from day one was play games with him. But Marcus bit his tongue, and it occurred to him that maybe he was learning.

"Settle down, Agent Reynolds. Got a pen? Okay, take down this address." After giving Reynolds the address of the Faradi residence in Canby, he told him to get in touch with the nearest Bureau field office—he assumed they had one in Portland—and send agents to that address. He detailed where the special room was and how they could find it.

"You got all that, Agent Reynolds? Good! Now, I want you to meet me at my brother Glen's house at nine this morning—by then you should already know what's in Oregon."

Before Reynolds could argue or question him, Marcus hung up and tossed the phone out the truck window and watched in the side-view mirror as it bounced off the asphalt and broke into little bits.

He pulled into the driveway of his brother's house about twenty minutes after nine. The two FBI agents on duty were standing in the driveway, and a second Crown Vic was parked at the curb.

As he parked, the boys came running out the front door. He hugged them fiercely. And for the first time in quite a while, they weren't all crying.

Marcus followed the boys into the house and heard Agent Reynolds angry voice coming from the kitchen. He sounded livid. Good, Marcus wanted him totally off his game.

"Agent Reynolds, always nice to see you!" Marcus said with a big, easy smile.

"Marcus, you are in deep shit. You need to tell me everything you have been up to, and then I am going to take you into custody, and if you don't want me to arrest your brothers as well, you had better start talking!"

Marcus walked over to the counter, grabbed a coffee mug, and poured himself a cup. "Want one?"

"NO, I don't want one! I want you on your ass in that chair—now!"

Marcus walked over and sat down in the chair opposite where Reynolds was standing. As Reynolds started ramping up to go at him again, the look in Marcus's eyes changed from mild amusement to stone.

"Agent Reynolds, sit down and shut the fuck up!"

He kept standing. "Don't want to sit down? Fine. Go look out the front window."

Agent Reynolds walked to the living room and peered out through the plantation shutters to see several news vans setting up for a live broadcast.

"What the hell is all this about, Marcus?" His tone was angry, but Marcus thought he detected a trace of nervousness as well.

"About twenty minutes ago, I called the local network news outlets and mentioned there might be a breaking story about the terrorist attack, and that they might want to get some crews over here before nine thirty. So now that I've got you focused on what matters, let's start with Canby—your boys go there?"

"Yeah, they went there, found a Mr. and Mrs. Faradi dead—some type of poison, maybe cyanide."

Marcus tried not to show any surprise. He had had every intention that the Faradis would be found alive. He hadn't spent any time searching the underground room. It seemed plausible that they might have some last-resort plan, some way of ending their lives if everything fell apart. Why not cyanide? In hindsight, this might work out better for him anyway.

"Your guys must've found some other stuff?"

"Yeah, they did. The computers and hard drives were smashed up pretty good. And from what the tech people are saying it appears that some type of virus was introduced to corrupt the data on the hard drive. But our guys are the best and if there is anything to be salvaged they will get it. There was also a filing cabinet with a lot of information about the cell phone devices and the parasite. It would seem that these people were directly involved."

After the data wanted had been downloaded he ordered Dr. Faradi to activate his fail safe protocol system which Ricky had told him would corrupt the data and make it very difficult to retrieve. Now that he knew the Faradi's were dead, Marcus wasn't about to fess up to smashing the computers. May as well let Agent Reynolds believe the Faradi's had done it. All that mattered was that Marcus was the only one with the information on the terrorist cell, at least for a few days.

"Yes, indeed they were. Maybe you'd like to sit down now?" Marcus pointed at the chair opposite him with a wave of his hand.

This time, Agent Reynolds sat.

Marcus leaned his elbows on the table, chin in his hands. "Now, Agent Reynolds, much as I hate to do it, I am going to give you your life back. My guess is that right about now you are not a very popular guy among the upper echelons of the FBI. In fact, I'd bet you're about one step away from a posting in whatever is the most godforsaken field office the Bureau has."

He paused for just a moment. The look in Reynolds eyes told him he was hitting pretty close to home. "You are going to do a few things for me, Agent Reynolds, and in turn, I am going to give you the means to go from delinquent stepchild to the prodigal son of the FBI, in one sweeping motion. What if I were to tell you that I have all the information you need—names, addresses, bios—of every person involved in the attack on *our* country?"

"Well, Marcus, that would be damn good news! So where is this information?"

"Hidden in a safe place."

"Of course, so why don't you tell me what is stopping me from just hauling your ass in and getting the information out of you any way necessary. These are extraordinary times, and they just might call for extraordinary measures."

This was what Marcus had been counting on—the man's predictability was laughable.

"That's what the reporters are for," Marcus said, cocking his chin toward the front yard. "If you and I can't come to some equitable arrangement, I'm going to walk out there, and in the span of, oh, thirty seconds I will ruin your life forever. When I'm done, the public image of the entire FBI will be dealt a crushing blow, and if you think the prospect of being banished to the hinterlands is bleak now, hell, you won't be able to get a job as a Wal-Mart security guard! Come on, Reynolds, what are you gonna do? You're the only agent in here with me, you think that you can stop me?" Marcus looked back over his shoulder. His brothers were standing right behind Agent Reynolds. He was certain they would be able to hold him off long enough for Marcus to walk out the front door and hand the USB drive to one of the eager reporters standing outside.

Looking Reynolds hard in the eyes, he said, "So why don't you just sit there for a minute and listen to me and let's see if we can't work this whole thing out?" He rested his hands on the table, palms up. "First, I want you to arrange for the boys and me, as well as Glen and his family, to be flown to Australia. Second, I want you to call my insurance company and put all the persuasive power of the

FBI to work, strongly encouraging them to pay Annie's life insurance policy promptly."

He could see that Reynolds was getting ready to protest, so he held up a hand to staunch the flow of bullshit before it began. "I didn't say that what I wanted would be easy, but you and I both know that diplomatic and military flights are leaving the U.S. every day. Get us on one and out of here. That's nonnegotiable."

Reynolds looked across the table at Marcus, sizing him up. "Okay, Marcus, for argument's sake, let's say I can arrange this—and I'm not saying I can. What guarantee do I have that you'll turn over the information, or, for that matter, that the information is worth a damn? I'm going to need something, some good-faith gesture on your part."

Marcus jumped to his feet and leaned across the table into Agent Reynolds' face. "Good-faith gesture? What the fuck do you think the address in Oregon was? Just because the people there killed themselves doesn't change anything. Didn't you find undeniable evidence that they were involved? I am done playing games with you, Reynolds. Let me be clear, you are going to make this happen. Now. Today. I want to be on a plane out of here by tomorrow. You send Agent Gibson, and only Agent Gibson, with us. The second my sons and Glen and his family have gotten off the plane, I will give him access to all the information. He can hold me on the plane until the information has been confirmed."

Reynolds said in a voice that came very close to a whine, "There's no way I can arrange a flight by tomorrow."

"You get on your phone right here, right now, and make this happen. If you don't, no matter what else happens, I'm going to squash you like the spineless invertebrate that you are. Do we understand each other?"

Marcus knew he had Reynolds backed into a corner. The man had no choice, nowhere to go. He only had to wait for a few moments before Reynolds pulled his phone from his inside jacket pocket.

For the next hour, he made one call after another, and Marcus had to give him credit, he was good. Despite the shit he had to be in, he was able to convince his bosses that he was on the verge of breaking the case wide open. He used the possible threat to the lives of the boys and Marcus as the reason to spirit them out of the country, and with his brother Glen just happening to live in Australia, that made it the best and safest place for them.

"Okay, Marcus," he said at last, "it's all arranged. Tomorrow morning at nine, Agent Gibson will pick you all up. I can't tell you how, or the route you and your family will be flying, but less than twenty-four hours from then, you will all be in Australia. As for the insurance money, I will handle it over the next few days. Before you leave, call them and give them your information so the funds can be transferred. It could take a week or so to finalize, but you have my word I will make it happen."

He sounded so sincere, Marcus wanted to believe him, but if there was one thing he had learned about the FBI, it was that they could lie with the best of them and not lose a wink of sleep.

Marcus motioned for Agent Reynolds to follow him as he walked toward the front door. When they were out of earshot, Marcus said in a low whisper, "Just so we understand each other, I have sent the complete computer file, in an encrypted format, to a major news network. If I don't cancel the time-stamped send command, they will receive the file. So if you get any bright ideas for trying some kind of end run or some covert spy bullshit, you will still lose."

He leaned in to Reynolds so their faces were mere inches apart. "Take a hard look at me, Reynolds, and ask yourself, do I look like someone you really want to fuck with? Think about it. So far, I've been right about everything. I'm the only one who has made any headway toward finding out who is responsible for the most horrific terrorist attack in history. So no matter what happens—you fuck up, the Bureau fucks up—you go down."

Agent Reynolds stepped back, looking at Marcus with what looked like a glimmer of respect. "I give you my word, this is going to happen. You just make damn sure that you live up to your end of the bargain, because if you don't, no matter what happens, I won't rest until I find you."

"Good for you, Agent Reynolds. Now you're actually showing some balls. And once this all goes down, shit, forget Melvin Purvis—you're going to be the most famous FBI agent of all time." Marcus grinned. "There is definitely a promotion in your future. Hell, you'll probably run the whole Bureau someday."

CHAPTER TWENTY-EIGHT
November 5

At nine sharp, Agent Gibson arrived in a big white passenger van, accompanied by Agent Reynolds in a separate car.

The luggage was in the driveway, and Agent Gibson was loading it into the back of the van when Marcus met Agent Reynolds at the door.

"I see you're ready to go," Reynolds said, handing him a large manila envelope. "You'll be needing these."

Opening the envelope, Marcus found their passports. He had forgotten all about them, forgotten that the FBI had taken them when they searched the house.

"Thank you!" Marcus replied, realizing this was the first time he had said those two words to Agent Reynolds without sarcasm.

"I've been assured that your insurance company will be paying out Annie's life insurance within the next two weeks,"

"Thank you again!" Maybe he and Agent Reynolds were on their way to forging a new relationship, one built on mutual respect instead of contempt.

"Marcus, I know you and I haven't exactly gotten off on the right foot, but if you have the information you say you do—and at this point, you're the only viable lead we have—I have to trust you. Our country is in a mess—fear, panic, and paranoia everywhere you look. We have to begin to rebuild, restore confidence, and get ourselves back on the path to recovery."

Standing on the front stoop, in the cool gloom of the overcast November morning and staring at Reynolds' face, Marcus thought he was sincere. "You know, you were right about one thing. This is bigger than Annie. What has been done to our country is beyond anything I could ever have imagined. That's bad enough, but you add in that her life was the price my boys and I had to pay—well, that's a debt that I plan to collect on, in full." His voice calm and cold.

Before Reynolds could launch into some BS about how individuals can't take the law into their own hands, Marcus continued. "The FBI are big on profiling. And I'm sure it works for serial killers, pedophiles and bank robbers, but on these guys …"

As Marcus paused, Agent Reynolds broke in, "So tell me Marcus how would you suggest we catch those responsible?" To Marcus's surprise, he sounded truly interested.

Getting into the van through the sliding side door, Marcus smiled back at the agent, "I know it sounds clichéd, but to catch a terrorist, you gotta think like one. And thanks to them—and you—I do."

***

Almost twenty hours later, in the early morning, the jet touched down in Sydney. Everyone but Agent Gibson and Marcus grabbed their bags and prepared to deplane.

Marcus helped the boys round up jackets and game stations and earphones. As everyone stood waiting for the door to open, the kids' chatter echoing off the plane's upholstered walls, Marcus turned to them.

"Hey, guys, I have some business with Agent Gibson. I want you to go with Uncle Glen. I'll be along in a few minutes."

Over the past few days, things had gotten back to some semblance of normality for the boys. There were moments when they played and laughed and even argued with each other. But there also were times when the enormity of what had happened hit like a brick to the face. They would act out and then become inconsolable. Marcus was so preoccupied with his plan, a plan that was constantly evolving as he went, that he was little help. But thanks to their aunts, uncles and cousins, their emotional needs were tended.

As Marcus looked at them, he could tell they were anxious about coming to Australia, but there it was, the same look that he had seen hundreds of times over the past three months. The look that said, *don't you dare leave us.*

"Hey, I got us all here, didn't I?" He said in his best *Dad-has-it-all-under-control* voice. "You think for one minute that I'm not getting off this plane? Now, go on, I'll be right there."

"Come on, guys," Glen said, coming to his rescue, "the quicker we're out of here, the sooner your dad can finish up, and the sooner we can all get to the beach."

Once Marcus and Agent Gibson were alone on the plane, they sat down. The agent gave him a quizzical look.

Giving him a sly grin, Marcus reached into his front shirt pocket, and withdrew a small black USB drive. He handed it to him. "This is all you need. Go ahead, put it in your computer and take a look for yourself."

"Mr. Diablo, I was led to believe that you had this in some type of encrypted format, that you had it on a preset time-send in case we reneged on our deal."

"The only part of what you just said that has any truth to it is 'led to believe.'"

Gibson gave him a bemused look, took the USB drive, and loaded it into his laptop.

As they waited for the information to load, Marcus spoke. "About this information, this shit is kryptonite—the scale is off the charts—but more important is the time frame. This thing's been lying dormant for decades. Long before Nine-eleven, these people were living in the U.S., pursuing careers, raising families. If it were to come out that these people had been living in our neighborhoods, working, sending their children to school, for almost thirty years, can you imagine the wave of vigilantism that would be unleashed? I mean the majority of Muslims are peaceful, decent people."

Marcus paused a moment to let his words sink in. "We've all seen firsthand what happens when society breaks down. I know you may not have much say in how this stuff is handled, but if you do, or if you have the ear of anyone with some juice, deal with it like it's radioactive."

Agent Gibson turned his attention back to the screen. There was a mountain of information.

"I told you, this is some serious shit," Marcus said. "All right, send that file and get your confirmation—my boys and I want to hit the beach."

The transfer took about ten minutes. When it was done, Agent Gibson talked on a cell phone, closed it, and turned to Marcus.

"Mr. Diablo, you are free to go."

Rising from his seat Marcus extended a hand to Agent Gibson and said, "It's a long flight home—put that inquiring mind to good use."

CHAPTER TWENTY-NINE
January 4

Garrett turned nine a few days after they arrived in Australia, bringing Annie's absence crashing down upon them all. The holidays came and went. There was little fanfare, in a season that had always been steeped in the traditions of gathering family together. This year, Glen, Ellie, and Marcus decided to keep it simple. Not being confined by short days and cold weather made it a bit easier.

The boys made the transition to a new school in a new country with a surprising ease. For them, it was all new and exciting. They seemed to blend right in and were making new friends from the start. Renée and Charlie treated the boys like their brothers and went out of their way to integrate them into their lives.

Two weeks after their arrival, Annie's two-million-dollar life insurance policy was paid. Agent Reynolds had done as he promised. Now Marcus and the boys wouldn't have to worry about their financial situation for some time.

Even here, on the other side of the world, the news of the attack on the United States dominated the airwaves. At least in Marcus's view, the latest updates were encouraging. The infection from the parasite was now fully under control. Agent Reynolds had cracked the case wide open, and those responsible for perpetrating the heinous attack on America were being located and arrested. Reynolds appeared on more than one broadcast, his handsome, buttoned-down persona tailor-made for the situation. And by all indications the Diablo family was no longer newsworthy.

Law and order was being restored, but the effects of some eighty thousand deaths and at least a trillion dollars in damage would mark America, the new America, forever. From the news commentators and the countless parade of everyday citizens being interviewed daily, it seemed to Marcus that complacency and apathy, so prevalent in America, had been replaced with a wary vigilance.

First on Marcus's mind was establishing a routine. In the morning after the kids got off to school, he ran for a few hours and then spent another two hours at the gym, training as if he were preparing for a high mountain climb or quite possibly—a battle. And after a few weeks, his five-eleven frame was getting lean and toned. His long brown hair came almost to his shoulder, curlier than ever in the humid salt air.

In the afternoons, before the boys got out of school, he spent time researching Adad al-Mohmoud. The guy was born in Syria in 1972, to Sheikh Nizar al-Mohmoud and his wife, Asilah. Although Marcus could find no information that the sheikh had any public political aspirations, he couldn't have accumulated his wealth without having friends and influence in very high places. The sheikh and his family controlled vast resources in oil, mining, and shipping, but it was not until after Adad took over the family financial empire in 1997, at age twenty-five, that their wealth seriously diversified, placing them among the five richest families in the world.

Adad was very accomplished in his own right. He graduated from the University of Cambridge and earned a Master's in economics from the London School of Economics and Political Science. Marcus could only assume that he had attended some college preparatory school in England as well. There was no mention of his being radical or even especially political at all in early life.

From what Marcus could infer, unlike Western multinationals, which operated under "normal" managerial systems with corporate hierarchies and boards of directors, Middle Eastern conglomerates were more tightly held. Being privately held made it difficult for anyone to discover more than just the most basic information on the companies under Adad's control. One thing was apparent, though; he was rich—one of the richest people in the world.

***

A few days after Christmas everyone was having dinner on the patio, relaxing in the soft warm air of early summer. "Hey, guys," Glen said, "I have a great idea. What do you say we all go up to Barrier Reef for a week?"

"Can we learn how to scuba dive, Uncle Glen?" Bodie asked.

Getting an assenting wink from Marcus, Glen answered. "Yeah, why not? We'll all go diving, it'll be great."

For the rest of the meal, it was one question after another, and by the end, the boys were so amped up, Marcus hated to break it to them that he wouldn't be going with them.

As Ellie and the kids cleaned up, Marcus and Glen sat back in their chairs, listening to the cicadas and enjoying a cold beer.

"What's up?" Glen asked. "You don't seem as excited as the boys."

"Well …" Marcus set the empty can on the table, "I'm sorry about that, but I have been struggling with a few things, and it seems you just provided me the best solution. The boys are content, thanks to you and Ellie. I need you to take care of them, to give them the love and attention I can't right now. When you guys fly to the Gold Coast I'm bound for Alice Springs."

Glen stared. Marcus had been dreading this conversation. Since he got here, Glen and Ellie had given him a lot of much-needed space. They had taken over the bulk of his parental duties, and now he need to ask them to do much more. He struggled to find the best place to start.

"Hey, man, don't just sit there like a lump! What's going on?" Glen's tone was more concerned than angry.

"Now, what I'm going to tell you will sound like I've finally gone 'round the bend,' but just hear me out." Glen nodded, and Marcus charged ahead. "Remember last Christmas, when Annie, the boys, and I came to visit, and you and I went down to the waterfront, to that bar in Kings Cross? What was the name—the Wicked Witch?"

"Wench," he said with a grin.

"Yeah, the Wicked Wench. Well, anyway, do you recall what we talked about when we got back to your house?"

This got him a blank stare. That day, almost a year before, the girls and the kids all went on a boat tour through Sydney Harbor, and Glen and Marcus opted out. Marcus wanted to go into Kings Cross, in the heart of Sydney's central business district. It was a mixture of rugged charm and rampant sleaze, tawdry shops, disreputable bars, and rooms that rented by the hour or the week. The Australian Tourist Bureau warned visitors that it was no place to go alone and that at night it was downright dangerous. Popping another can of beer, Marcus relaxed back in the patio chair. "Remember, we were discussing a comment I overheard about a retired American colonel who had a private security firm and training facility somewhere on Aboriginal land out near Alice Springs?" Glen still hadn't the foggiest idea what Marcus was talking about.

"We were talking about how, sometimes, in a bar you overhear someone say something that, for whatever reason, your ears pick up through a sort of acoustic window in the general din. Like, you might hear someone mention something about a hot stock or an upcoming IPO. Just a snippet, but then, days later, you see that a new offering went public, or there's a news release about some company that just had a new drug approved or developed some high-tech widget, and the price of the stock just shot through the ceiling in a matter of hours. Then the light bulb goes on, and it's that, *why didn't I put some money into that,* kind of hindsight moment."

"Yeah, now I remember. But what's your point?"

"Okay, this is where it gets a little crazy." Of course his brother already thought the whole thing was coming out of deep left field. "I can't tell you why I feel like this. All I can say is, I just know it's what I have to do. I have to find this retired colonel—he's the next step."

"Next step? Marcus, what the hell are you raving on about?"

Over the next half hour, Marcus told him all he knew about Adad al-Mohmoud. How he was the guy—the one main guy—responsible for the attack on the U.S.A. and how, ultimately, he was the one responsible for Annie's death.

"And you're going to do what exactly—go find this Adad guy and kick his ass? Listen to what you're saying! You and the boys have already been through hell. You haven't stopped for a second to grieve for Annie. I've gone along with everything you needed to do, but this—it's not just crazy, it's effing insane!"

"I know, and I haven't got it all worked out in my mind just yet, but I will."

"That's what I'm worried about, you working it out in that obsessive, never-stopping mind of yours. Don't you think maybe it's time to stop all this shit, that it's time for you to take care of yourself and your boys?"

Marcus sighed, gazing out into the yard. "In a perfect world, yeah, that's what I should do, but it's not a perfect a world, and I'll be damned if I'm going to stop. These people fucked with my life, with the lives of my boys, and with our country. Most of all, they killed my wife, Glen. I can't live with that, and until I've done everything, and I mean everything possible, there is no getting back to some type of normal existence for me." Marcus's jaw was set with a steely determination.

"All right, all right, calm down, Jeez! If anybody understands you, it's me. If this is what you have to do, then do it. Get it out of your system and come back whole."

Marcus looked into the face of his brother, a face filled with love, compassion, and a full measure of doubt. He knew Glen could read and feel his pain and would love to make it all better, but he couldn't. No one could.

Just then the boys came out of the house, their kitchen chores done. Glen stood and patted Marcus on the back as he left them alone.

"Hey, guys," Marcus said, "come sit down with me."

The boys sat, but before Marcus could begin, Bodie said, "You're not goin' with us, are you?"

Apparently, the look in his father's eyes was all the answer he needed. "Garrett and I've been talking about it for a while. He saw Mom again last night." Bodie turned to his brother. "Go on, tell Dad what Mom said."

Even though the boys were a little over three years apart, they were both about the same size, but at that moment, Marcus was struck by just how young Garrett was and how much older Bodie seemed.

Garrett looked up at his dad. "Mom was glad we're here with Aunt Ellie and Uncle Glen. She wanted to make sure we were being helpful. I told her we were. She said she knew that because she's been watching us." His lower lip quivered, but he went on. "But what she really wanted to see me about, was you. She said you had to go, and that Bodie and I had to be ready. She was worried about you. She thought you might be afraid to leave us, like that wasn't the dad thing to do. She told me to tell you it was time for you to go and that you're on the right track. From now on you have to really pay attention—she'll try and talk to you, but if she can't, she'll be watching over you, helping any way she can."

Garrett got up from his chair and slid onto Marcus's lap. "It's okay, Daddy. Bodie and I'll be okay. We all promised we'd do like Mom said."

Bodie got up and stood beside them, looking into his father's eyes with the same intensity that Marcus used when he wanted to get a point across to them. "It's time, Dad. You need to finish this thing, you know it and we know it. Nobody ever said life was going to be easy. You and Mom taught us that. Now it's time to dig deep, find the strength, and make it happen. We have Aunt Ellie, Uncle Glen, Renée and Charlie, and each other. We'll be okay. But I can see that you're not okay. It's eating away at you every day, so before it eats too much, put an end to it. When are you going?"

Bodie's voice never faltered. This twelve-year-old spoke like a wise and confident young man. Composing himself the best he could, Marcus explained that when they went to the Gold Coast he would be heading for Australia's

Simpson Desert. They never asked him what he was going to do or when he was coming back. It was as if they just knew it was something he had to do, and that, when it was done, he would come home to them.

***

They all stood in the domestic Qantas terminal. Marcus had been able to book a flight to Alice Springs that departed a half hour after the family's flight to Brisbane. He took a seat next to Glen while Ellie and the kids stood at the window and watched planes land and take off.

"Hey," he said, "you okay with all this?"

"Now that you mention it, there is one thing I'd like to know." Glen replied. "How are you gonna find this Colonel Webb? I mean, you don't have a clue other than some little snippet of conversation you overheard in a sleazy bar over a year ago."

Marcus rested a hand on his brother's shoulder. "Where is the best place to start when you need information on a guild, a climbing route, some remote trout stream or lake?"

"No way!" Glen said in a tone of disbelief. "Tell me you're not betting the farm on your half-baked 'people of the fringe' theory?"

Laughing, Marcus nodded his head. "Well, as I recall last time we were in Argentina looking for that stream with the big browns, it seemed to work out. And the year before, when we were looking for the guide to lead us to that steep couloir in the Monashee Mountains?"

"Yeah but we were talking fishing and skiing not finding mercenaries."

Marcus had explained a certain notion to Glen. He believed that people who lived out on the edge were basically of two types, those who actually did and those who lived vicariously through them.

"How many times have we stumbled into a small pub, in some BFE town or village and got all the information we needed from some half-crocked local?"

Glen took a moment before saying. "You might have a point."

As his brother pondered what to say next, Marcus reached up and slipped his chain with the Saint Christopher pendant over his head. He fingered the smooth backside of the medal as it rested in his hand, then slipped the chain over Glen's head. "I know I've asked you to trust me. To do things for me with little or no explanation. I need you to do one more. That St. Christopher—don't take it off until the day it can put it back around my neck. My boys are now your boys. It's your job to be their surrogate father, to care for them and love them. Consider this a link between us, and through that bond I'll remain connected to them."

With one hand on each of his brother's shoulders, Marcus went on, "You know we haven't talked about how long I might be gone. It could be months. I'll do my best to get word to you. But if I can't, Garrett will know."

Glen looked flummoxed.

"I can't explain it, but something is going on between him and Annie—something that's a lot more than just the dreamings of a young boy. They talk to each other almost every night. So if you need to know about me, ask Garrett."

Just then the gate announcer called their flight. The boys came up to Marcus their eyes glistening with coming tears, but before he could say a word Bodie beat him to the punch again.

With his arm around his brothers' shoulder, fighting to keep his composure Bodie said in a voice, clear and strong, "Let's not make a big deal out of this, Dad. You be safe. You make those people pay for everything they've done to us and everyone else."

Then Marcus's two sons, tears streaming down their faces, tapped their hands twice over their hearts and pointed at him, and turned, following their cousins through the door without looking back.

CHAPTER THIRTY
Four years earlier, Command Central, Green Zone, Iraq

"God damn it, Sam, I don't like it any better than you do!" General Walter Kittredge said slamming his palm down on the desk in front of him. "But you know as well as I, this is how the Army works." His voice wasn't angry so much as frustrated as he talked to his friend sitting across from him.

The general was a desk jockey, born for the politics that define the U.S. military complex. Even when they were back in West Point together, Colonel Sam Webb had been a doer, a hands-on man, who led by example, and he was damn good at it—in fact, the best Kittredge had ever served with.

"That's no excuse Walt, and you know it." The colonel's tone was hard but calm. "Hell, I've lost plenty of men in my thirty years. But this—it's unacceptable."

The general reached down, pulled open a drawer and got out a bottle of single-malt and two dusty glasses. Blowing them out, he poured four fingers of whisky into each and slid one across the desk toward the colonel. Holding his glass, the general appraised his friend. Webb looked ten years younger than his actual fifty-two years. At five-ten, and 170 pounds, he was still lean and fit. He had led covert black ops teams in the Soviet republics, Central and South America, equatorial Africa, South Asia, and every hotbed in the Middle East, going up against warlords, dictators, drug lords and, for the last ten years, terrorists. He took on every job no one else wanted. Hell, he took on projects no sane person would even consider, and often under the terms of plausible deniability—if the op went bad and he and his team missed their extraction deadline, they were left flapping in the breeze, to find their own way home.

Webb leaned forward and picked up his glass from the desk. As he settled back the general said, "You either let this drop, Sam, or…."

He didn't need to finish the sentence. The colonel swirled the scotch around in the glass, then tipped it to his lips and drained it in one swallow. Standing, he gently set the glass down and looked at his friend. Reaching into his camo fatigue jacket, he withdrew an envelope. "Well Walt, this time 'or' is the way it's got to be." He laid the envelop on the desk.

He saluted and turned on his heels to leave. To his back the general said, "Why is it, Sam, that I have this feeling I haven't seen the last of you?"

***

Colonel Webb returned to his small private room in the officers' quarters. At the desk, he pulled out several file folders from a cardboard box on the floor. Over his years as the commander of black-ops missions, he had led select groups on every continent and gone up against the worst the world had to offer. These missions required specific skill sets. There were always language and ethnic considerations, as well as specialized combat skills in explosives, long-range sniper tactics, or insertion by water or air. For these reasons, he had latitude to draw from every branch of the U.S. military as well as from U.S. intelligence agencies. He often needed personnel with specific local knowledge of the peoples and environs and for these his reach extended to the military and intelligence branches of several U.S. allies.

Because the parameters and specifics of each mission were different, he kept dossiers on all the people he served with, and some promising talents he might serve with in the future. Indeed, he was well known among his contemporaries for having a keen eye for raw talent—the kind of men who, with the right motivation and approach, could be molded into the right cog in an effective and efficient fighting machine. Hence, the stack of files before him now.

Staring at the manila folders, he mused, if the "new age" school of thought that outsourcing specialized protection and intelligence gathering to private security firms was the right strategy for modern-day warfare, then by God, those outfits should be composed of men and women whose motivations were based on the ideals of righting a wrong and not just kicking asses and getting paid. Not that he had ever seriously considered leaving the Army. It was his life, and he had been groomed from early childhood, not to play a sport, but rather to serve his country, to be a leader of men.

But the recent incident inside the Green Zone, in which contractors for a private security firm had mistaken his team for insurgents and opened fire, killing two members of Webb's command and badly wounding four others, was the last straw. The contract firm had been hired by the U.S. military to provide auxiliary support and security to the civilian service workers, and its employees were almost exclusively ex-military. The key was "ex." By and large, these men were working where they were because they couldn't cut it in the military. Certainly, the opportunity to make a boatload of money while getting to play with automatic weapons and explosives was a motivating factor, but those men lacked the discipline and commitment that the files before him represented. Then, to add insult to injury, when he pressed the issue, he was summarily told to drop it or take a hike. Well, it was time to lace up his boots and start walking.

He opened the top file and scanned the contents. He found it ironic that his plan to start his own security firm rested upon two individuals—one with no military background whatsoever, and the other a young, often rash hothead.

* * *

Colonel Webb studied the picture. Jonathan Tiberius, J. T., was an anomaly. At about five-six and maybe a 120 pounds, he was the archetypal scrawny nerd. His boyish looks belied his age—thirty-three going on twenty. His sandy brown hair was straight and sparse, and with the thick black-framed glasses, the only thing missing was the pocket protector.

He had graduated from MIT at eighteen, did a short stint with the CIA, and then went into the NSA. After MIT and before the NSA, he had embarked on a one-man mission to hack, undetected, into the most secure databases in existence. For relaxation, he developed and perpetrated massive real estate scams.

He sold land that he didn't own and that, in many cases, had never existed. It wasn't until he set up a scam to sell massive tracts of forest and wilderness in Bulgaria that he came up on the NSA's radar. One thing led to another, and instead of going to prison, he took a new job. The colonel had met him while the Army was setting up a logistics-and-protocol system for managing resources and manpower for U.S. forces in Iraq, during the beginning months of the invasion, when J. T. was in his early twenties. With the influx of close to a billion dollars a week, the task was both challenging and complicated, but for J. T., currently on loan to the private defense firm installing and maintaining the software, it was a walk in the park.

One of his many assets was his communications skills—not so much the one-on-one-type, but rather the sorting, analyzing and evaluating of the mountains of data spawned by the explosion of Internet, satellite, cell, and text-messaging systems. The information being communicated worldwide each day now comprised trillions upon trillions of bits. Text messaging had become a language unto itself, evolving daily and allowing groups to communicate in a code that had no mathematical or logarithmic basis. And terrorists' plans, disguised in even the simplest code, could easily become lost in the billions of messages transmitted each day.

But beyond that, J.T. was a technological wizard. In fact, among his peers his nickname was Mr. Wizard. He had countless patents on devices that gave the colonel and his teams communications and monitoring capabilities straight out of a science fiction novel. And the colonel knew that, in today's world of state-of-the-art gadgetry, if he wanted to compete for the best private security projects available, he had to have not only the best technology, but the best brain to manage and monitor it—someone also constantly on the cutting edge of the newest advancements.

Setting J.T.'s file aside, Webb turned his attention to the second file in the stack. If he was going to do this thing, he needed a base of operations. The requirements were simple, not in the States, but remote with an environment that was inhospitably arid, like much of the Middle East.

Jamie Marsden, aka Tracker, had grown up in Australia's Central Desert. He and his father had lived on a barren tract controlled by the Arrernte tribe of Aboriginal people. Jamie was the only child of a father who worked on a nearby cattle station, and a mother who died in childbirth. His father was a drunk who routinely used his son as a punching bag until, when Jamie was twelve, his father finally drank himself to death, leaving his son to fend for himself.

Jamie had been found, half starved, by the grandfather of an Aboriginal boy he had grown up with. From that point on, until Jamie joined the Australian army at nineteen, the Arrernte raised him. During those seven years, he learned to track and live off the desert and dry plains that were his home.

After joining the army, Jamie completed extensive commando training and was deployed to Iraq as part of the allied forces that supported the U.S. invasion. His superb tracking abilities had come to the attention of the colonel, who had commandeered his talents on several missions in Afghanistan and Pakistan. Not only could he track men over the most rugged terrain, he had an uncanny knack for observing a man's gait, the way he carried himself, and from that discerning critical information—a concealed weapon, or bomb, for instance, or an attempt to hide an injury. Small things that could make a difference.

At twenty-seven, Jamie was the youngest in the stack. He was also the most temperamental and unpredictable. In fact, he didn't give a shit what people thought of him. It was probably why he and J.T. were friends.

***

Geek Creek was a makeshift bar of sorts, which the mostly civilian tech staff had established in one of the portable buildings scattered around the centralized command post in the Green Zone. Colonel Webb, dressed in camo fatigues, that displayed neither name nor rank, entered to find Jamie and J.T. seated at a plastic table on plastic chairs having a beer, in what was essentially a glorified shipping container. Webb's particular field of expertise required that he move in and among the people he led. Often missions came up on a moment's notice, and he needed to have a good idea of where to locate them. Not that any of them could readily leave Iraq, but the Green Zone was a big, disorganized area, often with more chiefs protecting turf than Indians to fight the battles.

Grabbing a seat, he said, "Gentleman, mind if I join you?"

Jamie was immediately on his feet and at attention.

"At ease, son. This is an unofficial visit."

For the next little while the colonel explained his new situation. He tried to keep the conversation hypothetical, but the more he explained, the more interested his younger audience of two became.

"Well, Colonel," J.T. said, "you are the last guy I would ever have pegged for bailing out. I mean you're Army to the core. So now you want to go into the private sector, so to speak?"

"That's right. But if I'm going to do this, it's going to be the right way, with only the best personnel."

"I'm so flattered that you would think of me." J.T. lazily raised his beer to his mouth.

The sarcastic tone never fazed the colonel. He knew that J.T. had an ego the size of Texas. Of course, it made at least some sense, because when it came to raw brainpower, he had no equals.

Jamie said, "So, colonel, I guess you're thinking the Simpson Desert might be a good place to set up shop?".

"Well, son it fits my criteria, and maybe we can make this a win-win situation. I know that your tour is up in a few months, and I thought we might pay a visit to your grandfather. You told me the cattle station near where you grew up is on their land."

"That's right, sir," Jamie responded with a hint of excited anticipation in his voice.

"And J.T., I know that the company you're currently associated with is in the process of renegotiating its contract. I have no doubt they will be staying on. I haven't worked out the financial end of the deal yet, but I have a pretty good idea that our first client will pay handsomely, and I should be able to guarantee you a salary comparable to what you now earn."

"What, colonel, you think I do this shit for the money?" The kid sounded almost offended. "Hell, if my patents weren't almost all classified I'd be sittin' on some private island in the middle of the South Pacific, with naked girls and video games. I'm here because I get to play legally with obscene amounts of money and have carte blanche to hack into some of the most sophisticated data storage systems on the planet." Waving to the bartender for another round of drinks he said, "Truth be told, I'm a bit bored, so you can count me in—sounds like it might be fun."

***

Now that he had his genius and a strong lead on a location, the colonel had other people to see. Over the next several months he recruited every member who had made his short list. Due to their terms of service—and in some cases sensitive employment contracts—there were strings to pull and arms to bend. Webb had never burned a bridge in his life, and he had no intention of starting now. And so, with the help of his friend, General Kittredge, he managed to secure the discharge, from military or intelligence service, of every person on his list. The cost? A written agreement for the colonel's new firm to provide specialized personnel for certain sensitive missions for the duration of the U.S. occupation in Iraq.

A reasonable fee was negotiated and, although significantly less than what his team would earn on the open market, it was fair. And besides, it provided Webb with an inside track on potential clients, while maintaining relationships he had spent a lifetime cultivating.

CHAPTER THIRTY-ONE
Three years earlier, FOB Prosperity, Green Zone, Iraq

Colonel Webb, dressed in desert camo fatigues, paused outside the entrance to As-Salam Palace and surveyed the facade of what once had been the home of Saddam Hussein. The rubble from the attacks of those first days of the U.S. led "Shock and Awe" campaign, especially on the upper floors and roof of the building, were a clear and present reminder of the single-minded focus—find and eliminate Saddam Hussein.

It had been a year since the colonel had retired from the Army, but here he was moving through the green zone in military fatigues, just as if he had never left. Removing his sunglasses, he put them into his shirt pocket and walked into the lobby where a young National Guard lieutenant, standing by a low makeshift counter, greeted him with a crisp salute. "At ease Lieutenant. Colonel Webb to see General Kittredge," the colonel said.

Picking up a clipboard the lieutenant ran his finger down a list of names. Looking up he said, "Yes sir, Colonel. Can I have someone show you to his office?"

"No son, I know the way," the colonel replied as he walked into the grand foyer, across tile floors that were made up of hundreds of thousands of pieces of hand cut marble.

Of the six floors in the building only the bottom three were usable. Known as Forward Operating Base Prosperity, this had been General Kittredge's operational headquarters since shortly after the invasion. As the colonel walked down a granite-walled hall, he thought about how it had been the general's idea to keep his retirement as quite as possible. Oh, there were plenty of people who knew that he was no longer in the army and that he and his private security firm—Force 10— were working on contract for the U.S. military, it was decided that the less the rank and file knew the better. This allowed the colonel and his team, some U.S. Special Forces, some cherry picked from the elite crops of U.S. allies, and one quirky, very smart, intelligence operative, all individuals the colonel had personally recruited and worked with in the past, to move among the convoluted, military bureaucracy, with much more ease and efficiency.

At the end of the hall the colonel stepped though an arch that at one time held an elaborate set of carved wooden doors, which had either been destroyed or went missing during the rampant looting that typified that first several months of the invasion. "Colonel Webb sir," the Army captain who served as the general's personal assistant, said with a quick salute, as he came to his feet.

"Captain," the colonel said as he returned the salute. "Is the old man in?"

With a wry smile the captain said, "Yes sir, he's expecting you. Go right in."

The colonel entered through a open archway. Seated behind a wood and stone inlaid, museum quality, antique desk, sat General Walter Kittredge. Webb thought the fine grey stubble of his shaved head, and chewed down, unlit cigar stub hanging from the side of his mouth, gave the man an aura of the bygone days of rough-and-ready military commanders.

Standing, the general removed the cigar from his mouth and extended his hand, "Damn glad to have back you, Sam."

Colonel Webb shook the hand of the six-two, two hundred pound general. "I'm glad to be back, Walt."

Holding the cigar between his fingers, the general nodded to the chair in front of the desk, as he retook his seat.

"I can't tell you how much easier you taking over the advance set up and recon for our *visitors*," the word came out his mouth dripping with distain, "is going to make my life." Shifting his bulk in the chair the general went on, "Since the pentagon decided that particular task would be contracted out, and the leaders of our country, especially now that we are getting to the end of our part in this conflict, don't want to miss out on the political millage of a once in a lifetime photo opportunity in a war zone with real life soldiers, my life's been a nightmare."

For an hour the two old friends talked about the logistics and operational specifics of Force 10's new assignment. The colonel had come to Iraq in advance of his team to make sure everything was in order, that they had a base from which to operate, and had accommodations for what might be a fairly long-term project.

Measuring his words the colonel said. "I owe you, Walt. Without your help I wouldn't have been able to assemble the team I have, and your clout and connections cutting through the red tape are what got me here on such short notice." The colonel leaned forward in his chair, and said with a grin, "Besides, we each get do what were good at."

The colonel rose to leave pausing to look up and stare at the thousands of hand painted tiles that made up the ceiling of what used to be Saddam's bedroom. Shaking his head the colonel said, "No matter what Saddam was or wasn't, WMD's or not, he certainly was a greedy, egomaniacal bastard," the colonel turned and headed for the door, "and I for one, am glad he's gone."

CHAPTER THIRTY-TWO
One year earlier, Hotel Al-Rasheed Bagdad, Iraq

Colonel Webb sat at the desk in his room at the Hotel Al-Rasheed. The sun wouldn't be up for another hour, and he was going over the preliminary operational and tactical plan for an upcoming visit by members of the Senate and House Armed Services committees. In total the tentative plan was to have three members from each house along with two or three members of each of their respective staffs, somewhere between eighteen to twenty-five people in all.

The idea of having part of Force 10 housed in primarily civilian accommodation was by design, and had been arranged by General Kittredge. The Al-Rasheed, had been refurbished by the Army Corp of Engineers, and provided accommodations for much of the media and other civilian personnel working in Iraq. Also it was *the* place for U.S. and other western allied interests to meet with local Iraqi concerns in regard to economic development. This meant that wealthy and influential Iraqi's often passed though the hotel allowing the colonel and his team the opportunity to put faces to some of the individuals suspected of playing a part in the ongoing insurgent activity in Iraq in general and the Green Zone specifically.

The general had been right about the U.S. leadership using visits to meet-and-greet the troops as opportunities for big time political posturing and publicity and now that troop withdrawal was in full swing, the frequency of these visits, and the numbers involved, like the one the colonel was currently reviewing, surprised even him. The fact that these events always added significantly to the already existing threats to the lives of the young men and women serving their tour in Iraq, were apparently a secondary concern, overridden by the "star building power" of a picture and sound bite with the troops, from the front lines.

Not to mention that for each time a senator, representative, cabinet member or the President himself came, they brought with them an entire posse of staff and security personal, along with enough ego to make even a planned trip to the park a nightmare. Establishing a secure perimeter and ensuring that the specified area had been swept for explosives, all possible sniper locations identified and cleared, and a failsafe exit strategy was in place, was compounded by the fact, that no other conflict in the history of mankind, had the embedded media personal that were an everyday fact of life here in the Green Zone.

The team as a whole had been to the training headquarters in Australia only once. And that had been two years before, right after the colonel had put the team together. Since then the colonel or one of the other team members would make a periodic trip back to make sure that the improvements and repairs were proceeding as planned and on schedule. The compound had been in rough shape, and needed a lot of attention. So as time and money permitted the colonel was well on the way to establishing a state-of-the-art training facility, far from prying eyes, but for now their contractual commitment to the U.S. military was keeping them very occupied.

From the outset, the colonel had a concern that this project of basically babysitting U.S. and allied dignitaries, while they played dress up and smiled for the cameras, would quickly become routine for his team, and that keeping them focused and alert would be an issue as time drug on. But, staring out the window into the predawn haze, he realized, that just as the face of this awakening ancient city was in a constant and dynamic state of flux, so too, was each particular visit. Each mission came with its own shape, size and color, and presented the team with variables that were unique and specific to the time, location, and to the individuals involved, and fortunately boredom was not an issue.

The colonel picked up his go-bag, which contained everything he would need for personal survival in a hostile environment, and was a piece of equipment, in one form or another, he had not been without for over twenty years, and slung the pack strap over his shoulder and headed out the door. The general had provided him with office space in the FOB Prosperity headquarters. Since the general was in charge of overseeing the operational and tactical logistics for all planned visits by U.S. and foreign dignitaries into and out of Iraq, and Force 10 was contracted to secure all locations, establish exit routes and protocol if something went wrong, for each visit, it made logical sense to have the colonel and his team close.

Riding in the back of an armored Humvee, the colonel thought about Force 10 beyond working for the U.S. military. He had already secured the teams only other client, and currently the manpower requirements to fulfill that obligation were minimal, but someday he envisioned that Force 10 would have the opportunity to go after some of the major players in the war on terror. Those men who lurked behind the scenes, hidden behind a veil of wealth and family privilege, and financed insurgent activity, and planed terrorists attacks, not just here in the Middle East and South Asia, but all over the world. If he was honest with himself, that thought was at the root of his decision to leave the military. He didn't just want to be a successful private military contractor, he wanted to leave his mark on the world he had spent a lifetime protecting and defending.

Getting out of the Humvee, to head into his office and a daily briefing with the general and the Force 10 team, the colonel said quietly to himself, "Someday… someday."

CHAPTER THIRTY-THREE
Force 10 Compound, Simpson Desert, Australia
January 6

Colonel Sam Webb stared out the window, across the dirt yard of the compound, into the sere brick-red expanse of the Australian Outback. He and the team had been sucked into the news pouring out of the U.S. in regard to the fires, and the contamination of much of the nation's water. Millions of acres had burned, tens of thousands had died, hundreds of thousands had been sickened, and these...terrorists had beheaded the Diablo woman, and broadcast it around the world on a live Internet feed. The professional soldier in him, on one hand, wanted to do something, and on the other knew, beyond doubt, there was very little if anything he could do, even if he and his team were there.

He continued to stare out the window as Jamie drove out of the yard on one of the ATVs to check a stretch of downed fence. The boy had done well. Soon after their little chat in Baghdad they had visited Jamie's adoptive Aboriginal clan and arranged with the old man, Jamie's "grandfather," to lease the property. And as the colonel had said, the deal worked for everyone. It provided sorely needed income to a people whose lives were defined by limited resources and diminishing opportunities, and it gave him a base of operation 120 kilometers away from the nearest neighbor.

Turning away from the window, the colonel sat at his desk. It was bad enough that America was under attack, and he was half a world away, and no longer an active member of the U. S. Military, but he had his own personal crises to confront. Forcing himself to focus, the colonel looked down at the closed file folder sitting on the desk in front of him. For nearly thirty years, anytime he lost a team member, he took himself through a meticulous debriefing process. The problem was, for over a month now, he had been asking himself the same questions: What went wrong? What had he missed?

He opened the file and looked at the photo. He and Reggie Braddock, a Navy SEAL and a close friend, had served together for most of the past fifteen years. The colonel had a theory about leadership in small, specialized teams: you needed two leaders, one to pull and one to push. Reggie was the push.

The team was preparing for a Thanksgiving visit to Baghdad's Green Zone by the Secretary of State. It was ironic that even though troop levels were at an all time low, the dangers were at an all time high. Now that much of the internal security was being supplied by Iraqi personal, the danger from an insurgent attack, particularly to Americans, was as big a threat as it had ever been. They were on their final sweep, fine-tuning sniper assignments, clearing and securing the buildings, when gunmen ambushed the team. The colonel and Reggie found themselves pinned down in a narrow doorway. It took the rest of the team a few minutes to kill the seven attackers, and just when the colonel thought they were clear, a young girl perhaps seven or eight years old ran screaming out of a building. They both yelled at her, in Arabic, to turn around and go back inside, but she was too terrified to listen. From behind a half wall came another burst of rifle fire, and the kid stopped and stood in the street, screaming. Reggie set his weapon down and said, "cover me," and before the colonel could stop him, he had sprinted across the yard and swept the little girl up into his arms. Running back toward the colonel, Reggie came under fire. Miraculously, the two armor-piercing rounds went through his back high enough to miss the little girl, and he kept moving until he got her into the colonel's arms. His last words were, "I think she's okay."

Pull it together, Sam, the colonel chided himself. *Reggie just beat you to it.* In the Army, he had always kept some distance between himself and the teams he commanded. It allowed him to compartmentalize losses that he knew were part of the job. But now he was no longer part of a larger military machine. These were his people, and it was his job to get them back on track.

***

The slamming of the screen door disrupted the colonel's thought. A moment later Liam O'Hanlon walked into his office, red-ocher dust rising in small clouds from his stomping boots. "Colonel, it seems there's some bloke in town blowin' smoke and sunshine about you," Liam said in his heavy working-class brogue. "Some shit about bein' a civilian contractor in Iraq and you and him drinkin' pals."

Without speaking the colonel looked up and appraised the team's explosives specialist. If it could be made to explode, Liam O'Hanlon knew how to build it or disarm it. His IRA father had spent his life making bombs, and the talent seemed to be in the genes. Liam was a product of the UK Special Forces, Special Reconnaissance Regiment. He had a gift for spotting suicide bombers—a skill the colonel had made the most of for almost eight years now.

Still standing, Liam slid three color photos across the desk. The man in the pictures was in his late thirties or perhaps older, full beard, curly brown hair almost to his shoulders, and piercing blue eyes.

"Okay, son, what do we know about this guy?" the colonel said, studying the photos.

"His name's Marcus Diablo."

The colonel looked up, surprise, displayed on his face. "I know that name."

"Yeah. It's the guy whose wife got beheaded in the States—seems he broke open the case about the terrorist cell. J. T. hacked into the FBI database and got us that little nugget of info."

"All right, let's go get him and see what he wants."

As Liam turned to leave, the colonel said, "Be nice, Liam. The man's been through the worst kind of hell. And besides, I'm a little curious how he found us. So bring him back undamaged."

"Yes sir," Liam replied without turning around.

CHAPTER THIRTY-FOUR

After arriving in Alice Springs, Marcus went straight to one of the local pubs. On the flight in, he had cobbled together a story and plan of sorts. He was a civilian engineering contractor from Texas, working the past six years on the massive U.S. embassy compound in Baghdad's Green Zone. He had met Colonel Webb there and they had discovered a shared taste in single malts. They had lost touch, but he'd heard that the colonel might have set up shop near here. He had made a little money and had never been to Australia, so he was here to enjoy the sights and maybe look up his old pal. Marcus knew it was lame, but it was the best he could come with, and he could fake a fair Texas accent. Also, he was banking that with his long hair and scraggly beard he wouldn't be readily noticeable to anyone who might have seen his face on TV.

He asked around while having a few beers, then poked around the town. Alice Springs was a town of maybe twenty-five thousand, plunked down in the center of the continent, hundreds of miles from nowhere in the vast expanse known as the Central Desert. Sitting at the edge of huge tracts of Aboriginal land, it had become the hub for tourists seeking a taste of the real Australian outback, though it seemed a lot like many of the small towns Marcus had knocked around in while growing up in Eastern Nevada—arid scrub brush plains with lots of bare ground and not much shade.

He found a small hotel and rented a room. He had no idea what he expected, but he was betting that if the colonel was anywhere near, all he had to do was make some noise and they would find him.

In the late afternoon of his third day, while having a beer in the Wallaroo Saloon and reappraising his whole "people of the fringe" theory, which didn't seem to be working, he noticed a young man with a military bearing walk in. He appeared to be in his mid-thirties, wearing khaki shorts and shirt with the sleeves neatly rolled up to reveal sinewy arms tattooed from the wrists up. "Hey, Wally, how's about a pint?" he hollered to the bartender in an accent that wasn't Aussie or English, though Marcus couldn't place it at the moment.

Then, to Marcus's surprise, the man made a beeline for his little two-seat table. Helping himself to the other chair, he flipped it around and sat with his crossed arms resting on the chair back. "How do you do, Mr. Diablo?" he said.

Before Marcus could respond, his tattooed guest continued. "Seems you've been makin' a fair bit o' noise about Colonel Webb. Well, I've been sent to retrieve ya. The colonel'd like a chat. Name's Liam—Liam O'Hanlon." He didn't offer his hand.

Marcus just sat there, too unsure of himself to speak as Liam finished off his beer in a couple of large gulps, wiped the foam from his lip with the back of his hand, and rose to leave. Marcus followed him out, grabbing his pack from the floor beside him. He had gotten in the habit of not going anywhere without it. They got into a dusty tan Land Cruiser and headed southeast out of town, into the desert.

***

After two hours drive on dirt roads, during which time his chauffeur didn't utter a word, they came over a small rise, and entered what looked to Marcus like some sort of ranch. They parked in front of a rambling ranch house with a steep corrugated-metal roof that swept down to shade a wide deck and wraparound porch.

Marcus followed Liam into the house and was surprised at the tasteful decor, leather and fabric sofas and armchairs, dark wooden tables, and expensive rugs. He was led though the living room and through a set of double French doors. He found himself standing in a study paneled in dark wood, with bookshelves along two walls, and a big desk in the center. Along the wall to the right was a stone fireplace.

The man behind the desk stood up and stuck out his hand. "Marcus Diablo, I'm Colonel Sam Webb," he said in an accent from somewhere south and east of Memphis.

He was a solidly built man about Marcus's height and weight, fifty-something, with a high-and-tight graying crew cut.

"Thanks for making this happen, Colonel," Marcus said. "I'm in your debt."

The colonel nodded toward a leather armchair in front of his desk, and they both sat. "Well, Mr. Diablo, it seems you've been a very busy man." Marcus's face betrayed his surprise. "Oh, we vetted you. Hell, I probably know more about what you've been up to than the FBI. You see, sir, I'm a careful man. I've made my living in some of the worst shit-holes on the planet, and I have spent all of that time in the U.S. Army, the most bureaucratic, paper work loving organization there is. When it comes to my life and the lives of my people, well, let's just say I like to get my information firsthand."

There was a moment of silence, and he continued. "I'm truly sorry about your wife. No man should have to experience something like that, and your sons...." He left it there, as if there were no need to finish articulating something that was both tragic and self-evident. "I have to tell you, though, I am a bit curious about how you found your me."

Marcus told him about the bar in Kings Cross and the snippet of conversation overheard a year go.

Webb laughed, a deep, gleeful chuckle. "Well if that doesn't beat all!" He interlaced his fingers behind his head. "So, Mister Diablo, what is it you think I can do for you?"

"Well, Colonel—and please, call me Marcus—I'm on a mission to find the man responsible for Annie's death, the same man responsible for the most horrific terrorist attack of all time on *our* country. Not the men who took her—they've already been dealt with." The colonel's eyebrows rose in a *you don't say* kind of way. "As for the man who killed her, I'll take care of that, too, but I'm after a much bigger fish."

Marcus reached into his pack resting on the floor at his feet, pulled out a file folder, and handed it across the desk to the colonel. The colonel opened the file and leafed through its contents. His face was void of emotion as he closed the file.

"I know of Adad al-Mohmoud. You might have settled on someone less connected, maybe without quite so many resources. He's been suspected for some years now of being the money behind a number of terrorist attacks all over the world, the 1998 bombings of the U.S. embassies in Kenya and Tanzania, the 1999 Egypt Air flight off Massachusetts. His name has come up in the Nine-eleven attacks and, more recently, in the bombings of the four trains in Spain—not to mention car bomb attacks still going on today in Iraq and Afghanistan. But to my knowledge, there has never been any definitive proof, and at the end of the day, when you're one of the two or three richest men in the world, you can insulate yourself quite effectively."

"You see, Colonel," Marcus said, struggling to keep his voice even, "this man took my wife away from me, left my two sons without a mother, and attacked our country in my own backyard. If he's untouchable by legitimate means, then that leaves—"

"Let me get this straight. You think I'm your guy? That I would even remotely consider going after a man like this just to satisfy your need for revenge?"

His words cut deep. Marcus knew how it sounded, and the last thing he wanted was to have come this far only to get kicked to the curb—and the nearest curb was a long way off.

"No sir. I'm not here to hire you—or to convince you that this is your fight. I'm here for training."

"*Training?* Marcus, what do you think I'm running here—some kind of summer camp for wannabe mercenaries?" The amusement in his voice was laced with sarcasm.

"No sir. I have no idea what you're running here. But I'll tell what I know, or what I think I know. You're a distinguished career military man, in your prime in terms of command. Something happened. You probably watched young men and women die while in harm's way without proper equipment, training, and information. You got fed up with the bullshit, all that on-a-need-to-know-basis crap. My guess is one day you woke up and said, 'Fuck it. I can do a better job than these rookie security agencies they're using to provide personnel and equipment in conflict situations.' I think maybe the Blackwater bozos of this world were the last straw."

The colonel's expression changed from mild annoyance to curiosity.

"So tell me, Colonel, I'm not far from the truth, am I? You see, I did a little vetting of my own. Of course, I don't have the assets and connections you have, but I'm not a fool or a nutcase."

The colonel studied him with a bemused look. Then he said, "So just for argument's sake, let's assume in principle, you're right. What do you propose I can do for you?"

"You can train me. Teach me hand-to-hand combat, weapons, and most importantly, about the Middle East and Adad al-Mohmoud. All I want is to walk out of here with the best possible chance of getting this guy." Before the colonel could speak, Marcus hurried on. "I know, sure as I'm sitting here, that my chances of getting to Adad are practically zilch. But it'll help if you understand this about me. I cannot live with myself, cannot be a father to my boys, if I don't try. Right now I'm dead to my sons, dead to myself. And if, in the end, being dead is the cost, well, then so be it." Determination was on Marcus' face and his jaw was set tight.

"That's a bit fatalistic, don't you think?" the colonel said, cracking a smile, "but admirable. You say you know about me, but tell me, Marcus, what are you bringing to the table?"

"I'm prepared to pay. I have somewhere around a million U.S. I would think that might buy some training time. So, can you help me?"

"Well, Marcus, I like a man who gets right to the meat of things. I have to tell you I'm intrigued, and at the moment, the team and I have some time on our hands. We headquarter our business here, and due to...well, let's just say we're taking some time to decompress."

Decompress? Marcus had no idea what the colonel was talking about.

"So I'm going to deliver your proposition to the team. We have a democracy of sorts—either it's all in or it's a no-go. But, son, let me be real clear. This is no Boy Scout camp, and my people aren't babysitters. So you think long and hard about what you wish for. It's late. You'll be our guest. In the morning I'll give you our answer."

CHAPTER THIRTY-FIVE
January 7

Marcus awoke in the predawn, too anxious to sleep. He pulled on a pair of cargo shorts and went downstairs in search of coffee. In the kitchen, he found Liam and another young man seated at the wooden table with mugs of coffee. If they were surprised to see him, it didn't show.

"Morning," he said.

They nodded. They didn't appear to like him much, but then, he wasn't here to be liked.

He poured a cup of coffee and walked out onto the veranda. The vast expanse of desert scrub looked eerily beautiful in the light of the quarter moon. He could just make out what looked like low hills in the distance. Behind the house stood a big barn with the same corrugated galvanized steel roof as the main house. There were tractors and four-wheeled ATVs parked outside the barn, along with harrows and other farming implements. Also two corrals and, a large roofed pole structure containing several hundred bales of hay.

Maybe "decompressing" meant playing farmer, but Marcus didn't think so. There was another building, maybe a guesthouse, off to the right and a smaller barn behind it. To the left of the large barn was what looked like an obstacle course something straight out of military recruiting commercials.

Marcus went back upstairs, put on running shoes, shorts, and a tank top, finished off his coffee, and headed outside to work off some of the nervous tension. It was a little after five in the morning.

He walked through the obstacle course, stopping at an area about ten feet wide and thirty feet long, some twenty-five yards from the starting point. About a foot off the ground, barbed wire was strung from upright metal stakes in a tight grid— to crawl under, he supposed. After another short stretch, a wooden plank wall rose maybe fifteen feet high, with three ropes hanging limp against it. Then a much longer stretch of over a hundred yards, full of man-size craters and piles of rock and rubble. Beyond that sat a series of logs set horizontally with barbed wire strung below them, then a long stretch through a stand of bloodwood and ghost gum trees, and on the far side, a wide pool of nasty-looking brown water with a rope suspended over it. Marcus then observed a long honeycomb pattern of tires to step through, and finally, a looping path that came back around the corrals and the barn to the start point.

What the hell, he thought—*might as well.*

His first go was a nightmare. The barbed wire ate his shirt and gouged into his back. The rope on the wall burned his hands raw, as he fell like a brick and whapped into the baked earth, knocking the wind out of him. He fell and tripped a dozen times in the section with the holes and the piles of dirt and rock, and the logs were no better—every time he tried to climb over them, he caught his shoes and legs in the barbed wire. As for the pool, as nasty as it looked, it felt and tasted a lot worse. By the time he hit the tires, Marcus was panting like a worn-out dog. His feet felt as if he were wearing ankle weights, and he had no rhythm. The final stretch was surely meant to be an all-out sprint, but he could barely muster a half trot.

Feeling defeated, he limped up the front steps, looking right and left, not wanting anyone to see him. He went upstairs, rummaged through the drawers and found a pair of heavy khaki fatigues and a pair of lightweight brown desert boots that fit reasonably well. As he changed, the cuts and scrapes on his back stung against the rough cotton shirt.

Going back out to the course for another attempt, he took his time, paced himself, and mentally prepared for each section as if it were his only goal. He made it through—not easily or elegantly, but far better than the first time.

Over the next hour, he ran the course five more times, getting faster and more confident. His pants and shirt were in tatters, his hands raw and blistered, and he stank from sweat and putrid water.

As Marcus was preparing for another crack at the course, the colonel stepped out onto the veranda with a mug of coffee in his hand. Jamie was leaning on the handrail, watching Marcus.

"How's our visitor doing?" the colonel said.

Jamie chuckled. "His first go, in shorts and a tank top, I couldn't believe he didn't stop. Then he went inside and I thought, that's it—less than twenty minutes, and our Mr. Diablo's had enough. But no, he changes and goes right back at it."

"So how's he doing?"

"Well, I believe he'd give you a run for your money. Not that he's that fast yet, but the strange thing is, he's getting faster with each run—and not just by a few seconds, but by thirty seconds or more each go. If I didn't know better, I'd say he's getting stronger the more he exerts himself."

"O-seven-hundred meeting. Make sure our guest is present." And the colonel went back inside.

After Marcus's next run through the course, Jamie caught his eye and waved him over to the house. Jamie introduced himself. He appeared to be in his late twenties, stocky with short, curly red hair. Marcus took off his wet, muddy boots and socks, and as they walked into the house, Jamie said in a thick Aussie accent, "Time to meet the team, mate."

* * *

Around a large wooden dining table sat Colonel Webb, Jamie, and Liam. Also seated was the biggest black man Marcus had ever seen, as well as two other men, and a woman.

The colonel stood, and faced Marcus. "Marcus, we've decided to take you on as a project. Looks like you will be with us for a while."

Turning back to the table the colonel said, "All right, people, meet Marcus Diablo. Marcus, this is the team. You've already met Liam and Jamie. This is Sit."

Marcus took a step toward the seated giant, who extended a hand the size of a baseball mitt. His grip was surprisingly gentle. His eyes were the color of root beer candy. "Pleased to meet you...Sit?"

"Yessuh, Sit," His voice was Southern, slow and thick and sweet like molasses "Short for *Sit-yew-a-tion*. You be gettin' in one, I be gettin' you out."

"That's Ham," the colonel said, motioning with his arm to a young Arabic-looking man seated across from Sit.

"Pleased to meet you, sir. I'm the language guy," he said, with a sheepish glance to the woman at his right

"And that's Pete." The colonel pointed to a man at the far side of table, who raised his hand in greeting. "He doesn't talk much, but during your time here, you'll get to know him all too well."

At this comment everyone at the table shared a knowing, almost malicious grin.

"The runt over there," the colonel pointed to a scrawny young man at the head of the table, "is J. T." He looked all of twenty years old.

"Oh, don't let my youthful appearance fool you, Mr. Diablo. There's more brains in here"—he tapped his left temple—"than in the rest of the room combined."

He said it with such seriousness, Marcus wasn't quite sure how to take it.

"The boy has absolutely no modesty, Marcus, but he kinda grows on you," the colonel remarked.

"And this lovely lady," he said, laying a hand gently on the shoulder of the seated women he stood behind, "is our resident doctor, Chaya Lanner."

She nodded politely.

"So," he said, "this is the team known as Force 10. Two are currently on assignment, and we've recently lost a member." His voice held no hint of emotion.

So that was how these people grieved: they decompressed. Seemed reasonable.

Taking a seat and gesturing for Marcus to do the same, the colonel went on. "Okay, people, you've all been briefed. Marcus is our guest for the time being. We are going to train him in hand-to-hand combat, using weapons, and the peoples and environments of the Middle East. We're going to come up with a routine for him. First we need to know what he is capable of, mentally, physically, psychologically." They all looked at him, bloody, muddy, and smelling like pond slime in shredded, bloodstained clothes.

"One more thing, Marcus. Yesterday you mentioned 'all that need-to-know bullshit.' Well, we operate on a need-to-know basis around here, too." He paused looked around the table. "Everyone needs to know everything. Every day you will be trained by a team, have your ass handed to you by a team, and be critiqued by a

132

team. As for payment lets agree on a hundred thousand dollars. You get with J. T. in the next few days, and you can arrange the transfer."

"Thank you, Colonel." Marcus said.

"Don't thank me just yet. In a week you may wish you were in hell instead."

"I can appreciate that, Colonel," Marcus said, "but I've been in hell for months, and I'm doing my best to claw my way out."

Colonel Webb turned to the woman. "Doc, would you go tend to those scrapes? I'm pretty sure it's all from barbed wire, and from what I understand, Mr. Diablo might as well have been naked on his first run though the course." This brought smiles all around, and it occurred to Marcus that he had just signed up to be trained by a bunch of crazies.

The doc was beautiful—maybe forty, busty and athletic, with dark, tightly curled hair pulled back in a ponytail. Watching her walk toward him, it dawned on him that since they took Annie, this was the first time he had really looked a woman. He had just spent weeks living just off the beach, at the height of vacation and tourist season, without even noticing the scantily clad bodies all around him.

The doc said, "Mr. Diablo, get showered and cleaned up—I'll be up in ten." The accent sounded vaguely Middle Eastern, but from where, Marcus couldn't guess.

He showered fast and walked out of the bathroom to find her standing in his room. All he had on was a towel around his waist. He jerked to a stop.

"Mr. Diablo I live and care for a household of men," she said. "Think of me like your mom. Now, lose the towel and come here so I can see what damage your stupidity has caused."

Marcus walked over, dropping the towel on the floor. She turned him around and surveyed his backside.

"You would think that a reasonable, intelligent man, who has managed to track down the people responsible for abducting his wife, uncovered the cell responsible for the worst terrorist attack in history, and then managed to find us, would have more brains." She rubbed something that stung into the cuts on his back, butt, legs, and arms. "Now, this is going to complicate your training a bit," she said, and jabbed him in the buttock with a needle.

"Jeez, Doc, how about a little warning?" he said, wincing.

"That was an antibiotic...and this is a tetanus shot." The second needle went into the meat of his left upper arm.

He grabbed a pair of boxer shorts and stepped into them, then turned to face her. She was indeed beautiful, but, her strong, olive-skinned face and deep emerald eyes seemed to hint at some great sadness in her past.

"So, Doc, am I gonna live?"

"Yes, Mr. Diablo, for now." She smiled, then turned and walked out, leaving him standing in his underwear.

CHAPTER THIRTY-SIX
January 28

For three weeks, Marcus's routine didn't vary. He woke early and ran the obstacle course, got breakfast, then worked four hours straight. No training, fighting, or shooting—just digging postholes, mending fence, and bucking bales of hay. Every morning, Sit would go out with him, usually to dig postholes. Marcus had never seen a man that size except on a pro basketball court. He had to be six-eight and close to three hundred pounds and had arms the size of Marcus's thighs.

As they worked, Sit talked in a slow, smooth drawl that Marcus found soothing. According to Sit, it was only coincidence that his given name, Stanley Ignatius Thorn, formed the acronym that had become his handle. Perhaps even more arresting than his size was his color: gleaming-dark West African black, with a head as smooth and shiny as an eight ball.

A skilled and decorated Army Ranger, he was the sniper and all-around weapons expert on the team. When the colonel found him, he had been relegated to firearms instructor, being deemed just too big to be a high-value sniper. "He saw me shoot a coupla times and asked me what happens when I miss. I said I don't know, it's been so long, and next thing I know, I'm traipsing all over the world with him."

As the days wore on, Sit began describing weapons: caliber, action, weight, range, and a hundred other little details that Marcus just let in one ear and out the other. Only when they got to actually handling the hardware did Marcus realize that all those weeks of labor had not only hardened his body but allowed Sit's instructions, told in that easy Burl Ives manner, to sink in as if by osmosis.

In the afternoons, after working with Sit, Marcus spent three or four hours with Hamal Kamal, the only Arab-American member of Force 10. At thirty-two, Hamal—or Ham, as he preferred to be called—was one of the youngest members on the team. He gave Marcus the short version of his resume: A Yale grad with a master's in Arabic, he had been recruited and trained by the CIA. He had hooked up with the colonel while working as an interrogation translator in Iraq.

Ham was a patient and persistent teacher, giving Marcus information, country by country, on the geography, peoples, cultures, and religions of the Middle East and Central Asia. He spoke several Arabic dialects fluently but was quick to point out that his was the speech of educated, affluent Arabs—he could understand the Bedouins and most of the other pastoral peoples from the Middle East through Pakistan well enough, but his language skills, good though they were, wouldn't enable him to move freely among them. Every day he went over common phrases and words, but Marcus quickly realized it was going to take a miracle to get even a rudimentary grasp of the languages.

Late afternoon was PT. That meant running. Not the kind of running Marcus was accustomed to, in top-of-the-line shoes and running garb. No, this was combat running, in fatigues and boots and often with a fifty-pound pack, and in triple-digit temperatures. Although Jamie and several of the other guys could leave him in the dust on the short haul, Marcus had good stamina, and on longer distances through rough terrain, he held his own.

In the evening the team usually had dinner together, and although they weren't the most talkative crowd, whatever conversation did take place, almost always touched on what was going on in the U.S. J.T. as the team's information guy, was usually the one to begin the conversation. As surmised the parasitic epidemic was under control although eradicating the bug from the contaminated water systems was still ongoing. The upcoming spring runoff and rainfall were expected to bring unprecedented flooding and erosion problems. Loses had exceed one trillion dollars and the long-term costs were projected to be at least as much. But most disturbing was the daily violence being perpetrated against Muslim Americans, or any other of a number of ethnic groups who happened to have "that look." To Marcus it seemed that America was in danger of becoming too much like the thing they were trying to defeat.

***

On Tuesday afternoon of his third week, after finishing instruction with Ham, the colonel met Jamie, Liam, Sit, and Marcus on the porch as they were getting ready to head out on a ten-kilometer run. By now his cuts and scrapes had healed, and he was in the best shape of his life.

"I think it's time to take Marcus to the barn," the colonel said.

To Marcus, this sounded like a reasonable progression—anyone who bucked bales generally got to do his share of mucking out stalls. In the few weeks he had spent with Force 10, he had never been in the barn; in fact, he had been told explicitly to stay away.

"Liam, you take lead," the colonel said. "And please, let's not get him killed."

Marcus cringed inside. Clearly, this was not to be a stint of shoveling manure. And he would be answering to Liam, whose attitude from day one had been just shy of overtly hostile. He never missed a chance to disparage Marcus as some wannabe one-man crusader. "Gonna set the world right all by his lonesome, by taking out a man that the best in the world can't touch."

The colonel told Sit, "You run sweep; keep our boy in one piece."

"Yes suh."

Well, at least Sit was pleasant and helpful. But the colonel had warned Marcus, "Don't let his 'yessuh,' 'nosuh' bullshit fool you. The man's a stone killer—look you right in the face with that big grin and those liquid eyes and cut out your heart without blinking."

Marcus glanced at Sit, who gave him the kind of smile you might give someone before introducing them to the coolest thing they had ever experienced in their life. So why wasn't he feeling the thrill?

135

They walked across the yard and into a small tack room attached to the barn. There, Liam and Sit outfitted Marcus in full combat gear, chest, torso, and upper leg body armor, helmet, and rifle. What kind of rifle, he had no idea—his hands-on firearm training hadn't really kicked in yet. He knew only that it was an automatic weapon that could fire some astonishing number of rounds with a single squeeze of the trigger.

Sit looked Marcus up and down, checking to make sure all his gear was properly fastened. Then he took the rifle from him and ejected the ammo clip. "Don't want you blasting Liam all to hell first time out," he said. "And you gonna want to use *them*," he said, pointing to the goggle contraption strapped to his helmet. "Night vision goggles—dark in there. Now, things gonna seem all fucked up once we go through them doors. You stay close and do like you're told. We use live ammo—none o' that rubber bullet shit around here." His tone had lost all the joviality of their earlier encounters.

The only way Marcus could describe his first encounter with the Barn was that it was like skydiving without the benefit of jump school.

What had looked like an ordinary, weathered wood-slat barn door swung noiselessly open, and when they stepped in, it closed with a heavy metal *thunk*, leaving them in total darkness. It was as if he had stepped into another world. Marcus felt Sit's big hands pull the goggles down over his eyes, and the world came to life in an eerie pale green hue.

He heard Liam's voice over the comm device inside his helmet: "Force One, this is Force Five, ready to begin simulation."

Within seconds, the room filled with acrid, sulfurous smoke. Then came the noise—voices, yelling and screaming, loud music, and the sounds of people moving around seemingly in front, behind and above them.

"Ready for recon and extraction, Force Two?" said Liam.

"Ready, Force Five," Sit replied. No one asked Marcus if he was ready, but if they had, Marcus imagined his designation would have been simply F—for fucked.

Ten minutes later, when they came out of the barn, Marcus was so disoriented, even gravity seemed suspect. He couldn't imagine that anyone could get accustomed to that. But the fact was, these men were totally at home inside that haunted house.

The barn was an invention of both the colonel and Sit. The entire building was bulletproof—not to keep rounds from going in but to keep them from coming out. The walls and staircases inside were built on wheels and could be reconfigured to any number of settings and layouts. The noise and smoke were controlled from the command center inside the guesthouse, a few yards from the main house. Everything was computer controlled, including the languages that the voices spoke, screamed and shouted in. High-resolution cameras projected images that would appear and then just as suddenly vanish to provide the impression of enemy movement. Hydraulic rams provided thumping and banging, and these, too, could be positioned to provide a seemingly infinite array of effects. Everything that took place during one of these training exercises was recorded so it could be played back, reviewed, and critiqued.

After dinner, Marcus and the team gathered in the media room to review his first foray into the barn. To say that he looked like a boy among men would vastly understate what he saw on that tape. But to the credit of the Force 10 team, they all—even Liam—pointed out what he had done right, too. It wasn't much, but he hadn't turned for the door and pounded on it, begging to be let out.

After the critique, the colonel took him aside. "So you still want to pursue this, Marcus? I wanted you to get a taste of what it's like out there in our world."

"I'll do better tomorrow," Marcus said. And he went to bed.

***

The barn became a daily exercise. Marcus forced himself to remain composed, and to his surprise, by the fourth or fifth trip he was no longer a mere observer but a participant. The daily critique sessions became more and more positive. Besides the barn training, Sit spent a few hours a day training him on firearms—not shooting them, but recognizing makes and models and learning each one's range and characteristics and, most importantly, how to care for them. Sit had a genuine love for guns, and he wasn't satisfied until Marcus could identify a weapon, break it down, and reassemble it, all while blindfolded. Despite the rigors of his training, Marcus, riddled with anxiety about leaving his sons, and guilt because he had been unable to save Annie, was sleeping only three or four hours a night, so he had a lot of time in the dark to practice.

During this time with Sit, Marcus was introduced to Betty, Sit's sniper rifle. He had a lot of rifles, covering every range from a few hundred yards to over a mile. His favorite—his "baby girl," as he liked to say—was a Soviet-made Dragunov SDV, which fired a 7.62 x 54R round. Sit hand loaded his own rounds, and when they went out on the range, he never missed, ever. The colonel had told Marcus that Sit's most underappreciated talent, as a sniper was his ability to calculate range, windage, and elevation. "For him," the colonel had said, "those elements aren't so much complicated math as some kind of innate sixth sense."

Marcus also started spending time with Pete in the small barn, behind the guesthouse, that had been converted into a gym. It had the usual benches and free weights, but mostly it had heavy bags, speed bags, and pads—lots and lots of pads—on the floors and walls.

On his first day with Pete, Marcus walked into the gym to find him waiting, "Now, guy, we see what you know," Pete said. Marcus would come to learn that in Pete's heavily accented English, everybody was "guy."

"Come, guy, stand here," Pete said, pointing to a spot on the mat about five feet in front of him.

Everything about Pete was square, head, jawline, shoulders even his hands. His bushy brows and that rough stubble of beard that you could almost see grow gave him a menacing appearance. And even though he was of average height, he was as physically imposing, in his own way, as Sit's massive bulk.

"Okay, guy, now we start real training." Pete lobbed a knife at him as if it were a rubber ball.

Jumping back in surprise as the knife hit the mat in front of him, Marcus stared in disbelief.

"Pick up!" Pete yelled.

Marcus bent down and picked it up, noting that the end and edge were blunt. "Now, take me down."

Marcus fingered the knife, then, holding it in a loose underhand grip, nervously faced Pete.

"Ohhh, you loosey-goosey gang-fighter guy." Pete's grin held no friendliness.

Marcus had no idea what he was talking about. Pete made a beckoning motion with his hand, and Marcus stepped tentatively forward.

The kick came out of nowhere, whacking his hand and sending the knife flying. In the time Marcus's eyes instinctively closed when the foot struck his hand, he was on his back, in a chokehold, with a knife blade at his throat.

"Always hold knife like dis...."

Marcus strained to look at the blade pressed to his neck. Pete was holding the hilt so that the spine of the blade ran down along his forearm, edge out.

And just like that, Marcus was free and had the knife back in his hand.

"Again...."

And this was how it went with Pete, no matter what they worked on. The words he seemed to favor most were "Come, guy" and "again."

***

With each passing day, Marcus gained confidence. He learned to run the scenarios in the barn smoothly and on the fly. Pete continued to beat him like a rented mule, but there, too, he was improving. He learned to anticipate, to recognize his limitations, and compensate by using the element of surprise—and, basically, any other tactic he could come up with.

One evening, sitting on the veranda with Sit, Marcus asked him about Pete, mostly because he was to afraid to ask Pete directly.

Relaxing in a big sling-back chair, Sit smiled wide, all white teeth against the contrast of his black face. "You might say, the colonel is partial to misfits. We were in the Chechen capital, Grozny, in 2000—uninvited and officially not even there, mind you—when we came upon a badly wounded Russian soldier. You see, the Russkies were takin' a lot of heat from the West about the piss-poor job they were doin' handlin' the Chechen uprising. Bombing and killing was pretty much their whole bag of tricks. Anyhow, the colonel decides to take this boy out of the country with us. Turns out, our friend was a member of Spetsnaz, the Russian special-purpose regiment, and he had served on the teams that helped train the elite troops of Syria and Iran. Well, as you might guess, his knowledge was invaluable to the colonel. And besides, he's one bad-ass when it comes to hand-to-hand combat. Ya see, the colonel has a sense for people, like I have for rifles."

Besides the barn, languages, hand-to-hand, firearms, and PT, Marcus also began training in an area known as the "play yard." A few miles from the main compound was an abandoned village that had been repaired and shored up enough to serve as a real-time combat staging theater. It was just a few old mud-and-stone huts with one dilapidated old wood-framed larger structure that looked as though it might once have been a church.

Targets, both friendlies and unfriendlies, would pop up inside and outside the buildings while they did a sweep. Each participant was allotted a set number of rounds, and scores were based on "good kills" (bad guys) and "bad kills" (good guys).

On his first trip to the "play yard," Marcus went with Liam. He thought it a bit odd that he was going with the explosives expert. Liam laid out what was going to happen, and even pointed out where the targets would pop up, explaining that since it was Marcus's first time, he would go easy on him. Waiting nervously for the first target, Marcus sighted his pistol, but just as he started to squeeze the trigger, an explosion off to his right rattled him, sending his shot wild.

"'Point, aim, shoot' is not three separate movements, it's one," Liam said. "Don't let distraction influence the shot." Again and again targets popped up, and just as Marcus was about to fire, an explosion would go off and he missed the mark. But as with his barn experience, he learned to slow his mind and let his body move through the exercise, and over time, the explosions affected his aim less and less and, eventually, not at all.

There were some signs of grudging respect during the nightly critique sessions. But there was always a still, small voice in the back of Marcus's head telling him not to get too comfortable or confident. Then one night, almost a month into his venture, just after he nodded off, Jamie woke him.

"Come on, mate," he said. "We're going walkabout."

CHAPTER THIRTY-SEVEN
February 14

Marcus walked out onto the front porch with his pack slung over his shoulder and found Jamie waiting. Yawning, he glanced at his watch—not yet two in the morning. Marcus groaned inwardly. There wasn't much time for sleep, and those few hours he did get were precious.

"Drop the pack, mate—don't need it," Jamie said. "Everything we need is loaded in the Land Cruiser. Let's go. We have a good drive ahead of us, then a little hike." Even in the darkness, Marcus thought he detected a malicious glint in the young man's eyes.

They got in the Toyota, and Jamie handed him a canvas bag. "Put this on over your head. It's part of the drill."

They drove for about an hour, covering maybe sixty kilometers, before Jamie stopped. He helped Marcus out of the Cruiser, then tied a rope around his waist.

"Come on, let's get a move on, mate. I'm taking you to one of my favorite places."

They walked another hour and a half, during which Marcus stumbled and fell more than once, only to be dragged roughly to his feet.

"Almost there," Jamie said, taking the bag off Marcus's head.

They had crested a small hill and were standing on a bluff that fell abruptly off into a narrow gully below.

"Come on," he said. "We're going to visit one of the most revered places in all of Arrernte land." Revered for what, Marcus couldn't imagine.

They made their way down the steep hillside. Jamie seemed to know the route well, and when they got to the bottom, he dropped his pack and got out a liter bottle of water and a knife, which he dropped on the ground.

"Now we get to see what you're made of, old man. Let's see if you can get yourself back to the station. This isn't exactly where the colonel wanted me to strand you, but...anyway, there's water out here—you just have to find it. Mind the sun, though—by midday it'll be a hundred and ten out here."

And with that, he left. Why Marcus didn't argue or ask any questions, he would soon wonder.

On his way out, Jamie turned and yelled, "Oh, yeah, and you might want to watch out for the brownies." The only brownies Marcus knew of were chocolate, although he was pretty sure Jamie was referring to something else.

Marcus knew the most basic rule about being lost in mountains or wilderness, stay put. Even if help is not coming, give yourself time to assess the situation, orient yourself, take inventory of what you have and how long it will last, and, if something crucial to survival—water, for instance—is limited, see what you can do to replenish it before heading out. Spend a little time doing the right things *before* you start walking, and you just might make it out alive.

He had no idea where he was. And Annie and boys could all attest that he had the directional sense of a pinball. If he could find the road, it would take him back, but then, if it had taken at least an hour by truck, it was a good day or two on foot.

He still had a few hours before sunrise, and decided to scout around the arroyo—see if he could find any signs of water, or at the very least find a place to ride out the heat of the coming day. He spent the next two hours checking out his surroundings and—no big surprise—found no creeks or springs brimming with clear, cool water. Down in the center of the arroyo was a small stand of gum trees and some mulga bushes, which looked to be the only shade for miles. He would wait it out until evening and then try to find his way out.

As he neared the stand of trees, he noticed that what he had taken for sand was actually stone. It was just eight in the morning, and the ground was already hot. He looked at the trees and was lamenting the meager protection they were going to provide, when he caught movement at the edge of his vision.

He scanned the ground. Everything was the same tannish brown, the rock, the dirt, the bushes, and...a snake. Jamie's cryptic warning about the "brownies"—now it made sense. Of all the many highly venomous serpents in Australia, the brown snake was one of the worst—not just lethal but also aggressive. And this one was coming his way.

The gum tree above him suddenly looked inviting. The problem was, the lowest branch was maybe a foot higher than he could jump, and the bark, he knew, was too slick to get a firm hold on. He looked back to the edge of the little copse, and sure enough, the snake was slithering gracefully toward him.

Drawing the knife from its sheath, he took it in both hands and plunged it into the trunk as hard as he could. Then he picked up a hefty fist-size rock from the ground and, on tiptoes, pounded the hilt of the knife until he had driven the blade halfway in. Then, snatching up the water bottle, he tucked his shirt into his pants and dropped the bottle inside the shirt, grabbed the knife with both hands, and did a sort of thrashing, swinging pull-up...and fell on his ass.

He wiped the perspiration from his hand onto his shirt, pulled up again, then locked off with his right arm and got his left hand on the branch. If he fell now, he would land on top of a large snake with enough neurotoxic venom to kill him a dozen times over. Swinging a leg up, he hauled himself up and over the branch to relative safety, catching the water bottle just as it threatened to fall from his shirt. With a silent thank-you to Pete for all the pull-ups, push-ups, and core work he made him do every day before their training, he watched the snake poke around beneath his perch, looking for lizards. He made himself as comfortable as he could and waited for the reptile to go about its business elsewhere.

The hours wore on as the day heated up, and his meager liter of water was almost gone. His sunglasses were in his pack, on the front porch where he had dropped it when Jamie and he left. The sun was going to be tough on his baby blues, he thought, squinting into the distance.

Seeing no sign of the snake, he was about to scramble down from his perch, when he saw movement in the mirage along the hillcrest to the north—two dark shapes moving independently. As they descended the near slope, he could see that they were humans, one with white hair.

Still doubting his eyes, Marcus watched them grow steadily closer until they were in the bottom of the arroyo, no more than fifty yards away. A young man with a shaggy mane like a fright wig, and a much older man, walking with the aid of a tall stick. Both were shirtless, in tattered shorts and barefoot.

They approached him, and the young one looked up with a toothy grin. "Hey, mate," he said, "you look to be in a little spot of trouble."

Feeling stiff, hot, and thirsty, Marcus climbed down and looked warily around. "There was this big snake...."

The younger man spoke again. "No worries, mate. Brownies don't like the taste of Nunga blood." Marcus had heard this term before. Glen had told him it was a derogatory term for Aborigines. "And besides, Grandfather is of the brown."

"Seems like Jamie boy don't like you much, since he dumped your sorry butt here." He must have seen the bewilderment on Marcus's face. "Oh, Jamie—he's my mate, my older brother. We grew up here together, raised by Grandfather. Jamie, he's white enough on the outside, but he's Arrernte through and through."

"Grandfather has been waiting for you. He's seen you in Dreamtime."

Marcus had a general understanding of Dreamtime. He understood it as a way of perceiving or knowing directly the land and the animals that inhabited it, as in "wallaroo dreaming," or "brown snake dreaming." He had read that the aboriginal people of Australia believed that they, as individuals, existed eternally in Dreamtime, that this part of their consciousness had existed before they were born and continued after death. It was through Dreamtime that the present was governed and the future planned for.

"Let's go, mate," he said. "If we don't get you some water soon, you're going to dry up and blow away."

Marcus followed them for perhaps an hour in the direction they had come from. The old man easily kept pace with his grandson, and neither of them even broke a sweat. He, on the other hand, was scrambling along behind them, thirstier than he had ever been in his life.

They crested a slight rise and descended into another arroyo. In the bottom sat a cluster of mud brick houses amid a lush stand of gum trees. A few minutes later, Marcus was sitting in the dirt under a canopy of gnarled branches and green leaves, gulping cool water from a gourd. The young man gave him a rough wooden bowl of what he said was a mixture of yams and crushed bunya nuts.

As Marcus's strength and composure returned with hydration and food, the young man came and sat beside him. He squatted down and seemed to rest comfortably without his butt touching the ground. His skin was almost as black as Sit's, but whereas Sit had this almost shiny, oiled glow, the young man before him had chalky, dry skin that seemed opaque and sweatless.

In a lilting cadence that sounded almost like music, he said, "Grandfather wants to talk to you. He's a bit batty." He wiggled a forefinger in circles by his temple. "He thinks you're somehow important to our people. I don't see how some white guy who got treed by a brown snake can be of much help to us, but then, I haven't got Grandfather's sight." His tone seemed to imply that someday he might. "So you go talk to him, mate." He pointed to another, smaller copse of trees, where the old man was sitting on some kind of short stool with his back against the smooth bark of a gum tree. "You'll stay the night here, and tomorrow we're going to play a big joke on Jamie boy." There was no mistaking the mischief in his voice.

Marcus rose and walked over to where the old man was seated. He waved his arm, indicating that Marcus should sit on the ground in front of him. He looked old. His hair like a tangle of pale gray moss, and the skin on his face and arms was as weathered and creviced as the rocks and wood around him. Marcus had the sense that this weatherworn old man dwelt in a world he had no knowledge of.

Grandfather spoke quietly, his words coming in halting spurts. Though his accent was Australian, English was clearly a foreign language to him. His eyes pierced through Marcus as he spoke.

"I have seen you, my son. You are of the world of the white man, yet you have been drawn to the land of the Arrernte. You think you have come here as a means to an end. But one man's end is another man's means. My people have lived in these lands for fifty thousand years, and I carry inside me the memories of those years, the pictures and the history of the land and her creatures. Our young leave the land and go to the white cities, where alcohol and drugs destroy their abilities and their will. My people are dying. The old ways are disappearing, the languages forgotten."

He stopped talking and stared up into the sky. Marcus was both entranced and confused.

"My grandson, he is the hope of my people, though he doesn't yet know it. He believes he has returned to care for an old man in his last years, but his destiny has been foretold. Dreamtime—the youngsters think it's nothing more than make-believe, a fairy tale for the kids." His eyes fixed Marcus with an unsettling intensity.

"But you know about Dreamtime. You have a boy who knows about Dreamtime." How could this man possibly know about Garrett? Marcus wondered, as the old eyes seemed to drill deep into his being. "You are now and forever tied to the Arrernte. In you, I see one mouth with many tongues."

Grandfather fell silent, and in a moment, still sitting with his back to the tree, he began to snore.

143

Marcus felt as if, like Alice, he had blundered into some other world—down a rabbit hole or a wormhole and into a parallel universe or something. He left the old man sleeping and returned to find the grandson helping some other men with repairs to one of the mud dwellings. The two of them sat on the ground in the shade of the trees and talked. He told Marcus his name was Freddie Wanganami, though his Arrernte given name was Gelar, which meant "a brother." He was an only child, and his grandfather had always told him that a brother would be brought to him. And when he was ten Jamie came to live with them. Freddie never mentioned his parents, and Marcus didn't ask. His grandfather was Killara Wanganami. His first name meant "permanent, always there." They talked about Jamie and the presence of Force 10.

"Jamie's name among my people is Gilgandra," Freddie said. "It means 'walking alone.' He left here to join the Australian Army when he was nineteen. He was a member of an elite commando unit sent to Iraq as part of the Australian effort to support your country." From his tone, Marcus could tell that Freddie didn't think much of the notion that one people should impose its will on another.

"He learned to track from grandfather," Freddie said. "It's what his mates call him, you know? Tracker. But with him it's more than judging the when, how many, the weight, and the pace of a man or animal." He looked hard at Marcus, "No, he can tell the *temperament and attitude* of whatever he's tracking. It's almost as if he can actually *see* them—whether it's a goanna or a man or a red roo. As if their feet are his."

***

That night, Grandfather and Marcus went out into the darkness. They walked for a time, and it seemed that the old man could have found his way if he were blind. The night air was warm, and Marcus was aware of the sounds of the desert night: the scurrying of small animals, the buzzing of insects, the gentle sigh of the breeze. He could smell the dry earth and the scents of the desert life.

Grandfather stopped, raised his head, and scanned the star-filled sky, then sat. He pointed to a spot on the dry ground, and Marcus sat facing him.

"This is a sacred place," the old man said. "For thousands of years my people have come to this spot for guidance. It is here that the past, present, and future come together in Dreamtime. We believe that the power of Dreamtime is above men. The power of the earth, wind, and sky can make anything possible. It is only the limited foresight of the human being, the unwillingness to embrace the unknown, that prevents a man from reaching his true and full potential."

Sitting as still as a statue he continued. "My people have many needs. Our future is threatened. I have seen, with these eyes, my people almost wiped from the earth by the white man's bigotry, disease, and greed. You are going to provide us a path, provide us with the tools and resources to secure a future for our children and their children. It will rest upon my people to protect your gift. People like my grandson will have to bear the burden and responsibility."

As Grandfather spoke in cryptic rhythms, Marcus felt a tremendous weight in his words. If there were answers to the direction of his quest here in this ancient land, among these ancient people, what would the cost be?

Grandfather motioned for him to scoot closer to him, then reached out and took Marcus's hands in his. They were calloused and gnarled, bent from decades of work and arthritis. They felt warm, almost hot. As he sat holding those weathered old hands, Marcus felt the great loss and greater need of an ancient people. "You must clear your mind now. Let Dreamtime come to you."

He began to speak in his native tongue. Although Marcus didn't understand the words, the sounds came in a lulling singsong. It was the kind of sound that one felt more than heard. It encompassed his body, Grandfather, the land itself. He felt his mind begin to float. He felt himself drifting among sights, sounds, smells, and people. They were talking in many languages, and slowly, as he moved through the kaleidoscope of people and places, the words they spoke were as clearly understood as English.

When Marcus next became aware of the present, it was the beginning of a new day. At some point his hands and the old man's had broken contact, but otherwise, the two were sitting exactly as they had been at his last conscious memory.

He looked at Grandfather. He appeared to be asleep. Marcus felt rested and alert, not tired or stiff. Grandfather opened his eyes and spoke in his language, and Marcus gaped in astonishment. For he *understood the words*! How was this possible?

They rose and walked back to the village. Grandfather didn't speak, and Marcus was too dumbfounded to ask questions.

Grandfather left him with Freddie and set out across the desert in the direction they had led Marcus the day before. If Freddie had any curiosity about what the old man and Marcus had done all night, he never showed it.

"My grandfather believes you hold some key to our people's survival," Freddie said. "I can't imagine how, but I hope he's right. That man raised me since I was very young, after my parents died, and in that time I've seen more than my share of strange happenings."

For the next hour they talked. Marcus learned that Freddie was a very well educated young man. He had recently received his law degree from, of all places, the University of Notre Dame in Broome. How an Aborigine came to attend a well-respected private Catholic school, he never said. He had now returned home to care for his grandfather.

Abruptly Freddie stood, "Ready, mate? We need to go. We have three, maybe four hours before the colonel sends Jamie-boy back for you. Colonel's gonna be none too happy about where Jamie dropped you—I can't wait to see the look on his face."

Marcus had no idea what Freddie was talking about, but he did need to get back to the team. Along the way, he listened as Freddie laid out the joke he had planned for Jamie. As they walked, Marcus took in the surroundings. The land was dry and brown and, by all appearances, lifeless. But as he listened to Freddie, Marcus began to *feel* more than *see* the land around him. His eyes picked up the life and subtle hues of the vast desert, his ears caught the rustle of wind in the brush, and the sounds of a goanna's claws scuttling over sandstone.

The crux of Freddie's plan was that Jamie would find Marcus sprawled on his back at the base of the tree. It would look as though he had somehow stepped on a brown snake or angered it in some other way and that he had killed it before succumbing to its venom. Grandfather was already there, getting everything prepared. According to the plan, he would be found with a dead snake clutched in his hand. Freddie explained how his grandfather was making the arrangements with the snakes. Marcus had found himself in the middle of nowhere with people who talked to snakes—and, in Grandfather's case, many others things as well.

Arriving at the arroyo, Marcus saw Grandfather, sitting cross-legged near the base of the tree that had been his sanctuary yesterday. A brown snake lay at his feet. As they approached, Marcus slowed, and Freddie turned to him.

"No time to be a pussy, mate—this is going to be a hoot."

It was now midmorning, and according to Freddie, Jamie would be back within the next couple of hours. How Freddie knew this, Marcus had no idea, but from what he had seen in his short time with these people, he wasn't about to doubt him.

He drank two full bottles of water and lay on his back near the base of the tree. Freddie said, "Grandfather has asked the browns for a sacrifice." Feeling the heat of the baked dirt through the back of his shirt and pants, Freddie brought the dead snake over and, kneeling on the hot earth, leaned over and arranged its five-foot length across his chest.

"Okay, mate, let's see you scare that boy right out of his drawers," Freddie said. Grandfather was busy doing things to the ground around the base of the tree and near where he lay. "Jamie's as good a tracker as any Arrernte. He'll know exactly what happened here by looking at the ground. We have to make the struggle that supposedly took place look real, and only Grandfather can do that." There was a note of admiration and respect in Freddie's voice.

Then Grandfather approached him on sinewy, sun-wrinkled legs, and a strange memory flooded Marcus's mind. There was a novel by Paulo Coelho, *The Alchemist,* which he had read to the boys. It was a story about the Soul of the World, and a young shepherd boy's search for his personal legend. In that moment, Marcus knew that Grandfather was the Soul of the World, at least of *his* world, and that he had just received one of the keys to finding his personal legend.

Grandfather reached out with his walking stick and touched its tip to Marcus's forehead. In his Aboriginal tongue, he said, " *Yileen mayra.*" And as clearly as if he had spoken the words in English, Marcus knew what he had said—not just the literal translation, "Dream of the wind," but all its subtle shades of meaning. Marcus smiled up at that bent old man, and he smiled back, and then he and Freddie left.

Since he got here yesterday, everything had felt strange and dreamlike. What should have seemed impossible or crazy seemed the only logical path, so why not lie in the desert with a dead venomous snake draped over him? Trying to remain calm, Marcus realized, Freddie had failed to explain what he was supposed to do once Jamie found him.

He couldn't move to check the passage of time on his watch, but he felt this intense sense of calm and well-being. It seemed he hadn't been lying there long when he heard a low, worried voice. "Fuck...fuck! The colonel's gonna *kill* me! Fuck...." Jamie was back.

Marcus had his eyes closed, his head turned to the right, facing the tree, with the snake right up on his face. There were hurried footsteps, and he could sense Jamie looking at him. He heard a pack fall to the ground...heard him kneel next to him. The way Marcus was positioned, Jamie had to lean his body weight out and over him. He felt Jamie's sleeve brush over his chest as he reached across to check for a pulse. Just as the fingers touched his throat, Marcus sprang, and in one explosive burst he was astride Jamie's chest, with the snake's head in his hand, squeezed so the mouth gaped open, fangs almost touching the skin of Jamie's throat. One look into Jamie's eyes told Marcus he had him.

Marcus lowered his mouth to Jamie's ear and hissed, "Good to see you, Jamie. Now, don't get any crafty ideas, or my face—and your little reptilian friend here—will be the last thing you see on this earth. Now, you and I need to come to an understanding. You don't like me much. I get that. But what *you* need to get is, I don't give a shit. I'm not here to make friends or enemies. But understand this. If you ever do anything to get in my way, anything that might prevent me from returning to my sons, I'll kill you with no more thought than I give to wiping my ass. This soakin' in?"

Jamie blinked, too afraid to nod.

"Say the words, *boy.*"

In barely a whisper, he said, "Yes...sir."

Marcus stood and flung the snake away. "Good. Now, get me the fuck outta here." Jamie rose, the look in his eyes betraying more shame than fear. He dusted himself off and grabbed his pack, and they made their way back to the parked Land Cruiser and returned to Force 10 without saying another word to each other.

CHAPTER THIRTY-EIGHT

After a silent drive back to the compound, getting out of the Cruiser, Jamie said, "Sir?" His voice sounded subdued, almost meek.

"What's on your mind, pal?"

"Sir, I'm sorry about—"

Marcus held up his hand and smiled. "I know, Jamie. I know."

"Sir, about Grandfather...you should know that he has powerful magic. I've never told anyone, but my abilities to track, well, I learned some of them, but mostly it was a gift from Grandfather. When I track men, it's like I *feel* them. I feel the injury or the unbalanced load they might be carrying. It's not something I can really explain. It's like I'm walking in their shoes. All I know is that Grandfather has powers that are not of this earth."

Marcus appraised the young man standing before him. "Well, Jamie, that I can believe."

As Marcus walked into the house and headed for the stairs and a much needed shower, he saw Ham, typing on his laptop in the study that served as their classroom. Words and phrases in a dozen Middle Eastern and South Asian countries were scrawled on the large whiteboard behind him.

Glancing at the board, Marcus saw something ungrammatical in the Arabic version of the phrase. Without thinking, he stepped over to the whiteboard, erased two of the squiggly script lines with his finger, and rewrote them, then turned around and headed back out the door.

Before he reached the stairs, Ham had found his voice. "How...how did you do that!" he gasped.

"I don't know," Marcus replied, looking equally dumbfounded. "Say something in Arabic."

"*Ana al atakellem al arabi,*" Ham said.

"I don't speak Arabic?" The two men stared at each other. "Do you have any tapes or CDs in Arabic?"

"What do you think, man? No more than a few thousand hours' worth!"

"Let's hear one."

For the next hour, they listened and Marcus translated. Ham was sure it was some trick—it had to be, didn't it? Somehow, Marcus had known Arabic all along and had just decided to keep it a secret. But then he started playing taped conversations of interrogations. These were tapes of people from Afghanistan, Pakistan, Iran, Iraq, Syria, Turkey, and who knew where else, speaking not only Arabic but Pashto, Baluchi, Dari, Urdu, Farsi, and Turkish. Marcus didn't make a single mistake.

Finally, Ham said, "I don't know what happened to you out there in the desert, but whatever it was, I gotta get me some."

Just then the colonel's voice came through the doorway. "Marcus, have a good time with the natives?" The look he saw on both men's faces said it all. "Okay, gentlemen," he said, "what's going on?"

For the next half hour, Ham and Marcus put on quite a show for the colonel. Marcus felt like the three-armed man in a carnival sideshow. And yet, the colonel showed no surprise.

At the evening critique session, Jamie owned up to having stacked the "walkabout" so heavily against Marcus. Marcus thought he saw in the colonel's eyes a glint that seemed to say, *he's learning.* The origin of Marcus's new language skills was hotly debated. Most of the team chalked them up to a sun-addled brain. Pete was sure he had fallen out of the tree onto his head. But Chaya had the most fascinating theory. According to her, there were documented cases of people who had suffered a traumatic head injury only to awaken from a coma with newfound talents, the ability to do complicated math in their head, play music, or even, in some cases, speak another language fluently. That he hadn't fallen on his head, well, a person just might internalize the trauma in such a way that the brain rewired itself.

Marcus listened with amusement and turned to Jamie with a look that said, *oh yeah, something happened out there in the desert. But if we told you what, you'd put us in straitjackets.*

* * *

That night, Marcus fell into a deep sleep and dreamed, not of the boys or Annie, but of the world he was headed into. He was moving over the land, sort of "swimming" just above the ground. He traveled across the breadth of Australia, over his brother's home, over a turbulent, cold-looking ocean and then a clear, inviting aqua-blue sea. Over a sleek, black ship, over the dunes and rugged mountains of what had to be somewhere in Asia. And he didn't just dream it—he felt it, breathed it, tasted it.

CHAPTER THIRTY-NINE
February 15

Before dawn, Marcus's dreaming was interrupted when he was dragged from his bed, and for the second time in just days, a canvas bag was placed over his head. Without a word, he was manhandled down the stairs and out the front door. The hands moved in smooth, confident motions as he was forced onto his back and strapped down. They started at his feet and worked their way up, securing straps and finishing with one across his forehead. He was totally immobile.

His mind was sending a steady stream of commands to his body: *stay calm, slow your breathing and heart rate, go somewhere else.* It was a technique he used often when running long distances. He would force his mind to exist in a place separate from his body.

He was picked up, strapped to a board, and carried down the porch stairs and across the yard. They stopped. "It's time for a little anger management." It was Liam's voice.

The next moment, Marcus was lifted up, head down, and plunged into water. In that instant, a wave of terror swept over him. He realized that although this wasn't exactly water boarding, it was equally, if not perhaps more frightening.

He struggled to stay calm. But, after the fourth or fifth time under water, swallowing what seemed gallons, any thought of control escaped. He had no idea when he lost consciousness, but when he came to, he was on the front porch, staring into the first glint of sunrise. He was still on the board but no longer strapped down. Rolling onto his side, he puked. His throat was raw, and his head was pounding.

Shaking and weak he walked inside. It was almost six in the morning, and the Force 10 team, except for Colonel Webb, sat at the dining table. He walked past them and went upstairs, showered, and changed into fresh clothes.

Rummaging through his pack, he found the Ka-bar knife that was part of his barn gear. Tucking it, still sheathed, into the back of his pants, he pulled his shirt down over it.

He went downstairs, glanced at the team members at the table, and grabbed a mug and poured it full of coffee from the pot on the stove. He walked around the table to an empty seat next to Liam. Instead of sitting down, he sloshed hot coffee onto Liam's back, letting the cup fall from his hand and shatter on the wood floor. As Liam arched back in his chair, bellowing at the sudden scalding pain, Marcus pulled the knife from the back of his pants, whipped off the sheath, and, with his left hand, yanked Liam's hair back, exposing his throat to the Ka-bar's razor edge.

In the same tone he had used with Jamie, he said, "Boy, if you ever do that to me again, be very sure to kill me, because if you don't, I will certainly kill you."

And as the last word left his mouth, he let go of Liam's hair, laid the knife on the table in front of him, and beamed a big, sunny smile at Pete and said, "Did I hold the knife right?"

Liam was pouring cold water on his scalded back as Marcus causally asked, "Where's the colonel?" The doc pointed at the office.

Walking away, he heard the team talking. Probably trying to figure just who he was and what was driving him. If they figured it out, he hoped they would enlighten him.

He found the colonel in his office, looking at his computer screen.

The colonel looked up as he entered. "Well, you've had a full couple of days," he said. "What's on your mind?" The colonel asked, as Marcus took a seat in the leather armchair.

"Well, Colonel, I think I'm almost done here. But I have a proposition I'd like to put to Force 10. If there's one thing I've learned, it's that as a one-man wrecking force, I am seriously undermanned."

"Oh, I wouldn't be too hard on yourself. You took Jamie down and just about made Liam soil himself—you might be abler than you think." Marcus guessed Liam's screams prompted the colonel out of his seat to see what was going on in the dining room.

He handed the colonel the file folder he had brought from his room.

After opening it and scanning the contents, the colonel said, "The *Takbir*, Adad's base of operations. Hell of a ship. I've seen intelligence estimates that say he has over a billion—that is with a 'b'—invested in it. He spends most of his time on her when he isn't playboying around the world."

Marcus shouldn't have been surprised that the colonel already knew about the ship. "Well, the only way I'm going to get to him is while he's aboard it."

"What the hell, Marcus—you think they sell tickets like it's a cruise ship? Or maybe you think Adad's just going to invite you aboard for mai tais?"

"No, Colonel, that's where Force 10 comes in. I propose to hire you and the team to take control of the *Takbir*."

"And why in God's name would we want to do that?"

"For the money—and because it's the right thing to do."

"Marcus, you don't *have* enough money to hire us for a mission like this. We would go through your million like it was toilet paper, and probably the second million as well."

The second million—was there anything the man didn't know about him? "I know that, Colonel. I'm aware I don't have the money or the expertise to mount something like this. But my money will go a long way toward getting things started. The rest will come from you."

The colonel gave him a quizzical look. "Are you proposing we become business partners?"

"That is exactly what I'm proposing."

"And what, might I ask, is the return on investment?"

"The way I figure it, if this is Adad's base of operations—his command center, so to speak—and given the cash-and-carry nature of so much of the business in the Middle East, I'd be willing to bet there's a shitload of cash, gems, art, and God only knows what else on that ship."

Since the man wasn't interrupting, Marcus forged ahead. "I would also assume that he has significant security, though I would also bet that that security is pretty complacent. And we all know what happens when people get complacent." He couldn't resist the veiled allusion to Jamie and Liam.

"If you look a little deeper in that file, you'll find some information about a satellite the Saudis are going to launch this year. I don't remember what they call it, but it roughly translates as 'God's Eye.' It's supposed to be the latest in high-tech communications satellite technology. But if you follow the blogs of all the conspiracy nuts, there's some speculation that it is also the latest in surveillance spy shit. Now, if I were one of the richest guys in the world, and my hobby was wreaking havoc on the West, I might just want a piece of that kind of technology. I know it sounds far-fetched, but hell, everything I've *done* is *so* far-fetched. With no help and almost no information, I've connected the dots, and the picture is frightening. All I ask is that you consider it—do a little research and see what shakes out."

Marcus paused a moment as the colonel watched him thoughtfully. "So Force 10 gets whatever's on the ship. You know I'm good for only two million, but if I have to, I'll liquidate every asset I have, use every last dollar, to finance this. If you haven't figured it out yet, I have no choice. And if there is no money, you said it yourself: the ship is worth upwards of a billion dollars. International salvage law applies to all ships in international waters—at the very least, it would be worth ten percent of value to the insurance company."

The colonel rolled his neck and stretched. "Okay, Marcus, for the sake of argument, let's say I present your proposal to the team and recommend we go forward. Are you sure you're prepared to become an active participant? You see, it would seem that you are the only one with the requisite language skills to pull something like this off. The only way we can gather the intelligence is to come up with some scheme that puts our people in direct contact. That means being able to move in and among some of the most hardened, committed zealots on this planet."

"Well, colonel, that would be your call. But I'll do whatever I can to make these people pay for what they did to Annie and to *our* country."

The colonel looked at Marcus his expression softening. "So it seems that this one man quest for revenge has taken on a broader context."

CHAPTER FORTY
February 23

A week passed without any word. Marcus continued his daily training regimen and decided it was time he got to know the doc a little better. One perk of his sessions with Pete was that he got to see her most days. From the start, he had felt a certain tension between them. She was beautiful in an exotic, wounded sort of way. It was the way she looked *into* him rather than merely *at* him, that he found himself drawn to, as if somehow she understood his pain. Since Annie's death, Marcus had not looked at another women with even a hint of sexual interest. But he had to admit that, when he was with Doc, he felt a stirring and need. Still, every time he came to her after Pete had pummeled him, Chaya's approach was clinical and direct.

On the second day after his meeting with the colonel, Marcus found her, just off the kitchen, in the room that served as her exam and treatment area. She looked up at him as he shuffled toward her, holding his arm, blood dripping through his fingers.

"I told you to be careful!" she yelled. "Did you break open the wound again?" When he nodded, she said, "Sit."

As she unwrapped the bloody gauze, Marcus said, "So, Doc, I've managed to find out at least a bit about the rest of the team, but I don't know anything about you except that you're a doctor and you're from Israel."

"What is it you'd like to know?

"I don't know, Doc. How about something that gives me some insight into who Chaya Lanyer is?"

She didn't immediately respond as she swabbed the wound on Marcus's forearm. When she spoke, her voice had a detached, distant quality. "I was in love once, a long time ago. He was Palestinian. We meet at university, as part of a cross-cultural exercise. We were young and idealistic, convinced that we could change the world. We thought we could be examples to our peoples of how two cultures, two religions, could live side by side. He was going to be an engineer, but in my final year he was killed in an Israeli bombing raid on a suspected Hamas stronghold."

She looked up from her work to see the question on Marcus's face. "I don't know if it was true. At the time, I wanted to believe...but I've learned a lot since then. I graduated and went to the United States to attend medical school at Stanford, then did my residency in Detroit." Lightly shaking her head, she looked up at Marcus. "That city was like an urban war zone. I'd never seen so many knife and gunshot wounds. After that, I returned to Israel, and that's when I suffered a serious crisis of faith."

The doc didn't elaborate, but Marcus sensed that whatever she was alluding to was another, possibly much greater loss.

"So I took my medical training and language skills to Mossad. I figured that if I couldn't change the world from the outside, maybe I'd have better luck working from inside the best trained, most efficient and lethal intelligence organization in the world." The statement seemed contradictory, but her tone was dead serious.

She applied a butterfly bandage to close the wound. "My language skills are all of Ham's and probably then some." There was no brag in her tone. "The problem is, I'm a woman, and in much of the Islamic world, and even in Orthodox Judaism, women are of little consequence. A look of sorrow came over her face. "I'm sorry, Marcus. I didn't...."

He touched her arm, "Hey, it's all right. I understand all too well how some feel about women." They looked at each other, and for first time Marcus felt a mutual connection.

She gave him a look that reached inside and grabbed him. "You truly believe you can get to Adad?"

Marcus got up from the chair, "It's a funny thing about belief, Doc—at least for me—every day I have to reevaluate it. But if things work out, yeah, I'll get to him." He walked toward the front door, flexing his arm, then turned. "Hey, thanks for patching me up, again."

From then on, he made it a point to spend time with Chaya. He learned that her language skills were indeed remarkable. She was fluent not just in English, Hebrew and Arabic, but French, Spanish, Italian, Greek, Turkish, Farsi, and a half-dozen other languages—and to Marcus's surprise, every language she could speak, so could he.

***

Gasping for breath, Marcus struggled up from the mat to find the colonel watching him. "You know, you shouldn't let him win all the time," the colonel said to Marcus with a sly smile.

Marcus looked from the colonel to Pete and back. He had been so focused on his training and trying to gain acceptance among the members of Force 10, he hadn't really noticed the almost fatherly relationship the colonel had with the younger team members. And why not? This was his family.

The colonel asked Pete, "How's he doing?"

"Not bad. Needs more training. Needs more...." He hit his palm with his other fist.

The colonel chuckled. "I need to borrow him for a while, but I promise you'll get him back."

Marcus groaned inwardly as a big smile spread across Pete's square face. For the man had just gotten official sanction to beat him even harder.

Marcus followed the colonel over to the command center. The only time he had been in this building was when he arranged with J. T. for the transfer of the hundred-thousand-dollar training fee.

Entering the state-of-the-art ops center complete with a wall of HD monitors and stacks of electronic monitoring, routing, and satellite interface equipment, the colonel said, "All right, J. T., show Mr. Diablo what you've found."

J. T. looked back over his shoulder at him, then returned his attention to the wall in front of him, with its massive HD monitors displaying multiple applications simultaneously. "All right, Mr. Diablo," he said, "there's Google and then there's *my* version of Google."

He hit a few strokes, and an image of a satellite appeared on the screen. "May I present God's Eye. Ain't she a beaut? Seems that maybe you were right about this little baby being more than just the latest in communications technology. This unit is loaded—and I mean loaded—with the most tricked-out hardware on the planet. Of course she's got high-res imaging capabilities, but she's also got parabolic sound interception technology that, until now, was nothing more than theory. If this works the way I suspect it does, not only can this baby zoom in on home plate at Yankee stadium it can pick up the jaw-jacking between hitter and catcher. There's even some infrared, ground-penetrating, thermal-imaging capabilities, which I haven't quite figured out yet—but I will. Billions and billions have been invested in this little piece of hardware.

"Now, as for our friend Adad...." The image of the satellite now occupied half the screen, and a picture of Adad the other half: a handsome, sharp-featured man with jet back hair, tall, lean, and exuding confidence.

"It wasn't easy, but I uncovered that through many of his companies, he has invested heavily in this project. So I would say that your assumption that he wanted a piece of this is right on track." J. T.'s voice held a note of undisguised admiration.

The screen divided again, and the new frame showed a ship. It was the same ship in the file Marcus had given the colonel—the same ship he had flown over in his dream after his time with Grandfather.

"The *Takbir*—now, this is not your average billionaire's mega yacht. She's right at six hundred feet long, built in a shipyard in Vladivostok. Seems Adad is a big investor in the new Russia. He has huge oil, gas, mining, and timber holdings throughout the continent. The Russians may lose points for style and sophistication, but when it comes to building shit that lasts, they're the pros." Marcus was a little confused by his statement. The ship he was looking at was as sleek and sophisticated as anything he had ever seen. Her lines were sharp and clean, and she had this science fiction, state-of-the-art look about her.

As if reading his mind, J. T. continued, "Seems our young prince brought in a team of ship designers and architects from the Italian shipbuilder Brilinie. This baby has all the brawn of the hammer and sickle, but with the style of Armani. By every definition, it's a floating palace, but more than that, it's is his home, his corporate headquarters. She carries a Sikorsky H-92 Superhawk—a beast of a transport bird—as well as a Bell 407, the Ferrari of copters." The view of the *Takbir* changed from a profile to an overhead shot. From above, she looked like an anvil, with a sharp bow spreading widely back to a broad foredeck and then tapering back to a, squared-off, narrower but still substantial afterdeck. "There is a ramp aft that lowers to launch one of several high-speed boats. Retractable decks fore and aft are for storage. As for hardware, she has it all, the best in electronics and satellite interface technology, as well as propulsion, navigation, and automated operating systems. If I'm right"—he said this as if there were no way he could be otherwise—"this ship can be operated by a crew of a dozen, maybe even less."

"One more thing, the satellite is set to be launched from French Guiana next month. The window is March twenty-fourth through twenty-seventh. Allow a couple of weeks to fine-tune the telemetry, check all onboard systems, and upload software, and she'll be ready by mid to late April. If our boy wants to connect, he's going to have to dock for a least a week. The sophistication and sensitivity of the software will require very specialized, skilled people and multiple system interfacing that would be too complicated while the ship's at sea."

J. T. swiveled in his seat to face Marcus. "So all you have to do is figure out where she's going to dock." His tone of voice said *no problem, right?*

***

The colonel looked across his desk at Marcus, who sat facing him, doing his best to appear relaxed. "Okay, I presented your plan, and as crazy as it is, the team's decided to proceed. It just so happens that we need a project to redirect our focus and...well, let's just say that the timing and the objective seem to work. We get the first hundred million plus expenses. Anything after that is yours. For now, you'll put up five hundred thousand, as will Force 10. You see, we've been quite successful, and we get well compensated for our services. Besides, for some time now we've been discussing the idea of branching out, looking at projects that satisfy not only our financial needs but, more importantly, our sense of what's right. I don't want to come off like we're crusaders for the oppressed and downtrodden, although I could see a time when that might be a part of the Force 10 mandate."

The colonel leaned back in his chair. "You see, Marcus, before I left the Army, I secured a client for my new firm. In fact, at the moment, other than the U.S. military—and, I guess, now you—they are our only other client. During the first Gulf War, after Saddam invaded his and the Saudis' mutual neighbor Kuwait, the Saudi royal family immediately requested help from the United States. My team was sent in to provide protection for them, keep them safe, and come up with a contingency plan should the war spill over into Saudi Arabia. Since then, I've spent considerable time with the House of Saud and have developed strong, long-standing relationships with them. They spend an obscene amount of money on private security, so my new firm was a natural fit. Mostly we do glorified bodyguard work, such as helicoptering various members of the family around the country or accompanying them on one of their many yachts in the Gulf or the Med. All in all, it's a low-risk, well-paying gig."

He leaned forward, elbows on his desk, his tone suddenly dispassionate and austere. "Our timeline is tight. From today, you are a provisional member of the team. It would seem that you have a skill set absolutely vital to any chance of success. That said, you will take orders and follow them to the letter. The first time you put one of my people in danger, it ends on the spot. Now, if we're going to find the location and date when the *Takbir* is going to dock, we have to be in country in less than four weeks. So the remainder of your time here will be spent training, every hour of every day, if necessary. And if you think we were hard on you before, prepare yourself."

He pointed out the office door, indicating the team. "There's something going on here, and somehow, you've drawn me in and you've drawn them in. You managed to refocus us. Something we desperately needed. But, now, I want to impart a little advice to you. Where we're going, the people can't conceive of God and politics as separate. These men, the men we need to find, are committed to the point of death. For them, dying is a privilege and an honor."

The colonel got up and walked to the window to stare out across the bare yard of the compound. A few silent moments passed, then he turned back. "Also, they distrust everyone but those closest to them. It appears that you can speak and understand the languages, and that's wonderful, but speaking and understanding aren't the same as being accepted by the locals. We don't have the time to teach you customs, mannerisms, or nuance, so you'll have to improvise, something you seem a natural at. But listen to me, if you want to survive, if you want to go home to your boys, you stay RAW. You keep every sense, every nerve ending, tuned and alert, all the time. You feel it, taste it, smell it. You trust your instincts and the members of this team. You trust them with your life, and you protect their lives with your own, and just maybe we'll all walk out of this in one piece."

"Once we go into mission mode, everything changes, time schedules, training, diet, everything. You just need to adapt, and something tells me that will be the easiest part of the whole thing for you."

Leaving the colonel's office, Marcus mumbled to himself yet again, *what have you gotten yourself into?*

CHAPTER FORTY-ONE
March 11

The next three weeks passed in a blur. The daily scenarios in the barn took on a whole new character now that Marcus could understand every word blasted through the sound system. In his training with Pete, the blunt-bladed knives and rubber guns, were replaced with the real thing.

Every training exercise was amped up in both duration and intensity. And although every member of the team had a specialty, they each, including Doc, had skills with small arms, knives, and bare hands that were downright frightening.

Two weeks into the intensified training phase, Ham, Doc, and Jamie left the Force 10 compound for Saudi Arabia to set up logistics, establish a base of operations, and gather information about Adad that could help them determine when and where the *Takbir* was going to dock and take aboard the equipment for the God's Eye satellite interface. According to the colonel, the satellite's launch was the big buzz among the U.S. and Western European intelligence agencies.

Now that he was a quasi member, Marcus wondered a bit about the name "Force 10." He knew that it signified the number of team members, and he had heard some of the colonel's philosophy about ten being an ideal size—something to do with his fascination with college basketball, and his belief that with nine other dedicated, well-trained individuals running both offense and defense, there would not be a mission he couldn't accomplish.

But by Marcus's count there were eleven members: the eight in Australia, two on assignment in Saudi Arabia, and Reggie, the guy who died rescuing the kid in Iraq. When he asked, the colonel told him that J. T. didn't carry a numerical designation. If the colonel was running ops, J. T. functioned under the colonel's designation: Force 1. And if the colonel was tactical, J. T.'s designation was simply "Force."

***

Shortly after his arrival at the compound, Marcus had made arrangements with the colonel to talk with Bodie, Garrett, and Glen at least a couple of times a month. The boys never asked him what he was doing. It was as if Annie and Garrett's special connection somehow provided them with the assurance they needed that he was okay. Meanwhile, the intensity of his training and the revelation of his new talent kept him busy and focused. He had not suffered from overwhelming guilt about being away from them until the day he and the rest of the team left Australia.

The morning of their departure Marcus called his sons. They both sounded so *normal.* School was going well, and they both were playing point guard for their basketball teams.

"Hey, Dad, you okay?" Garrett said. "Mom said you've been working hard and basically getting your butt kicked." He could hear a hint of a chuckle in his son's voice.

"Yeah, I'm okay, pal, and yeah, I have been getting worked over pretty hard."

"That's good—we wouldn't want you to get soft, now, would we?" He paused. "You're getting ready to leave Australia, aren't you?"

Marcus had long since stopped being surprised by the things his youngest son seemed to know. Somehow, Annie was with them. She was watching over them, her light shining brighter than ever. From beyond this realm, she had assumed his role in the parenting process. It had always been his job to prepare the boys for the difficult challenges in their lives, but now she was doing it. He hoped he would be able to assume her role as easily when this whole ordeal finally came to an end.

He finished up with Garrett and talked to Bodie. "Well, Dad," he said, "time to move on to the next thing!"

"Yeah, bud. I guess your brother's been keeping you up to speed on his conversations with Mom?"

"Of course," he said, with an implied *duh, Dad* in his tone. "Now, you be careful. It would be a real bummer for you to have put in all this hard work and then fall to pieces now. Garrett and I are good. Mom's keeping us informed. You know, as weird as it is, I kind of like it. It's almost like she isn't really...gone."

"I know what you mean, buddy," Marcus said, unconsciously reaching for his missing Saint Christopher. "So listen, I'm not sure how often I'll be able to check in with you. But somehow, I'll figure it out."

"Seems like you always do." Was that pride he heard in Bodie's voice? "One last thing, Dad, make sure you survey the slope, spot the potential danger zones, plan your exit route, and if the whole mountain starts to come down, you get the hell out of there."

This was the last thing he and the boys always went through when they planned to ski a backcountry slope. He approached it with a kind of lighthearted, joking banter, but the boys knew that it was deadly serious.

"Will do, son, I have to go. You take care of your brother. I love you."

Marcus tapped the phone hard twice to his chest, put it back to his ear, and heard the same double thump on the other end. Then the line went dead.

***

In the early afternoon, the colonel, Liam, Sit, Peter, J. T., and Marcus drove to Alice Springs and boarded a brilliant white jet with a green emblem on the tail showing two crossed swords and a palm tree.

All Marcus knew was that they were flying to Saudi Arabia. Ham, Jamie, and the Doc had already been in country for three weeks, having rendezvoused with the two members of Force 10 he had yet to meet: Bronson Daughltry and Weathers Fisher.

As they boarded the private jet, the colonel motioned Marcus to the seat beside him. The jet's interior was well appointed with seats of plush, creamy leather. It seemed that Force 10 had some serious resources at its disposal.

As the jet soared into the clear sky the colonel turned to Marcus. "You remember when I told you to be careful what you wished for? Well, son, things are going to ramp up. If we're going to be successful, we'll know in short order. I want to warn you about getting your expectations up, though. But beyond that, Marcus, I'm curious what it is you want."

"You want the long or short answer?" The colonel's look told him he wanted *the* answer, however long or short it was.

"Adad. His life is the price for Annie's life; the rest is for my sons."

"The rest of what, Marcus?"

"All of it, Colonel. The man controls billions and billions of dollars—I intended to take it all."

With a tone of exasperation, the colonel asked, "And how in the name of heaven do you plan on accomplishing that?"

With a stupid grin, he replied, "I don't have the faintest idea, but I'll make you a promise. If it can't be accomplished within the scope of the mission, it won't happen."

"Why is it, Marcus, that every time you say that, I just know that more shit is going to take place than I ever planned for?"

For the next half hour, the colonel talked about his operational approach. From what Marcus could discern, he was man who refused to play by the rules if those rules put his people needlessly in harm's way. In Marcus's mind, this explained why the man had agreed to train him, and why he was now an active part of Marcus's crazy journey, because Marcus, too, refused to play by rules that made no sense.

At some point, he drifted off to sleep, and Annie came to him. It was the first time she had visited him. They were in their cabin in the High Sierra Mountains. It was night, and she was standing before the glass patio door, staring at the star-filled sky. She was wearing a loose pair of gray sweatpants and a baggy fleece top, her blond hair falling free over her shoulders.

"Hey, Marcus, long time no see," she said, turning around to have a look at him. Marcus tried to speak, but no words would come. "You can't speak to me, baby." She said a big smile spread across her face, dimpling her checks and crinkling her nose. "That's okay—you always talked too much anyway.

"Well, look at you. You did it. These people you're with—they're good, really good people. You need to know that what's coming up is going to be tough, tougher than anything you can possibly imagine. Do you trust me? *Really* trust me?"

He nodded.

"Okay, then, you're going to have to make some hard decisions, decisions that could get you killed. But that's why you're here, so I can tell you. Then they won't. You know how you're always going on about pain, about how you like it because it sharpens your awareness and reminds you that you're alive? Well, honey, you're about to get your wish. Now, listen close. When the time comes—you'll know what I'm talking about—you think of me. I will get you through it. Okay, I love you. Time for me to go."

She walked past him, and Marcus could feel the heat of her body, smell her. She passed by him silently, like an apparition. She walked out the back door, and he ran after her. She was walking up the stone steps to the patio. Turning, she blew him a kiss and said, "Listen for the singing, baby, the singing. Listen for it." Then everything went black.

CHAPTER FORTY-TWO
March 13

In early morning, they landed at King Khalid International Airport in Riyadh. Bronson Daughltry and Weathers Fisher, the other two members of the Force 10 team, were there to greet them. As Marcus descended the gangway steps from the jet, the baking heat and harsh, dry smell of the air seemed strikingly like that at the Australian compound.

He had been spending every second of his spare time educating himself about the Islamic peoples, customs, and religious beliefs of this part of the world. After his little adventure with Grandfather he had begun reading the Koran and at least a dozen other books that Ham had given him. It seemed that along with his affinity for language he also had an enhanced ability to comprehend and retain whatever he read or heard. Maybe Chaya's theory had some validity.

He knew that the Middle East had seen dramatic changes in the last half of the twentieth century. It was a land ravaged by wars, revolutions, military coups, and social turmoil. But even with the changes, partly due to the country's vast petroleum deposits, much remained of the old ways. Borders between countries were still viewed as relatively unimportant compared to the sovereignty of tribal allegiance.

Their entry into the country seemed to be handled without any formal customs inspection. They were ushered into an air-conditioned Hummer and driven to a hangar, where Doc met them. There were vehicles waiting, along with what seemed like a mountain of gear. Tables and chairs were set up in front of a huge map of the entire Middle East.

They took seats, and Weathers Fisher, one of the men Marcus knew only by sight, began a briefing. They had located one of Adad's chief minions, one Fazil Rafanjani. He was Afghan by birth and served as the conduit between Adad and his people.

The benefit of maintaining this conduit was one of the many things Marcus had learned from Ham. There was part of the Islamic mind-set here that no matter how powerful a man is, no matter how much wealth he might have or control, he must keep a direct line of communication, a direct link, to *his* people. This was accomplished through a go-to man who was part of the inner circle. It was the grand backup plan if everything should fall apart. When things went badly, one needed a place to go to ground—a place so remote, so hostile to one's enemies, that with the right allies, a man could just drop off the face of the earth.

The team spent the next several hours inventorying ammunition, rifles and pistols, smoke grenades, mortars, food, water, tents, fuel, medical supplies, clothing, and body armor. It looked as if they were planning a war.

The colonel was not present. Right after their briefing, he had left with an official-looking Saudi gentleman. When the colonel returned late in the afternoon, they had the Land Rover and truck loaded. Again they took their seats at the table in front of the map, and the colonel briefed them. The word in the desert was, a meeting was going down soon. Its subject and its exact location were unknown. Tonight they would drive to Jubail, on the Persian Gulf, some 386 kilometers northwest of Riyadh. From there, they would load their gear, trucks and all, on a military transport ship bound for Karachi, Pakistan. Marcus now understood what the colonel had been doing, pulling some very important strings.

"All right, people, listen up," the colonel said. "As of this moment, we are in full operational mode. J. T. and I have Ops. Marcus, you are here as an observer, a consultant, if you like that term better. Things are going to happen fast. We need to have our head in the game. Let's get the information we want and get out."

It was well after midnight when they arrived at Jubail. There was not enough time or light for Marcus to take in more than brief glimpses of his immediate surroundings. He did know that Jubail was the home of the Royal Saudi Navy base and that it contained the world's largest seawater desalination plant. Although these facts had no particular relation to each other, they were the only things that had stuck in his mind.

A guard waved them through the gate at the port entrance to the Naval Base, and they drove the vehicles up a large gangway and into the hold of a ship. The two days it would take to cover the nine hundred nautical miles gave the team time to plan the route from Karachi to Peshawar, in the foothills of the Pakistani Hindu Kush.

CHAPTER FORTY-THREE
Aboard the Takbir, somewhere in the Arabian Sea

"Fazil, you and I have been over this. You must to go to Afghanistan and arrange to meet up with the American." Adad said, in a calm, even tone, as he glanced up from his desk.

"So I am to assume that this American is a worthy recruit?" Fazil asked with distain.

Pushing back in his chair and removing his reading glasses, Adad said, "Did not you tell me to trust you in this matter? I did not say you were to welcome him into our circle, but our people must know that we are honorable, and that our American brothers, at least on the face, are respected for the sacrifices they have made. We are going to need the support of every Muslim as we strive to put in place a new world order."

Rising, Adad strode to the sofa and sat. With his hand Adad indicated he wished Fazil to take a seat in the chair opposite him.

"This is the most delicate part of our plan. You know as well as I that the American *jihadists* are much talked about by our people. They have gained an almost legendary status for the success of their attack. We must give this American his due."

"You do not know if it is the one called Abbas that I am supposed to meet?" Fazil asked.

"I am sorry to say, no. I have not had contact with him or his father, since I made arrangements for the women, a few days before the fires began. Although in our last communiqué the elder Faradi had an alternate plan if Abbas was unable to make his way out of America."

"I still do not like this idea of bringing an American into our fold. But you are correct that we must save face with our people and that means honoring our word."

"Thank you, Fazil," Adad said, rising from his seat. Embracing Fazil he said, "Now be safe my brother and I will you see you in Istanbul."

As Fazil took his leave, Adad walked through his palatial office that was part of the nearly four thousand square feet, executive suite. Although he spent much of his time while aboard the Takbir, in his smaller, though no less opulent, office behind the command bridge, this was his favorite space on the ship. With every amenity a person could want, he was certain that he could remain in these rooms, for months if required. And now that the New Islamic Dawn was about to have at its disposal the means, to not only unite the Islamic nations of the earth, but to place this new alliance at the very top of the world most influential power brokers, he might well be confined to the *Takbir* for some time.

CHAPTER FORTY-FOUR
March 14

The transport ship lacked the relative comfort of the Australia compound, but the team's mood was relaxed and easy. Marcus could tell that this was well within their comfort zone, and the division of labor was natural and smooth. There was little need for words, with each member organized and on task, planning rendezvous coordinates, rechecking supplies, while he just hung around like a fifth wheel.

"Marcus." The colonel waved him over to a table set up against a bulkhead. A laminated map of Pakistan and Afghanistan had been taped to the metal wall.

"Our information puts the meeting somewhere in this area." He drew a circle in red around Peshawar, over eleven hundred kilometers north of Karachi. "This should be right up your alley, Marcus—we're heading into the mountains. This is where the really bad guys like to hide out, mainly because of the rugged, harsh terrain but also because of the equally rugged people who call this home."

Moving his finger along the map, he continued, "This area, with its lush fields and glacier-fed streams, makes for a self-sustaining way of life. Osama spent a lot of time here—hell, he might still *be* alive if he'd just stayed here."

The colonel shifted his attention from the map back to Marcus. "Now, from the information you supplied about the terrorist cell in the U.S., J. T. has developed two legends that will withstand a fair degree of scrutiny. The plan is, once we've established the location and time of the meeting, these legends will be our way in. We're working on the assumption that the information Ricky gave you about being promised a position in Adad's organization was true. Men who show that kind of initiative and self-motivation are highly valued. Combine that with the fact that he was a U.S. citizen, and he or someone just like him would be a hell of an asset. The discovery of the terrorist cell was always part of the bigger plan. Make no mistake, they *want* the American people to know there are enemies living among them. That Ricky and his parents might not survive was always a strong possibility."

Stepping away from the map, he leaned, palms down, on the table, his eyes hard and intense. "What role you have to play in this, to be honest, I don't know yet. But for now, you listen and learn. When the time comes for you to be involved, you'll make subtle adjustments. Blending in is all about slight modifications. Improvise within yourself. The goal is to be an unremarkable face that leaves no impression." The colonel tilted his head the way an inquisitive dog might, and looked at Marcus. "Have you taken a hard look at yourself lately, Marcus?"

He waved, and Doc came over. She placed a picture of Osama bin Laden in front of him. It was a head shot: his thin, gaunt face with its sharp lines, his head wrapped in white cotton swathes, the grizzled gray-black beard and dark, glowering eyes. Then she put a mirror on the table. What Marcus saw was unbelievable. But for the eye color, if he were to wear the right clothes, they could be brothers. He had lost a lot of weight, and although he thought he looked like a haggard, half-starved mountain man, the question now was, from what mountains?

Over the next few days, Marcus continued to educate himself on the lands and peoples they would be encountering. That first night in the hold of the ship, while sitting on his cot, he felt the same gnawing anxiety he had that day when he saw Annie through the binoculars, with the three terrorists, in the bottom of Buck Creek Canyon.

He was lost in thought when the sound of someone clearing his throat startled him. Marcus looked up, reeling his mind in from a distant place. Before him were the two members of the team that he had met only informally. Both appeared to be in their mid-thirties. One was tall and broad-shouldered with wavy sun-bleached hair, giving Marcus the impression of a rough and ready Southern California surfer. The other was built like a bulldog, short and stout, with tight-cropped black hair and a face that conveyed a low tolerance for bullshit.

"I'm Bronson Daughltry, and this here's Weathers Fisher," the tall one said.

Marcus stood up and stuck out his hand. "Good to meet you. I'd like to say I've heard a lot about you, but—"

"Yeah, the colonel and the team can be pretty tight-lipped, especially about personal info," said Weathers.

As they each pulled up a chair, Marcus sat back down on the cot.

"Well, since we're going to be working together, we thought we should get acquainted. Heard you did a passable job of impersonating someone from my home state," Bronson said, grinning. "Well, I'm the team's resident pilot, although a few of the others can fly, too. And my good friend here"—Bronson gave Weathers a conspiratorial look—"he's in charge of anything to do with the water. You see, the royal family spends most of their time either flying from one point to another or cruising around on one of their many yachts, so unless there's something special goin' on, we spend the lion's share of the time with them."

Marcus learned that both Bronson and Weathers, like many on the team, came from military families, and, like everyone else, were unmarried. Bronson was a Navy pilot, and Weathers was a Navy SEAL. They discussed their talents matter-of-factly. Bronson could fly anything from a Piper Cub to a Blackhawk, to the most sophisticated fighter jet to the largest commercial airliner, and Weathers could pilot anything from a rowboat to an aircraft carrier.

"Well, we'd best hit the rack," Weathers said, getting up.

Then Bronson said, "I would've given my left nut to see you take down Liam. He must have gotten quite the ego check when you put that knife to his throat."

"And taking Jamie down—I'd have given your *other* nut to see that." Weathers said, grinning. "Seems like you've made quite the impression on the boys—and, of course, Doc."

As they walked off, Marcus wondered about Chaya Lanyer. What would make a smart, talented, beautiful woman throw in with a bunch like this?

CHAPTER FORTY-FIVE
March 21

They arrived at the port of Karachi, on the coast of the Arabian Sea, in the evening and offloaded under the cover of darkness. Ham and Jamie were already at the rendezvous point near Peshawar. To cover the distance from Karachi would take four days over rough roads. They traveled in daylight only, stopping at small villages. Marcus was amazed at how many people spoke English and how many knew, or knew of, the members of Force 10. In this way, they refueled, found lodging, and gathered intelligence. It also provided Marcus the opportunity to observe some of the customs and habits of these people and test out his newfound language skills.

* * *

They plodded north, through the Sulaiman range. It was a rugged, mountainous land, and not with just any old mountains—these were the highest, most spectacular peaks anywhere on earth. And the people of these mountains also had a weathered toughness to them. Almost no one was fat, and they all had a look of intense, hawk like wariness in their dark eyes, and a wild, animal-like tautness in their walk and bearing. Their manner was not something one learned; it was something born into and lived. With his unkept beard, lean, hard body, and his sun-weathered, Spanish-Italian complexion, Marcus still didn't realize how closely he resembled these people in his look and movements.

Marcus had worried that he would be uncomfortable, that he would appear as someone contrived, someone trying to be something he was not. But he needn't have worried. He naturally fell into conversation, and as Annie was constantly reminding him, he was listening, really listening.

In the early evening of the third day, they arrived in Nowshera, forty-four kilometers east of Peshawar. From his time with Ham, Marcus knew that Nowshera sat on the Iranian Plateau along the Kabul River and was home to the Pakistani Army's School of Artillery. Ham had also impressed on him that the area's many Pashtun tribes and clans were almost never politically united. In this part of Pakistan, the border with Afghanistan was a mere artifice and of no importance to anyone. Political demarcations came and went, and through it all, these people continued to move over and through these lands just as they had for thousands of years.

They pulled the vehicles through an iron gate and into a courtyard, where Ham and Jamie met them. Marcus was learning very quickly what "operational mode" meant. There were no greetings. They left the trucks and entered the simple concrete-walled dwelling. A detailed map of the Khyber Pass area and the bordering lands of Afghanistan was taped to the wall.

Ham was on the advance team because of his knowledge and language skills, and Jamie for his superb tracking ability. They had spent weeks in the lower Hindu Kush range, and they confirmed that Fazil Rafanjani was in country and that something was going down.

Ham had been spreading the word that an Iranian-American, one of the warriors of the attack on the United States, was here to meet with Fazil. Something had happened to Ricky and his parents, and he was following the contingency plan. To the FBI's credit, no information had been leaked about the death of the Drs. Faradi, and as for Ricky, no one would likely ever find him.

The meeting date and location were still unknown, but it was going down soon. That night, Ham and Jamie left, and everyone else would be leaving in the morning for Aradu, on the Pakistani-Afghan border. If Marcus had thought he was going to get some time to acclimatize to his new surroundings, it was only because he hadn't fully understood "operational mode."

CHAPTER FORTY-SIX
March 22

In the predawn darkness the team dressed in light wool salwar kameez—long, loose-fitting tunics and baggy pants, in colors ranging from drab gray to dark brown. They also wore kaffiyeh-style headdresses, which could be used to hide the face, with well-worn leather lace-up boots to complete their native attire.

They were en route to the barren mountainous region of Arandu, on the Afghan border. Ham explained to Marcus that this was a land riddled with hidden canyons and caves, which had always made it a favorite hiding place for anyone bent on not being found. But most importantly, this was not a land where Westerners could move without drawing instant notice.

Marcus was surprised at how many small villages they drove through—one every ten kilometers or so. To spread out the language skills, he drove the Land Rover with the two young men he had met at Nowshera, and Ham drove the big supply truck with the other eight Force 10 members and the supplies all loaded into the back. It was about a hundred and sixty kilometers, but the terrain and road conditions made it a six-hour journey.

As he drove, Marcus pondered how he would handle his role in what, even to him, was beginning to seem a bit insane. On the day the colonel told him the team would take on his project, Marcus had given him all the information he had taken from Dr. Faradi on the terrorist cell. J. T. had worked with the material and developed two legends, one for Ham and the other for Marcus. He now had a richly detailed past, and he had better know it cold.

They stopped frequently and were stopped several times by armed men wanting to know their destination and the purpose of their travel. Marcus had spent some time with Ham going over their cover story: they were carrying supplies to an important man, Fazil Rafanjani; and, more importantly, Ham was one of the men responsible for the attack on the United States.

All the team members could speak some Urdu, well enough to be understood, and seemed to have a reasonable idea of what was being said. The strange part was the virtually unanimous approval and awe that everyone they met had for the attack on America. Ham's heroic status was instantaneous. What Marcus found incongruous was that Force 10 also seemed to have allies almost everywhere they went.

For cover, Ham was Farid Tehrani, born in the States to parents who were among the first *Petit Amérique* couples to immigrate with the Faradis in the early 1980s. When he was fourteen, both his parents were killed in a tragic car wreck, and members of the Muslim community in Rochester, New York, raised him. He had met Ricky only once, but they had made a connection. They were about the same age, very well educated, and committed to the proliferation of radical fundamentalist Islam. Each had been chosen to organize teams to plant the fire-starting devices. And each was chosen to lead a team. Ricky led a team in the West, and Farid, Frank, as he was known in the States, in the Northeast. It had been in the contingency plan established by Abdurrahim Faradi and Ricky that if something should happen, Frank was to take Ricky's place as part of Adad's organization. The fact that Frank had been arrested by the FBI and was currently being held in Gitmo, in complete secrecy, meant they just might pull this off.

The cover fit well with Ham's language skills. He had no problem speaking in a manner that implied that Arabic, Urdu, and Farsi were all secondary languages to English—indeed, this would be assumed.

Marcus, on the other hand, came off as a native speaker, Frank's much older distant cousin, Nouri Ganji. Although he was born in Iran, he had lived all his adult life in Afghanistan, in the foothills of the Hindu Kush. He was a simple farmer, raising goats and yaks. His wife, son, and daughter had been killed in a U.S. air raid on Kabul in 2001. From then on, he had been living in the Tora Bora Mountains near the Pakistani border. That no one knew him, the colonel and Ham had assured him, was not that unusual. Simple, poor, and uneducated, he had been living the quiet, unnoticed life of a lonely, dispirited man. The whole thing seemed too simple to be believable, but then, who was Marcus to question what people would believe?

As they neared Arandu, at about four thousand feet on the eastern slope of the Karakorams, Marcus was awe struck. He thought of himself as used to rugged mountains, but he knew these twenty-thousand-foot monsters were something altogether different. They passed through Arandu and took a dirt road northwest to a camp some ten kilometers up in the mountains.

Ham drove in first and greeted two men with AK-47s slung over their shoulders. It had never occurred to Marcus that Force 10 could have allies in a place like this, providing advance setup and security and auxiliary support during its covert operations. But they kept magically showing up.

The camp consisted of three large wall tents, rather like those Marcus had used on extended hunting trips back home. Though the accommodations seemed fine, he couldn't escape the feeling that they would not be here long.

CHAPTER FORTY-SEVEN
March 25

For three days, Ham, Jamie, and Marcus would set out at the crack of dawn. They never traveled the same path twice, each day setting off in a different direction as they wound along the trails between villages scattered among the cave-and-canyon-riddled foothills. The objective was to seek out, as inconspicuously as possible, any information about the meeting with Fazil. Whenever conversation was required, Ham or Marcus did the talking. Like in all small communities, important people and events were topics of conversation. Marcus's newfound language skills were key, especially his ability to match dialects. But in keeping with his goat-farmer cover, he hid his ability by stumbling through phrases, using the wrong tense in conversation, and feigning incomprehension whenever someone spoke fast or didn't enunciate clearly.

On the afternoon of their third day, things went to hell. They were crossing a narrow ridge between two small villages when Jamie slipped on the loose scree and slid fifty yards down the slope, toward a group of armed men.

Alerted by the noise of the sloughing rock and rising dust, five men were on him an instant later, guns at the ready. Marcus knew that as soon as they removed his headscarf, and saw his red hair, or tried to speak to him, they would know that he didn't belong. He was about to scramble down the slope after him, but Ham restrained him.

"Come on, Marcus," he said. "We can't help him right now. We need to get back to camp and organize an extraction." He seemed oddly detached and thoroughly unperturbed about the whole thing.

An hour later, they were back in camp, with everyone assembled in the mess tent. A detailed topo map was hanging on the sidewall. The colonel and Ham led the briefing.

"Okay, people, it was only a matter of when, not if, and the when is now. We can assume they'll transport Jamie to a nearby village or camp. The problem is, these mountains are a maze of hidden canyons and caves. J. T., are you up?"

"Just a few seconds, Colonel," J. T. replied from the folding card table where he sat hunkered over a laptop.

Marcus had no idea what the colonel was talking about.

"Got him," J. T. called out.

On J. T.'s computer screen was a blinking red dot, labeled with a small "F8." The confusion on Marcus's face must have been obvious. Doc walked over to him and held up a bottle of small white pills. They looked like the allergy pills he had been taking every day for weeks.

"Inside is a tiny ceramic chip, undetectable by even the most sophisticated body scanners. The downside is, you pass them through your body every day. The chip is so small—we're talking nanotechnology here—that even if someone were to crush the pill, all they would do is crush the transmitter. The design is courtesy of our friend over there." She nodded toward J. T. "You've been taking them every day since you arrived at Force 10."

Marcus had been dutifully taking various pills at Doc's suggestion—vitamins and other supplements to ensure that he stayed healthy. So it made more sense now, how the colonel always seemed to know where he was.

"They send out a burst every ten seconds, as long as they stay in the system and as long as you don't die, and even then they'll transmit for a good ten or fifteen minutes, until the body completely shuts down. The problem is range. J. T. has them tapped into an NSA communications satellite, unbeknownst to them, but when we're in mountainous terrain or have thick cloud cover, the range can be iffy."

"Looks like they've stopped, about twenty clicks from our position," J. T said.

The colonel pinpointed the location on the map. It was in a small canyon, with steep rock walls on three sides

"Okay, people, let's gear up. J. T., set up a secure link so the team can talk text."

"Roger that, Colonel, but we're going to have some dead zones."

"Just get it set up. Sit, take Betty. I need you to find a spot up here on this ridge." The colonel drew a black line on the map. "Make sure your position gives a clear view of the enemy camp and that you're in constant contact with J. T."

"Sit, Ham, Liam, Pete, and Marcus, Weathers will drop you here." He scrawled a black X. "This'll put you about five clicks out. Gotta move fast—we all know what these boys are doing to Jamie."

"Doc, get ready. Bronson, give her a hand and then make sure that bird will fly if we need it."

No one spoke; they just began moving. Sit handed out gear. Now Marcus understood all the barn and play yard time. It was less about the actual exercise than about *getting ready* for the exercise. There wasn't a single wasted motion.

As Marcus was putting on his body armor, the colonel came up to him. "Here you go, son. Time to see just how good a job we did." He handed him his pack. "There are some things in there you might need. Okay, time to go."

Marcus thought he had gotten past all the cryptic innuendo—what was it that he still wasn't getting?

As they left the tent, the sun was dropping behind the mountain, and the sharp chill of night was descending quickly. He noticed Bronson pulling a big camo tarp off what he had assumed to be a huge pile of firewood fifty yards behind the tents.

Ham said, "It's an old—and I mean way old—Russian helicopter, left over from the Afghan-Soviet war. Bronson found it and got it running, sort of. At least he got it here. Don't worry, though," Ham added with a grin, "he wouldn't put us in anything he thought was unsafe."

Sit, Ham, Liam, Peter, Weathers, and Marcus loaded into the Rover and took off. A half hour later they were at their drop-off point. Sit handed him what looked like some sort of PDA.

"This is our comm device." He touched the screen with his finger, and it came to life with a faint red glow. Pulling out a small stylus from the side of the device, he held it up and said, "You just write on it, that's it. Whatever you write will be transmitted to J. T.'s and our screens, provided we have a signal. Each is programmed with a designation number, so we know who's sending. Your designation is F-Ten. The boys know the signs to get a message to me if we don't have a signal. I'll have eyes on you the whole time. Soon as you guys make your move, I'll call for evac and move to your location."

Sit laid a huge hand on Marcus's shoulder, and their eyes met. "You make sure and bring our boy home!" Then he shouldered the Dragunov sniper rifle and headed up the east slope to his observation spot. The others made their way around the right side of the canyon, staying tight to the slope. They were just above and right of the camp were Jamie was being held when they heard voices. Pete held his right fist up, and everyone stopped.

"He will break," a voice said in Pashto. "It is the American pigs who sent him. Rahim will make him talk, and then he will die."

Marcus could tell just by looking that Ham had gotten at least most of what was said. They moved back about a hundred yards so they could talk. Pete and Liam looked from Ham to Marcus.

Marcus took off his pack. Inside was his salwar kameez, the local Pashtun garb. Did the colonel know something he didn't? He put them on over his gear and wrapped his head. No one questioned him. "Okay," he whispered, "you guys need to move up to our point of insertion. I'm going to figure out how many bad guys we have. Just wait there for me."

As Marcus was preparing to skirt around the camp toward the voices, Pete handed him a coil of thin wire cable with a strong plastic T-grip at either end. The garrote was one of the many weapons he had trained with, although, unlike with knives and guns, it was impossible to train effectively with something designed to cut a man's throat in one clean, fast motion.

He made his way toward the voices. There were two men standing side by side, sharing a cigarette. In a moment they separated, one going right, the other left. Marcus followed the one going left. He walked for a few minutes, then stopped to take something from his woolen jacket. Marcus approached him, moving slowly, careful not to kick up a rock or step on a twig. Holding the T-grips loosely, he slunk up from behind, and whipped the wire over, and pulled tight. The taut wire sliced through skin and tracheal cartilage like a hot knife through butter. The only sound was a low, deep gurgle as warm blood spilled over Marcus's hands.

Moments later, he dragged the lifeless body behind a boulder. Then, circling left, he came around the back of the crude stone hut where they were holding Jamie

Four men were standing guard outside, two right, two left, about thirty yards from the hut. Out front were two battered old Russian jeep-style quarter-ton trucks. Then he heard the scream and saw a flickering light coming from one of the hut's unglazed window holes. Then, in a thick Aussie accent, "'Zat all the juice you camel shaggers got? I've had more of a shock from a carpet on a dry day." The flickering light again, and this time the scream was primal and deep. Then came the sound of a fist on flesh, but no taunting reply.

Quietly working his way back toward the team, Marcus had reached the point where he had seen the other man, when he heard the splash of running water. The guy was relieving himself, and the sound of his piss hitting the rocky ground masked Marcus's approach. As the garrote bit into his throat, the pissing stopped, before resuming a few seconds later as a mere trickle.

As Marcus reached the rise where the team was waiting, Ham held a finger to his lips, calling for silence. They all looked at the blood on Marcus's hands and on the front of his salwar kameez. They must have heard Jamie's screams, but it seemed to make no visible impression on them.

Marcus held up two fingers, then moved his hand across his throat. With a stick, he drew a square in the dirt. Inside the square, he scratched "F8," then drew two X's to the right and two to the left. He pointed to Ham and indicated the right side, then pointed to Pete and the left X's. Just then Sit approached. Marcus found it eerie how a man that size could move without a sound.

He nodded to Sit, then held five fingers up to Ham and Pete, signifying five minutes. Then he pointed his finger at his chest and stabbed at the center of the hut scratched in the dirt. Ham and Pete nodded and left. Marcus motioned for Sit and Liam to follow him back a short distance so they could speak.

He whispered to Sit, "You and Betty cover me."

The big man nodded.

"Okay, Liam, when you see me come out of that hut, pop the smoke."

Dressed like a poor Pashtun, Marcus approached the structure as the flickering continued from the window openings. He pulled out a silenced HK 9 mm, then yelled out in Pashto, as if he were one of the now dead guards, "Rahim! Men coming!" "Rahim!" he yelled again as he burst through the door.

In the dimly lit stone shack, he quickly spotted three men, two standing and a third rising from a stool. In the space of perhaps two seconds, he fired three shots, and all three men fell to the floor.

Marcus was not prepared for what he saw next. Jamie was strapped naked to a rickety wooden chair that was secured in place by what appeared to be sandbags draped over the bottom braces. His head was hanging against his chest, his face a bloody, battered mess. His feet were in a galvanized tub of pinkish-brown water. There were alligator clips hooked to his scrotum and his nipples. The clips were

175

attached to wires that ran to a wooden crate, where a dial control was wired to several car batteries.

Marcus felt suddenly sick. What had he gotten this boy into? He felt for his pulse—weak, but there. He unhooked the alligator clips and lifted Jamie's feet out of the bucket of bloody water. Without the ropes holding him to the chair, Jamie slumped forward, almost falling off the chair. Marcus knelt in front of him.

"Jamie, you hear me? Come on, kid, stay with me." Pulling a bottle of water from his pack, Marcus gently tilted his head back and poured a trickle between his split and cracked lips. "Come on, kid, come back to me."

Jamie's eyes were almost swollen shut, but he forced them open into tiny slits.

"We're leaving—you ready?" His eyes started to roll back up into his head, and Marcus slapped his face hard. Through gritted teeth, he said, "Now, listen up, kid, you aren't dying, not here, not today!" Detecting a faint mumble, he pressed his lips to Jamie's ear. "Do you hear me? Say the words, boy!"

"Yes...s-s-sir...."

"All right, then!" Squatting down with his back to him, Marcus got Jamie's arms draped over his left shoulder, then used his right arm to get his legs over the other shoulder and hoisted him. Staggering under the weight, he walked outside, into a cloud of beautiful white smoke.

Headlights were coming up the rough road. Marcus knew it wasn't the team. Then he heard the loud crack from Betty, and before the echoes died away in the canyon, the approaching headlights had stopped their forward progress.

In moments, Jamie was being lifted from his back, and Marcus heard the welcome *whop-whop* of an approaching helicopter.

While Bronson transported Jamie and Marcus back to the camp, the rest of the team stayed on site to do what the colonel called "cleanup"—Marcus assumed it was that *we were never here* thing.

Doc was ready for Jamie with a triage area already set up in the mess tent. She worked quickly and efficiently, checking the airway and starting an IV of fluid, antibiotics, and morphine.

Marcus just stood there in shock. He had not felt like this since the day he witnessed Annie's murder. There was something about this young man that reminded him of what his sons might be like in not so many more years.

As Doc was attending to Jamie, he started coming around. He groped and found Marcus's hand and tried to speak. Marcus put his ear close and heard, in a feeble whisper, "Sir, thank you." Jamie's eyes were now almost completely swollen shut. "Sir, I have...your back." And he was out.

Still holding Jamie's hand and fighting back tears, Marcus looked down at his battered and bloody teammate and said, "I know, kid, I know."

The team got back two hours later. Doc had Jamie stable, and she assured Marcus he was going to be all right.

They were all seated around the mess table. There was no reassuring required, no visible anger or regret.

"Let's debrief," said the colonel. He looked at Sit.

"Well, Colonel, Marcus assumed tactical command and laid out a concise plan. He took the initiative and executed per the plan. From an analytic standpoint, it was the best possible solution, and all the players had their abilities put to highest and best use." There was not a trace of the earlier shuck-and-jive in his voice.

The colonel said, "Marcus, I've been waiting for this to happen. I don't mean Jamie getting captured, but waiting for a situation to present itself that would put you in a decision-making position. Part of the responsibility is in the execution, but more importantly, it's in dealing with the unknown, the unexpected, and any aftermath. Every member of this team, at one time or another has been a prisoner, been beaten or tortured, or worse." Marcus noticed Doc stiffen slightly.

"In what we do, there is no perfect plan. All we have is the ability to keep our head, make a plan, and act. Right now we have a bigger problem. When Jamie came in, he told me the meeting is set for three days from today. That boy is a real piss-cutter. He told his interrogators he was here hunting one of the men responsible for the terrorist attack on the U.S.—an Iranian-American who was in country to meet with Fazil—Adad al-Mohmoud's go-to guy. He knew damn well that a story like that was going to bring some serious punishment. The meet is set for a location near Samanaknesha, on the Afghan side of the border. It's at least eighty kilometers north, over rough country. But I think we can assume they'll be expecting you." He looked at Ham, then Marcus.

"We move out at first light. Doc and Bronson will stay here with Jamie. The rest of us are going to relocate. I want to be ready for a speedy exit from Osamaland. Once we've obtained the information, we are out of here. Now, Marcus, you and Ham are going in alone. We'll have Sit in a long-range position to provide cover if necessary. Liam, Pete and Weathers will be support if we need extraction. We have no idea what to expect, so let's expect everything. J. T. and I will run Ops on the move. This will complicate things a bit, but you've all been in this situation plenty. So let's get some rest. It'll be a few days before any of us get our next good night's sleep."

Everyone made their way to the bunk tent, but Marcus couldn't bring himself to leave Jamie. He sat next to his cot, listening to his breathing. Other than the damage to his face, he looked peaceful, thanks to the morphine.

"Marcus, you need to get some rest," Doc said, putting a hand on his shoulder. "The next few days are going to be tough."

"I'm going to sleep right here tonight," he said. "There's an extra cot; I'll be fine. Besides, I can keep you company. I hate being responsible for almost getting this boy killed."

She grabbed him by the shoulders and turned him to face her. Her eyes were a smoky emerald against her olive skin. "You listen to me, Marcus. No one in this group is a boy, no matter what their age. Everyone here is packing around their own personal pain, and as much as you have, they have more, trust me. Now, for whatever reason, you've managed to strike a chord with every member of this team. So you keep your head in the game. This is no time to feel sorry for yourself or anybody else. We're now two men down, and it appears that you need to step in. So step in."

"Up," Marcus said. "It's 'step up.'"

"Up, in—whatever." She handed him a blanket. "Now, sleep."

CHAPTER FORTY-EIGHT
March 28

Marcus woke to the smell of coffee. He dressed, and the team did an equipment check. He was impressed by how routine it all seemed, the sorting of rifles, pistols, ammunition, explosives, and all the gear required for making armed camp in the wilderness. Everything was loaded in the Rover, and they prepared to leave.

As they drove in silence along the rutted, rock-strewn road to Samanaknesha, Marcus realized that he had not once had the impression that anyone on Force 10 entertained the slightest doubt about their success.

The advance team had already scouted out the area and selected the location for their next base camp. While J.T. got his gear organized, the team assembled for another briefing.

Ham took the lead, and much of what he said was directed at Marcus. "There's this thing in Islam emphasizing hospitality. It's very bad form to turn a stranger away."

"So what, Ham—you and I are just going to walk right up and knock on the door?" Marcus said.

"Yeah, pretty much. They already know we're here—word travels fast among these people. I'm sure our cover will hold. But what happens once we get in is anybody's guess. Now, Marcus, remember about proper greetings. You're the native; it'll be crucial that you follow protocol. You're low on the food chain, just a simple, uneducated man. Don't worry about the way you look—the fact is, you look more like them than I do. But that fits, too. I'm an American, an idealistic zealot. These people don't quite understand me, but on some level they respect me. I would expect that we'll be tested, subtle things, so think about your responses. Your language skills are helpful, but they could bite us, too, so don't just start spouting off. They'll expect you to be nervous and basically subservient. You're kissing my ass to some degree." Ham shrugged his shoulders as if to say, *you're the one who asked for this.*

"Okay, so we know the meeting's in two days," he continued. "All we need to do is find out where. Marcus, you and I are out of here in about thirty minutes. We're going to start walking northeast. The plan is that we won't be returning to this camp. We'll find lodging among the locals. We keep moving until we find or are directed to where we need to be. This is some of the most rugged terrain in the region, full of possible locations for a clandestine meeting. This will give you some time to dial in your approach, interact with some of the locals. Again, I want to remind you of the way you greet people—it's very important and absolutely expected."

Marcus's understanding was that these types of meetings didn't hinge so much on a specified time as on when everyone arrived. It wasn't as if one could just drive up or fly in. The players all had to be assembled, many coming a long distance over difficult terrain. Ham kept insisting that thanks to Jamie, they were a part of the meeting, and the most important items wouldn't be discussed until they arrived.

***

For two days, Ham and Marcus combed the hidden canyons under gray skies that hinted at the coming monsoon season. They increased their search parameters in an ever-widening arc. Marcus was surprised at how many of the people they met knew who Fazil Rafanjani was. If their information was correct, the meeting window was open.

As Ham had promised, they found lodging. In fact, he was the most famous man anyone around here had ever met, and they welcomed him with open arms. They shared the people's meager supplies of food, drank strong tea, and smoked the hookah.

In what became a well-established routine, they would walk into a small village, Marcus would ask the questions, and Ham would listen. The pecking order was clearly evident to the people they encountered. Ham was dressed in clothing of a visibly much higher quality than his, and Marcus always followed behind him and kept his head bowed, eyes averted from his. He prepared their food, boiled the water for their tea, and never ate until Ham had been served. They kept up the pretense even when alone, because, as Ham was so fond of reminding him, the hills had eyes and ears.

The villages they encountered were all haphazard collections of rough concrete or stone hovels, many of them built mainly of rubble, with crude wooden doors and unglazed, wood-shuttered windows. Every village had a gathering area, where men sat on the ground near a small stone fire pit with its ever-present kettle of hot water. It was here that they began their inquiries.

First Ham would motion for him to approach and, in hushed whispers, would pretend to give him instructions. Then Marcus would approach the villagers, always with the same greeting: "*Assalamu Alaikum,*" peace be to you. Then came the reply, "*Wa Alaikum assalam wa rahmatu Allah,*" and to you peace, together with God's mercy.

Ham had pounded into him that when two strangers used this greeting, they immediately established common ground even if they did not speak the same language. As he was preparing him for this leg of the journey, he frequently quoted the Koran. Regarding greetings, he had a favorite: *When a greeting is offered you, answer it with an even better greeting or with its like. God keeps count of all things.*

The whole greeting thing was so much more than the simple "Hey, how's it going?" that passed for a salutation in the West. These greetings imparted something much deeper. They conveyed a sense of common purpose and belief that instantly obligated one man to another. And this approach never failed them. Time after time, they were greeted and then invited to eat a meal or share tea.

Marcus had memorized his cover, down to his linage going back five generations. Often someone would say, "Ah, yes, I remember your grandfather. He was a true and faithful man of God, may his spirit and soul reside in peace." This, too, was a common subject in conversation. It was never "My name is...." Rather, it was "I am the son of...son of..., son of...."

In the afternoon of the second day, they approached a group of men smoking strong tobacco through a hookah and drinking tea with goat's milk. Ham and Marcus went through their usual dog-and-pony show. Marcus made his greeting and received a greeting in kind. Then one of the older men in the group stood.

Marcus was having some difficulty determining people's age. The harsh living conditions, constant exposure to the elements, and limited diet meant that a man who looked to be in his mid-fifties might well be in his early thirties. Everyone had bad teeth, and bathing was a rare event.

Ham and he were prepared, though. Neither had bathed in over a week, and Doc had outfitted Marcus with a bridge that gave his teeth a ragged, broken appearance. There had been some discussion about knocking a couple of his teeth out for authenticity, but luckily for him, it was decided not to take his imposture to such extremes. Ham, of course, had perfect, straight teeth—as an American, he was supposed to.

The thin, gaunt old man turned to Ham and spoke to him in guttural, uneducated Pashto. Ham turned to Marcus, indicating that he did not quite understand, his cue to act as interpreter. The gist of the conversation was that he had been waiting for them. In fact, there were men waiting at several villages in the area for the American *jihadist* hero. There seemed a certain reverence toward Ham in their discussion. He was one of the chosen of Allah who had brought the mighty American Satan to its knees. Everything was rhetoric, and Marcus had no problem dishing it out. It just rolled off his tongue with impassioned vigor, all of it merely the means to an end.

Their little welcoming committee had been instructed to lead them to a location some ten kilometers away. Finishing their tea, they left. Just at dark, they came to a small house nestled at the base of a canyon, beside a small creek bed.

There was no sign of vehicles of any kind. At the door, they were greeted by a huge man with a great, unruly beard that hung to his collarbone. They exchanged greetings and bade farewell to their guides.

Keeping his gaze on the ground in front of him, Marcus followed Ham in. The house was lit with kerosene lamps that gave off an oily smell that you could actually taste. Greetings were again exchanged as they approached four men who were seated on rugs around a small stone fireplace. One of the men motioned for Marcus to sit across the room near the far wall. He had never felt discriminated against until that day. He didn't mind it a bit, though, for it meant that so far, their ruse was working.

Introductions were made. Ham, or Farid, was on center stage. A middle-aged man with a tall turban, clean white robe, and well-groomed salt-and-pepper beard and fashionable wire-rimmed glasses introduced himself as Fazil Rafanjani. He was cut of very different cloth than the other three men—cleaner, more educated, and clearly more important. In fact, the only other person in the room who seemed his peer was Ham.

They spoke in Arabic at first but quickly switched to English. Marcus was sure it was so no one else in the room could understand what they were saying. Fazil spoke in precise English, with an accent indicating some education in the UK. In questioning Ham about the attack on the United States, he was eager, animated. He wanted to know everything: How had they pulled it off? Were the fires not amazing? What was it like to see the fear and panic first hand? And the parasite— what was it like to see hundreds of thousands of infidels fall violently ill?

Marcus had to give it to Ham. He never missed a beat. For over an hour he had Fazil on the edge of his seat, grinning and periodically shouting exuberant praises to Allah for his wonderful vengeance on the Great Satan. How great was God for providing the cause of *jihad* with such committed and mighty warriors from the very heartland of the infidel! And what a great addition to the cause he would be!

And yet, something in the tone of Fazil's voice had shifted, setting Marcus instantly on edge. He only hoped that Ham had also heard it.

"So you are the young warrior whom Allah has sent to Adad! Adad is a gift to Islam from Allah himself. Where others have failed, he will succeed. You should be thankful for the opportunity to serve such a man." There it was, that word *opportunity*. To Marcus it always implied a cost, but what?

Ham never betrayed any nervousness or anxiety. And as for Marcus, he was of no more consequence than a cockroach. "So, my young Farid," Fazil continued, "in two days' time, the *Takbir*, the great and glorious ship of Adad, will make port in Istanbul. There she will be equipped with the technology that will forever change the way the world views Islam. If you are worthy, then you, too, will be allowed to be part of the awakening of the army of Allah. Are you worthy, Farid? Do you have a faith that burns in your soul? You have been tested, but are you willing, are you ready, for the ultimate test?"

"Yes, Hajji, I am ready. Just tell me what I must do. My only purpose in this life is to serve God, to be his humble servant." Ham gushed with the excitement of a young zealot. But Marcus had a feeling that something bad was about to happen.

"You are familiar with the body of law known as *Sharia?*"

"Yes, of course, Hajji."

"Yes, I am sure you are. But among the chosen, those special few who serve the mighty Adad, we have interpreted the ancient law in a new light. You see, those who truly believe, those who are pure of heart and faith, must prove their worthiness, their allegiance. You must understand, we cannot be too careful! The enemies from the West, the infidels, want to crush us, so we must be stronger. We therefore must demand absolute allegiance from the members of our innermost circle. You are the first American *ever* to be considered."

"I understand, Hajji. I am willing to prove my worth. Just tell me what is required."

I understand! Marcus had never heard such a line of utter horseshit in his life.

"Your cousin here, he is a worthy man, a true man of God?" This was the first acknowledgment of any kind that he had received since they arrived.

"Oh, yes, Hajji! Nouri is far more virtuous, more pious, than I. He has never left the lands of the righteous, never lived among unbelievers and seen their depravity and their greed. Never has he seen the way women flaunt their bodies. He is uncorrupted, and his children and his wife were taken from him by the American infidels."

"That is all very good and admirable. So one of you will have to endure sixty lashes from the whip. If, in the morning, you are still alive, then you and I will be reunited on the *Takbir.* Now, the choice is yours. Your cousin seems a fine man, but the question is, can he further the cause? He appears to be a hard man—maybe he can survive and, in so doing, help pave for you the path to true and everlasting glory. I will give you a moment to speak to him. You may go outside if you wish."

Ham came over to where Marcus sat crouched against the wall. He looked up at him with the dumb smile of someone wholly ignorant of what was going on.

They walked out the door and into the dark gloom. Moving out of earshot, they faced each other, maintaining their roles as members of two distinct castes. Ham spoke in a low, hushed voice. "Marcus, I'm sorry!"

Keeping his head deferentially lowered, Marcus said, "Don't be sorry. We got what we came for. Now we just have to get out of this alive. Keep pretending to talk to me. Here's what's going to happen." He whispered while Ham's lips moved and his hands made animated gestures. "When we go back, you're going to ask the hajji to let me have a moment to pray. You need to get a message to Sit, saying that no matter what, he doesn't do a thing till you give the all go. This is important. You can bet your ass Fazil won't leave till the beating's over. If we take these guys down now, we lose the *Takbir.* If Fazil doesn't return, our window of opportunity vanishes. I have this strong feeling that this may be our only shot."

"But, Marcus, who can survive sixty lashes? People go into shock and die from half that!"

He pulled him into an embrace, his mouth close to his ear. "Hear me on this. I don't have time to explain it, but I have a guardian angel with me. I'll survive it. But you have to stand there, proud and righteous. You *can't* let your emotions betray our purpose."

"Okay, Marcus," Ham said in a resigned whispered. "I understand."

Marcus pulled back and faced him. "Okay, then. Let's do it. And you just pray I don't yell out in English."

They made their way back to the hut, where Fazil waited for them in the doorway, his body silhouetted in the lamplight. Ham approached him. "Hajji, Nouri is proud that he can be tested. He asks only that he be allowed to pray before we begin."

"I would expect nothing less from a true man of God."

Ham nodded at him, and Marcus knelt in the dirt facing southwest, toward Mecca. Bowing with his head to the ground and mumbling that there is only one God and Mohammed is his prophet, he was thinking, *You have done some really stupid shit in your life, Marcus, but this has to be, hands down, the stupidest yet!* He had no illusions about who would be wielding the whip. It had to be the big door guard.

Sure enough, the big man led him around the back of the stone building, where two wooden posts stood about six feet apart, joined by a crossbeam some ten feet high. Hanging from the crossbeam, maybe four feet apart, were two thick ropes, each running through a rusted metal eyehook in the beam. The guard had him stand between the posts and remove his woolen jacket and shirt. One of the ropes was tied to either wrist; then two of the men who had been in the house pulled him up until I was standing on tiptoes.

Marcus had taken note of the coiled leather whip hanging from the big man's belt. If he recalled correctly, such a whip, in the right hands, could move with such speed that the sound of its crack was actually a small sonic boom. There were times he wished his mind would just shut off.

Marcus heard the whisper of the evening breeze, and the shuffling of feet on the dirt behind him—the sound of a man establishing his footing, like a pitcher on the mound preparing to throw his fastball. The first lash was like nothing he had ever felt. There was pain, to be sure, but it felt hot, as if someone were running a blowtorch across his back.

He yelled out in a voice that came from the deepest recesses of his soul, "*Allahu Akbar!*"—God is great! *No English, Marcus, no English,* he said to himself again and again. Then, correcting even his own self-talk, he switched this mantra to Arabic.

The next lash, and the next, came in rapid succession. The tail of the whip wrapped around his side, cutting deep, the heat of one lash melting into the next, the burn rising to unbearable intensity. To keep from blacking out, he tried to keep count: four...five...six...ten...thirteen. He was fading out. The pain was beyond comprehension. And in that instant before the world turned black, Annie's voice was in his head, hard and insistent.

"Marcus, baby, you hold on, do you hear me? You hold on to me and don't you dare let go!"

How much time passed, he had no idea. His first conscious thought was of lying in the dirt, racked with pain no words could describe. His skin was on fire, and the cold night breeze seemed only to fan the flames. He couldn't move arms or legs, and each breath required a supreme effort. Then he heard it: the sound, the singing. It wasn't Betty's voice, though—no, this was the Fat Lady, the .50-caliber. The sound echoed off the mountains, the vibration of pure, raw power moving at over two thousand feet per second and then pounding into its intended target with the force of a freight train. So this was what Annie had meant when she'd said, "Listen for singing, baby, the singing."

He felt hands on him. "Don't touch me," he tried to say, but the words wouldn't come.

Then voices: "Marcus, hang on. We'll get you out. Stay with me!"

Ham—thank God.

Summoning every last atom of will still in him, Marcus forced his right hand to crawl out over the dirt. Ham's hand was on his, and imperceptibly Marcus's fingers moved on his. Somewhere, he found his voice, the voice of one desperate to utter his final words. In his mind, he could hear it, but he knew that it wasn't even a whisper.

"Ha...m-m-m...."

Ham's voice answered back. He could feel his breath on his neck. "What is it, Marcus?"

"Before I go out for good, I need to talk to Doc. You make sure...."

***

He woke up on his stomach, but no longer in the dirt. He was on some sort of bedding. It felt soft and smelled of stale sweat and wet wool. He couldn't open his eyes, though he could hear concerned voices.

"Colonel, we need to evac him now." A women's voice—it had to be Doc, or was he dreaming? "As bad as the damage from the whip was, the kicks to his torso broke several ribs and one of his lungs was punctured during transport."

"Bronson has the chopper ready. You take Jamie. Liam can help you with Marcus during transport. The team and I will follow."

"Doc...." *Please make the sound come out.*

"Marcus, don't talk. You're going to need every ounce of strength you have left."

"My...pack," he croaked.

"Yes, Marcus, I have it right here."

"Open it...the brick."

"This, Marcus?" He could just make out a blur of the greasy brown waxed paper she was holding in front of his eyes.

"Yes...when you get Adad, use that."

He didn't have the strength to explain, but Doc was smart. She would figure it out. When he had helped rescue Jamie, after killing his tormentors, one of the things he had noticed in the stone hut was a pile of bricks wrapped in brown waxed paper. In that moment, he hadn't known what they were, but when he pulled his water bottle from his pack, he stuffed one in. During Ham's conversation with Fazil, some of the discussion was on the business of poppies and the refining of their sap into heroin. Fazil found it ironic that such a beautiful flower could be used to supply the Western world with such an addictive drug. That's when he knew what the brick was.

"Colonel...."

"Marcus, you need to stay quiet and let Doc keep you alive!"

He moved his hand, and the colonel touched it. He was standing by his side, but he couldn't see him, let alone move his head. "Adad...he's mine."

And then the sweet angel Morphine spread her wings and swept him up into her velvety-soft arms. Her lips were on his, breathing life and comfort into him. The wind blew sweet and warm and smelled like coming rain. And the rain came, bathing him in compassion, washing away his pain. Through the clouds, fluffy and light, she carried him, and he thought, *am I going to heaven?*

How long the angel carried him, he couldn't say—an eternity, maybe, and at that moment he hoped it would be. All he knew was that he was safe and warm and at peace. He could feel the earth below him, breathe in her scent and feel her life force, her strength, her age, and her infinite mystical power.

Somewhere along the journey, he lost his blessed angel, and the next instant, he was again back at the cabin.

Annie was seated on the leather sofa, legs tucked up under her. She was wearing a thick flannel robe and held a steaming mug in her hands. He could sense the warmth from the wood stove, and hear Van Morrison's "Into the Mystic," floating softly in the air.

"Hey, my gypsy has come home," Annie said, a little smile creasing her face. "You don't look so good, baby." Annie's tone sounded so inviting and lighthearted when in life she had always been much more realistic, sensitive, and practical.

"Come here, baby," she said as she patted a spot on the sofa next to her. "It's time to rest. You come lay your head right here in my lap. Come on, now, I won't bite." Again the sexy smile.

Marcus walked to the sofa, stretched out, and laid his head in her lap. He could feel her fingers combing through his hair and down the nape of his neck. He could feel the heat of her body, and smell her sweet cinnamon tea–scented breath on his face.

"You did good, Marcus. You held on tight. I thought I might lose you, but you didn't let go. But, damn, the cost was high. I know you're always going on about the pain, but, honey, you *never* felt pain like this. You've been banged around some in your life, had your share of broken bones, but this is a whole new level of hurt. If chicks dig scars, then they are going to be all over you!" She laughed in a sort of little-girl way that made his heart glad. "So now you have to rest. I'm going to stay with you. I'll let you know when it's time to wake up. I'm so proud of you, baby. You've come such a long way. Now, you just stay here with me and let me take care of you. Close your eyes and sleep!"

And he drifted into the most peaceful sleep he had ever known.

CHAPTER FORTY-NINE
April 5

J.T. read from the screen of his laptop. "Ham is on board, Colonel," he said. Since arriving in Istanbul, the colonel, Sit, Bronson, Weathers and J.T. had been sequestered in the sub-basement of the U.S. consulate. With the help of General Kittredge, some strings had been pulled that gave the colonel and his team quasi-official sanction to proceed—a sanction that, everyone knew, was good only if they succeeded.

"Now we wait for Ham to contact us," the colonel replied. "Let's keep Jamie, Liam and Pete in play for now."

He had chosen those three to keep tabs on Ham as he made his way to the *Takbir* mostly because they fit the profile of young, eclectic tourists whose notion of vacation had a prerequisite exotic bent. It also helped that they weren't American.

Chaya had Marcus in a drug-induced coma while she did her best to keep him alive. And until the team secured the *Takbir,* she would remain there with him in Jeddah, at the King Faisal Specialist Hospital.

The colonel looked around him at the dingy underground confines of their temporary headquarters. As with every mission, the waiting was the hardest part. At the meeting, in Saudi Arabia, he had been surprised at the intensity with which the team insisted that they proceed. Ham was understandably adamant that they move forward and take the *Takbir.* For he had to stand and watch while Marcus was beaten to within a sliver of death. And afterward, when they cut Marcus down, he had overheard Fazil tell the big man wielding the whip to "see that he does not breathe the air of a new morning." So, as Fazil prepared to leave, Ham had no choice but to stand by as the big man slammed his steel-toed boots again and again into Marcus's ribs. And not until Fazil was well away had Sit put a stop to the brutal beating.

Chaya had been equally passionate, though in a somewhat different vein. She insisted that Marcus could not be left alone in Saudi Arabia, even in one of the most advanced and well-staffed hospitals in the world. Her point was that, if their hosts should find out what the colonel and the team were up too, Marcus's life would be over. Her observation brought home the fact that despite the colonel's personal relationship with the royal family, at the end of the day, they ruled one of the most fundamentalist Islamic nations on earth, and their relationship with the colonel was still just business.

The colonel called Sit, Bronson and Weathers, to gather around J.T.'s monitor. "Sit, we need a weapons plan, preferably silent and nonlethal. The deal we've made requires us to get some high-value human assets to turn over to the U.S. command."

"We're all set, Colonel. We'll be using air pistols with Fentanyl darts. Them boys won't know what end's up. All's you gotta do is get the team aboard."

The colonel looked at his big friend whose eyes glowed with a cold fire when he gave his aye vote to continue with the mission. The colonel thought about the direct impact the attack had on his team, when Sit shared that his family home in Tennessee's Cherokee National Forest had burned in the terrorists' fires. And even those members of the team who weren't U.S. citizens, had all spent time training or studying in the U.S., and they too had suffered some loss or knew someone who had. Now, it seemed, Marcus had provided a rallying point, not only for their skills, but for their rage as well.

"I'm up to speed on the *Takbir,*" said Weathers. "As soon as we take control, J.T. has the communiqué ready so the ship can leave port immediately. She's moored just one berth away from the port entrance, so getting out quickly should be no problem."

"Once we're in helicopter range, I'll head back to Jeddah and pick up Marcus and the doc." Bronson added.

"J.T. tell us what you know," the colonel said.

Without turning around J.T. started his briefing, changing images on the screen as he went. "The *Takbir* has been in port six days. By my estimates she has at least another four of five days to complete the up-link with the God's Eye satellite. I hacked the dock surveillance and I've monitored a lot of traffic coming and going, mostly supply and repair companies. It would appear they're preparing for an extended stay at sea. I found something interesting though. This black Mercedes sedan,"—the picture zoomed in—"arrived the day after the *Takbir* docked." Images of two men appeared on the screen.

"Well-known Indian software engineers, both with ties to the fundamentalist Islamic movement. But if you ask me, their real bond is with money. Anyway, four arrived, as I said, the day after the *Takbir* docked. The other two's faces weren't picked up by the camera, but it's safe to assume they're all part of the team installing the hardware and software for the satellite interface. And even if they don't quite finish before we take the ship, the gear will be aboard and I can complete the link." The colonel looked at J.T. It was out of character for him to speak so modestly of his abilities.

***

Ham approached the gate to the berth where the *Takbir* was docked. He noticed several large trucks and a constant stream of men and equipment going up and down the gangway. At the chain link gate, he was met by a well-dressed Arab whose shoulder holster and pistol bulged beneath his unbuttoned suit jacket.

Offering a greeting in Arabic and receiving one in kind, he introduced himself as Farid Tehrani, one of the American *jihadists,* responsible for the recent attacks on the United States. The guard made a call on his radio, and a few minutes later

Ham was led through the gate, onto the berth, and up the gangway to the hold of the *Takbir*. There he boarded a service elevator that rose quietly and opened into a very masculinely appointed wood-paneled room, with mahogany-hued leather sofas and club chairs and several pieces of exercise equipment. He had to consciously hold back his rage when he saw Fazil and a handsome younger man seated in the leather club chairs.

The man with Fazil stood as Ham entered. "My brother Farid, how nice to make your acquaintance." He said warmly, embracing Ham. "I am Adad al-Mohmoud."

Ham didn't have to put on an air of nervousness as he stepped back and said, "It is I who am honored Sayid. That I can offer my humble service to the cause is a gift from Allah."

"Yes, Allah works in ways no man can predict," Adad said with a quick glance at the seated Fazil. "God's will is God's will, and who are we to question. Now, you must be tired from your arduous journey. Tell me, how fares your cousin?"

"He suffered greatly, Sayid. But Nouri is a true and faithful man. He will wear his scars with pride at being allowed to do his part for the cause of Islam."

"Fazil, take young Farid to his quarters and give him a tour of his new home," Adad said without taking his eyes off Ham.

Fazil led him through the main salon, several thousand square feet of far and away the most ostentatious, lavish, décor he had ever seen. The scene was like something out of *Architectural Digest*: elegantly adorned with rich, thick carpets over pale yellow marble floors. Art work and antiquities, some obviously thousands of years old, hung from the walls or were arranged on wood and glass tables throughout the space.

It wasn't until they arrived at his suite that Fazil spoke. "It is very fortunate that those misguided separatists, those who believe America is their friend, arrived when they did. From what I am told, your cousin was only barely alive. Certainly he would not have survived unattended until morning."

Ham wanted to break Fazil's neck right then and there. But resisting the impulse, he said with a sad, serious voice, "Yes, Hajji, the beating he took was severe, but as the great Adad said, the will of God is unknown to mere men."

"Yes-s-s," Fazil responded, giving Farid a suspicious look. "That is so true. Now, settle in and make yourself at home. We have another four, maybe five days and then we depart, and the fight to make Islam the one and only faith, begins." With that, he turned and left Ham amid the palatial trapping of his suite.

* * *

The colonel was uneasy leaving Ham without back up, but more troubling were all the unknowns of the mission. He and the team would have to be prepared to move at a moment's notice, and they would have to develop their incursion plan on the spot, once a viable opportunity to get aboard the *Takbir* presented itself.

Before Ham left Saudi Arabia the doc had outfitted him with another of J.T.'s ingenious communications and tracking devices, a porcelain-polymer crown over

189

one of his molars. It worked along the same principle as the tiny ceramic GPS transceivers that the team members ingested daily. It was charged by the body's own electrical impulse. By gently tapping his teeth together, Ham could send Morse code messages via a reliable low-frequency analog signal. J.T. had programmed his laptop and the communications PDA's to receive and decrypt the coded transmissions. For twenty-four hours the only message from Ham, "Not yet."

Ham spent his time aboard the *Takbir* orientating himself to the ship's layout and determining how many men Adad had aboard. Late on the morning of the third day, he found Fazil and Adad on the command bridge. It looked like something out of *Star Trek,* with high-backed leather swivel chairs the color of freshly churned butter, behind countertop-mounted flat screens. There were no buttons or switches; it seemed that everything was controlled by touch. All this faced a huge bank of tinted windows that looked out over the expansive bow of the *Takbir.*

"There must be something I can do, to make myself useful," Ham said to both men, who were watching four younger men at work at the consoles.

Fazil turned to him and said, "Yes, Adad, and I have thought the same. Tomorrow a load of crates will be delivered. It is furniture and art work. It will be your task to unpack them and inventory the contents. Will that suit you?"

"Yes, of course, Hajji."

"Good then. Here is the manifest from the company delivering the goods. Some of the crates are very large. Once they are secure in the hold, make sure everything is accounted for and is undamaged."

Adad never so much as looked at him, as he took the paper from Fazil and left.

***

The team located the warehouse where a shipment of crates awaited delivery to the *Takbir.* Access was easy, only an unguarded chain link fence and a simple door lock. Working with night-vision goggles, Sit and Bronson quickly assisted Pete, Weathers, Liam, and Jamie, into the shipping crates, along with all equipment necessary to effect a quite, nonlethal, takeover of the *Takbir.* Ham had notified the team that there were five guards—two always stationed outside the ship and three doing cursory patrols of the interior—plus Adad, Fazil, and the four software engineers. The actual crew was not scheduled to be aboard until just before departure.

The next day, the crates were loaded on a truck and taken to the *Takbir,* where Ham awaited with one of the guards to unload them. Some of the crates held large upholstered pieces that were perfect for hiding the men.

Ham got right to work checking the crates against the manifest. The task seemed to be beneath the guards and once all was stacked in the cargo hold, he was left on his own. It took him two hours to free the Force 10 incursion team. Since the *Takbir* was operating on dock-supplied power, J.T. was able to hack into the onboard video surveillance system and was providing a looped feedback to the monitors that showed, just as they had for the past few days, no suspicious activity in the cargo bay.

That night, while Adad, Fazil and the engineers slept, all five guards were subdued and secured in the hold. Weathers quickly got the ship ready to set sail, as a supply truck arrived. Under cover of darkness, the colonel, Sit, Bronson, and J.T. boarded the *Takbir*.

***

In Fazil's suite, Ham's bare feet made no sound as he crossed the thick carpet. When the lights suddenly came on, Fazil woke, rubbing his eyes. "What is it, Farid?" he said. "Why have you woken me?"

Then he saw the knife. Fully awake, he pulled his flabby form up into a sitting position. "What is the meaning of this?"

Ham fought his rising rage down. "I am not Farid Tehrani, but soon enough you will know that." Quickly he pulled a hypodermic needle from his shirt pocket and stuck the soft flesh of Fazil's upper arm. In seconds, the man was out.

What to do with Fazil had been a topic of much debate between Ham and the colonel. Ham wanted nothing more than to slit his throat and watch him die, but as was often the case, calmer heads prevailed. And he had to agree since the team had no intention of turning over Adad to the U.S. Military, that Fazil, Adad's number one, would be the next best thing.

By midnight the Takbir was making her way through the Aegean Sea in route to the Mediterranean. As far as those in Adad's circle were concerned everything was exactly as it should be.

***

Two days after departing Istanbul an unmarked Blackhawk transport helicopter landed on the bow of the *Takbir*. Fazil, the five guards, and the four engineers, all with their heads bagged, were marched out on to the bow deck. Ham held Fazil to be loaded onto the chopper last. "Now you get to experience *my* version of Sharia." Ham growled through the black cloth, into Fazil's ear, and pushed him into waiting arms that hauled him aboard. As the helicopter took off into the night sky, Ham found it a bit ironic that Fazil and his cohorts might well be on their way back to Turkey. It was known, after all, as one of the most moderate Muslim nations of the region, and a favorite unknown and unsanctioned location for interrogating suspected terrorists.

Shortly after they were rid of the unwanted passengers, the hydraulic rams opened huge deck doors on the *Takbir* bow, and the Bell Jet Ranger helicopter rose from the interior hangar. Bronson and Jamie did a quick pre-flight check and took off to get Doc and Marcus.

CHAPTER FIFTY
May 7

No matter how hard Marcus struggled, there was no air.

"Marcus...Marcus!"

Annie, are we in heaven? Where are you, baby? Don't leave me! Somehow, Marcus knew the words were only in his mind. Then he felt the touch of hands.

"Marcus...Marcus, come on! Fight, now—fight, damn it!"

It was a woman's voice, but not Annie's. So who...? Where the hell was he?

"Come on! That's it, Marcus, open your eyes."

A brilliant white glare blasted his eyes. *Annie, I can't see you. Where are you?*

"That's it, Marcus...take your time. Give your eyes time to focus. You can do this."

It was like opening his eyes underwater, everything was a blur, just hazy images surrounded by dazzling white light. The woman in front of him was coming into focus as if she were walking through smoke into clear air. *Doc? Doc, is that you? Where's Annie?*

As his vision slowly drifted into focus Marcus found himself looking into the green eyes of Chaya Lanyer.

"You've had a rough go, Marcus. You need to listen and do as I ask. Can you do that? Blink your eyes twice." Her voice sounded so calm, so in control. It took every ounce of concentration he could summon to make his eyes blink.

"Okay, I want you to breathe out with everything you have, and I'm going to slip the tube from your throat. Ready?"

Two blinks, and Marcus exhaled. If he thought blinking was hard, forcing his breath out felt like an elephant was standing on his chest.

"It's going to take a while before you can talk, so don't try. I'm getting some ice for you to suck on. One step at a time, okay?"

Two blinks.

God, he was tired! And he hurt beyond describing. He shifted his eyes from side to side around the room. It was definitely a hospital room. There was equipment everywhere, and he seemed to be hooked up to all of it: IV tubes, oxygen, electrodes stuck to his chest. But where was he?

Doc returned with a cup of shaved ice, and with a gentle touch, she fed him the tiny chips. The first few just touched his lips and fell out. His eyes were darting around, the questions running through his mind, echoing silently in the air.

"Calm down, Marcus. You've been in a drug-induced coma for almost a month. You need to give your body time to reacclimatize and restart. It's going to take a few days before you can talk, and it's going to take a few weeks just to get you out of this bed." The Doc's eyes looked tired and concerned. "We're on the *Takbir.*"

Marcus tried to force his eyes open wider. *How?* Chaya put her hand on his chest and leaned close. "We have Adad, and I figured out the brick. Our boy is now a full-blown junk man." Marcus attempted to raise his eyebrows in that *what,* kind of way.

She gently patted his chest, "No wait, that isn't right. Not junk man...*junkie.*" Then she smiled, and for the first time, since he had met her, the smile seemed to contain more joy than sorrow. "That's all for now Marcus. You have to rest and let me take care of you."

Marcus couldn't reach up to wipe the tear that slid down his check. Hadn't Annie said those very same words to him just minutes ago? He closed his eyes and drifted away.

* * *

Over the next week, each day was an exercise in pain and revelation. All Marcus could remember was the whipping—he had no recollection of being kicked almost to death, though it felt as if it had happened yesterday. From the look on Doc's face and the worn, dark circles under her sad eyes, he was sure she hadn't left his side.

Marcus wasn't the least bit surprised to learn that the team had proceeded with the mission. Somehow, he had known they would. Besides Doc, Ham was the first one allowed to see him. One glance told Marcus how responsible he felt. His voice was still not back to normal—the rawness in his throat from the intubation gave it a raspy, gravelly tone.

"Hey, look at me, Ham!" Marcus said. "I told you I'd make it! No regrets pal, not today, not ever."

Staring down at the white marble floor, Ham said in a voice thick with shame, "I did as you asked, Marcus. I stood there and watched that big bastard flay the hide right off of you. There was nothing ritualistic about that shit. It was meant to kill, and by all rights, it should have. All the time, the look in Fazil's eyes, that sick, evil grin—he was certain you wouldn't survive and that I would never join him on the *Takbir.*" His voice caught, and he shook his head in disgust. "And when he ordered that...to make sure you didn't live to see the morning, and that goon started kicking you, well, imagine his surprise when I showed up in Istanbul. It's how I got aboard—after you surviving that beating, there was no way he could *not* welcome me. If Arabs have one unshakable quality, it's their honor. They must always save face."

Marcus nodded to a chair, and Ham sat. "So tell me about Adad."

Ham's face cleared a bit, the shame replaced by what looked like pride.

"Well, as Farid Tehrani, I've become Adad's closest and most trusted confidant, especially since I convinced him, he was betrayed by Fazil." A smile crossed his youthful face. "Between J.T. and me, we've extracted every scrape of information about his financial empire. We are now in control of an amount of money with so many zeros, I can't really comprehend it—though J.T. apparently can."

"Good for you, Ham," Marcus, said. "Look at me. I know you've been trained to be dispassionate, not to let personal feelings invade a situation. But sometimes that's exactly what's required. Now, you put that guilt up on a back shelf somewhere, and if you ever need it, you can reach out and take hold of it, but don't you think for a minute you can pack it around because of what happened to me. You know, the last thing I really remember was the echo of the fifty—sweetest sound I ever heard."

Ham got up to leave. "Yeah, it's a great sound if you listen just right. Sit plowed the road from near two thousand yards, but you need to know, making him watch you get beat when he knew he could prevent it—well, let's just say he's not any happier about it than I am."

Jamie came next to visit. The last time he had seen the kid, his face was beaten almost unrecognizable and he was unconscious.

"You look like chewed meat, mate," Jamie said in a cheery voice. "Just had to go and outdo me, now, didn't you, you bloody wanker!"

Marcus managed a lopsided grin. "Yeah, well, if it's any comfort, as bad as I look, I feel worse. How about you? You look pretty much back to normal."

"To be honest, mate, I haven't had a chance to try out the ol' hydraulics since shock therapy, but everything else appears to be in good working order. Anyway, there'll be plenty of time for that. Right now we need to get you up on your feet and finish this thing, whatever it is." Hearing a shuffle behind him, he said, "Oh, hey, Sit's here, so I think I'll duck out. Anyway Doc's clocking our visits with an egg timer. Be warned, though—you're not too high on the big man's list at the moment."

Marcus waved weakly as Jamie left.

Sit's shadow fell over him. It wasn't easy, trying to move his head. The muscles in his back, shoulders, and neck had been ripped up terribly, and with a month of total immobility, he was basically paralyzed.

The man who, since they first met, had always seemed to have a big, easy smile on his face now glowered down at him. The look wasn't one of anger, exactly. It was more like indignation, an expression of *how could you put me in such a position?* Marcus didn't know what to say to him. Whereas Jamie felt more like a son to him, Sit was much closer to his own age—not a man he could buffalo with experience and well-honed bullshit.

Marcus looked at him and said, "Grab a chair. We need to talk." For the next half hour, he told Sit about Annie, about what she had told him in his dream and about her cryptic instruction to listen for the singing.

Sit never interrupted—just sat as quiet as a very big church mouse. "Okay, Marcus," he said, "For your Annie, you get a walk, but hear this: never again will I watch that happen to one of my people, not when I have the ability to prevent it. If that's the only option, then it's not worth it."

Sit leaned forward in his chair "I'm damn thankful to have you back."

Telling his story had left Marcus tapped out. Despite his daily improvement, he could manage to stay awake only five or six hours a day. So when the pain became too much, a click of the button controlling the Demerol drip would allow him to fade away to a place where time had no meaning.

When he floated back up out of the fog, J. T. and the colonel were standing by his bedside. "Well, Marcus, that was quite the stunt," the colonel said. "I hope you have some inkling of just how lucky you are to be alive."

Marcus gave him a weak nod. "That's what you call this—luck? Anyway, at the time, it didn't seem like such a bad idea"

"Not such a *bad idea*? " the colonel said. "How in God's name did you ever think for one second that you could survive such a beating?"

Marcus could see the concern and disapproval on the colonel's face. What he had somehow failed to consider was the effect that his lashing would have on the members of the team.

"This is going to sound a little nuts," he said, "but I have this thing—I believe I'll know when it's my time, and I knew for certain this wasn't it. And look where we are, on the *Takbir,* with Adad a full-blown heroin addict."

The colonel sighed. "Someday, you and I are going to sit down, son, and you are going to explain what goes on in that fucked-up mind of yours!"

"Hey," Marcus said as his eyes found J. T.'s face, "how's everything been going with our pal?"

In his animated, geeky fashion, J. T. told him how, with Ham's help, they had begun to extract information from Adad. After just the first week on a heroin drip, Adad was a devoted slave to one of the most addictive drugs on earth. Ham, in his guise as Farid Tehrani, was the only person Adad was allowed to see. He was of his people, spoke his language, and, as a committed *jihadist* against America, shared his vision of the best way to advance the reach of the holy war. In Adad's state of drug-induced euphoria and paranoia, Ham convinced him that his closest advisers had betrayed him and that, to survive to fight another day, he had to restructure his financial holdings. Ham managed to tease out the codes and passwords for his various numbered accounts, and J. T. had determined what documents were required to sign over control of most of the vast financial empire he ruled over. Adad was unable to separate reality from the drug. His dependency had become his reality, and J. T. and Ham were able to lead him like a lamb to slaughter. Force 10 was now in possession of billions in cash and assets. An empire of oil, gas, shipping, mining, technology, manufacturing, real estate—almost everything was now in the capable hands of J. T., a.k.a. Mr. Wizard.

"Colonel," Marcus said, "I would like your permission to have J. T. work on a personal project."

With a wry grin, he said, "What the fuck, Marcus? You've been directing this whole thing from the beginning—how much more personal a project could you possibly have?"

Marcus assumed this qualified as permission. "So, J. T., I want to avail myself of your special talent for real estate deals. Go at this like one of those scams you used to pull. I want you to find ranching property up in British Columbia. It needs to be a minimum of a hundred thousand acres, with a paved runway that can handle private jets. It must have a large main compound that can accommodate at least seventy-five people. Now, this is important: I want you to approach it like a scam, so that you give full rein to your creative energies. But that's where the scam ends. Once you locate it and are satisfied that it meets our criteria, I want you to buy it. Offer so much money they can't refuse. Don't dick around. I want the deal done in sixty to ninety days. One more thing—you and I will not discuss the location or any of the particulars—all I want to know is that it's done."

To the colonel, he said, "I assume that our agreement on Force 10's fee has been met to your satisfaction?"

"Uh, that would be an unqualified yes."

"Colonel, I think, given the sums we are talking about, that some renegotiation is in order. In fact, you decide. Take whatever you think is fair."

"Uh, Marcus, do you have any real conception of what kind of money J. T. is talking about?"

"Not really, Colonel, and I don't especially care."

"Well, son, you'd *better* care, because we're approaching a trillion dollars— that is about six more zeros than most people can even imagine. The question now is, what are you going to do with it?"

Marcus grinned up at the colonel through the pain that was beginning to throb through him. He pressed the button on the Demerol drip, and just before he slipped off into that fleeting paradise, he said," I haven't the slightest idea, but when I figure it out, I promise you'll be the second to know."

CHAPTER FIFTY-ONE
June 21

"Marcus, we need to bring you off the opiates," Chaya said to his back, as she held onto his waist. This had become his daily routine, either with her or one of the other teammates' help, Marcus would struggle to take one agonizing step farther than the time before. As he shuffled his feet across the marble floor, she continued. "It's going to be a challenge. Not so much coming off the drug, because we can supplant it with other pain meds, but as far as pain relief, you're going to really start feeling it. This is going to affect your ability to sleep, but we should see a substantial improvement in your progress. You've spent the better part of the past two months in bed, and I think you're ready. And besides, you told me once...how did you put it? 'Doc, the pain is nothing!' Well, we're going to find out."

Marcus would often catch a glimpse of his reflection in one of the glass wall partitions that divided the sick bay into specific exam and lab areas. With his atrophied muscles and sallow, translucent skin, he resembled a ninety-year-old man. He wasn't surprised that the sick bay on the *Takbir* was like a miniature version of the best-equipped, most technically advanced hospital in the world. Designed strictly for Adad's use, its nearly three thousand square feet included a fully equipped lab, MRI and CAT scan equipment, and a complete stock of the latest pharmaceuticals. And he thought longingly about those drugs as he started coming off the opiates. Doc had warned him—it was no picnic. The first night without the drips, Annie's voice came to him. It was the first time since the beating.

"Oh, Marcus, Marcus," she said, "what are you *doing*? It took you long enough to drag your sorry ass out of bed. Oh, yeah, and the dope? You *love* that stuff. Well, baby, it's time again, time to start figuring out the next move. By the way, the boys are good. They know you can't call them, but there's this anxiousness in them. It's time for you to feel it, too. So the time has come for you do something stupid. Come on, I know you have it in you."

In her teasing tone, Annie was making an unmistakable allusion to something only she and Marcus shared. During their twenty years together, he had managed to injure himself a few times. And each time, he had languished in a drug-induced fog until Annie decided it was time to cut him off. Then he did something stupid, or, at least, something that Annie thought was stupid. He had broken his ankle, and the day after Annie took away his drugs, she returned home to find him on the stationary bike, his foot cast duct-taped to the pedal, his face and back drenched in sweat, and on the verge of blacking out from the pain. She chewed him out, but every day from then on, he strapped his foot to the pedal of that bike and rode,

197

until he could go for two hours nonstop. Recalling it, he thought, *Yeah, Annie, I suppose I do have it in me.*

Annie's chiding provided the motivation, and over the next two weeks he made dramatic strides toward recovery. He wasn't running laps around the sick bay yet, but at least he could walk unassisted. And his wounds were healing now to the point of scabbing over and itching like crazy.

Besides changing the bandages and redressing his wounds the doc drew blood from Marcus daily and ran tests in the lab. As he became stronger and more mobile he would frequently stop in to chat with her. Back at the compound, they had just been getting to know each another when Chaya had left Australia for the Middle East. And once Marcus and the rest of the team arrived—and ever since— they had not had more than a few moments of private conversation.

Sitting on a rolling stool, because it hurt to have his back pressed into a chair, Marcus wheeled up to her desk. "So Doc, we were just getting to know each other when—"

"Look Marcus," she said, not smiling. "I care about you probably more that you could know. But you have this thing about you that is...let's say, not healthy, for you or me."

Seeing that he wasn't going to get any further, Marcus rose and said, "Okay, Doc, you win, for today."

***

Marcus was taking a lap around sick bay when he almost collided with Jamie, who was coming out of the elevator.

"Hey, mate, no walker," Jamie said in surprise. "I thought for a while we were gonna have to buy some Depends and sign you up for AARP." He snickered at his own joke.

"Come on, walk with me," Marcus said. "Tell me, where's the gym in this tub?"

Jamie looked him up and down. 'Don't shit me, mate."

"I'm serious, Jamie."

"Okay, for the sake of conversation, which gym do you want: basketball, racquetball, squash, weight room, yoga, or Pilates studio—or maybe the private gym?"

"The private gym—where's that?"

"Well, it's quite the deal—right behind the control bridge. I think it was Adad's personal domain, a place he could hang out and still be right next to the bridge. It's pretty tricked out: state-of-the-art treadmill, bike, climber, free weights, HD monitors on the walls, kick-ass sound system, huge private bath, and sleeping quarters."

"How do I get there?"

At this question, they stopped moving and he leaned close. "Listen, if I tell you, you can't let Doc know. You may think the men on this team are bad-ass, but she is a whole different animal. If she finds out I told you how to get out of sick bay, and especially how to get to the private gym—which, by the way, is a very bad idea—she will kill me, and by that I mean she will stop my heart and all other vital functions. You see, you've become something of a special project for her, and we all have express orders not to interfere."

Marcus laughed, then grimaced in pain. What Jamie had said about the Doc, reminded him of the times he and the boys had planned to do something not entirely risk free, without telling Annie. They would pick a pitch to ski and, unbeknownst to her, change their route as they were skinning up, only to have her instantly on the radio. They had it all rehearsed. Dad would come up with some bullshit story about the snow conditions requiring them to change their plan on the spot. Annie's response was always the same: "Marcus, if you do anything to hurt or endanger my boys, you will deal with me. Do you hear me, Idiot?"

"Okay, I promise, no one hears it from me." Marcus said, reaching out painfully to pat Jamie on the shoulder.

"Okay, then, bloody fool, take the elevator. Just hit 'B' and it'll take you right to the workout area. I hope you know what you're doing, though, because Doc's not gonna be amused."

* * *

Marcus waited two more days before he got the nerve up to approach the elevator. Staring at the door he thought, hadn't Jamie mentioned *buttons?* Seeing a touch screen to the right of the door, he tapped it, and it lit up instantly. He found the right symbol, and the door slid open without the barest whisper of sound. So far, this was the only other room on the *Takbir* he had ever seen. As he should have expected, the inside of the elevator was opulent—solid slabs of black granite with brilliant silver veins covered the walls, ceiling, and floor. Another touch screen displayed letters in a grid like that on a digital calculator. Marcus touched "B," the door swished shut, and the elevator rose.

It opened into a big room of perhaps twenty by twenty. Facing one wall were a spin bike, an elliptical track, a stair climber, and a treadmill.

The walls were a rich dark mahogany', in front of the equipment was a massive flat screen. The floor was thick black rubber that felt as if it floated on a cushion of air. His footsteps made no sound on it. But the most impressive feature was the clear wall that faced the bridge. The room on the other side was some kind of high tech command bridge that looked like what Marcus imagined a modern-day version of Nemo's *Nautilus* might be like.

Marcus could see the colonel, J. T., and Ham, and even though they were looking directly at the glass wall before him, it appeared that they could not see through it to him. Turning his attention back to his immediate surroundings Marcus wandered through a door at the back of the workout room, and lights automatically came on. He found himself standing in the most ostentatious bathroom he had ever seen. The whole room, far bigger than the workout room, was covered in forest green marble. It had a steam room and sauna, a huge Jacuzzi tub that appeared to be carved out of a single block of reddish stone, and a shower so big and with so many heads that a dozen people could have bathed at once. There were stacks of thick cotton towels the same forest green as the marble, with the letters *A. M.* embroidered in calligraphy on each one. Terry cloth and silk robs hung on gold hooks. In the huge walk-in closet, Marcus found everything he needed—brand-new shorts, T-shirts, and running shoes. Relieved that he didn't have to wear anything that Adad had once worn, he still found it troubling that he and his enemy were roughly the same size.

Marcus dressed, which took a lot more effort than he had anticipated, and made his way toward the treadmill. On the way, he sorted out the audio system, and seconds later he had music.

He stepped cautiously onto the treadmill, set it at a five percent incline and hit the start button. He walked slowly, increasing the speed one-tenth mph at a time, and when he got to two mph, barely half a fast walking speed, he knew he was maxed out. He had walked maybe five minutes when the elevator door opened.

The look of concern in Doc's eyes was gone, replaced with emerald daggers of righteous fury.

"What the fuck do you think you're doing, Marcus? You think I've been caring for you night and day for the last three months so you can come up here and pull this bullshit?"

He stopped the treadmill and grabbed the hand rails to avoid collapsing. Doc was immediately by his side. She helped him off and into a leather stuffed chair; he was a sweaty mess. She went into the bathroom and returned with a towel, which she promptly threw in his face.

She was pacing back and forth, much as Annie would do when she was so exasperated with the boys and Marcus that she didn't know whose neck to ring first.

"Hey, Doc, come on over and sit down," he said in his best contrite tone.

She wasn't buying it. "Marcus, you are some piece of work. First you go and get yourself beaten to death's door and halfway through it; then you pull this crap." She looked on the verge of spontaneous combustion.

He motioned to the matching leather chair beside him. "Sit, please."

She stalked over and flung herself down into the chair

"Think you can sit there and listen to me for a minute?" he said.

Although she nodded, he was pretty sure she didn't much care what he had to say.

"You're right. It's been almost three months, three fucking months. If I'm going to get better, you need to let me do it my way." Marcus waved off her objection. "I know you think I'm crazy, that I'm pushing it. But if you haven't figured me out yet, that's how I work. I push it—sometimes a notch too far, I admit. But it's what works for me. Three months, Doc. It will be a year since the attack pretty soon, and I need to bring this whole ordeal to an end. I need to get back to my boys."

He was feeling light-headed, and Chaya must have noticed, because she got up and brought him a bottle of water from the fridge.

He drank it down in big gulps. "So this is the deal. You can help or not. But either way, I'm going to get myself back in shape—I have to!" He paused for a minute and noticed the anger fading, replaced by a sad, melancholic concern.

"Look at me, Doc. There is a history here," He pointed first at himself, then at her. "It's being written every day. It started the day we first met. What that history's going to look like, I have no idea, but I want to know—*need* to know. And I think you do too. So the questions are, can you help me? And can you trust that I know that the time is right?"

Her eyes had a wounded, hurt look, but her voice was strong and clear. "About a month after I returned to Israel...I was celebrating the completion of my medical training. My entire family was gathered at a restaurant in Tel Aviv." Marcus watched her face as she seemed to detach herself from the moment. "My whole family, Marcus—parents, brothers, sisters, grandparents, aunts, uncles, cousins, nieces, nephews, they were all there when a car bomb exploded just outside the restaurant." She looked at him, her face contorted in a mask of anger and guilt, "I walked out without a scratch. I had gone to the bathroom." She averted her eyes toward the floor. "No one else survived. In the blink of an eye, all the family I had on this earth was gone."

Marcus could feel his shirt sticking to the scabs on his back as he moved his weight forward to the edge of the leather chair. "Chaya—"

She held up her hand. "I swore a long time ago that no man would hold power over me ever again, and then you had to show up, and I began to think, maybe— So yes, I'll help you, but the first time your stupidity threatens your health, I'll pull the plug. You're a strong man. There's something about you...." Leaving, she turned at the elevator door and smiled at Marcus. Her face seemed to radiate light. It reminded him of the smile Annie would give him when he had been forgiven.

CHAPTER FIFTY-TWO
July 2

As Marcus ran on the treadmill he thought about his boys. Tomorrow would be his oldest son Bodie's thirteenth birthday, and Marcus wouldn't be there. He hadn't spoken with either of them or his brother since the day he flew out of Australia in mid-March. Although he was sure that Annie, their lighthouse, was keeping them informed and comforted that he was safe, the sense of inadequacy and failure overwhelmed him, pushing him to run like a man possessed

Doc did as she agreed and two days later, they moved from sick bay to Adad's private quarters. Doc took the bedroom, and Marcus stayed in the workout room, sleeping on a mattress on the floor. Everyone thought his idiosyncrasies were finally getting the better of him. They all wondered, why would he sleep on the floor when some of the most opulent accommodations anywhere in the world were available? Marcus never tried to explain to anyone his aversion to the *Takbir*. He had promised himself, when he first regained consciousness that he would have as little to do with that ship as possible. And to that end, he would avoid every area of the ship that was not absolutely essential to his *getting off* the ship.

At Marcus's insistence, he returned to the simple diet of rice, chickpeas and raw yogurt, the team maintained during their time in Pakistan. Daily, he was requiring less and less sleep, and by bunking in the workout room, he could get on the treadmill anytime, day or night. The stronger he got, the harder he pushed, and the harder he *could* push. His biggest immediate problem was his back. His motion on the treadmill made the scabs crack and bleed, and the doc reminded him daily that it was going to make the scarring worse.

All Marcus really knew about their location was that they were somewhere in the Mediterranean, one of the bodies of water where Adad spent a lot of his time. And for all anyone in Adad's world knew, everything was normal. Marcus knew that the Middle Eastern mind-set of patriarchal control played to the team's advantage. It was not unusual for one man to be the sole controller of vast financial resources. In that world, there were no chairman, board of directors, and CEO to answer to—there was only the boss.

Marcus had been spending some time on the bridge with J.T., who was thoroughly enjoying playing with more wealth than Marcus could even comprehend. And he had found and secured a property, already fully staffed, in British Columbia. He and the colonel had vetted every employee, and although the former owners would need another month to be completely gone, the main compound was vacant and ready for occupancy.

Marcus was also able to check on what was going on back in the states, he hadn't had any news since leaving Australia. There had been significant flooding, and the wind was creating storms of dark, sooty ash that left a charcoal film over everything in its path, not to mention the often deadly effect the particulate filled air had on those with repository problems. And eliminating the parasite from the water systems was going to take at least another year, so periodic wide-spread out breaks of sickness would have to be managed.

Everyone was waiting for Marcus to decide what to do with the vast resources now in their control, and Marcus had been giving the issue a lot of thought when the colonel entered the private quarters. He motioned for Marcus to get off the treadmill and sit with him. Mopping his face Marcus sat.

"We have some serious issues that must be dealt with," the colonel said, "the least of which is all this money J. T. is playing with." He smiled, looking through the one-way glass wall to the bridge, where J. T. sat watching a series of numbers flit across one of the huge HD monitors.

"I know," Marcus said, "I need you to do me a personal favor. My brother Glen—I need you to go to Sydney bring him back to the *Takbir*."

"Couldn't you manage that just as easily with a call?"

"It's more than just bringing him here. I need you to put the kids and his wife, Ellie, on a jet in route to Beginnings." Seeing the colonel's puzzled look, Marcus shook his head and laughed. "Sorry, 'Beginnings'—that's what I'm calling the property in BC. Also, I need you to arrange for a security detail to stay with them, until we can get there. I have an idea about all the money, and I think that between J.T. and my brother they can work it out. You see Glen, is as much a financial wiz as J.T. As for you going to get him, well, my brother is a world-class skeptic. He needs validation and confirmation for everything he does, and short of me going, you're the only one I can think of who will be able to convince him."

"And what about Adad? Have you given any thought to him?"

"One problem at a time, Colonel. Isn't that what you taught me?"

"Oh, so *now* you're going to start listening to me?" The colonel cracked a smile. "Okay, Marcus, I'll go get your brother. But when I get back, I expect you to have a plan ready to present to the team."

***

Now that Marcus had the form of a plan in his mind, he needed to regain the sense of purpose and motivation he had when he began the hunt for Annie's killers. And though he was clear that what had happened was much bigger than Annie's murder, and that in fact, she would disapprove if he were to ignore the death and destruction that effected so many Americans, for now he needed to cling to his own sense of personal injustice. So, to that end he had J. T. make a tape of Annie's murder and load it onto the hard drive in the gym so that it ran in a continuous loop. For three days he ran, watched that tape, and let his soul bleed. And the more it bled, the more determined he grew, and the more he wanted to see Bodie and Garrett.

Through the glass wall, which was in reality a one-way mirror from the workout room side and functioned as a massive display screen from the bridge side, Marcus saw Glen step into view. His hair was a bit grayer, and his six-foot-one frame was carrying a few more pounds than when they last saw each other, six months ago.

The colonel led him into the workout room. Still running, Marcus slowed the treadmill to an easy walk and looked at his brother. Glen stared back at him.

"Marcus?"

Until he heard the hesitation in his brothers' voice, he didn't realize just how much his appearance had changed. "What—you don't like the new look?" Marcus said, stepping off the treadmill deck and embracing him. Fighting back his emotions Marcus said, "I've missed you. How are my boys?"

Glen pushed him back and held him at arm's length. His eyes were beginning to tear up. "They're good, Marcus, no, they're great. It's been an absolute joy to have them with us. Ellie isn't going to know what to do when the day comes that they're not her boys."

"How is she? And Renée and Charlie—they're good?"

"Cut the shit, Marcus. You know damn well they're okay. The question is, how are *you?*" He was looking at the bloodstains on the front and back of Marcus's sweat-soaked T-shirt.

From the way he asked, Marcus knew that the colonel had told him everything. "I'm good, much better now that you're here and, I know that Ellie and the kids are safe."

"What's going on, Marcus? Why all the secrecy and urgency?"

"We're on the home stretch, bro, and I know you have a thousand questions, but you need to let me do this in my own way. I promise I'll answer everything. But for now we need to get to work."

"Okay, Marcus, I've gone too far with you not to know that whatever's going on in that weird mind of yours will come out in due time. The colonel's told me what has happened, so, like you said, let's get to work. Oh, by the way, nice letter."

He was referring to the letter the colonel had brought from Marcus.

Dear brother,

You remember when I made you promise that if the day came and I asked you to do something for me that went against every instinct you have, you'd do it, no questions asked? Well, I'm asking. The man delivering this letter is Colonel Samuel Webb, one of the finest men I have ever met. I trust him with my life, and I need you to trust him with the lives of Ellie and the kids. I can tell you they will be absolutely safe, and when you see where they're going, you'll approve. I don't have the time to explain it, but I need you

here with me—now. So ask the colonel whatever you want. Satisfy yourself.
Like I've always said, I save the hardest jobs for you.

Love,
MD

Glen looked around the room. "I need to take a picture of this," he said. "Is this the same man who can't go to sleep until he's bathed, no matter where we are? Hell, I've seen you wash with snow and dry with a T-shirt, after fourteen hours of climbing and skiing."

Marcus laughed. "There are occasions when being too clean can be a bad thing, but I can tell you that when this is done, the first thing on the agenda is a haircut and a shave and nice, long, hot bath. But, not just yet. Anyway, you'll get used to the way I look and smell."

The colonel gave Glen a look that said, *maybe not.*

"All right," Marcus said, "let's go—there's someone you need to meet."

They walked out onto the bridge. "J. T., I'd like you to meet my brother Glen," J. T. swiveled his seat around. "J. T., good to meet you," said Glen. "I understand you have some, uh, specialized talents. By the way, you wouldn't be the guy I've been getting the cryptic e-mails from, the ones that read 'DM KO'?" Marcus looked at the colonel, but he looked just as mystified. J. T. never answered, and Glen didn't pursue it, so Marcus let it go.

"What I will tell you is that when it comes to compiling, understanding, organizing and disseminating information, I'm the best." J. T. said.

"Well, it's nice to have a good opinion of oneself," Glen replied with a puzzled look on his face.

"J. T., would you mind showing Glen your progressive slot machine thing?" Marcus asked. J. T. made a few keystrokes, and the flitting, growing line of numbers appeared on the big monitor. "Tell him what it is," Marcus prompted.

"Well, I thought that since you work for a big gaming company, it might be interesting to look at the assets we control as if we were looking at a progressive slot machine, linked to hundreds of other machines in multiple locations. So, using some complicated math that we won't go into right now, I've set up an extrapolation of gain and loss so that we can see, with reasonable accuracy, the value of our assets at any given time. As you can see, the numbers are steadily increasing, sometimes moving so fast you can't really see them. It's dependent on a set of ever-expanding variables. Say we move a huge chunk of cash from one location to another, or we sell or buy or expand one of our enterprises. It affects how the numbers move. What I can tell you is that with just a few very minor exceptions, we have seen nothing but up. Over the past six weeks, we are averaging an eight-to-ten-million-dollar-a-day increase in the value of our holdings."

"Do you mean to tell me I'm looking at over eight hundred and fifty billion dollars?" Glen gasped.

"Yeah, I would say that's about right," J. T. said offhandedly.

"Holy shit," Glen replied, and plopped down into the next seat.

"Okay, J. T.," Marcus said, "are we done showing off for the moment, so we can get down to business? Glen, I asked J. T. to begin segregating the assets into two columns, those of high value and those of lesser significance, with the goal of dividing them into two halves of roughly the same value. Now, here's the tricky part. I'm assuming that to do what I am asking, we'll have to divide a particular asset, keeping part in column A and part in column B. That's fine, but I want the portion of the asset that's held in the first column to be the controlling portion of the asset. The more important and profitable the asset, the more control is needed. I want all the less important ones to be in column B. Shouldn't be too hard for a couple of financial wizards. Now for the really tricky part: this needs to be done in two weeks, preferably less. J. T., can you set Glen up with a workstation? We need to go over some stuff, and then the two of you can get to it."

Marcus sat next to his brother at one of the empty computer consoles. He knew Glen wanted to start firing off questions.

"Ready?" Marcus asked.

"Hell no, I'm not ready! What's going on, Marcus? How in God's name did you lay your hands on this kinda money? What are you doing? And *look* at you! You look like some kind of crazy, deranged...I don't know what."

Marcus leaned forward and put his hands on Glen's shoulders. "Hey, hey, slow down and breathe. It's a long story, brother, one we don't have time for right now. I know how I must look to you, but we—you and I—have to finish something."

Marcus took a deep breath. "You promised that when the time came, you'd do what I asked, no questions. Now I'm asking. I give you my word, when this is done I'll answer any question you have, but right now if I let the immensity of this ship, the money—everything—get to me, I'll lose my mind."

"Okay, bro," Glen said with a resigned sigh, "but there is one thing you need to know. A few months ago your boys and I flew back to Reno, all arranged by Agent Reynolds...." Glen's voice trailed off as he looked away.

Marcus reached out and laid his hand on top of his brothers, "Hey, it's all right, whatever it is you can tell me," Marcus said as Glen composed himself.

Glen looked up and found Marcus's eyes, "We took care of Annie...her body."

Marcus took in an audible breath.

Swallowing hard Glen continued. "Garrett insisted that we have her ashes put in that OLD PEACH can you guys kept on your mantel. He said that's where she wanted to be."

Marcus listened impassively. He had been so focused on his goal that he had almost forgotten about Annie's body.

"Hey, look at me," Glen said, his tone all business, "I'm supposed to tell you that she knew you didn't forget, and that when this thing is done, whatever that is...." His eyebrows raised in that, *I wish someone would enlighten me*, kind of way, "then you and the boys can find the perfect place for her." A smile returned to his face, as if a tremendous burden had been lifted from his shoulders, and he asked Marcus, "So what is it you need me to do?"

With his elbow on the counter, and head in his hand, Marcus massaged his forehead and forced his mind back on task. Looking up at Glen, he took a deep breath and began, "First, I want you to call Mario. Tell him he just got a new job. Between the two of you, put together the best group of international corporate attorneys you can find. At some point, we'll need to buy a building, or, for all I know, we might already own one somewhere that will work. You can tell him whatever you want; I just don't want him to tell Marie yet. We're in possession of literally billions of dollars in cash that can be at your disposal in a matter of minutes. Second, I want you to set up a trust for the Arrernte tribe in Alice Springs. Use your contacts in the Australian government to reach the people you need to talk to. I want this done fast, and I'm willing to pay to have the accommodation made. The trust is for one billion dollars. The trustee is Freddie Wanganami. Jamie, you haven't met him yet, but he can give you all the necessary information to put you in contact with him. I don't care what concessions are required, but in the end, I want the lands of these people legally secured, and enough money in place to provide for their people and their culture, for a long, long time."

"Marcus, it's coming up in just a minute," J. T. interrupted.

Glen gave Marcus a questioning look, as the brothers turned, focusing their attention on one of the big HD monitors. CNN Australia was up on screen. At the bottom, the reader script read, BREAKING NEWS, and then a male reporter began to speak.

> CNN has just been informed that World Wide Gaming, which maintains its Pacific Rim Headquarters in Australia, has been sold to a group of private investors. The terms of the sale have not been released, but our source tells us that the sale price is reported to be double today's closing share price. Glen Richard Diablo, managing director of WWG's Pacific Rim operation, is said to be the CEO of the investment group that has purchased WWG. Our source close to the deal informs us that COO Marion Daily will assume the managing director's position, effective immediately. In a statement issued by WWG, all current operations will remain in place. As this story unfolds, CNN will bring you the latest news.

Glen sat staring openmouthed.

"Hey, I need you with me," Marcus said. "And I know how you are. You can't just walk away from a commitment. Now you don't have to worry about that. We can talk about the how later. Right now we have bigger issues to deal with."

CHAPTER FIFTY-THREE
July 14

For almost two weeks, Glen and J.T. worked day and night sorting through the assets that once belonged to Adad. A daunting job, to say the least, but the biggest problem was the short timeline Marcus had set.

With J.T. and Glen on task, Marcus focused on getting his body ready for the next leg of his journey. He told the colonel that he needed some more time to work out the details. The fact was, he had it worked out, but he wasn't sure yet how to present it to the colonel and the team. Glen found it odd that Marcus was living in the gym when he could have had his pick of the ship's many luxury suites. Marcus tried explaining to him that he wanted as little as possible to do with the *Takbir* and especially with Adad's excessive lifestyle. The truth was, he didn't want the opulence of the floating palace to distract his focus. What he needed now was, as the colonel had stressed before, to stay RAW. Marcus was certain that the colonel had been using the term figuratively, but now the flayed skin of his back and chest gave the term a more literal meaning.

Glen was perhaps the only one who understood his brother, logging mile after mile on the treadmill while watching the gruesome tableau of Annie's beheading play out over and over. Before marriage and kids, they had gone on numerous expeditions together. And even after wives and children, and living on opposite sides of the globe, they still managed a couple of "guys only" trips every year. They had been in many situations, where the terrain was difficult and the weather worse, where an extreme sense of motivation was required if they were going to be successful.

As a team, Glen was the analytical one, the one who saw things black or white. But Marcus's strength was his ability to see options that existed in a rainbow of colors and dimensions. When it came to their lives, to their safety, Marcus was never hampered by ego, morality or convention. He always said that the day he no longer felt the fire inside, was the day he would quit. Glen knew that, after all he been through, all he had suffered, this was perhaps the only way for Marcus to keep that fire burning. Every time Marcus watched it, every time he saw Annie's lips making her impassioned plea, Glen knew, a strength born of grief and motivating rage surged through his brothers' veins like a drug.

Marcus knew that Ellie and the kids, along with a security team, had arrived safely at Beginnings. It also didn't surprise Glen that Marcus didn't know any details about the place, or the team sent to keep them safe, and that he didn't want to know. It was a personality trait they shared, defer to those who know better than you. When lives were at risk, it was the ultimate show of trust.

It was three in the afternoon when Glen entered the workout room. Marcus switched off the treadmill and the video. Glen shook his head slowly, no doubt feeling that his brother had gone 'round the bend.

"Done," was all Glen said. "We have the assets divided basically in half, with the most important and profitable ones in one column and the less important and minority positions in the other. Now what?"

"A herculean task, but you're gonna think that was a walk in the park compared to what I need you to do now." Marcus said, trying to sound light and upbeat. " I need you to sit down with J. T. and call your parents and each of your brothers and sisters." This was something Marcus always did with Glen. In their conversations, Marcus always said "your mother," "your father," "your sister," never "our." It was an inside joke, as if maybe Marcus were adopted and thus somehow immune to the crazy dynamic that made up their family.

"Before we left Reno, I gave Harold letters to be delivered to each of them. They're actually a version of the letter I sent you, but you know how they are, especially *your* sisters, Ruthie and Lynn. This is nonnegotiable. Within an hour of your conversation, a van will arrive at each one's home, and they will get in and be taken to a private airfield and flown to Beginnings. J. T. has made all the arrangements; transportation is lined up and ready. Most of them are going to want explanations and they'll all have lots of questions. I'm sure you'll figure it out. Good luck!" The mischievous grin on Marcus's face said, *I'm glad it's you and not me making the calls.*

"As soon as you're done, it's time to have a meeting and get you out of here."

"You aren't coming?"

"No, but I'll catch up to you in a month or so." Marcus hoped his face didn't betray any of the trepidation he felt. Leaving Glen with J. T. to make his calls, Marcus went out to the bridge and sat down beside the colonel, who was working at one of the computer consoles. Up until that moment, he hadn't realized just how little attention he had paid him. The colonel always had this sort of omnificent presence that Marcus had just taken for granted. But sitting there in his wrinkled khaki pants and short-sleeved shirt, with a tattoo, high on his right arm, that read, *ALL GAVE SOME, SOME GAVE ALL,* he looked as worn and tired as Marcus felt.

The colonel looked up from the screen, as if waiting for Marcus to hit him with his next wild-assed idea.

"I would like to put a proposition to you and the team," Marcus said. "It's the proverbial one last job. And if you don't mind, I'd like to make the pitch myself, say, around five o'clock?"

The colonel rubbed his screen-strained eyes with his hand. "Marcus, why is that you always ask me what seem like questions but are actually statements?"

"Sorry about that, Colonel," he said. "Guess it's just my nature."

"Well, according to your brother and those two sons of yours, it's one thing about you that hasn't changed."

What conversations had gone on between the colonel and his brother and sons, Marcus didn't know and didn't want to know.

"No problem," the colonel said. "I'll assemble the team at seventeen hundred. I'm interested to hear what you have on your mind."

"One more thing, Colonel. Do you think it would be all right if Glen was present? He needs to hear what I have to say, and I'd just as soon kill two birds with one stone."

"No problem. See you in while."

Marcus left the bridge, got back on the treadmill, turned on the tape, and ran.

* * *

At five o'clock, the team was assembled on the bridge. "Okay, listen up, people," the colonel said. "Our friend Marcus has something to say."

Marcus walked to the polarized-glass windows, gazed out onto the azure Mediterranean, then turned around and looked at the team and his brother. Everyone was sitting in one of the creamy leather swivel chairs or half standing, half leaning, on one of the console counters.

"Before we get to new business, I want to thank each of you for all you've done for me. It's pretty obvious that on my own, I wouldn't have made it out of Australia." The faces Marcus looked into were in full mission mode, impassive and quietly contemplative.

"I would like to hire Force 10 for one more mission."
Sit stood up. "We don't work for one of our own—it's a hard and fast rule." When Marcus gave him a puzzled look, Jamie stood up and said, "We found a replacement for Force 10." Marcus knew Jamie was referring to their lost member, Reggie Braddock.

"That's good, Jamie. I know how hard it's been on all of you. I'm sure they will be a great addition," Marcus said.

"You don't understand, sir. *You're* the replacement."

Marcus stood there in stunned silence. It seemed that there was much happening that he didn't see or comprehend. He was standing before a group of the most capable people he had ever met—people who had put their lives on the line for him. This was not something one could answer with "Well, gee, guys, thanks for the honor, but no thanks." All eyes were on him, especially Glen's.

Marcus, cleared his throat, "Imagine me being at a loss for words. I can see you've thought this through. I would consider it a privilege to be a part of Force 10." Not knowing what else to say, he thumped his chest twice with his right fist.

Sensing that Marcus had lost focus the colonel took up the slack. "Okay, people, Marcus has ops."

Facing the entire assemblage, Marcus said, "I imagine you all would like to know what's going on, so here it is. I'm going to return approximately half the assets we took from Adad." Only J. T. showed any hint of surprise. "I know, J. T., it's a lot of cake, but I have to put an end to this thing. We've made some powerful enemies, and I don't want this particular group coming after us—at least,

210

not until we have time to structure what we intend to keep and we all get a world away from here. Make no mistake, we're keeping a lot, all the best stuff, in fact. From this day forward, Force 10 will never have to worry about what projects it takes on. We'll be able to work as we choose, take on the fights we want, protect those who deserve protection. Bronson, I need you to fly for me." Bronson gave his acknowledgement with an almost imperceptible nod. "Sit, you think you and the Fat Lady would cover my ass one last time?"

Sit looked at Marcus with his big root beer–colored eyes and broke into a big grin. "Suh, my girl would have it no other way." Standing, his bulk rising like an ominous shadow, he walked to stand directly in front of Marcus. "I have your back, Marcus, so that means it's my call. Are we clear?" Sit's voice was calm but menacing.

Marcus looked up and nodded affirmation.

"Good, then let's get this goin, this dog is ready to hunt." And with that Sit returned to his seat.

Getting back on track Marcus said, "Colonel, I need you and J. T. to run ops from the *Takbir.* Liam, I need your talent with explosives. You're going to fashion a vest out of C4. You need to figure out a failsafe detonation method. It must be powerful, lightweight, and concealable under a djellaba and I need it today.

"Ham, Liam, Pete, Jamie, and Doc, you will be leaving with my brother and flying to Beginnings, in British Columbia."

Jamie was on his feet again. "Sir, I respectfully request that I remain here."

"Jamie, I know you promised to always have my back, but what I'm asking you to do is much more important than me. My sons, my family, are your responsibility. You keep them safe until I get there. Can you do that for me?"

"With my life."

"I want those who are going with Glen to Beginnings to be ready to leave in the morning. J. T. has all the appropriate documentation. On the morning of the new moon, August first, I'm going to walk into the oasis at Palmyra, to the summer palace of Adad's father, that is, if J. T. can make contact." Marcus said it as if it weren't a foregone conclusion—he just couldn't resist ribbing his ego a little.

"So that's it. Questions?"

"Uh, yeah, Marcus," Ham said. "What the hell—you just gonna walk right in and knock on the door?"

"Something like that. I'm still working it out in my head. I'm thinking simple and direct." He gave him what he hoped was a confident grin.

"Whatever, Marcus. You are about the craziest man I have ever met. Then again, I never imagined we'd get this far. So, I guess I'm in." Ham looked around at the other members of the team, waiting to see if anyone else had anything to add. No words, just nods all around.

As the meeting broke up, Chaya remained seated. Marcus motioned for her to follow him back into the gym. They sat facing each other in the leather club chairs. "What is it, Marcus?" she said. "I haven't saved your foolhardy ass enough?"

He could see the hurt in her. He leaned forward and took her hands, "Chaya, I know I've put you through a lot more than you ever bargained for. I've asked too much from you, from everyone, but I have to finish what I started. But if I have learned one thing from Force 10, it's that we must have a plan if everything goes to shit." Marcus paused, then said, "Look at me!"

Lifting her eyes to his, she gave Marcus a reluctant, acknowledging nod.

"Good. I have no intention of dying on you, Chaya. But if, by some fluke, this thing goes bad, there's nothing you'll be able to do for me. But if anyone comes after my family, then you need to be where they are. Will you do that for me?"

"Yes, of course, Marcus, damn you. I will." And she threw her arms around his neck and hugged him fiercely. Marcus knew in that moment that he would never call her "Doc" again.

CHAPTER FIFTY-FOUR
July 31

The morning after Marcus's induction as a member of Force 10, Glen, Chaya, Pete, Liam, and Jamie flew out of Marseilles en route to Vancouver, British Columbia. Marcus knew only that the newly purchased compound was in B.C. Everything else, location, size, character, was and would, for now, remain a mystery. He couldn't risk that such specific knowledge might be used against his family. That someone wishing to do him harm could eventually locate it, he had no doubt, but Marcus also knew that once a substantial contingent from Force 10 was on site, they would be able to secure the facility and keep his family safe—at the expense of their lives, if necessary.

Through a series of coded messages, J. T. was able to set up a meeting with Sheikh Nizar al-Mohmoud, Adad's father. Unlike in the United States, where financial turmoil made the news with light speed, in much of the world, financial transactions were veiled in layer upon layer of secrecy. Still, Adad's father, a rich man in his own right, could not have missed the massive transfer of ownership of family assets. For months, Ham had been able to lead Adad and keep his father informed that something very big was coming that would require patience and understanding. But when over $800 billion is transferred out of family control, even the most trusting father would have to get a bit nervous.

The *Takbir* was holding a hundred miles off the coast of Israel when, in the early morning, Sit, Bronson, Weathers, and Marcus lifted off from her deck in the Sikorsky Superhawk. Their route would take them over the blue waters of the Mediterranean, across Israel and the northern border of Jordon, then northeast into Syria and the oasis of Palmyra. The colonel had personally secured permission from the king of Jordon and the Israeli prime minister to fly through their air space. The Israelis were even going to provide jet cover under the guise of regular patrols of the Israeli-Syrian border. There was the added risk of the ongoing civil war in Syria, but Palmyra was basically in the middle of nowhere, and if the sheikh could get there so could they. Although the trip there and back was near the edge of the Sikorsky's range, Bronson assured Marcus, that they would make it, "one way or another"—whatever that meant.

About thirty-five kilometers from Palmyra, the helicopter set down on the arid plateau. From the air, the surface looked like sand, but stepping out of the chopper, Marcus found himself standing on rough, course ground the color of toast.

Marcus had been unable to explain to the Force 10 team, or his brother, why he felt it necessary to cross that desert on foot and alone. All he knew was that he needed to arrive on the doorstep of Sheikh Nizar al-Mohmoud's summer camp, in all appearance, as one of his people, just a poor simple man who had walked across the parched desert for an audience with a powerful and respected leader. Marcus needed the Sheikh arrogant and all full of himself. Also he needed to resolve the issue of what to do about Adad. It would be his final hurdle before he could return to his sons and he was hoping that time alone in the harsh desert, would put him in the right frame of mind and enlighten him about ending Adad's time on this planet.

Marcus had allowed himself all night to cover the distance to Palmyra. Bronson, Sit, and Weathers would fly into about ten kilometers from the oasis, where Sit would go on foot to a vantage point where he could keep eyes on him.

Marcus's plan was basic. Glen and J.T. had the assets segregated and broken down. All Marcus had to do was convince the sheikh that this was the best deal he was going to get. Then a straight forward computer interface between J. T. on the *Takbir*, and the sheikh's financial advisers, and the transfer of wealth would begin.

Marcus was dressed in a light-tan T-shirt, compression shorts, and running shoes. In his pack were a coarse off-white cotton djellaba and a pair of rough leather sandals, three gallons of water, and the C-4 vest.

The plan was for him to set out at dusk so that he could cover the distance in the cool of the night. J. T. had programmed the GPS in his communication device with the route. All he had to do was follow the red line.

As the sun began to set, Marcus gazed at a vault of sky that seemed to extend forever, blushed with pale pink, then tangerine orange, darkening to deep, flaming red before finally fading to purple. And as he left, with the temperature still hovering right at a hundred degrees, he felt like he had just witnessed something holy.

Shouldering his pack Marcus set out at a fast walk. He had given a lot of thought to that pack. It had belonged to one of the men who first involved him in all this. It seemed almost as if that pack had a life of its own, as if something about it were trying to make up for the evil associated with it. Marcus knew how weird it sounded, but time after time that pack had carried the things necessary for him to take one step further on his journey.

Three hours into his running/walking trek, Marcus was thankful for the absence of sand. His mind wandered to what he might encounter in Palmyra. He knew that for centuries this oasis had served travelers crossing the Syrian desert. That it had extensive, excavated Roman ruins. At first, when Ham had suggested Palmyra as the meeting place, explaining it was where the sheikh had his summer palace, Marcus had this picture of a large white stone structure with chiseled columns, marble floors, and sweeping desert vistas. But what he would see instead in this Bedouin caravan town, were elaborate round tents woven of mohair, furnished with thick Persian rugs and lush, richly colored cushions.

Marcus thought it strange that Sheikh Nizar would chose to spend two months at the oasis of Palmyra, especially during the hottest time of the year. But according to Ham, it had something to do with staying true to one's roots and honoring their ancestors while trusting in the same God that had provided for them during their crossing of this scorching hot, inhospitable land. And now with Damascus a war zone, the refuge of the oasis, was all the more significant.

No matter what the rational though, the sheikh and his entourage of personal staff would already have arrived from Damascus and been here for several weeks. Marcus had no doubt that among the people the sheikh had with him, would be several personal bodyguards.

Running over uneven terrain, in the dark demanded his constant attention. Unlike the treadmill, where he could let his attention wander, here his focus had to be razor sharp, for a rolled ankle could mean not just failure but death. Also his conditioning was not anywhere near where it been before the beating. So Marcus ran on, alert to every contour and shadow, and the night passed, the stars wheeling slowly above him, his only companions the whispering desert breeze and the ceaseless whirling of his mind.

CHAPTER FIFTY-FIVE
August 1

At six in the morning, the moon still visible in the morning sky, Marcus looked down on the oasis of Palmyra, an emerald set into a sea of sand, its pale ruins lit by the rising sun. He quickly changed into his djellaba after first putting on the vest that Liam had devised. It was really quite a work of art. It fit over his shoulders and covered his chest but left his scabbed and still healing back open. A small electronic receiver was mounted on the left, just below his collarbone. Once it was activated, the colonel and J. T., aboard the *Takbir,* would pick up the signal and, with a keystroke, turn Marcus to mist and send anyone within a hundred yards to his long-awaited tryst with the promised "seventy-two virgins." This was his one and only insurance policy if the whole thing went bad.

Marcus laid his pack on the ground and walked toward Palmyra. The sun was already hot, and the sweat trickled in warm rivulets down his chest.

With his gray-black beard and lean, furrowed face shaded with ragged brown cloth, Marcus looked like just another traveler who might walk into this oasis. At least, that's what he hoped.

Marcus approached the largest and most colorful of the tents, and two men stepped forward carrying automatic weapons. He made his greeting and was greeted in kind. He told them he was the man who had come to meet with Sheikh Nizar al-Mohmoud. Ham had said that the likelihood that he would be patted down was next to zero, that among the Arabs of the desert there was this implicit trust that one came to such a meeting as this unarmed and on peaceful terms.

He was led through a flap into the large, airy main tent. But the interior was unlike any tent Marcus had ever seen. The floor was covered in thick, colorful plush carpets, and rising as much as three feet along the perimeter were large, elaborately colored cushions. In the center of the tent, the carpet was exposed, and an old wooden table similar in height to a coffee table was set up. On this was a large computer monitor and keyboard. Outside, Marcus had noticed a small satellite dish, mounted on a portable tripod a short distance from the main tent. A man sat cross-legged on the floor in front of the monitor.

Marcus was struck by the smells inside the tent—smells so natural, so real, he could taste them in the air: orange, lilac, jasmine, honeysuckle, and rose. It was as if he had stepped into a magnificent garden on a windless day.

Marcus kept his eyes averted from the man seated on the raised pillows. He was lean, with a well-groomed gray beard and dressed in a crisp white robe and matching turban. Marcus bowed and dropped to his knees, placing his head almost on the carpeted floor. "*Assalamu Alaikum,*" Marcus said as he made the sign of obeisance, a touch of his right hand to his forehead followed by a slight motion, palm up, toward the seated man.

" *Wa Alaikum assalam wa rahmata Allah,* "the man said. "How can you be the one who is responsible for stealing my family's money?" Marcus could sense the arrogance and outrage in his voice. Good—he needed him angry. "You have come here alone—a man who is, by all appearances, of no consequence. I must warn you that I am a man with little patience for the games of ignorant schemers." At least the sheikh and Marcus had that much in common.

Lifting his head, Marcus looked into the eyes of Sheikh Nizar al-Mohmoud. In Arabic he said, "I have come in peace as a man of God. We have important business, and it would be unwise of you to misjudge me."

The sheikh rose from his place above Marcus and came down to the floor and stood before his kneeling, supplicant form. "You must tell me what has been done to our fortune," he said. "And it must be returned to me immediately. I have not spoken to my son Adad in several weeks. Do you know where he is? Is he well?"

Marcus sat back on his heels, "May I rise, Sayid?"

"Yes, but my tolerance is near its end!"

Marcus stood and faced the father of the man responsible for Annie's death and the horrific terrorist attack on the U.S. "I have come to you as one of your people, but I am not of your people." Marcus slowly unwrapped his head and let his long hair fall to about his shoulders. He sensed movement behind, heard the soft click of safety catches on rifles being flicked off.

Keeping his voice controlled and even. "Look into my eyes, Sayid. What do you see?" Marcus had not known until he was preparing for this part of his journey that his blue eyes were considered the mark of evil in Arab culture, something to be both respected and feared. "As unfathomable as it may seem to you, I am the man responsible for the loss of your wealth. And although I am not from the land of mankind's beginning, I wear certain marks of Allah nonetheless."

Marcus pulled first one arm then the other through the top of the lose djellaba, revealing the pale yellow vest that covered his chest. With his right hand, he touched the small black receiver in the left side of the vest, and a red LED blinked on. "You see, it is somewhat ironic that I come to you as a human weapon, like the ones so readily used to further the ideals of Islam. But the most ironic part is that this particular device is controlled by your own satellite, God's Eye." As Marcus said this, he turned to reveal the crisscrossing purple scars and scabs on his back.

He turned back to face the sheikh.

"You! *You* are the one? I have heard there was a man who survived the ritual of Sharia—and at the hand of Bahir, no less."

Marcus smiled. "So you know about me."

The sheikh studied him. "We must speak in English. I find it disturbing to converse with one who speaks as if he were a believer, born in my land, and who, moreover, looks so as well."

"As you wish, Sayid." Marcus switched to English, knowing that his accent would tell him he was a Westerner.

The look on the sheik's face was one of complete stupefaction.

"Yes, Sayid, I am American, but I am here simply as a man. I am here to seek retribution for a grievous injury to my people and for the murder of my wife." In the sheik's eyes Marcus could see it all coming together.

"Now, our time is short." Marcus looked at his watch. "We have less than one hour to complete our business before this vest explodes and makes martyrs of us all." In an instant, six armed men surrounded him. Marcus held up his hands. "I would not be hasty," he said in Arabic. "This vest is wired in such a way that if my heart rate varies by more that fifteen beats per minute, either up or down, it will go off. And any attempt to remove it will break the connection that is charged by the electrical impulse of my body—again, causing it to go off. You are familiar with the capabilities of the new God's Eye satellite, of course. If we do not complete our task quickly, a signal will be sent to this receiver, and *boom!*"

"What do you want?" the sheikh said.

"Now, is that not better?" Marcus spoke in the formal English so common among foreigners educated in the UK. "It is not so much what I want as what I offer. This is not a negotiation; it is, as the Americans say, a take-it-or-leave-it proposition." Marcus paused to let the words sink in. This man was certainly not accustomed to having terms dictated to him.

"I am prepared to return to you approximately four hundred billion dollars of assets," Marcus said. "You will have no choice in which assets. I see you have done as instructed and brought your financial adviser with you. This is good!"

"I want *everything* back, not just part of it! My understanding is that the value of what you have stolen is twice what you are offering to return."

Marcus steeled his gaze on the sire of the egomaniac who had stolen so much from him, his sons, and his country. "I will not say it again. You are in no position to make demands. The Koran says, '*On the day that every soul shall find present what it has done of good and what it has done of evil, it shall wish that between it and that evil there were a long duration of time; and Allah makes you to be cautious of retribution from himself; and Allah is compassionate to the servants.*' Don't look so surprised, Sayid. I know well your holy book."

"Adad—where is Adad?"

" '*Go back to your father and say: O our father! Surely your son committed theft, and we do not bear witness except to what we have known, and we could not keep watch over the unseen.*' I am willing to accept that your son is responsible for his own sins against Allah, but as his father, you must bear the cost of some of those sins. The Koran is clear on the price one must pay for taking the life of another: Qisas—an eye for an eye. What it did not teach you was the price one must pay to the *children* of those whose life has been unjustly taken. According to the Book of Marcus, the cost is four hundred billion dollars."

The sheikh seemed to have gone away from the moment. He was looking at Marcus, but Marcus was not sure he was hearing him.

Right on cue, Sheikh Nizar's cell phone rang. From the pained and confused look on his face Marcus knew that he was talking to Adad. The sheikh kept trying to interrupt, but as scripted, Adad had been coached to keep the conversation short and to the point. Within less than a minute the sheikh flipped his phone shut. Reluctantly and with visible self-restraint he nodded at Marcus and then to the table holding the computer.

Marcus stepped to the monitor, knelt on the thick carpet and typed in a code accessing a secure link to the *Takbir.* A few seconds later, the financial data began to scroll across the screen.

Marcus stood and faced Sheikh Nizar. "Adad...where is my son?" His question lacked the force of his earlier superiority.

Like so many of the notions that had come to Marcus, along his insane journey, so it was with what would ultimately happen to Adad.

At the sheik's question, in a flash Marcus knew. " '*So we caught hold of him and his hosts, then we cast them into the sea, and see how was the end of the unjust.* ' The Koran is clear: the hand of the one and only Allah will punish the sins of man—I am a mere servant doing his work. So, I am afraid we have no more time, Sayid."

It was evident to Marcus that the sheikh was a defeated man. His one and only son lost to him. No matter what his son had done, the sheikh was his father, and despite his feelings about Adad, Marcus felt a father's loss. "Will you walk with me, Sayid?"

They walked out into the glaring morning sun. The ruins cast their long shadows over the ground. As they stepped away from the tent, a small boy ran up to the sheikh, who bent and picked him up and embraced him, then set him back down, and with a nod indicated he wanted the young boy to return to the tent.

The sheikh did not tell Marcus who the little boy was, but he assumed that this was his grandson—Adad's son? As they walked, Marcus said, "It would seem that Allah has blessed you with a second chance. Don't squander it." Just then a cloud of dust erupted behind Marcus and the sheikh. Marcus shifted his attention as the report of the fifty caliber echoed across the oasis.

Marcus leaned in close to the sheikh. "Tell your men to stand down, or in the next second you will find out if you have truly been a faithful servant of Allah."

The sheikh turned and ordered his men to lower their weapons.

As if the whole thing were no more than a normal part of such an encounter, the sheik clasped his hands behind his back and resumed walking toward the ruins.

They walked in silence for a few moments, Marcus forcing his mind and body to remain calm. Then he spoke. "One of the things I find so endearing about your people is the love of stories, teachings given through analogy and metaphor. So let me tell you a story. You should look upon me as one of your wives. No, that is not right—look on me as your *number one* wife—the one who knows your deepest desires and secrets. The one who is responsible for the instruction of your lesser wives in the art of pleasing their master. The one who is the mother of your heirs. The one person to whom, despite the demeaning position of women in your culture, you feel bound. The one who sees all and whose wrath you do not want to incur. So, one man to another, one father to another, I must be clear. If you renege on our agreement, if you try to find me or in any way threaten my family, I will return like the fire of hell itself and will scorch your seed from the face of this earth."

They had stopped a few hundred yards from the camp. Marcus took one last look at Sheikh Nizar al-Mohmoud. He had wanted to rail against him, revile him. But he only felt empty and anxious. "Go in peace, Sayid. May the blessings of Allah forever rest upon you and your family. May you and I both see wisdom and forgiveness as a road to redemption and peace."

Marcus turned his back on Palmyra and walked into the rapidly warming desert. Several hundred more yards away from the oasis, he removed his vest and set it on the ground. He continued walking away, and a few minutes later heard the explosion, felt its concussive wave. As he strode away, for the first time in over a year, Marcus felt free.

CHAPTER FIFTY-SIX

When the helicopter landed back on the *Takbir,* Marcus went straight to the bridge, looking for the colonel. In his absence, a crew of men he had never seen before, had come aboard. Marcus had not given any thought to what they would do with the *Takbir,* but it seemed the colonel had.

He found the colonel in a discussion with a tall, broad-shouldered, middle-aged man in desert fatigues. With a nod from the colonel, the man left.

Not looking up from his console, J.T. said to Marcus, "Everything's coming off as planned. It'll take weeks for the transfers to be finalized, but so far so good."

"Heard we had a bit of excitement?" The colonel said.

Marcus had to think for a moment...Sit's rifle shot. "Yeah, I don't think Sit trusts me much. Anyway colonel, it's time to finish this thing. Adad's time is up."

The colonel studied him for a moment. "I need to qualify what I'm going to say, Marcus. I agree that Adad's time on this earth is up. But that said, if you think killing him is somehow going to lift some huge weight from your shoulders or unburden your soul of the guilt you're packing around, you're in for a disappointment."

Stepping closer so that he stood right in front of Marcus, he said, "I told you when we first met that revenge has no place in what we do. And it's true. Finishing Adad is no more and no less than an operational necessity. He is no longer a viable source of information, or anything, for that matter. So how do you want to do this? We're not really in a location that would be conducive to getting rid of him."

Marcus grinned. "I have no intention of getting rid of him anywhere remotely near here." He turned to J. T. "You think you can get me to Dutch Harbor, up in the Bering Sea?"

J.T. beamed a conspiratorial smile. "No problem, my man. One of Adad's newest acquisitions is in Marseille—a Boeing 777—sort of his aeronautic version of the *Takbir.* We can be in helicopter range in twenty-four hours. But we have one serious problem. There is no way you're landing a private jet in the U.S. without going through customs. In theory, we can fly direct to Anchorage and then take a Gulfstream G5 into Dutch Harbor. We just happen to have one there, by the way. It belongs to one of the oil companies you now control. So you work out that little problem, and I'll have you on your way."

"I need to make a phone call, Colonel," Marcus said. "Can we make that happen?"

"Depends on who you want to call."

"Who else? The FBI."

From the bridge, J. T. set Marcus up with an untraceable secure line. Then in a display of the sort of computer hackery that had earned him the moniker "Mr. Wizard," his fingers flew over the keys and Agent Reynolds's direct line rang in Marcus's headset.

"This is a secure line!" a familiar voice spluttered. "Whoever you are, you'd better have a damn good explanation how you got this number."

"Well, hello to you, too, Agent Reynolds—oops, make that *Deputy Director* Reynolds."

"Marcus?" There was a long pause.

"I'm flattered that you remembered my voice. Now, if you're trying to trace this, don't waste your time. There's not a chance in hell you'll be able to. I just wanted to let you know so you could leave it alone and focus on the actual conversation."

"Glad to see you haven't lost your confidence, Marcus. How are the boys?"

Marcus had to give it to the man: he was FBI to the core. "Let's cut the crap, Reynolds," he said in a cheery tone. "I need a favor. We'll just consider it a partial payment for your rising success."

"You know, Marcus, you've been on my mind of late. Seems that a lot of...interesting things," he held the s for a second, "are going down in various places. You wouldn't by any chance know anything about that, would you?"

"Haven't the foggiest idea what you're talking about, Deputy Director. And even if I did, that would require a face-to-face, and that's not going to happen just yet. So listen close. I need you to arrange for me to land in Anchorage, in three days. I need to be there no more than seventy-two hours. No customs, no questions, no nothing!"

Reynolds started to give Marcus a hundred and one reasons why he couldn't do it, so he cut him off before he could start. "I know, I know, but you are a very resourceful, and, now, very important, highly placed man. I'm sure you can figure something out. I'll make you a deal. You make this happen, and I promise that in the near future, you and I will have that face-to-face. And I guarantee you'll find it worth your while."

There was a pause. "Okay, Marcus, call me back in an hour. You obviously have the number."

An hour later, Marcus was on the line with the deputy director of the FBI. "Okay, Marcus, you're cleared. Just make sure you're out of U.S. airspace seventy-two hours after you land—and I'll be waiting for that face-to-face." The call ended without Marcus ever saying a word.

CHAPTER FIFTY-SEVEN
August 5

After his conversation with Deputy Director Reynolds, Marcus was feeling as wired as he had in months. He asked the colonel if they could speak in private.

As they sat down in the stuffed leather chairs, Marcus said, "Seems you've made plans for the *Takbir?*" referring to the men he had seen on board when he got back from Palmyra.

"You do know that's what I do, don't you—make plans?" The colonel said offhandedly.

"Yeah, I know. Sorry."

"Hey, don't get all sentimental on me now, Marcus. We still have a ways to go. Seems like the shipyard where the *Takbir* was built is one of the many assets in your control. So until we can figure out what to do with her, I've arranged for a crew to sail her, and remain there until we do, all on your nickel, of course," he said with a friendly smile.

The two men sat in silence for a moment; then the colonel said, "Okay, Marcus, spit it out. How is it you'd like this to work?"

"I'd like to take Bronson, Weathers, Sit and Ham and of course, our substance-dependent friend with me and head for Alaska. I'd like you and J.T. to arrange to meet us in Calgary when our business is done."

"Anything else?"

Marcus studied the colonel for a moment. "Yes Sam, there is—another personal favor."

The colonel shifted in his chair, crossing is legs. "You know, Marcus," he said, "I believe that's the first time you ever used my first name."

"I know. I had to a build a wall between us. It was the only way I could think of to get to your team. I needed to be an active part of it, needed to participate. So, though I never intended to become a member of Force 10, I *absolutely* intended on being a part of this particular operation, and for that to happen, you had to see me as you see them.

"I'd like you to check on my family and the team at Beginnings. Make sure that procedures to protect them are in place, and formulate contingency plans if we—"

"Hold on there, Marcus," the colonel said in his, *I have ops,* voice. "I've been in contact with the team at Beginnings every day since they arrived. Everything is fine. It seems those boys of yours have made quite the impression, especially on Chaya." The colonel fixed his gaze on Marcus. "She told you, didn't she?"

Marcus didn't need to answer.

"Well, that's good. If there's any member of this team that needs what you seem to have in abundance, it's her. So for now it would be best if you quit worrying about my job and took care of your own shit."

***

After their conversation, Marcus returned to the bridge to see J. T. "I need to make one more call." Marcus handed him a slip of paper.

Ten minutes later, Marcus had the headset on, and a deep voice on the other end said, "Scott Bohannon and the *Lucky Lady*. Can I help you?"

"Scott, my name is Marcus Diablo. I think you and my wife, Annie—her maiden name was Annie Mitchell—are distantly related."

There was a moment of silence on the other end. "Marcus *Diablo?* I know who you are, and yes, your Annie and I are related—some cousin-of-a-cousin's-cousin thing. I'm really sorry for your loss. But I hope you don't mind me saying, that girl showed some serious balls before those bastards took her life. So to what do I owe the genuine pleasure of this call?"

Here was the moment of truth. With little more than a line of bullshit, Marcus hoped to get this stranger to become a willing participant in his crazy plan.

"Well, it's my understanding that you're a crab fisherman."

"That's right, son, been doing it my whole life, second generation. And if I can keep my dumb-ass sons on track and our luck holds, it'll be three generations. You know, that whole *Deadliest Catch* thing has given our industry a much-needed shot in the arm."

Marcus took a deep breath and dived in. "Well, Scott, I have a business proposition of sorts. I was hoping you might lease your boat to me for a few days. I can provide you with whatever you need: insurance, deposit, prepayment."

"Hold on there, son. Does this have anything to do with your Annie, her death, and the attack on our country?"

"Yes, that much I can tell you. Beyond that, you don't want to know—trust me."

"So you want to lease my boat for a few days. You know it's over in Dutch and you're calling me in Anchorage?"

"Well, as it happens, that works out real well for me, Scott. You see, I've been thinking about a little sightseeing tour of the Bering Sea."

"Don't bullshit me, boy. Nobody in their right mind goes sightseeing there. The Bering is Satan's own cesspool." He let out a deep laugh. "Tell you what, I can hear in your voice a great need, just call it fisherman's intuition. If you need the boat for a few days, it's yours, but I'm a little unclear on how you expect to pilot it. This isn't like taking a Boston Whaler out for a run around the bay."

"Tell you what, Scott," Marcus said. "You think you'd be willing to meet me in Anchorage on the fifth? And if you can spare a few days, we'll fly to Dutch together. You can meet my skipper and decide for yourself. I would expect to compensate you very well for your time and, of course, pay you for the use of your boat."

224

After a momentary pause on the line, Scott said, "Your timing couldn't be better. It just so happens I need to take a trip over to Dutch and check on some gear I've been waiting for. I've been putting it off. I had a new Doppler radar installed. Supposed to be some state-of-the-art weather forecasting genie. And, well, let's just say the guys in Dutch tend to work at their own pace." He laughed and went on. "As for payment, let's just wait till we meet. I'm sure you and I can work something out. I can't explain it, but I've got a feeling about you and when you've spent your life on a small boat in scary seas, you learn to follow your gut."

"Excellent! Then we're on. I'll contact you when we're en route to Anchorage, and let you know our arrival time."

On the afternoon of August 4, Bronson, Weathers, Ham, Sit and Marcus, loaded into the Bell with Adad and flew to the private jet port at the international airport in Marseille. Upon landing, they were met by two men from, according to Bronson, the Directorate-General for External Security (DGSE), the French version of the CIA. Everyone but Marcus seemed to know them, and they spent a few moments exchanging pleasantries. Marcus knew they would need some official clearance to fly out of France. And once again the Force 10's connections came through.

J. T. had the appropriate documents that the team and Marcus needed, and they had recovered Adad's French passport from his safe. Bronson was the pilot, and as it turned out, Weathers had adequate flight credentials to serve as copilot. It was a stroke of coincidence and good fortune that Adad's newest toy, a Boeing 777, just happened to be in Marseilles, one of his most frequented playgrounds. With a range that would easily make the more than five thousand miles to Anchorage, it was, as J.T. had said, a flying palace. Although less spacious, it was as elegant and plush as the main salon of the *Takbir*.

Four hours out of Anchorage, Marcus called Scott and gave him their ETA. An hour out, he talked to the team, with Bronson and Weathers listening in on the intercom from the cockpit.

"I want everyone to remain on board until I make sure everything's clear," Marcus said. "I have a funny feeling there might be someone there to meet us. Bronson, clear with the tower for an immediate takeoff, and if you get the high sign from me, I want you out of there. I don't think we'll have a problem, but I'm not very popular with the FBI."

They landed at almost eight in the evening, with the sun still shining bright. It felt good to be back Stateside again. Marcus got off the plane alone and was met at the bottom of the stairs by none other than Special Agent Gibson.

"Why, Agent Gibson, what a surprise!" Marcus exclaimed in a very unsurprised tone.

"Mr. Diablo, good to see you again."

"I take it that you didn't end up getting posted in South Dakota?"

"No sir, I have done all right for myself. I'm working directly under the deputy director."

"So how is our illustrious Mr. Reynolds?"

"He's doing well, sir. I think he learned a lot from his experience with you, and once he broke the terrorist cell, it was an elevator ride straight to the top."

"So what's the deal, Agent Gibson—you here to babysit me again?"

He shifted from foot to foot and, with an embarrassed expression on his face, said, "I am here to accompany you to wherever you're going, and then to make sure you leave per your arrangements with the deputy director."

"Of course you are! All right, let me just get my passengers organized and we'll meet on that jet right over there," Marcus said, pointing to a sleek G5 being fueled and prepared for takeoff about a hundred yards away. "You'll be riding in the copilot's seat—my guests are very private individuals; I'm sure you understand."

"Oh, by the way, there's a man waiting for you in the terminal," Gibson said.

Marcus walked over to the private jet terminal and entered through the glass double doors.

A guy in a Sea Hawks ball cap and brown Carhartt coveralls, a bit on the pudgy side, was sitting by a TV monitor. It had to be Scott, though somehow, Marcus had expected him to be bigger and tougher looking.

Walking up to him, Marcus said, "Scott?"

"You must be Marcus," he said, and bounded up from his chair to clasp Marcus in a bear hug. Marcus tried not to flinch from the pain the warm embrace inflicted on his still scabbed and healing back.

"You ready to go?" Scott said, reaching down and hefting a large canvas duffel bag.

Marcus explained that he had to go and get his guests, pointed Scott toward the jet, and said he would join him in a few moments.

Back aboard the 777, Ham had Adad bundled up in a baggy wool sweater and a knit cap pulled low over his forehead, and so doped up he was like a well-behaved dog on a leash.

Ten minutes later they were all aboard the G5. After taking off on the two-hour flight to Dutch Harbor, Marcus introduced Scott to Weathers. A few minutes later, Scott was ready to hire him on the spot as a crab boat pilot. Then they spent some time going over a nautical map.

"How long will it take us to get...here?" Marcus asked Scott, pointing to a spot some 230 nautical miles southwest of Dutch Harbor.

"Figuring, say, fifteen knots, oh somewhere around sixteen, seventeen hours. But, Marcus, there's nothing out there, just some really deep ocean."

"Yeah, well over ten thousand feet," Marcus said. "That will suit my purposes just fine. Now, you think you can come up with a plausible story for the folks in Dutch, so they won't be suspicious when we take your boat out for a few days without a regular crew?"

"Long as you let me take your boy Weathers into the bar for a few minutes."

Marcus had no idea what story Weathers would come up with, but if there was one thing he did know, every member of the team was seriously adept at improvisation. And besides he had Agent Gibson to deal with.

Marcus went up to the cockpit and squeezed in. Dutch Harbor was just a tiny blob of light on the horizon. Stooping over, Marcus said, "Agent Gibson, do you trust me?"

"Well, to be honest, I have no reason not to. You've always lived up to your end of the bargain anytime you dealt with the Bureau."

"Good," Marcus said, resting a hand on his broad shoulder, "because you're going to stay in Dutch with my good friend Bronson here." Marcus gave a slight nod to the pilot. "Now, don't argue with me—where I'm going and what I'm doing, you don't want any part of. Tell Reynolds we ambushed you and tied you up—whatever. But this is as far as you're going. I'll be gone less than forty-eight hours. Then we're back aboard the jet to Anchorage, I'm gone, and everyone's happy."

"I guess I don't need to tell you that if the deputy director finds out I let you out of my sight, he'll be, um, less than pleased."

Marcus laughed. "So I guess what the deputy director doesn't know won't hurt you. When we land, you'll give your cell phone to Bronson. I think, if you ponder the situation, you'll see that it works out best for everyone if you'll just humor me on this."

Agent Gibson looked around him and must have felt a little outmanned and outgunned. "You know, Marcus," he said, "the deputy director's expecting me to check in." He looked at Marcus, as if to see how he would respond.

"Tell him we had bad weather and no signal, or that you got so seasick you couldn't lift your head from over the rail, let alone make a phone call—tell him whatever. Bottom line, I need you to stay put in Dutch and not to make any calls to the deputy director while you're there."

Agent Gibson gave him a disgruntled nod, along with a wary glance at Bronson, and Marcus returned to the main cabin.

When they landed in Dutch, Scott took Weathers into the bar, and it was after midnight when they finally boarded the *Lucky Lady*. Scott had to give Weathers a full rundown of the ship, engines, and navigation and communications systems. He assured them they had a "heaven-sent" weather window for the next four to five days, and since the ship had just gone through a complete overhaul and retrofit, Weathers should have no problem dealing with anything that came up. Odd, Marcus thought, but it seemed perfectly natural that a man he had never met would, on the strength of one phone call, lend him the single most valuable thing in his life, which represented everything he had spent a lifetime working for. But then, over the past months Marcus had often been amazed by people who evaluated others in an instant and then bet their life and livelihood on their instincts.

CHAPTER FIFTY-EIGHT

They motored for eighteen hours and all the while Marcus felt on edge. His wounds seemed to throb in rhythm with the thrum of the diesel engines. In his months on the *Takbir,* Marcus had not spoken a word to Adad, or so much as laid eyes on him, until they departed for Alaska. It was a deliberate decision, so he wouldn't be tempted to kill him on the spot.

Marcus was sitting in the galley of the *Lucky Lady* as the boat slowed and the engines came to a full stop. He asked Ham to get Adad up from the cramped bunk where he had ridden out the journey in a methadone haze, and bring him out onto the deck. As Marcus waited at the rail, in the crisp gray morning, a seething rage surged through him. A few minutes later, Ham walked out the bulkhead door with Adad.

Marcus turned and began walking toward Adad, who was standing, clinging to one of the posts that supported the stairs to the upper bridge deck. Ham made to go back inside, but Marcus said, "Stick around for a few minutes, Ham." Stopping before Adad, Marcus saw the man was shaking, even though it wasn't that cold, and his eyes were darting around giving him the look of the wild, strung out junkie, he was. Before Doc had left the *Takbir* for Beginnings, she had begun weaning Adad off of the heroin, and for the past week Ham had been giving him just enough methadone to keep him from crawling out of his skin. And since they boarded the *Lucky Lady,* he hadn't had a fix. Marcus wanted him, jonesing and frantic.

Marcus had rehearsed this scene in his head a thousand times: the grand denouement, with the arch-villain now at the victor's mercy. Reaching out Marcus snatched the cap from Adad's head. Adad cowered, clinging to post like a frightened child to a mother's leg. With hate seeping from his every pore, and without taking his eyes off Adad, Marcus said, "Ham, why don't you tell our friend here who you really are."

Ham walked over and stood next to Marcus, and for the next few minutes, speaking in Adad's native tongue, as Farid Tehrani, explained to Adad.

Marcus watched as awareness began to spread across Adad's face, like a light being turned slowly from dim to bright.

Adad's eyes flashed from Marcus to Ham and back.

Marcus said, "I see you've figured out who I am."

"You...." Adad murmured. "No, it cannot be. You are the...husband? How...? It is not possible! Where am I?"

"At the end of the fucking world," Marcus said.

Despite Adad's hallowed, drawn, sickly completion, Marcus could see that, although temporary, a transformation had taken place, and in that moment, the confident, arrogant Adad was back.

Holding the post with one hand, Adad straightened up, and spoke to Marcus. "You think that by killing me, that will make a difference?" He sneered, "So typically American, always so shortsighted. You don't think we made plans? That there are not others who, like me have the resources and the commitment to carry on the fight? My value as a martyr will be immeasurable."

Marcus was unconsciously balling up and releasing his fists, as he stood, transfixed by Adad's voice. Then a hand touched his shoulder. "Marcus, you all right?" Ham said.

Taking a couple deep breaths Marcus looked at Ham, "I'm good." Ham gave Marcus that *sure you are* look. Marcus, nodded, "Yeah, I'm good, go on."

After Ham went back inside, Marcus focused on Adad. Despite the arrogance in Adad's voice, he was unsteady on his legs, and the rocking and swaying of the boat in the lazy swells was enough that he couldn't let go of the pole. Marcus got very close to Adad, their face so near he could smell Adad's stale breath. "You don't get it, we control, in one form or another, nearly all of your family's wealth. We have the *Takbir* and the God's Eye Satellite." The indignation was building hot in Marcus, like the rising of the summer sun. The questioning look in Adad's eyes, begged for an explanation. "And you...you have nothing. Being a martyr only works if people give a shit that your dead."

Adad was shaking his head side to side, "No, that cannot be, my father would…"

"Would what," Marcus was crowding Adad, forcing him to cower against the pole, "never abandon his son? Don't you be so sure. The truth is, your father and I have reached an understanding. You see Adad, you fucked with the wrong American." Marcus hissed as he stabbed his finger in the air right in front of Adad's face. Then as Marcus was warming up to lay into Adad, to attack his manhood, his faith, his very existence, a group of sea gulls came sweeping down toward the deck searching for an easy meal, distracting Marcus for a brief moment.

In a sudden, lucid rage, Adad sprung from the pole, like a wild animal bolting from a just opened cage, and launched himself at Marcus. With his teeth bared, his face drawn and pale, Adad looked like one of the undead from horror movies, as he wrapped his arms around Marcus, and propelled them both towards the rail. Marcus was franticly backpedaling, the soles of his rubber boots unable to get purchase on the wet deck. Adad was screaming, "Now you can join your infidel whore of a wife. My cause will survive without me, it will, it will."

In that instant when Marcus's back hit the rail, time stopped. As if it were a prelude to the drowning that awaited him, Marcus's mind, running at the speed of light, replayed the event that had driven him to this place, and as Annie's head rolled from her shoulders and the geysers of blood exploded from her headless neck, Marcus and Adad plunged into the thirty eight degree water. Locked in Adad's death grip the shock of the freezing water sucked the little remaining air from Marcus's lungs.

In full-blown survival mode and knowing that he had only seconds, Marcus swung his head forward with all the force he could muster, making contact with the middle of Adad's face. Marcus was so numb he barley felt the hands that gripped him relax their hold. Kicking franticly with legs that were heavy and sluggish it seemed like he would never break the surface. Between his drenched clothing and water filled rubber boots, it required every ounce of strength he had. Once his head broke the surface, he tried to breath, but his teeth were chattering so hard that instead of a huge gulp of life giving air all he got was a sip.

It was then that Marcus realized that the boat had drifted. He was at least fifteen feet away from it, *and it may as well have been a hundred miles* that little voice in his mind said. God, he thought, to have come this far to only die in this frigid water, all because he let his guard down, because *he* got *complacent,* for one stupid second.

Just as he was about to let his hypothermic body fade into oblivion, Marcus felt something hit him in the head, then voices screaming, "Grab the buoy, God damn it. Marcus, grab the buoy."

"What," Marcus tried to say, as his hands involuntarily thrashed about and made contact with the hard foam cylinder.

"Hold on to it, hold on!" He heard, but this time it was Annie's voice in his head. Then he wasn't sure, but he thought he felt hands dragging from the water. To Marcus it seemed like a dream, in which he was floating in the air, looking down at himself, as he lay on his back on the deck of the *Lady Luck*, with a small smile on his blue lips, while Sit, Weathers and Ham, worked to remove his clothing. Then Annie's voice was in his head again, hard and angry, "You're an idiot, Marcus. You just about screwed everything up. Now, if you had gone and gotten yourself killed, after all we've been through, well, I'd be kicking your dumb ass for all eternity, so you wipe that stupid grin off your face." Marcus took one last look down at himself, then everything faded from view and he again felt the deep, dark cold devouring him.

***

For the second time, Marcus wasn't sure if he was dead or not, as Annie's voice invaded his mind. "You're a lucky man Marcus. Your friends...they're always looking out for you. You remember that! Now you listen to me, the colonel was right—you can't banish what you're holding inside by ridding yourself of this man, and damn near getting yourself killed to boot." Marcus could feel more than hear the chastisement in her tone, then her voice softened, "Come on, honey, you know that can only come from a life well lived. So live well. You've surrounded yourself with the most incredible people. And with our family, they'll help you—let them! Chaya's pretty, Marcus." He detected no chiding or jealousy in Annie's tone. "You take care with her. This is not a woman you can just bowl over with

230

your baby blues and bullshit. The pain in her is deep, too deep for me to read. But, baby, you can. In fact, you may be the only one. Give it all the time it takes. Don't worry about me. I expect you to get on with your life, to be the man I always loved and always will. But you can't live if you're not whole. Our sons need you whole. *I* need you whole. We're almost home; it's almost done. Now, rest, my love."

When Marcus woke, the sun was filtering through a round porthole window. His head and chest hurt and his throat was raw. His naked body was wrapped in a rough, scratchy wool blanket, and he was covered by a thick comforter as he lay on his back in the bed that occupied most of the small, neat cabin. As he was attempting to sit up the cabin door swung open.

Sit's massive bulk took up the entire doorway and he had to duck to enter the cabin. "Well boy, you just 'bout fucked the whole thing up." Hadn't Annie said pretty much the same thing a little while ago, Marcus thought, as he got his back propped up against the wall? "You always gotta go off half cocked, do shit all by yourself." Now Sit was standing next to the bed, his menacing gaze smoldering down at Marcus. In all the time Marcus had known Sit, he had always been able to find, at least a hint of friendliness in his face, even after the beating, but not this time.

Sit held up his big hand, "Don't even say it, Marcus. You know what those guys wanted me to do?" Marcus knew Sit was referring to Weathers, and Ham. "They had the nerve to suggest that I get naked, and crawl into that bed with you. Use my big body to warm you up." And just like that a smile broke across his black face, and with a little laugh he said, " I tol' them that if anybody was gonna get all Johnson to ass with you, it sure as hell weren't gonna be me. Anyway, I don't know what makes you tick, but whatever it is you best never lose it, cause my friend, you have a knack for surviving shit no man should survive. And another thing, Marcus," Sit's serious tone was back, "you make damn sure that when you tell the doc, what happened here, that the three of us are no where within a hundred miles." Marcus looked back at Sit inquisitively. "That's no shit Marcus. Now were gonna be in port in an hour or so, so you git yourself together."

As Sit was turning to leave Marcus said, "Adad?"

Sit stopped and with his back to Marcus said, "You were the only one in the water, Marcus, and if we had been just seconds later...." And with that Sit walked out and shut the door behind hm.

Marcus rummaged through the cabin and found cloths that fit reasonably well. As he was getting himself dressed, Marcus wondered what it was about Chaya that could put the fear of God into the most bad-ass men he'd ever met. An hour later he walked up onto the deck, his body still in shock from spending more time than should have been possible in the world's most deadly waters. As Weathers piloted the Lady Luck into Dutch Harbor, Marcus, standing at the bow, could make out Scott, Bronson, and Agent Gibson standing on the dock.

As Marcus was readying to walk off the boat, Scott met him on the deck. Scott looked at Marcus and then at the crab pot still seated on the hydraulic lift. "I half expected to see that pot gone," Scott said. Before they left Dutch Harbor, Marcus had asked Scott to load one of the steel crab pots onto the boat, and to give him a crash course in how to operate the lift that would dump the pot over the rail into the water. That had been Marcus's big plan, to have Adad caged inside that pot like an animal, while he described in detail the cold icy, death that awaited. Scotts voice interrupted Marcus's thought, "And hey, aren't those my clothes?"

"Well," Marcus said, "as to the crab pot, that would have just been a waste." Out of the corner of his eye Marcus caught Sit's expression that said, *Oh yeah the whole going swimming thing, that was a lot better,* "as for the clothes, mine kinda got all wet." Scott gave him a no-matter shrug. As they walked down onto the dock Marcus continued speaking, "Here's a promise, Scott. I'm coming back with my sons, and we're going to get to know one another and, at some point, get seriously drunk." He gave Scott a big hug. "I can't thank you enough!"

Scott would have no talk of payment, not even for the fuel they used. But Marcus was sure the day would come when he would have the opportunity to repay him in kind. Scott would stay on in Dutch for a few more days readying the *Lucky Lady* for the upcoming king crab season.

Agent Gibson said, "Seems you're one short, Marcus."

"Oh, Jerry's been violently seasick ever since we left," Marcus said. "He's resting. We'll get him on board as soon as the jet's ready."

Bronson took the cue. "All right, Copilot, let's go preflight the jet!" he said, leading Agent Gibson to the truck that would take them to the airport.

* * *

In Anchorage, Bronson returned Agent Gibson's cell phone.

"Tell Reynolds he'll be hearing from me."

"No problem, Mr. Diablo, but what would you suggest I tell him about...?" he asked in an unsure tone that seemed at odds with the trained, professional mien of an FBI agent.

"I'm sure you'll figure it out," Marcus said, walking away.

CHAPTER FIFTY-NINE
August 6

Landing in Calgary, Alberta, Marcus, Ham, Bronson, Sit and Weathers met the colonel, once again accompanied by officials who knew him personally. Was there *anyone* this man didn't know? After a couple of routine questions, passports were stamped, and they were aboard another G5, en route to British Columbia and Beginnings.

The colonel motioned Marcus to the seat beside him. Giving him an appraising look, he said, "We get you a little rest and put some meat back on those bones, and you just might pass for human."

Marcus just grinned.

"You did it! Despite your 'Polar Bear Club' stunt," the colonel said. "If I hadn't seen with my own eyes, I'm not sure I'd believe it all happened. Now it's time for you to finish what you started."

"You know," Marcus said, "this is gonna sound strange, but during this whole ordeal I've never been particularly afraid, even when I was in that water. And maybe that's just plain, arrogant stupidity. But now that it's over, what if my boys don't recognize me? What if the man I've become is not the man, the father, they need?"

"Somehow, I think you'll measure up, Marcus," the colonel replied, his voice taking on a soft quality.

"I hope so, Sam."

The colonel looked hard at him then spoke in the cold, analytical tone he always used when briefing the team. "Now, I want you to hear this. You don't wear self-pity well, Marcus. It hangs off you like a cheap suit. So what you're going to do now is pull your head out of your ass. From day one you have bulled your way along, somehow enlisting the support of the finest group of people I have ever had the honor of commanding. And now you are damn well going to sit back and get some rest. And when we land, you're going to march off this plane and take your boys in your arms, and you're going to hold them and begin the process of healing. Along with your family, it's our job now to help Bodie, Garrett, and you."

"Roger that, sir." Marcus said with a grin.

"Get some rest."

Marcus sank back in the lounge chair and let the vibration of the plane lull him to sleep. Annie came, or maybe it was Marcus that came to her. It was early morning, and she was sitting on the front deck of the cabin, sun glinting off the granite peaks behind her. She wore a plaid flannel robe and had thick, fuzzy slippers on her feet. Steam rose from the mug she held cupped between her hands. Her gaze was toward the mountains, and she didn't turn to Marcus as he walked to her. He tried to call out, but the words still wouldn't come, so he knelt in front of her. But she just gazed up at the mountains, a gentle, peaceful smile on her face.

Then he felt her hand running through his hair. "Hey, baby, I've been waiting for you. You look good!" The way she said "good" implied *good enough to eat.* "I like you better without the beard. I'm glad you left your hair long, though. It reminds me of when I first met you.

"You did good, Marcus. It was a hard road, and you've suffered, but now it's almost over. I wish I could tell you this is going to be the easiest part, but you and I know that's not true. But remember what you always tell the boys: nothing is ever as bad or as hard as you think it's going to be, ever. The colonel's right, you know. Self-pity doesn't fit you; it never has. I've done the best I can with our sons. I've done your job. Now it's time for you to do mine. I know you're worried, but I see you and I feel you—the Marcus Diablo we all know and love is still there. I think maybe he might even be a bit better." Her hand massaged his neck.

"It's time, Marcus. Our boys need you. You did what I asked. Now go to them and let the people who love you help you. By the way, Beginnings is quite the place. The boys love it; it's a place where they can thrive." She giggled. "You know, I've really come to like this, you listening and me talking. One last thing: you think it was your language skills that enabled you to pull this off, but you're wrong. It helped, no doubt, but the thing that allowed you to overcome every obstacle, to see the path to the next destination, was your ability to draw people in. It's your gift. You've always had it. It's been the *force* of your life. I am so very proud of you, baby. Now, go to our sons. They're waiting for you." As she said these last words, she began to fade before Marcus's eyes, her voice trailing off into silence.

* * *

They touched down, and as the jet rolled to a stop at the west end of the tarmac, amid a lush meadow surrounded by stands of pine, fir, tamarack, and birch, Marcus could see the boys wedged between Chaya and Jamie standing by a pickup truck at the edge of the runway. As the door opened, and the stairs folded out Marcus could see the boys coming toward the plane at a run. He felt as though he were somewhere else. His body was moving, but his mind wouldn't focus. As he reached the last stair and stepped onto the tarmac, the boys were twenty feet away. They were smiling, their blond hair fluttering, but Marcus couldn't hear their words over the jet engines winding down.

He took a few more steps and dropped to his knees, and in an instant his world was whole again. His sons poured into his arms, both crying with joy and relief. Marcus held them tight and smelled their skin and hair mixed with the fragrance of woods and clean mountain air.

While time stood still and waited, Marcus brought his emotions under control, and the boys stepped back a little from his embrace. Their eyes—Annie's eyes—were bright and full of life. They had grown so much. Garrett hugged him again, and as he did, Marcus felt something slide over his head. Looking down at his chest, he saw two St. Christopher medals hanging there: Annie's and his. Kneeling there on the tarmac, surrounded by majestic mountains, and with his sons in his embrace he knew he was home.

EPILOGUE
Mid-September

Heading northwest, away from the main ranch compound, along the gravel road that ran parallel to the river, Marcus, Bodie and Garrett drove in silence. The pickups headlights bounced, giving the landscape an eerie, surreal feel in the predawn darkness. The previous night, Bodie and Garrett had been adamant that Marcus go with them. There was something they wanted to show him, and it could only be done at dawn's first light. As he drove, Marcus looked over at his sons seated next to him. So much had happened in the last year and yet, right then, at that moment, it seemed almost like they were back in their old lives.

After a few miles, Bodie said, "take a right where the road Y's. That'll take us up away from the river and into the foothills." The boys kept sharing furtive glances at one another, the *cat that ate the canary* kind of looks. But, what the hell Marcus thought. Since his return, if it wasn't the boys, it was one of his brothers or sisters, or one of the members of Force 10, who were always organizing his life, gently prodding him in this direction, or that. Marcus knew that they were just giving him time to reacclimatize, to come to terms with all that happened. And the truth was, he was enjoying not having any responsibilities.

"Be careful through this next part Dad," Garrett said. "It's sorta twisty." By the light of the high beams, Marcus could see that they were driving through a stand of Aspen and Birch, their leaves showing a hint of the colors that would soon be splashed about this canyon.

"So I guess you guys aren't going to tell me what's up?" Marcus said.

"No way dad." Bodie said. "It's a surprise. You're just gonna have to wait."

Ahead Marcus could see that the dirt road took a sharp left. As they approached the curve, Garrett pointed to the four-wheel-drive shifter. "It's steep, and the road is full of ruts and loose rock."

Marcus engaged the 4WD, drove up the steep, winding incline, and after twenty minutes came to a large landing area where the road ended. As soon as he pulled to a stop, the boys were out of the truck.

"Hurry up guys." Garrett said. "Grab the pack from the back of the truck Bodie," he continued as he grabbed his father's hand. "Come on Dad, we only have a few minutes."

Still in the dark, literally and figuratively, Marcus followed the boys, by the beam of a flashlight, up a well-worn trail that led them up hill for a few hundred feet. Stepping out of the trees, Marcus could make out a small cabin situated on the crest of the hill, with a commanding view of the river valley bellow and the snow-capped peaks in the distance.

Setting the rucksack on the stone steps that led up to the cabin, Bodie said, "Garrett you get the rock on this side, I'll get the one on the other."

Marcus watched as the boys approached a waist high, stacked rock wall that was built at the edge of the bluff, in front of the cabin. In one bound, Bodie vaulted the wall, and ceremoniously the boys stood, one on either side, facing each other, then at the same time they reached out and leaned a rock down so that it lay flat on the top of the wall. Squinting, Marcus thought he saw something inside the small niche that was now revealed.

Returning, the boys stood on either side of Marcus. Garrett looked over at Bodie, who gave him an encouraging nod. Garrett reached out and took his dad's hand. In a soft, innocent voice, he said, "We wanted to wait a little while, give you some time." Marcus looked down at his youngest son. Garrett pointed at the stone wall, "Watch!"

As the sun rose over the hogback to the east, and the sun peeked above the mountain, Marcus watched the mornings first tendrils of light shine on the spot Garrett was pointing at. Nervously the boys tucked their bodies in close next to their father. Marcus bent slightly forward and strained his eyes. There in the center of the little rock enclosure was the OLD PEACH can.

Garret looked up at his dad and, without a hint of sadness in his angelic face, said, "Mom really likes it here, Dad. I mean she likes Beginnings, but she likes it right here the best. She told me, you would know that."

Marcus smiled and shook his head. It had always been something they'd joked about. Whoever died first, got the OLD PEACH can, and it was the survivors' duty to find a place for it that had a spectacular view. Hugging Garrett to him, Marcus said, "Yeah, I do know. And I couldn't have picked a better place for her."

Garrett gently pulled away from Marcus and walked the few steps to the wall. Reaching out he laid his hand on the OLD PEACH can. "Good morning, Mama. I brought him, just like you asked. You don't need to worry, Daddy's going to be okay." Garret said with a quick look back at his father. "The sun really did a job this morning, just like you said it would. Love you Mom, always and forever."

Marcus marveled that Garrett, standing on the top of a mountain, talking to his mother in the OLD PEACH can, seemed like the most normal and natural thing in the world.

Bodie picked up the rucksack, pulled out a thermos and three stainless steel camp mugs. He gave one each to Garrett and Marcus, then filled all three with steaming hot chocolate. Sitting on the wall Bodie raised his mug and with a tinny clink they touched cups in a wordless toast to Annie. As they sat there, the world awakening anew around them, Marcus thought, just as he had a year before, *what have you gotten yourself into?* But unlike on that fateful day, today he had no premonition of dread, rather he was filled with a wondering curiosity about what this new life held in store for him, Bodie, and Garrett and of course the Force 10 team.

Smiling at his boys and at peace for the first time, in what seemed like forever, something that he often said to his sons popped into his mind: *The end of one adventure is just the beginning of another.*

About the Author

I live in Reno, Nevada with my wife and two teenage son. I own a hardwood floor company that specializes in the use of reclaimed and hand distressed materials. For many years I imported centuries old building materials, beams, wood planking, limestone and terra cotta, primarily from Western Europe, for use in the high-end U.S. housing market. I enjoy skiing, backpacking and fly fishing and spend as much time as I can in the Western and Eastern Sierra Nevada Mountains. As a voracious reader I, like many, have finished a novel only to say I could write that! Well, that's what I've done, and now only time, and hopefully, a boat load of readers, will tell if I have the chops to be a viable fiction author.

To contact the author, please visit his website:
http://www.markshaff.com.hostbaby.com/index/

THE STORY CONTINUES

SAINT OR SINNER

The Next Marcus Diablo Adventure

As America recovers from the latest attack, a new wave of terror is unleashed. Fear is the weapon. Make people feel unsafe in their towns, their neighborhoods, their homes. To save a nation Marcus Diablo and Force 10 will have to walk the fine line between, *Saint or Sinner.*

WATCH FOR SAINT OR SINNER AVAILABLE SOON FROM MOONSHINE COVE PUBLISHING

CHAPTER ONE
New York City

Standing in the lobby of the Western Union building at 60 Hudson Street, in New York City's Tribeca neighborhood, Peter Revant took in the classical art deco design of the historic landmark. With its patterned marble floors, bricked columns and walls, barrel-vaulted Guavastino tile ceilings, as well as chandeliers, wall sconces and furniture, the inside of this iconic building harkened back to a time ninety years in the past. Oddly he thought, dressed in his custom tailored, navy pinstriped suit, white Egyptian cotton shirt with a purple polka dot silk tie, and highly polished black wing tips, he fit into the décor in a perverse sort of way. It made him wonder about America and Americans fascination with a past that went back only a few decades, while most other places in the world went back centuries or even millennia. But then again it did explain why it was almost impossible for the citizens of this country to comprehend the commitment required to preserve a faith and lifestyle that was as old as civilization itself, that customs and tradition didn't simply change to fit new ideas or the whims of a new generation.

The tap, tap sound of black four-inch stilettos echoing off the walls and floor of the cavernous lobby, drew Peter's attention to a stylish, attractive young woman, walking his way. Stephanie Aldridge represented the leasing company brokering office space in this particular building and Peter had met with her once before, now almost a month past, when he had begun negotiations to lease the entire eighteenth floor. Dressed in a light grey wool pant suit that was as tailored to her form, as his suit was to his, Peter had to admit, that using a late twenties blond, who was not only beautiful, but had the where-with-all to use her feminine sexuality to her company's advantage in coming to terms on a multi-million dollar lease agreement was not only shrewd business but, was also something that, at the very core of who Peter was, appalled him. In the part of the world Peter called home, this type of overt display by a woman, any woman, could be considered just cause for her death. Yet here in America a women dressing or behaving so provocatively, as if she were on equal footing with men, was not only considered acceptable, it was a large part of the democracy the U.S., subtly and not so subtly, preached about and exported around the world.

"Mr. Revant, how good to see you again," Stephanie said, as she extended her hand.

Taking the young women's hand in his, Peter smelled her perfume, sweet and seductive with a hint of musk, and thought for the briefest moment what it would be like to taste the fruit of this tree. Peter knew that he was a handsome man and that women found him attractive. At thirty-eight, six- foot- two, one-hundred and ninety pounds, with jet black hair, parted on the right side and feathering back behind his ears, combined with a day's growth of beard, he had an aura of sophisticated business man, mixed with a touch of carefree bad boy. With brown eyes that went from sparkling bronze to the color of cold coffee, depending on his temperament, combined with an olive skin tone that made his ethnicity impossible to pin down, Peter Revant, was an enigma, one moment a worldwide entrepreneur, the next a lusted after lover from some exotic port, and it didn't hurt that he was rich. Just as Stephanie dressed and prepared for her role, so did he.

"Ms. Aldridge, the pleasure is mine," Peter said in an accent that intentionally implied he was from England, although he could speak unaccented English as well as she. Still holding her hand, which she made no effort to withdraw, Peter went on, "I take it that you have received the revisions to the contracts sent by my lawyers and that all the documents are prepared?"

"Yes, Mr. Revant, all is in order."

Releasing her hand Peter continued, "Would you mind terribly if we first went and looked at the space? I have thought of little else these past weeks, and…well as I am sure you can imagine this is a milestone for my company."

"By all means Mr. Revant. Follow me."

***

Peter entered the eighteenth floor that was now nothing more than concrete floors and columns, and of course windows that provided spectacular panoramic views of the Manhattan skyline. Ignoring Stephanie, Peter moved through the empty, naked space in a daydream. Over the next week he would replay this scene at two other locations, in two other U.S. cities: One Wilshire Data Center in Los Angles and the Westin Building in Seattle. Stopping at the expansive windows, Peter stared down onto West Broadway, the people and cars looked so small. There was a certain calm to the chaos from up here. A smile came to Peter's lips as he imagined the same scene—without the calm. A voice brought Peter back to the moment as he picked up Stephanie's words mid sentence, "…and as I'm sure you know, having your telecommunications company, *Visionary*, housed in one of the world's most concentrated internet connectivity hubs is a huge advantage, because," Stephanie spread her hands wide as if she were speaking to a audience from atop a stage, "the world is all about communication."

Turning Peter faced his attractive host. With a broad smile that reveled brilliant white teeth, he nodded his head in asset, "Yes, today's world is all about information."

What he didn't say was, "or the lack there of."

CPSIA information can be obtained at www.ICGtesting.com
Printed in the USA
LVOW112145200513

334729LV00005B/122/P

9 781937 327217